A Note from Melissa

I have been looking forward to writing Clay Braden and Pepper Montgomery's love story for years, and I'm thrilled to finally bring it to you. Clay is an NFL quarterback known to millions as "Mr. Perfect," and he is determined to show scientist Pepper Montgomery the benefits of hands-on research. Pepper, however, has other ideas. Their story is funny, sexy, and healing in special ways for both of them. Their journey starts in Paris and ends in the States, but their monumental love knows no boundaries. *Playing Mr. Perfect* is the first book in the Bradens at Ridgeport series. If this is your first Love in Bloom book, each of my love stories is written to stand alone, with no cheating or cliffhangers, so dive in and enjoy the ride.

Be sure to check out my online bookstore for pre-orders, early releases, discounted bundles, and exclusive sales on ebooks, print, and audiobooks. Ebooks can be sent to the e-reader of your choice and audiobooks can be listened to on the free and easy-to-use BookFunnel app. shop.melissafoster.com

The best ways to keep up to date with new releases, sales, and exclusive content are to sign up for my newsletter, join my fan club on Facebook, and follow my social pages.

Newsletter: www.MelissaFoster.com/Newsletter

FB Fan Club: @MelissaFosterFans

FB: @MelissaFosterAuthor

IG: @MelissaFoster_Author

TikTok: @MelissaFoster_Author

Playlist

"Do I Make You Wanna" by Billy Currington
"Good Girl" by Dustin Lynch
"Love I've Been Jealous Of" by Rachel Grae
"All That Really Matters" by Illenium and Teddy Swims
"Ain't Too Proud to Beg" by The Temptations
"Slow Dance in a Parking Lot" by Jordan Davis
"Heart Attack" by Demi Lovato
"Infinitely Falling" by Fly By Midnight
"Best of Us Go Down" by Aquilo
"Need a Favor" by Jelly Roll
"Last Call (NOW What's Next!)" by Will Linley
"Don't Ya" by Brett Eldredge
"In the Woods Somewhere" by Hozier
"Broken Glass" by Sia
"Walk Through Fire" by Chuxx Morris
"Ruin My Life" by Zara Larsson
"Confident" by Demi Lovato
"Your Bones" by Chelsea Cutler
"Just Because" by Sadie Jean
"Little Bit More" by Suriel Hess
"Get Ready" by The Temptations
"Before You" by Benson Boone
"House on Fire" by Mimi Webb
"Feels Like I'm Falling in Love" by Coldplay

Chapter One

Clay

 I drop my suitcase and head directly to the minibar in my Paris hotel suite to pour myself a shot of whiskey. It was a long-ass flight, and my shoulder aches. *Fucking injury.* I'm downing the shot when my phone rings, and my youngest brother's name flashes on the screen. I pour myself another shot and answer on speaker. "Hey, Noah. What's up?"

"I'm here with Clay Braden, the quarterback for the New York Giants," he announces in his best sportscaster voice. "Clay, you lost the playoff game for your team, and they won't let you into Disney World. Fans want to know what's next for Mr. Perfect."

I down the shot, trying to drown out my recent distaste for the nickname the media graced me with a decade ago. As far as Noah goes, we've always given each other crap to lighten the mood when tough shit happens. It usually works, but last weekend's loss is still raw.

"You still there, old man?" Noah urges. "I'd get you your hearing aid, but I have no idea where you are."

"I'm in Paris, asshole, and thirty-five isn't old." As true as that is, I'm past my prime in the world of professional football, and I'm starting to feel it. I no longer recover as quickly as I used to, and it's affecting my ability to nail a pass. Then there's the young up-and-comer, Russ Staley, who's gunning for my position. I grit my teeth against that reality. I'm in a contract year, and my agent has an extension waiting for my signature. One minute I'm ready to sign my life away for as many years as they'll have me, and the next I want nothing more than to walk away from the game and all the limelight and pressure that goes along with it, because the sport I once lived and breathed for has lost its shine. The trouble is, football has been my life for so long, I can't even begin to think about who I'd be without it.

"Dude, you're in *Paris* and you didn't invite me? What the hell? You know I'm into French women."

"You're into just about any woman." And with the same playful nature he possessed as a kid, Noah draws them like flies. "It was a last-minute trip. Dash invited me. He's here with Amber and some of her family to see her sister Sable's band open for Bad Intentions on the last leg of their European tour." Dash Pennington is one of my closest friends, and the best wide receiver I've ever played with. He retired a few years ago and married Amber, the love of his life—and a sister to the real reason I'm in Paris. *Pepper Montgomery.* The only woman on the planet who won't give me the time of day.

"Are you fucking kidding me?" Noah complains. "This is Johnny Bad's last tour. Where is the love, man? *Wait a second.* Pepper's there, isn't she? Holy shit. You were afraid she'd be into me, weren't you? That's why you didn't invite me."

I scoff. "Hardly."

I wasn't even going to come on this trip. I didn't think I'd make very good company, but then Dash said Pepper was coming, and the thought of seeing her again was enough to get me here. I need a distraction, and she's the perfect one to hold my interest. I've known a lot of beautiful women in my life, but there's something about the brilliant scientist that hit differently from the first time I met her. It was more than the sizzle and burn that sears between us every damn time I see her, more than her beautiful face and gorgeous figure or her thick golden-brown hair, which I've thought about tangling my fingers in more times than I care to admit. It's the depth that resonates in her hazel eyes that drew me in and has had me thinking about her ever since.

"You know she's going to take off the second she sees you," Noah says, jerking me from my thoughts.

"Fuck off." I pace the floor, knowing there's a good chance he's right.

The combination of my good looks and fame has paved an easy road with women for me, but it hasn't opened any doors with Pepper, and my siblings love teasing me about it. Believe me, I've tried to get to know her better, showing up every chance I get under the guise of visiting Dash when I know Pepper will be in town to see her family—and reaching out after she leaves nearly every time for a work emergency. Not that she responds to my texts. I should probably forget about her, but there's no forgetting Pepper Montgomery, and if she wants to play hard to get, I'm game. I love a challenge. Especially one as beautiful and as intelligent as her.

"You know I'm just giving you shit," Noah says. "I mean, she'll probably take off, and she'd be into me over you if I were there, but since I'm not, I can give you some advice if you'd like."

"*Noah*," I warn.

He laughs.

"Is there something you need, bro? Or did you just call to

give me a hard time?"

"Giving you a hard time is the most fun I've had all day, but I did call for another reason. We're putting together our summer programs for the Real DEAL, and we were hoping you might be interested in doing a few days of football camp with the kids." Noah is a marine biologist, and he's the only one of my siblings who doesn't live in New York. He lives in Colorado, where he and a few of our cousins run the Real DEAL (Discover, Experience, Appreciate, Learn), a total immersion exploratory park for kids that includes educational exhibits and hands-on activities.

"When are you thinking? I've got workouts in May and early June. I don't think Flynn and Sutton have picked a wedding date yet, but I'm sure it'll be between minicamp and the start of preseason." Our brother Flynn recently got engaged.

"I spoke to Flynn," Noah says. "They're thinking of the second or third weekend in July, but I'll take whatever time you're willing to give."

"Then count me in, and we'll firm up dates as soon as they make their decision. I love working with kids."

"I know you do. Thanks, man. This'll be a big draw."

"Anything else? I need to run. I'm meeting Dash and everyone to grab dinner and go to the concert soon."

"Just one thing. If you run off Pepper, give her my number, will ya?"

"Goodbye, asshole." I end the call, cutting off his laughter.

Mark my word, Pepper will be mine by the end of this trip. I couldn't make a hard play for her during football season, but now that I've got nothing but time, the only place she'll be running is into my bed.

Chapter Two

Pepper

"*Please don't hold the reports until I get back. I don't want to get behind,*" I say to my empty hotel room as I lean over my laptop and reply to an email from one of my employees, Min Zhao, a brilliant medical engineer. I swear owning a research and development company requires forty-eight hours in each day. I don't like taking time off work, but my siblings pressured me into coming to Paris with them to support my twin, Sable, the lead singer for Surge, on her international concert tour. Now that I'm here, I'm glad I came, but work won't stop because I'm on vacation.

A knock sounds at my door.

"Pepper, open up!" Brindle hollers. My youngest sister is about as patient as a gust of wind. I open my mouth to respond, and she knocks again. "Pepper!"

"Hold on," I call out as I type.

"Move your butt, Pep!" Brindle demands. "We're going to be late."

"Give her a second," Amber, always the mediator, says.

"She's had *hours*," Brindle complains.

"The guys *are* waiting for us downstairs," Morgyn chimes in, in Brindle's defense.

I huff out a breath, trying to tune them out as my fingers fly across the keyboard. I'm used to tuning out my younger siblings. I love them dearly, but I know once I open the door, they'll sweep me into their chaos and I won't have another chance to think clearly all night.

"Hey, Pep!" our only brother and the youngest of our brood, Axsel, yells. "Is that guy who tried to pick you up last night in there?"

As if I would sleep with some guy I barely know? Axsel knows me better than that, but I can't help smiling as I type, because while I'm thrilled that I've had the last couple of days with my siblings, I'm especially happy to have had that time with Axsel. As the lead guitarist for the band Inferno, his schedule is insane, and we don't see him often enough.

"Yeah, *right*," Brindle says, her laughter carrying through the door.

Tension tightens across my shoulders as I click send on the email and then stalk over and open the door. Four sets of eyes land on me. Brindle's are filled with impatience, Morgyn's shimmer with happiness, Amber's are apologetic, and Axsel's smirk reflects in his eyes like trouble waiting to happen.

"About time," Brindle snaps, strutting past in a black leather jacket over a concert T-shirt, a red suede miniskirt, and black boots, with her blond hair pinned up in a highly teased ponytail. She looked more like a college student than a high school English teacher and mother of a toddler.

"Sorry. I was working," I say as the others file in.

"You're in the City of Love," Morgyn says as she breezes by. "You're supposed to be having fun, falling in love with this romantic city, and forgetting about real life." Her fair hair is loose and wild over the shoulders of her bejeweled green velvet jacket, which she's paired with jeans that are ripped and patched strategically. She embellished both items of clothing herself—proof of her incredible creative side, which I've always been a little envious of. Morgyn could make a paper bag beautiful.

I've been in Paris for two days and have yet to see what's so romantic about it.

"Is everything okay with your project?" Amber asks gently. She looks sexy in leopard-print leggings, a black turtleneck, and matching boots. Her brown hair falls halfway down the back of her black cropped jacket. She never would have worn a curve-hugging outfit like that before falling for her husband, Dash.

Amber would worry all night if she knew I was stressed about work, and I don't want to stress her out for fear of exacerbating her epilepsy, so I lie. "Yes, it's fine."

"Work, my ass. Fess up, sis. Where's the hottie hiding?" Axsel plants a hand on the hip of his leather pants, his shaggy dark hair trapped beneath a backward baseball cap, the ends curling around his ears. The sleeves of his long-sleeve black shirt are pushed up, revealing the tattoos he's accumulated over the last few years.

"You think I'd let you near any man I'm interested in?" Axsel was handsome, gay, charismatic, and a shameless flirt with all men. "I made him climb down from the balcony."

Axsel laughs. "Smart move."

"If *only* it were true," Brindle exclaims. "I'd love to believe Pepper cut loose, but the evidence says otherwise."

"Evidence?" Amber asks.

Oh, Amber, why couldn't you just let it go?

"The laptop is open," Brindle points out. "The bed is perfectly made, and there's *no way* a man's fingers were in that perfectly combed hair of hers."

I roll my eyes. Brindle has owned and flaunted her sexuality since she was old enough to understand the power behind it. She mostly only used it on her now-husband, Trace Jericho, who she's been in a relationship with since she was fourteen, but compared to her and Sable, I might as well be a nun. Okay, that's an exaggeration. I'm just careful and private.

"Your pinched expression says it all," Brindle says. "If you got a few good Os, you'd be grinning like a fool."

I can't even remember the last time I had an orgasm from a man. "Not everyone thinks about sex all the time."

"They don't?" Axsel asks with a baffled expression.

"I'm trying to make a point," I say exasperatedly, and turn back to Brindle. "Some of us keep our sexual escapades private, and some of us show up at events with our shirts on backward because we couldn't keep our clothes on for an entire night."

"That happened *once*," Brindle says.

"More like twice," Amber corrects her.

"I can think of three times," Morgyn says. "Wait. *Four.* Remember two years ago at the Valentine's Day Festival, and the year before that at the Turkey Trot?"

"Don't forget the barn bash the summer after her first year of college," Axsel said.

"What*ever*," Brindle says, and we all laugh. "Trace and I have a great sex life. I'm proud of that, and I want Pepper to be with a guy she can't keep her hands off, too, so she doesn't have to make up stories."

"I was *kidding*, and my sex life is just fine, thank you very much. Why don't you focus on Axsel? *He's* single." These three sisters are all happily married, and they've been on some kind of mission to couple me off since Sable got engaged to business mogul Kane Bad last year.

"Axsel isn't sitting home alone at night," Brindle explains.

"Neither am I." Okay, I am, *mostly*. But that's by choice. Dating is not all it's cracked up to be, and it's not like I'm sitting at home staring at a television. I left my corporate job to follow my heart and develop medical devices to help people with disabilities who can't find relief through products that are currently on the market. That means working harder for less-profitable contracts, putting in more hours to run and market the business, and missing some outings and get-togethers. But at the end of the day, I'm helping others and changing lives, and that makes me happier than any man ever could. My sister knows this, and now I'm done with this conversation.

"Can we go, please?" I grab my room card and shove it into my pocket as I head out the door.

Amber hurries after me. "I'm with you on keeping it private, but I'm also with Brindle. I want you to find love, and I have a feeling you're going to meet your match soon."

"I think we all have that feeling," Axsel chimes in.

"Did you guys start day drinking or something? You're more annoying than usual." I push the button for the elevator.

"Can't you feel the magic in the air, Pep?" Morgyn looks up at the ceiling with a wide grin and throws her hands up. "The universe is finally on your side."

I love Morgyn's faith in the universe, but while she's all about fate and love and all things mystical, as a scientist, I believe in facts, quantifiable evidence, and results. "Please tell the universe to mind its own business."

Brindle nudges Morgyn. "How could you forget our practical sister doesn't believe in magic?"

"Oh! *Practical Magic!* I love that movie," Morgyn exclaims.

Axsel cocks a grin. "A young Aidan Quinn? Yes, please."

I sigh as we step into the elevator. I'm not a big drinker, but

I could sure use some wine right about now. "Actually, I *do* need the universe on my side tonight to give me the strength not to throttle the four of you."

They laugh, and the elevator doors start closing, but a large hand shoots between them, and they open again, revealing six-plus feet of broad-chested, hard-bodied man and the insanely handsome face of Dash's close friend Clay Braden. The man I've been trying to forget since Dash and Amber's wedding. But forgetting him is impossible when he randomly shows up to see Dash and attends events in my hometown, then texts me afterward like it's his *right*. I could kill Dash for giving him my number.

Clay's mesmerizing blue eyes lock on me, and I swear they sear into my brain like lasers, making the neurons misfire. A slow grin slides into place, bringing out his dimples as he says, "Looks like the universe is on *my* side tonight."

My stupid heart skips, and my thoughts turn on that confused organ. *Do not go there or I'll throttle you, too.* I am *not* getting worked up over the man the media calls Mr. Perfect. Clay oozes charm like Amber exudes sweetness, as if it's innate and he can't help it. I don't have to be on social media or follow football to know better. There are so many rumors about the pro-baller's active personal life, they carry in the wind. He is a total player with an ego bigger than the football fields he plays on. He's the farthest thing from *my type* that a man can be, and yet as my siblings greet him with enthusiastic *Clays!*, I can't take my eyes off him in a leather bomber jacket that makes him seem bigger than life and probably cost as much as my monthly mortgage.

His megawatt smile glints beneath the harsh elevator lights as he steps inside, taking up far too much space. "Ladies. Axsel," he says as the doors close behind him.

"I'm sorry you lost your playoff game, but I'm so glad you were able to join us," Amber says, hugging him.

What? You knew he was coming?

"It sucks that we lost." Clay's gaze locks on me again as he says, "But it looks like my luck is changing. Nice to see you again, Pepper."

"You, too." The words are hard to get out, which is a strange occurrence for me. But so are most of the ways he makes me act and feel. Except for my smile. That comes naturally, because he *is* a beautiful man, and I don't see many of them in my lab.

His eyes gleam arrogantly.

I realize I'm staring, and force my gaze away, looking straight ahead. But there's no escaping our reflection in the shiny elevator doors, or his decadent scent, a mix of cedarwood and pure potent male, bringing a rush of hot, tingling aware-ness. Clay holds my gaze in our reflection as he shifts behind me, his chest brushing the back of my shoulder. The touch echoes in the seductive narrowing of his eyes, sending electric currents slithering through me like asps, and I wonder if anyone else feels flames licking up their skin.

"Is it hot in here?" I tug at the neckline of my shirt beneath my blazer.

"It sure is," he says low and deep, the edges of his lips tip-ping up.

"From so many people in a tight space," I clarify.

"Exactly. One hot body makes all the difference."

My cheeks heat, and I'm vaguely aware of my siblings' chat-ting as the elevator descends, but Clay's presence holds me captive. The feeling of being under anyone's spell is so foreign to me, I'm not sure I breathe the rest of the way down to the lobby.

When the doors open, I hurry out, relieved for the space, but at the same time, I want to chase that rush of adrenaline he caused. Which is precisely why I need to put distance between us.

Clay has a way of making me feel like the swoony-eyed teenager I left behind a long time ago. At least when he shows up at community events in my hometown, I can claim a work emergency and hightail it back to Charlottesville, where I live. Then the most I have to deal with are texts from him, which I simply ignore. But I can't jump in my car and drive home from Paris.

I steal a glance at him as he talks with Axsel. He must sense my gaze, because he looks over and our eyes connect. My body tingles and burns again. I know better than to be sucked into that enticing vortex, but it taunts me like only an equation with a missing parameter ever has.

"There they are," Morgyn calls out, bringing me back to the moment. She's waving to her husband, Graham Braden, one of Clay's cousins, who is standing by the entrance with Dash and Trace. The three of them look like they walked out of a lifestyle magazine, tall, built, handsome, and as different as can be. Graham is wearing a worn MIT baseball cap and a Henley, Dash is in a crisp button-down, and Trace is wearing a flannel shirt over a plain-white tee, his ever-present cowboy hat firmly in place.

As we head in that direction, I snag Amber by the arm, tugging her traitorous butt back to me as the others forge ahead, and lower my voice. "Why did you invite Clay?"

"His team didn't make the Super Bowl. We thought this

would lift his spirits."

"Hasn't he won a few Super Bowls?"

"How do you…?" Amber's eyes widen. "Have you been googling him?"

"*No.*" There's no way I'll admit *that*. It was only once, and I never made it past drooling over pictures of him. "You guys rave about him like he's some kind of hero. It's hard to miss."

"I know football isn't your thing, but he is a hero to his fans."

I roll my eyes as we make our way across the posh lobby toward the others. "The whole thing is ridiculous. He gets a ring and worldwide notoriety for throwing a ball, and I get a pat on the back for building life-saving medical devices."

Amber looks amused. "Are you jealous?"

"*No.*" I realize I sound like I am and nip it in the bud. "I'm just annoyed that he's here. I wish you'd given me a heads-up."

"I didn't think you'd care. You take off every time he's around."

I give her an imploring look, whispering as we near the others, "Doesn't that tell you something?"

A mischievous grin curves her lips. "Actually, it reminds me of how I used to avoid Dash, and now he's the best part of my life." She beams at her husband, who's looking at her like she's his world.

"There's my gorgeous wife." Dash draws Amber into his arms and kisses her.

I glance at Graham and Morgyn holding hands, their foreheads nearly touching as they talk, and Brindle and Trace, his arm around her like he never wants to let her go, his hand resting on her butt. I might not be a starry-eyed romantic like Amber or Morgyn, or a sexpot like Sable or Brindle, but watching my sisters fall in love, seeing them change and grow with their partners, has brought a longing that takes effort to ignore.

"They almost make you want it, don't they?" Axsel asks as he sidles up to me.

Yes, hangs on the tip of my tongue, but I notice Clay heading our way, and that tingling starts low in my belly again. The past slips in like a ghost, reminding me of what those feelings can lead to, and I tuck that *yes* down deep. "*Almost*. You?"

"Oh yeah," Axsel says. "But only for a night."

I laugh.

Clay lifts his chin. "Care to share?"

"Hell yeah." Axsel eyes him lasciviously. "My room or yours?"

"Dude, if I swung your way, I'd be all over that," Clay says without missing a beat.

"My loss," Axsel says, and heads for the others.

"Let's go, you guys," Brindle calls out. "The limo is here."

As we head for the door, Clay falls into step beside me and says, "You know, if you wanted me to be your date for the concert, you could have just asked. You didn't have to ask Dash to do it for you."

"I didn't ask him to invite you."

"If you say so." His cockiness rivals Axsel's. "How long are you going to play hard to get?"

"I'm not playing hard to get."

"Then why haven't you responded to any of my texts?"

He puts a hand on my lower back as we follow the others outside. Cold air stings my cheeks, but my body is warm from his proximity. "I don't text people I haven't given my number to." It turns out that talking about his texts is as nerve-racking as fighting the urge to respond to them.

"I got your number from Dash, who got it from Amber," Clay says. "That has to count for something."

"It does. Bad judgment on their part." We wait as Trace and Brindle climb into the limo, and all I can think about is how I'll probably spontaneously combust if I have to sit close to Clay. After Brindle climbs in, I snag my window of opportunity to get away from him. "I'll get in next," I call out, rushing forward to slip inside the limo before Morgyn. I feel bad for being rude, but my sanity is on the line. I breathe a sigh of relief as I settle in beside Brindle, pleased with my strategic move to sit between her and Morgyn.

"Clay, you can go next," Morgyn offers.

Are you freaking kidding me? Is this some kind of conspiracy to make me as uncomfortable as possible?

Clay flashes those disarming dimples as his big body lands beside me, and he claps a hand on my leg, giving it a squeeze as the others pile into the limo. "Of all the limos in all the towns in all the world, she's sitting in mine. It must be fate."

As if trying to ignore my quickening pulse isn't hard enough, the heat of his hand sears through my jeans, and I like his quick wit so much, I'm smiling like a teen with a crush. What's worse is that I can't seem to *stop*. It's so infuriating, an incredulous laugh slips out. "Does that kind of pickup line ever work for you?"

"I don't know. I don't usually have to speak to pick up a woman."

And there it is. The perspective I need to keep my distance from Mr. Perfect. I lift his hand off my leg, meeting his gaze as I place it on his leg.

Big mistake.

His blue eyes are no longer mesmerizing.

They're *challenging.*

Seductive.

Dangerously alluring in a way that would appeal to rebellious souls like Sable and Brindle, not to a rational woman like me.

Only they do.

My skin goes hot, my heart races, and suddenly I understand what Sable and Brindle have been claiming forever—that there are certain types of chemistry that are so all-consuming, they seep into your pores and saturate the very air you breathe. Inescapable.

That's when I realize I'm wholly and completely screwed.

Chapter Three

Pepper

Drinks are flowing and the air feels electric in the VIP lounge of the Paris Lá Defense Arena, where dozens of men and women are moving to the beat, as captivated by my talented twin and her band as I am. Well, maybe a little more so, given that even across the crowded room I can feel Clay's eyes on me. The heat of his gaze has had me in a choke hold since dinner. I fight the urge to look over, and fighting it makes me worry I'll accidentally glance in his direction and those all-seeing eyes will catch me doing it, erroneously feeding into his belief that I'm just playing hard to get.

My nerves flame with the pressure not to look over.

I know he's with my brothers-in-law and a handful of men and women who were here when we arrived. Another group had converged on Axsel right away, but a few others had flocked to Clay and Dash, thrilled to be among the American football players. I don't know how Amber deals with it. Dash is retired and people *still* consider him public territory. At least Dash kept his distance from the ladies. Clay, on the other hand, hammed it up, putting his arm around the women as they took selfies.

I try to quell the pang of jealousy that I don't even understand. Clay is *not* for me, so why do I care? A voice in my head whispers, *Because there's something there. Something hot and sharp and enticing.*

The roar of the crowd rises with the crescendo of the music, drawing my attention from my runaway thoughts to Sable strutting across the stage, playing the guitar like it's an extension of her fingers. A dozen crisscrossing lights call her out like the celebrity she's become. I get chills watching her, so confident and unafraid, living out a dream she never wanted and few could ever achieve. We shared a womb, but that's where our similarities end. Sable is loud and rebellious. She has a gorgeous voice and an ear for music, and she has always taken what she wanted without allowing anyone's criticism to affect her actions. I, on the other hand, speak my mind but would rather walk away than raise my voice. I just don't see a need to fight every possible battle. On top of that, I couldn't carry a tune if it came in a suitcase, and I pick apart criticism to see if any of it is applicable before setting it aside to overthink it later.

Sable throws her head back, her long dark hair whipping around her as wild and free as she is. Her raspy voice booms through the packed arena as she belts out the end of the song. The fans, and all of us, explode into cheers and applause.

"Listen to that crowd. Sable is killing it!" Brindle grabs her glass, holding it up. "To Sable!"

"To Sable!" we all cheer, and clink glasses before drinking our mojitos.

I usually have wine, but I'm so far outside my comfort zone tonight, I'd drink gasoline if it would take the edge off my nerves.

"I can't believe Sable doesn't want to *live* on that stage," Brindle says.

Surge was a hometown band before billionaire Kane Bad

walked in and offered them a chance to tour with his brother Johnny's band. Sable never wanted to tour, but she agreed for her band's sake, which was why this would be her first and only tour.

"She wants to spend time with Kane," Amber says.

"I don't blame her," Morgyn says. "The man owns half the East Coast, and he looks at Sable like she's worth more than all of it put together. He's also generous to a fault." Kane paid for all our rooms at the lavish Hôtel de Crillon.

"You *know* he's got to be all *that* and a whole lot more in the bedroom to have hooked Sable's heart," Brindle says.

"This is Sable we're talking about," Morgyn points out. "He's got to be a hell of a lover in every room, on the roof, in the yard, in her truck."

We all laugh.

I lean in so they can hear me over the music. "You know darn well she wouldn't want to live on that stage even if she wasn't with Kane. She doesn't like being a public commodity." My thoughts race back to Clay, who seems to gobble up the attention his celebrity status brings. And just like that I'm fighting the urge to steal a glance at him again, which annoys the crap out of me.

I take another swig of my drink and watch Sable burn up the stage, refusing to let Clay's presence rattle me to the point of stealing the joy of watching her. I focus on the beat of the music and the excitement of the crowd, welcoming it as the mojitos work their magic. I dance with my sisters, giving myself over to the music until it becomes a part of me, like I did as a kid when our grandparents would take us to concerts. I had forgotten how that could happen, and as the beat thrums through my veins, I feel more alive than I have in years.

"Is it just me," Amber says loudly, "or has Sable's music gotten even better since she fell for Kane?"

"Haven't we *all* gotten better with love?" Morgyn says. "I felt a change the minute Graham and I came together."

Swinging my hips to the beat, I say, "That was your hormones speaking."

"Maybe partially, but I knew he was the one when I met him at the music festival, and the universe did, too," Morgyn insists. "That's why it answered my manifesting and brought us back together at Grace's wedding," Grace is our oldest sister. She's three months pregnant, and after suffering a miscarriage last year, she is playing it safe, opting to stay home instead of joining us.

"Because it couldn't have been a coincidence that his friend was marrying our sister," I say sarcastically. Sometimes I think about how much easier life would be if I were more like my sisters and could believe that merely existing, or manifesting, was enough to make all my dreams come true. I had some of that dreaminess in me when I was younger. I had even, on occasion, thrown caution to the wind, but that was before I knew how dangerous that could be.

I take another drink, reveling in the cool liquid sliding down my throat.

"O ye of little faith." Morgyn points to me as we dance. "One day you'll understand that all those facts you believe in don't hold a candle to the power of the universe. With Graham, I'm happier and more creative than ever, and I get to live every moment with my best friend by my side. *That's* the universe's doing."

"That's the power of *love*," Amber chimes in. "Dash makes me see myself and the world differently. I'm stronger because I know he'll love me through whatever else life throws at us…"

As Amber goes on about her amazing husband, I can't imagine a man making me stronger. If anything, one particular man is making me weaker, because the draw to look at him is too strong to deny. I cave and steal a glance at Clay. He's watching the band, flanked by two beautiful women. Maybe it's the alcohol speaking, but I have the strange thought that he's more beautiful than the women are.

He reaches up to rub the back of his neck, turning his head slightly, and catches me staring.

Again.

Shitshitshit. If I turn away, it'll look like I am staring at him, which is true, but I don't want him to know that. He grins and winks, and I tell myself to look away, but I'm like a deer caught in the headlights. Suddenly all I see is that spark of interest in his eyes, the tempting curve of his mouth, and his big hand moving up the back of his neck. I remember the heat of that hand on my thigh and imagine how good it would feel beneath the denim. My body goes hot just as he flashes an exasperated look, yanking me from my ill-timed fantasy.

I don't know if that look is aimed at me for reacting to his wink with a blank stare, or if it's a conspiratorial look. Like he's letting me in on a secret that I don't understand. In any case, I go for the nothing-going-on-here move, shifting my gaze slightly to the left, as if I've been looking beyond him at Axsel standing by the bar the whole time, then quickly return my focus to Amber, who's still talking about Dash.

"He makes me want to do things and see places I was afraid of before he came into my life." Amber glances at Dash with a dreamy expression.

"He makes you want to do *him*," Brindle says.

"*In* places you never dreamed of," Morgyn adds.

Yes, Clay does. The thought comes unbidden, and my gaze flicks back to him without any thought. My heart nearly stops. He's still watching me, and this time there's no hiding the fact that I purposely looked at him. I tear my gaze away, gulp down the rest of my drink, and set the empty glass on a table.

Amber blushes. "That's the power of love, too."

"More like lust," I say, realizing after the fact that she was responding to Morgyn, *not* talking about me ogling Clay. The man really does make my brain misfire.

"To lust!" Brindle raises her glass, and they all drink as another song comes to an end.

We cheer along with the roar of the crowd, and the band starts playing one of our favorite songs. My sisters and I break into a hip-swaying, shoulder-rocking dance.

Brindle dances closer to me and says, "You and Clay looked awfully cozy in the limo, and he hasn't taken his eyes off you since we got here."

"I'm sure you're mistaken." My nerves prickle with the lie, but thanks to the alcohol, the anxiety doesn't take hold.

"When it comes to lust, I'm never wrong. But I guess we're about to find out," Brindle says just as I hear the guys behind me.

"Sable's kicking ass out there," Trace says as he wraps his arms around Brindle from behind and kisses her cheek. "Just like old times, huh, Mustang? Want to sneak off and find a dark corner like we used to at concerts?"

"Heck yeah," Brindle exclaims, eyeing her ruggedly handsome cowboy over her shoulder. "Right after Sable's done with her set."

"I'd like to see *you* strutting across a stage, Sunshine," Graham says as he drapes his arm around Morgyn.

"You find me a stage, and I'll totally do that for you." Morgyn goes up on her toes and kisses him.

Amber waggles her finger at Dash and says, "Don't look at me like that. I don't do stages or dark corners at concerts."

Dash laughs. "That's just one of the many things I love about you."

As he lowers his lips to hers, I feel myself teetering on longing for what my sisters have. Not just the love, but their friendships with their husbands. The part that appears to take no effort at all for them. I realize with an unexpected pang of disappointment that Clay didn't join us. I turn to see if he's still with those women and see him closing in on me with a drink in each hand, watching me so intently, my chest flutters.

His penetrating gaze never wavers from mine as he hands me a glass. Our fingers brush, and a zing of electricity shoots up my arm. He leans in so close, his breath warms my cheek as he says, "You were looking a little *thirsty*."

The way he said *thirsty* made it sound like an innuendo, sending my thoughts back to when I googled him and found pictures captioned *Thirsty Thursday*. He was shirtless, wearing those tight football pants, pouring water over his head after a game like some kind of fan porn.

Now I really do need that drink.

"Thank you. As a matter of fact, I am thirsty." Still caught up in the image of him shirtless, it comes out flirtier than I intend, but I kind of like the way I sound. I haven't flirted in so long, I'd forgotten how uplifting it can be, so I go with it and take a sip of my drink, telling myself not to overthink the situation. "You seem to be enjoying yourself."

"I had to heal my bruised ego after offering to be your date and getting turned down."

"I didn't realize you were so fragile," I tease.

"Am I? Or was I trying to make you jealous?"

"I can't imagine Mr. Perfect trying to make anyone jealous."

The muscles in his jaw bunch, but in the next second he cocks a brow in amusement. "I guess that means it didn't work."

I shake my head, laughing softly. He steps closer, sliding his hand to my lower back, sending my pulse sprinting. I eye him curiously. "What are you doing?"

"Entering your personal space."

"I can feel that. The question is, *why?*"

"Because I want your personal space to be mine."

God, this guy is never at a loss for a comeback. "That's not really how personal space works."

"It is now."

As cheesy as his lines are, I find the fact that he never runs out of them oddly intriguing. "You're awfully cocky."

A playful grin appears. "Thank you. I don't usually get such bold compliments about my body so early on in conversation, but I appreciate you noticing."

My cheeks burn, but I laugh. "I didn't mean it like *that.*"

"Oh, I think you did." He lifts his brows and takes a drink.

Applause erupts around us, startling me out of the moment. I was so focused on him, I lost track of everything else.

I kind of liked that, too.

Clay

That little startle was so fucking cute. I like a woman who can give as good as she gets. I'm glad I accepted Dash's offer to join them. Even on the heels of that devastating loss, I feel lighter than I have since spending the holidays with my family. Pepper is watching her sister with pride in her eyes as Sable thanks the audience, and not for the first time, I'm drawn to Pepper's love of her family. She's as close with hers as I am with mine.

"They were awesome," I say, leaning closer so she can hear me over the roaring crowd.

She beams. "Yeah, they were."

"It's hard to believe Sable's going to give all this up." My older sister, Victoria, who goes by Victory, owns Blank Space Entertainment and reps Bad Intentions. Last year she offered to sign Surge to her label, but Sable turned her down. She ended up signing several of Sable's bandmates, and Sable walked away without her band, or a deal.

"You probably can't relate to this, but she doesn't like the limelight."

"I can relate to that more than you know." It's not something I want to think about, and I'm glad for the distraction when Sable announces Bad Intentions. The crowd goes wild as the other band takes the stage.

"Hello, Paris!" Johnny Bad's voice booms through the arena, inciting more excitement. "This song is for my beautiful fiancée, Jillian, who's holding down the fort with our three kids back in the States. I love you, baby!" Jillian is Graham's sister.

Johnny breaks into "Star Crossed," and the crowd goes wild again.

As Pepper's sisters and brothers-in-law couple off to dance, I set down my drink and take Pepper's glass from her, placing it beside mine on a table.

"Hey," she complains. "I need that."

I draw her into my arms. "Not while you're dancing with me, you don't."

"I need it even *more* if I'm dancing with you." Her gaze darts around us nervously.

"Why is that? We're both good dancers." I hold her tighter, keeping her focus on me.

She doesn't respond, but as I sway more seductively, she moves with me. I dip my head, speaking into her ear. "Why are you fighting our connection? You feel incredible in my arms. Doesn't it feel good to you?"

"Reasonably good," she says breathily, but there's no missing the battle between desire and rational thinking looking back at me.

"It's okay to admit we feel phenomenal together."

Her eyes narrow. "Why are you even dancing with me? Didn't your pickup lines work on your other lady friends?"

I grit my teeth against the accusation, but I can't blame her for saying it, and it confirms the hint of jealousy I thought I sensed earlier, which I fucking loved. "Do you really think I'd come all the way to Paris to see you and then try to pick up other women just because you're playing hard to get?"

She gives me an incredulous look. "You're not here for me."

"Do you think I came all this way to hang out with Dash and see a concert? I love the guy, but this wasn't a two-hour plane ride."

Her eyes widen as understanding hits.

"Now that we're clear, do you really think I was trying to pick up those women?"

She schools her expression. "Based on your reputation, I'd be remiss to think otherwise."

"That stings," I admit. "Don't get me wrong, I appreciate your honesty. It's refreshing, since most women don't give a damn as long as they get a piece of me. But I'd think an intelligent woman like you would know better than to believe the rumors."

"They're rampant. They can't *all* be unfounded."

"I didn't say they were. It sounds like I need to give you reasons to believe I'm not a total scoundrel. I didn't try to pick them up. They're fans of the game. I was just giving them something to post about on their social accounts. It comes with the territory."

"Well, I'm not on social media, so you don't need to do that with me."

"I know. That's just one reason I find you so intriguing."

Her brows knit and her eyes narrow, like she's weighing my response.

The song ends, and she tries to pull away as applause rings out, but I keep her close, forcing her focus to remain on me. "That's right, Pepper. I searched for your nonexistent social accounts in an effort to find another way to connect with you after you ignored my attempts last year." I let that sink in as the next song begins and sway to the beat, enjoying the feel of her against me. "Why are you so determined to avoid me?"

"Because we have nothing in common."

"How do you know unless you give me a shot?"

"I'm a scientist and you're an *athlete*," she says, as if that should explain it all.

"Which means I'm dedicated to my career, a hard worker, and a team player. I'm determined to be the best, and I'm in great shape because of it. From what I've read about you, and from what I've seen, we're not so different." I skim my hand down her back and wrap my fingers around the curve of her hip, keeping her close. A sexy gasp escapes her lips, and I can feel her heart hammering against me. "Does my touch make you nervous?"

"Maybe a little," she admits. "I told you I need my drink."

"You make me a little nervous, too." I take her hand and press it over my heart so she can feel how fast it's beating.

Surprise rises in her eyes, and she looks like she's going to say something, but she just skims her teeth over her lower lip, looking innocent, and too fucking sexy.

"Damn, Pepper. You're killing me."

"I didn't *say* anything."

"You didn't have to. I've been thinking about kissing that sexy mouth of yours for a long damn time."

"I...*You*..." She presses her lips together, tensing in my arms. "Don't tell me that."

"Why not? Does it embarrass you?"

"What do you think?"

"Then I probably shouldn't tell you the other things I've been thinking about doing to you."

Her cheeks flame. "If you're going to say things like that, I definitely need my drink."

I chuckle, but I'm relieved and thrilled that she didn't slap me or walk away.

"I bet you say that kind of thing to all the women."

"I don't," I say firmly, biting back my annoyance at continually having to fight my reputation. If she were anyone else, I might walk away. But she's finally right here in my arms, unable to run away, and whether she wants to or not, she's looking at me like I'm a decadent cake she wants to gobble down but knows she shouldn't. I'm going to hand her a fucking fork and feed myself to her if that's what it takes. "How about we make a deal?"

"What kind of deal?"

"Give me one night to show you who I really am. Let your guard down. Allow yourself to have fun with me tonight. Pretend I'm not an athlete with a reputation that scares you, but just an incredibly good-looking guy you met through Dash."

"Not that you're conceited or anything," she teases.

"Confidence is not conceit. You're a beautiful woman. You must know that."

Her cheeks pink up. "I don't think I'm beautiful, but if I were, I wouldn't go around saying it."

"You're either incredibly humble, or you don't see what I see. I'll tell you what. You leave my reputation out of tonight and see me for the man I show you I am, and I'll try to look uglier."

She laughs. "Lucky me. Remind me what I'm getting out of this deal."

"You mean besides the best night of your life, sexy arm candy, and most importantly, debunking the myth that I'm nothing but a dumb jock?"

"I never said you were dumb, and that's not what I was implying. I meant we have nothing in common."

"I'm glad to hear that, and again, you can't know if we have anything in common until we spend some time together. As I was saying, give me tonight to prove myself. If you don't have fun, you can tell me to get lost." The song ends, and she tries to step out of my arms as applause and whistles ring out around us, but once again, I hold her tighter. "Do we have a deal?"

"Why does it feel like I'm making a deal with the devil?"

"Because I'm devilishly handsome."

That earns a genuine smile and a reluctant, "*Fine.* I'll make a deal with a dimpled devil, but don't make me regret it."

"You're really fucking cute." Before letting her go, I lean in and say, "For what it's worth, there's not a woman in here who can hold a candle to you."

Chapter Four

Pepper

"*Okay, okay!* I've got one! Never have I ever…" Brindle's voice trails off, her rascally gaze moving around the table. Anticipation hangs in the air like bait as we await her claim in our game of Never Have I Ever.

We're at the hotel nightclub for a private party with the bands and their crews. They're leaving early tomorrow morning for their next stop on the tour. Music is blaring, and the club is teeming with people dancing and drinking. Johnny has already come and gone, and his and Sable's bandmates are scattered around the club. I'm tipsy from alcohol, high from the excitement of the night, and my every nerve ending is ablaze from the darkly handsome man beside me. It's been hours since Clay and I struck our deal, and he's been *right there* ever since, driving me out of my mind with furtive glances, hidden touches, whispered jokes, and sexy innuendos that catch me off guard, wreaking havoc with my ability to think about anything other than the dirty things he says.

"Never have I ever," Brindle, the drama queen, repeats, "had sex in public."

Everyone reaches for their shot glass *except* me.

I swear my siblings are out to either embarrass me or find

out *all* my secrets, and this is just one more thing that sets me apart from them. As banter and laughter ring out, even Amber, my most demure sister, is whispering and giggling with her husband. It's like they're all in some kind of naughty-fun club that I'm not privy to.

Clay leans in and whispers, "I can help you remedy that."

Yes, please tramples through my tipsy mind, and my body takes it as a promise, throwing a little party, which is crazy because I'm *not* a public-sex person. I don't know *what* is going on with me right now, but I'd be lying if I didn't admit that it's as exciting as the hungry look in Clay's eyes. None of the men I've been intimate with have made my body ignite the way he does. I never thought I was missing out by not having one-night stands or meaningless trysts, but with him looking at me the way he is, I'm beginning to think I am.

"Really, Pep? Not even in college?" Brindle asks, pulling me from my thoughts.

"Not even in college," I say with exasperation, because I can't understand why it's so hard for her to comprehend.

"Not even when you went out with Ravi in high school?" Morgyn asks.

Ravi Bhandara grew up with us in Oak Falls. He's always been as science minded as me, which is what made us fast friends as kids and has kept us close ever since. But I'm not about to give my gossipy sisters the down and dirty on him. "Nope."

"I always thought you two snuck out to a field or some other place to fool around," Morgyn adds.

"Gosh, you guys," Amber says. "You jumped straight to sex with her and Ravi, and I always thought she was doodling *Pepper Bhandara* in her notebooks."

"Well, you were all wrong. Can we move on, please?" I take a sip of water.

"Ravi Bhandara, huh?" Clay says for my ears only. "Was he your first?"

"I'm not telling you that."

"Not here. Got it." He winks. "We'll talk about him later."

"Don't count on it."

"Now that we've got the skinny on all you exhibitionists," Brindle teases, "I'm changing the game. Whoever has the best answer doesn't have to drink. What's the hottest place you've ever had sex?"

"One partner or multiple?" Axsel says.

"Ohmygod." I shake my head at my brazen brother, and Clay chuckles.

"Your choice," Brindle announces.

"I don't know what you'll find hot, but I've got a few good ones," Axsel says. "The Jerichos' barn roof, a construction elevator, at a bonfire on a beach with three other guys, under the lights onstage before a concert."

"Our barn *roof*?" Trace snaps.

"You'd be even more surprised if you knew who it was with," Axsel said.

Trace frowns. "Do *not* tell me. I don't want to think about you doing some dude on my roof."

"I want to know," Morgyn exclaims.

"Let it go," Sable says, leaving no room for negotiation.

Sable has always been everyone's greatest protector. I don't know if she's protecting Trace from finding out what he doesn't want to know, or the guy Axsel was with, but Morgyn murmurs, "Fine."

"*On*stage, Axsel? In front of people?" Amber asks, wide-eyed.

I'm still trying to process the *three other guys* part.

Axsel's brows knit in concentration. "I think there were a half dozen people milling about."

As Axsel and the others discuss his varying trysts, Clay places his hand on my thigh, leaning closer, and says, "I can't wait to hear your answer."

"I am *not* answering that question," I whisper harshly.

"Aw, come on, Pep. You can tell me. I won't tell anyone."

His charm is addicting. "I am not telling *you* anything."

"I get it. You're a bedroom-only girl. Probably vanilla, too. There's no shame in that. It's cool."

"I am *not* vanilla. I've done things. I just don't feel the need to broadcast them."

"Mm-hm," he says disbelievingly. "If you say so."

"Oh my God. *Fine*," I whisper harshly. "I'll have you know that I've used syrup."

He laughs. "Sounds sticky."

"*Chocolate* syrup." Now I'm laughing, too. "There was a lot of licking, and it *was* sticky, but it was fun."

"Wait a second. You mean you went for sundaes, right? That almost counts. *Sex. Sundaes.* I can see the correlation."

"We did *not* go for sundaes." We're both cracking up.

I swat him, but he grabs my hand, tugging me so close, our mouths nearly touch. We both fall silent, the air crackling between us. The others sound far away. He reaches up and caresses my cheek with the backs of his fingers, sending heat scorching through me as he says, "I'd like to get my mouth on your sundae. Maybe add a little whipped cream." He licks his lips. *"Mm."*

I can barely breathe for the lust pooling inside me. I grab a shot and down it.

"You might want to slow down on the shots." He moves the water he'd gotten me earlier closer. "I'd hate for you to wake up with a hangover."

He's been watching out for me like that all evening, making sure I'm staying hydrated, asking if I need anything. When I went to the ladies' room, he insisted on walking me there. It's easy to forget who he is when he does things like that. What isn't easy to forget is that when I came out of the ladies' room and found him waiting for me, it was just the two of us in the dimly lit hallway, and I wanted to kiss him so badly, I ached with it.

That ache still hasn't left me.

"I'll be fine. Thanks."

His lips quirk up. "I might have ulterior motives. Especially now that I know you like the idea of sharing your *sundae* with me."

I go for a deadpan stare, but I'm betrayed by my attraction to him and fail miserably. "Didn't I tell you not to say things like that?"

"And miss seeing that sexy blush? Not a chance, sweetheart."

Futilely trying to hide my smile, I say, "I'm going to get you back for that."

"I can't wait." He picks up his shot glass and whispers, "To sweet revenge," and eyes me as he tosses it back.

"Hey, what's going on down there?" Brindle shouts.

We both look over and find everyone watching us. My stomach knots up. "Nothing," I say, sounding like I've been caught naked. *Ugh.* Now I'm thinking about Clay naked.

"You're drinking and we didn't get to hear your answers,"

Brindle complains.

"I don't have an answer," I say.

"Oh, come on," Axsel urges. "You must've rubbed one out with Ravi in the science lab or something."

"I did *not*." Okay, maybe I did, but I'm not going to announce it. It turns out it doesn't matter what I say, because once again they start discussing all the places they *thought* Ravi and I snuck off to all those years ago.

Clay leans in, his breath like fire on my skin. "I'm making a mental note to get you into a science lab."

"Ohmygod. Why am I even playing this game?"

"Because you want to know the hottest place I've ever had sex."

"No, I definitely *do not*. I don't want to think about you having sex with anyone else."

"Good to know," he says with a grin.

I realize my mistake and quickly backpedal. "I mean I don't want to think about you having sex at *all*."

"Yes, you do." He squeezes my thigh, and my entire body gets hot. "And just so you know, the hottest place I've ever had sex is yet to come. But don't worry, you'll be there with me, so you'll get to see it firsthand."

I blink once, twice, three times. That's how long it takes for me to realize I'm mentally ticking off all the places in Paris where we could have sex. I scramble for something to say. "Enjoy that fantasy." In an effort to take the attention *off* me, I lean forward, peering down the table, and say, "I haven't heard Sable's answer yet."

Sable and Kane exchange knowing glances, and she says, "I don't kiss and tell."

"Since when?" Morgyn retorts.

Sable eyes her handsome fiancé. "Since Kane."

Kane looks like the billionaire badass he is, with tattoos creeping out the collar and cuffs of his crisp white dress shirt, as he presses a kiss to the back of Sable's hand. "If you're thinking about what I'm thinking about, there wasn't a lot of kissing going on."

"Only because I couldn't reach your lips," Sable says.

Kane leans in and kisses the hell out of her, earning whistles and cheers from all of us.

"Our hottest place was in Belize," Morgyn announces, leaning into Graham. "Remember the swing?"

"Sunshine, what we did on that swing should be illegal." He pulls my giggling sister into a kiss.

Relationship envy is a thing, right? Because it's hitting me pretty hard right now.

"You're up, Amber," Brindle says.

Amber's cheeks flush. "Ours was a study room at the public library."

"What?" I practically shout, unable to believe my ears.

Everyone laughs, and Brindle says, "Maybe Amber can teach you how to loosen up."

"I'm loose," I insist, causing more laughter.

"That's not what he says," Morgyn teases.

Clay grabs my ankle and lifts my foot onto his lap, his silver bracelet catching the light.

"What are you doing?" I ask.

"Making sure you don't put your foot in your mouth again."

We all crack up.

He gives my calf a squeeze before releasing my foot and tosses me a charming grin that makes him look so boyish, my stomach flip-flops.

"It's my turn," Morgyn announces, and taps her fingernails on her glass. "Never have I ever had a threesome."

Everyone stills.

"You'd better not reach for that fucking glass," Sable says to Kane, and we all laugh.

Clay reaches for his shot glass, and my stomach twists. The guys give him halting looks.

"*Dude.*" Dash shakes his head. "Don't do it, man."

"Fuck that," Axsel says, and drinks a shot.

Clay shrugs. "You've got to try everything once, right?" He downs the shot.

Now I'm wondering why he's even interested in me. He might not know me well, but he knows I'm not the threesome type. Even more curious is what it says about me that I'm still attracted to him.

"Damn right, brother," Axsel says as they refill their shots.

"God, Axsel. Is there anything you haven't done?" Amber asks, spurring our brother on to brag about things I have no interest in hearing.

Clay leans closer again and says, "It really was only once."

"You don't have to explain yourself to me."

He puts his hand over mine, holding my gaze. "You're the only person I've ever wanted to explain myself to."

The honesty in his eyes is as inescapable as the heat between us.

"I was pretty drunk when it happened," he explains. "Bragging rights and all that. But once was enough to know sharing isn't for me."

And just like that, my thoughts are reeling again. I may not have had a lot of interesting sexual experiences, but I don't need experience to know that I'd never be comfortable in a non-monogamous relationship.

"Let's get it *all* out there," Brindle suggests.

"I don't think I can take any more revelations tonight," I say.

"Sure you can. This is fun." Brindle looks around the table and says, "How old were you when you lost your V-card? The youngest person drinks."

I shrink back in my chair, wishing I could disappear.

"On that note, I need to dance. Let's go, Pep." Sable pushes to her feet, coming to my rescue.

As I stand, Clay grabs my hand and says, "Save me a dance."

Such a simple request should not make my heart race, but as Sable and I head to the dance floor, I'm practically vibrating at the thought of being in his arms again. "Thanks for saving me from further mortification with that drinking game."

"You have nothing to be embarrassed about. I never understood your need to keep your sex life private until Kane and I got together. I get it now."

We find a spot on the dance floor and begin dancing. "Does that mean you no longer think I'm a weirdo?"

"I never thought you were a weirdo. I just didn't understand why other people's opinions mattered to you so much."

"It's not about anyone else's opinions. Sharing private moments belittles them."

"I understand that now. Sorry if I ever made you feel bad about it."

"Thanks." It feels good to hear that. Sable isn't one to make me feel bad about anything, but I like that she cares enough to apologize just in case she ever has. "How does it feel knowing you're just a couple of weeks away from the end of your tour?"

"Bittersweet. How does it feel knowing you're maybe an hour away from an incredible orgasm?"

Laughter bursts from my lungs. *"Sable!"*

"Don't pretend you're not thinking the same thing. I'm surprised you haven't dragged his ass up to your room yet. I've never seen you so into a guy."

"I'm not—"

"Save it. We both know you want him."

I dance closer so I don't have to talk so loud. "I was going to say that I'm not the kind of person who drags a man into my hotel room, but I kind of wish I *were*." Sable is one of only two people I can be this honest with. She knows most of my secrets.

"Then become that person. And you're welcome for my Never Have I Ever turn." She'd said *Never have I ever had an STD*, and nobody had done a shot. "Now you know he's okay to sleep with."

"That's why you said it?"

"Why are you surprised? I've always got your back."

"Thank you for that, but I don't know how to go from being *me* to doing *that*."

"You just do it," Sable says, like it's easy. "Look at me. I never thought I'd settle down, and there's nothing I want more than a life with Kane. Clay's a good guy, Pep. I've been watching him. He's looking after you, and he makes you laugh and blush and *want*."

"That he does, but he's also an athlete, and you know I don't date athletes."

"Yes, and for good reason when you were in college. But Clay's not a stupid college kid, and who said anything about *dating*? You're having fun. You're in Paris. If ever there was a time to cut loose and enjoy yourself, it's now. Nobody's going to know what you do except you and him." The song ends, and we start dancing to a faster song. "When's the last time you've felt like this about a guy?"

"I don't know. *Never*. He makes me feel rebellious and like I want to rip off his clothes, which is *so* not me, and knowing it's not me makes me want to hide. But I *really* don't want to hide."

Sable laughs. "Girl, you've got it bad."

"No kidding. But, Sable, he's got *loads* of experience."

"Which means he'll know how to make you feel good."

"Sure, but what if I throw caution to the wind, and I don't make *him* feel good?"

"You're overthinking. Everything feels good to guys. They're not that complicated."

"I wish I had your confidence."

"You *can*, and you will. Trust me. When you're with someone who really turns you on, it all comes naturally. Even the confidence."

I cling to that as we dance, hoping it's true, and try to lose myself in the music. But between the alcohol and Sable's encouragement, all I can think about is getting up the nerve to be with Clay.

"You've got a gorgeous guy watching your every move. Are you going to show him what you're made of, or go home from Paris wishing you had?" Sable encourages.

I chance a look, and sure enough, those keen blue eyes are trained on me.

Clay grins, like he's heard every word we've said. Even *that* feels dangerously exciting. The dance floor is hot and crowded with couples bumping and grinding. I don't know how I muster the courage, but when "Lose Control" comes on, I close my eyes for a moment and give myself over to the music. Fueled by desire, I open my eyes, dancing dirtier, more seductively.

"You look *hot*. Get it, girl," Sable encourages.

The tethers of my inhibitions fall away with every thunderous beat, until I feel free and a little wild.

Sable takes my hand, pulling me closer, and says, "Tonight is your night."

She twirls me away, and my hands land on a hard chest. Cedarwood infiltrates my senses as I look up, finding Clay's piercing blue eyes boring into me. He falls into step with my dirty moves, and "*Hello there, handsome*" sails huskily from my lips. I don't recognize my own voice, but his eyes flame, and I refuse to give in to the urge to overthink my behavior.

"Have fun," Sable says, and saunters off the dance floor.

"I think this means Sable approves of me." Clay wraps his arms around me as we dance.

"I wouldn't be so sure," I tease.

"How about you?" His expression turns serious. "How much does it bother you that I've had a threesome?"

There go my nerves again. I expect instinct to kick in and my insecurities to pour out, but Sable was right, and confidence shoves them aside. "Let's just say, never have I ever seen myself as someone who would be into a guy who's had a threesome. Yet here I am in your arms again."

Relief washes over his features. "Good. I was worried it intimidated you."

"It did" comes out before I can stop it. *Hello, rational brain, please go away.* "You have a lot of experience. I'll surely pale in comparison. I've only had twosomes, and lately, it's been more onesomes."

He holds me tighter. "I like that about you. Fewer men I have to kill."

I laugh.

"Tell me more about those onesomes."

"No." God, he makes me smile.

"I'm kidding. Spending the evening with you has already been more fun than anything I've done in a long time. If you succeed in seducing me, I know it'll be better than anything I've ever experienced."

"If *I* seduce *you?*"

"Don't play innocent. You've been doing it all night with your coy smiles and sassy comments. Don't even get me started on that sexy laugh or the cute way you fidget when you're nervous. It's a little embarrassing the way you've been undressing me with your eyes."

I laugh again.

"Seriously," he says with the warmest expression, making my insides go soft. "Cards on the table. Never have I ever thought about a woman day after day, month after month, the way I've been thinking about you. I have no doubt if we take this where I think we both want it to go, we'll be great together, and I think deep down you know it, too."

Time stands still as I try to process the truth in that, and Sable's voice tramples through my mind. *Are you going to show him what you're made of, or go home from Paris wishing you had?*

"Confident" comes on, and I take a page from Morgyn's playbook, counting it as a sign from the universe. Before I can overthink *that,* I step out of Clay's arms and start dancing seductively, his heated gaze fueling my confidence. His hands skim over my waist and up my ribs, stopping just short of my breasts. I have a fleeting thought about my family seeing me, but the dance floor is even more crowded, and that thought is no match for the things he just confessed and the desire coursing through me.

I run my hands along his chest, his muscles flexing beneath my fingers, and we fall into sync, moving erotically to the music. When "Body Like a Back Road" comes on, he turns me around, and I gyrate my hips, dancing with my back to him. He gathers my hair over one shoulder and slides his arm around my waist, tugging my back to his chest. I feel every hard inch of him against my ass.

"You're so fucking sexy," he rasps in my ear, sending shivers down my spine as he bites my earlobe. I gasp at the mix of pain and pleasure slicing through me. "That's for taunting me," he growls. He sucks my earlobe into his mouth, his arm tightening around me.

Sweet baby Jesus. I feel myself go damp.

This man is going to be my undoing, and I *want* to unravel.

I angle my head, giving him better access. He lowers his mouth to my neck, kissing, licking, and nipping, setting my entire body on fire. "A Little Wicked" starts playing, and he turns me around. The hunger in his eyes makes me feel bold and brave and sexy.

"Get in here, you wicked thing." He tugs me to him.

We're swaying and grinding, our hands roaming, eyes trained on each other. His touch sears through my clothing, and the music pulses beneath my skin. The sexually charged atmosphere magnifies every sensation. When "Play with Fire" comes on, he holds me tight against him, our hands on each other's asses, our hips grinding. He brushes his lips over mine, electrifying me all the way down to my toes. Time moves in a blur of *want* and *need* as one song bleeds into another until I'm dangerously close to ripping this man's clothes off right here on the dance floor.

I force myself to take a step back. "I, um…" I'm breathing hard. My brain won't function. "I need a minute." I hurry off the dance floor, making a beeline for the ladies' room.

I push through the bathroom doors, blinded by the bright lights. I pace, trying to calm my racing heart. I run my hands under cold water and wet a paper towel, pressing it to the back of my neck, trying to cool off. But this isn't just heat from dancing. My body is an inferno of desire. I've never felt anything like it. I toss the paper towel in the trash and look in the mirror. My hair is tousled, my cheeks are flushed, and I look as hot and bothered as I feel.

Who is this wanton woman?

Okay, Pepper. Think rationally.

Yes, it feels good to want and be wanted, but this is not you.

Some rebellious part of me fights that, but I work hard to squash it. After a few deep breaths and a long-winded pep talk, I feel a little more in control. I head out of the ladies' room and nearly crash into Clay. We're alone again in the dimly lit hallway.

"Everything okay?" His fingers wrap around mine.

My nipples tighten with awareness as he closes the small gap between us. My back hits the wall, the beat of the music vibrating through it, competing with the hammering of my heart. "Uh-huh," I manage as the rational part of my brain battles with the needy woman being enveloped by his masculine scent.

"You sure?" His thick thighs press against me, caging me in with his big body.

"Better now," that needy woman says, earning a devilish grin.

"Good." His hard length presses into my stomach, and he

threads his fingers into my hair. "I know you're a private person." He skims his teeth along my jaw, sending prickles of heat through my core. I close my eyes, savoring in the sensation. His lips brush over mine, soft as a feather, as he says, "This is what I really wanted to do out there."

His mouth comes coaxingly down over mine in a slow, sensual kiss. He doesn't press his body harder into mine, and I know he's giving me a chance to change my mind. Rational thinking be damned, I want this night with him. I slide my arm around his waist and go up on my toes, hungrily returning his efforts. He growls in appreciation, and the sexy sound unleashes something wild in me. He intensifies his efforts, his hands fisting in my hair, his tongue delving deeper, rougher, more possessively. *Yes! This is what I want!* We're grinding and moaning, feasting on each other like ravenous animals. Our kisses go on and on, and when he tears his mouth away, I'm so caught up in us, I pull it back to mine. But he kisses me for only a minute before breaking our connection again. My eyes fly open, and the passion staring back at me has my knees weakening.

"Not here," he says gruffly. "Unless you want your family and everyone else in this place to hear how thoroughly I'm going to pleasure you. Let's get our jackets and get out of here."

Chapter Five

Clay

Pepper tells the others she has a headache, and I offer to make sure she gets up to her room safely. We play it cool as we head to the elevator, but the second the doors close, we drop our jackets and devour each other, grinding and groping as the floors tick by. I've wanted her for so long, I feel like a fucking teenager, so damn greedy for her I can barely think straight. My hands are everywhere at once, on a mission to feel every lush curve. Her mouth is hot and sweet and so fucking willing, my dick aches to be inside it.

When the elevator stops on my floor, we reluctantly part, snag our jackets, and rush down the hall. Once inside my suite, I strip off her blazer between ravenous kisses and tear her shirt over her head. She's pushing at my shirt, and I make quick work of taking it off. Her bra goes next, and I take a long lascivious look at her gorgeous tits and swollen lips.

"You're fucking beautiful."

"*Me?* Look at you. Those abs can't be real."

I laugh. "You think that's impressive. Just wait till I take my pants off."

She blushes a red streak, which makes her even more adorable. "Don't be conceited when I'm half-naked."

"Okay. I'll save it for when you're fully naked, but for what it's worth, nothing is as impressive as that unstoppable smile of yours."

Her gaze softens, and I can tell she finally believes me. That trust untethers me, and I bury my hands in her hair, angling her luscious mouth beneath mine, devouring her as her back meets the wall. We're finally flesh to flesh, her taut nipples and soft breasts turning my skin to fire, but it's nowhere near enough. I want to possess and pleasure all of her at once, but I can't stop kissing her.

Keeping her mouth exactly where I want it with one hand, I palm her breast with the other and brush my thumb over her nipple. She moans, and the sound goes straight to my cock. I grit out, "*Fuck*," and lower my mouth to her breast, teasing her nipple with my teeth and tongue, earning more sexy sounds. "So damn soft and gorgeous."

She clings to me, moaning and arching. I want to strip her bare and lay her out where I can worship every inch of her, but I'm too impatient to cross the room to the couch or the bar or go into the bedroom. I suck her nipple to the roof of my mouth, and she cries out.

"Sorry," I murmur against her skin.

"*I like it*," she pants out.

I do it again, sucking harder, and she clings to me, her fingernails piercing my flesh.

"Feels so good." Her voice is husky and raw.

I use both hands, rolling one nipple between my finger and thumb as I tease and taunt the other until she's writhing and begging for more. Only then do I trail kisses down her stomach and use my teeth to open her jeans. She giggles, and *man*, I love that sound. I kiss the silky skin I revealed, rubbing her through her jeans, and she inhales a ragged breath. Sinking down to one knee, I press a kiss between her legs through the denim and grit out, "I cannot wait to taste you."

Her cheeks flame, but she watches me take off her boots and socks. "I like your beautiful eyes on me."

"I like your everything on me."

I strip off her jeans. "Silk panties," I say as I tease her through them, then take them off. "You secret little sex kitten."

"My guilty pleasure," she pants out.

"No guilt allowed." I rain kisses over her thighs and kiss the bare flesh just above her glistening pussy as I slide my fingers through her wetness, earning another hungry moan. "Do you know how many nights I have fantasized about burying my mouth between your legs?" Her pussy clenches, and she bites her lower lip. "Spread your legs for me, baby." She does. "Now watch me pleasure you."

Her eyes brim with desire as I circle her clit with my tongue and move lower, taking my first taste of her. "So damn sweet." I do it again, and again, circling her clit and licking her sweet, hot pussy.

"*Ah....so good...Clay...*" Her voice is drenched in desire, and my cock throbs for her, but I've waited too long to rush. I continue licking and teasing, building in intensity and speed with every slick of my tongue, until she's writhing against the wall, her arousal coating my mouth. "*Please. I can't take it.*"

I push two fingers into her slick heat and drag my tongue over her swollen clit, earning a long, sensual sound that rockets through me. "That's it, baby. Let me hear how much you want me." I tease and lick and flick that sensitive bundle of nerves as I find the magical spot inside her that makes her pussy clench and her legs tremble. I suck her clit between my teeth, and she gasps, riding my fingers. "I can't wait to fuck you."

"*Clay*," she pants, her entire body shaking. *"I'm going to—"* She cries out, clawing at my shoulders, her pussy clenching tight and hot around my fingers, her hips bucking. I stay with her, eating the best meal of my life, as she rides out her pleasure to the very end, and then I send her careening again. My name flies from her lips like a fucking prayer, and I know I'll hear it long after we're apart.

She goes limp above me, her hands on my shoulders, panting out, "Wow, you're good at that."

I laugh and lift her into my arms. She gasps in surprise.

"I have legs, you know," she says as I carry her into the bedroom.

"I'm well aware of those sexy legs and look forward to having them wrapped around my neck and wrapped around my waist while I'm buried nine inches deep."

I strip down the blanket and lay her on the sheet. Moonlight spills in through the windows, giving her an ethereal glow. She looks so sweet and sated, I have the urge to climb into bed and hold her. That's about as foreign, and as startling, as the fact that I haven't thought about the playoff loss since I first set eyes on her tonight.

She goes up on one elbow, watching me toe off my shoes and strip off my remaining clothes. As I step out of my boxer briefs, her eyes lock on my cock, shimmering with appreciation. She sits up. "You weren't lying about *that*."

"Yeah, I'm not big on lying." I wrap my hand around my erection, giving it a stroke. "Guess Morgyn didn't tell you about the Braden curse."

"Thankfully *no*. She doesn't talk to me about her husband's junk. Were you honest about never having an STD?"

"Like I said, I'm not big on lying."

"In that case." She moves to sit on the side of the bed and crooks her finger, beckoning me.

I didn't think it was possible for her to get any hotter, but a lady in the streets and a vixen in the sheets? *Fuck yeah*. She is scorching. "Does my sexy scientist want to do a little hands-on research?"

"Hands. *Mouth*." She says *mouth* just above a whisper, and it sounds so fucking sexy, my cock jerks. "You're not the only one who fantasized about this." She licks her sultry lips as she wraps her delicate fingers around my cock. Her gaze flicks to mine, and her eyes narrow. "If I'm giving myself one night with you, I'm going to enjoy it, so please don't thrust so hard you choke me."

I don't think a woman has ever told me what to do in the bedroom. They're usually just happy to be there. I fucking *love* that she's not willing to be used for only my pleasure. "Baby, I want to do a lot of things to you, but turning you off to sucking my cock is not one of them."

"Good." She begins licking me from base to tip, getting me nice and wet, and swirls her tongue around the broad head.

"That's it. Feels good." I thread my fingers into her hair. "Look at me." Her hungry hazel eyes flick to mine, and she lowers her mouth over my cock, stroking as she sucks me off. "*Ah, yeah.* Tighter." She tightens her grip, chasing her mouth with her hand, working me into a heart-pounding fervor. She quickens her efforts, and I grit my teeth against the pleasure coursing through me. I focus all of my willpower to keep from taking control and driving my cock down her throat. "Feels so fucking good. Can you take me deeper, baby?"

She grabs my hip with one hand, pulling me closer and

taking me to the back of her throat. Then she takes me deeper. Pleasure rockets through me. *"Fuuck."* She strokes me faster, tighter, taking me just as deep, over and over. Lust pounds beneath my skin, mounting like a volcano readying to blow. "Feels too good," I hiss. "I'm gonna come if you keep doing that."

Her eyes turn feral, and she works me faster, taking me so fucking deep, I see stars, and grit out, *"Fuuck,"* as I come down her throat. She swallows everything I have to give. When the last shudder rumbles through me, I utter, *"Christ,* Pepper," and rub her jaw as I pull out of her mouth. "I didn't hurt you, did I?"

She shakes her head, eyes at half-mast. I tighten my grip on her hair, lifting her to her feet with a gentle tug. "I knew your mouth would wreck me."

The smile that earns twists me up inside. I take her in a kiss so fierce and possessive, I know I should break the connection, run from those feelings. But I don't. I intensify my efforts, chasing them, wanting to consume them. When I finally tear my mouth away, she's beautifully breathless, and I'm hard again. "I'm not done with that stunning mouth of yours, but climb up on the bed, sexy girl. I'm going to make you feel so good, you'll never want to leave."

"One night," she says as she climbs onto the bed. "That's all this is."

"We'll see about that." I leisurely explore the dips and curves of her body with my hands and mouth, taking her right up to the edge of release and holding her there. She moans and gasps with every touch, begging me for more. Hearing her beg only makes me want to stave off her orgasm longer, to revel in her greediness for me. When I finally give her what she needs,

"*Clay*—" flies from her lips, and I devour every last drop of her essence as she writhes against my mouth, moaning and mewling.

When she finally collapses to the mattress, gasping for air, and runs her fingers through my hair as I kiss my way up her body. I soak in that intimate touch until her hands slide off my head, landing lightly on my arms, and I drink her in. Her skin is flushed, her eyes closed, and her hair a mass of shiny locks spread over the pillow. I've never seen anything so beautiful. "Still with me, sweetheart?" I'm not an endearment guy, but with her, *sweetheart* comes naturally.

"*Barely*," she whispers, her eyes fluttering open.

My chest tightens at the sweetness and trust staring back at me. I lower my lips to hers, intending to go slow, but I can't hold back. Passion builds so fast, and I kiss her for so long, we both nearly lose it. I tear my mouth away, gritting out, "Your mouth fucking owns me. I *love* kissing you."

She pulls my mouth back to hers, and our bodies meld together as we feast on each other. I grind my hips, and she bows beneath me, grabbing at my back, moaning into my mouth. I give her the friction she craves, grinding my erection against her clit. We're a brewing storm, thunderous and sharp, gaining strength with every rock and moan. The need to be inside her is primal. I reluctantly tear my mouth away and get up to grab a condom from my wallet, quickly sheathing my cock. She reaches for me as I come down over her.

Our mouths fuse as our bodies become one, and she's so fucking tight, my vision blurs. "*Ohmygod*," she whimpers, and I know she feels it, too. I move slowly at first, trying not to give in to the exquisite pleasure coursing through me. I lift her leg at the knee, spreading her wider, taking her deeper. "*Ah*," she says against my mouth. "*So good.*"

Her pleasure heightens mine, and she gazes up at me with a mix of lust and something akin to confusion. I get that, because we fit together like two pieces of a fucking puzzle. I'm overcome by a feeling of rightness like I've never known. Nothing has *ever* felt this good. Before that can fuck with my head, I reclaim her mouth, and we begin to move. When we find our rhythm, we're in perfect sync. Our kisses turn feverish, my thrusts deep and purposeful. Our bodies take over, and there's no holding back. We grope, claw, and *claim*, kissing, biting, and sucking. Our skin grows slick with sweat, her moans and my curses filling the air. This is not just sex. This is something all-consuming. Something unstoppable and wild, and I want more of her.

I slide my hands under her ass, lifting and angling her hips. She hooks her feet around the backs of my thighs, taking me impossibly deeper. *"Clay."* The desperation in her voice is underscored by the way she's clinging to me like a lifeline. I realize with a start that I want to be that lifeline. I want to be the anchor that grounds her the way nothing else can.

As if she can hear my thoughts, she kisses me harder, meeting my every thrust with a rock of her hips. The pleasure is torturous, drawing me deeper into the soft, trusting beauty beneath me. I quicken my efforts, pounding into her, rough and greedy.

Her legs are tight around me, and her head falls back, her face a mask of pleasure. I seal my mouth over her neck, sucking hard. Her breaths come in fast bursts, fingernails cutting into my skin as she surrenders to our passion. *"Clay—"*

This time my name sounds like a fucking curse. Her pussy pulses tight and hot around my cock, and my release crashes over me like a bullying wave. I bury my face in the crook of her neck, gritting out her name as the world disappears, and I'm lost in a sea of pleasure so vast and new, I never want to hit shore.

Chapter Six

Pepper

Wakefulness comes with a faint throb in my temple, eased by the luxurious feel of soft sheets, the scent of something sweet and spicy, and the blissfulness of being completely and utterly sexually satisfied. Panic flares in my chest, and my eyes fly open. I lie stock-still for fear of waking Clay as last night comes reeling back in vivid color and surround sound. Images flash in my mind of Clay's face buried between my legs, his eyes gleaming with lust as he made me moan and writhe and *beg. Beg! Nonononono.* I don't beg for sex! I squeeze my eyes shut against that mortifying reality, and his voice traipses through my mind—*Spread your legs for me, baby. Now watch me pleasure you*—sending my traitorous body into a heated shudder with the memory of his talented mouth, hands, and body giving me the best orgasms of my life.

Shitshitshit.

How could I let this happen? This is all my sisters' fault with their stupid drinking games and flaunting their happy coupledom. All that kissing, cuddling, and whispering with their men!

Breathe, Pepper. Just breathe.

It was just sex.

Three rounds of hot, vocal, dirty sex, to be exact.

And a blowjob.

The memory of beckoning him to the edge of the bed hits. *Oh God.* What was I thinking? I don't even like giving blowjobs.

But I enjoyed it with Clay. I wanted it. I *craved* it.

So much that I did it twice.

And *swallowed.*

That was a first.

Everything about last night was a first.

Holy cow. Who was that woman?

My stomach knots up as the full scope of my debauchery rolls in.

How could I go against everything I believe in and have a one-night stand with an athlete?

I cringe inwardly, knowing I'm just one of many women he's used to satisfy himself. But he said so many nice things, and it felt like he meant them. Nothing is as impressive as my smile? He knew my mouth would wreck him? Those things felt monumental last night. Special. *Intimate.* Now, with a clearer head, I realize he probably would have said anything to get me to agree to have sex with him.

Ugh. This isn't helping. I can't erase what's happened.

All I can do is minimize the damage.

I'll sneak out before he wakes up and pretend it never happened. It's not like I have to see him anymore. He's probably got plans for today, and I'm leaving tomorrow. That makes me feel a little better. I try to remember where I left my clothes, so I can make a swift and silent escape.

I hear the faint chime of a text message, and the memory of us tearing off each other's clothes as we came through the door of his suite comes rolling in. Solution in hand, I feel a tad more in control. I open my eyes, but I don't dare move. Instead, I shift my gaze to Clay's side of the bed. My attention locks on the tented sheet above his hips. My body ignites as more dirty memories flood in.

"Morning, Pep."

I whip my head to the side, feeling like I'm watching one of those movies that zoom in too fast, bringing Clay's bright eyes, panty-melting dimples, and Cheshire cat grin into focus. My nerves flame. "Hey."

"That was fun last night." He shifts onto his side, and his erection lands on my leg.

Lands on it. Trying to ignore the heat and heft of that appendage is like trying not to breathe. "Yeah. Loads of fun," I manage. My phone chimes in rapid succession, making my heart race even faster. *Oh God. My sisters!* If they find out I spent the night with Clay, I'll never live this down. I begin weaving an excuse for not answering their texts. "What time is it?"

His arm snakes over my waist. "Time for me to eat breakfast, and for you to come." He yanks the sheet down, sending cool air over my naked body. My nipples rise to greet his mouth as he lowers it toward my breast.

"I don't have time." I push out from under him, but he tugs me back, his eyes playful, which makes me smile, *damn it.*

"We'll be quick," he promises.

My phone is chiming, my pulse is hammering, and my stupid body is already revved up. "No. We can't be quick. You'll start with your mouth, and then I'll want my mouth on you, and we both know where that leads."

He flashes a wolfish grin. "Yes, we do. *Hello, nirvana.*"

"*Yeah*" comes out breathy before I can check it. "*No!* There will be no nirvana." I start to get up, but he tightens his hold on me.

"Why so adamant, sweetheart? Last night you were all about pleasure. I believe you said I was the best you've ever had."

I wince as *that* memory strolls in like a fucking champ. It was right after our third round of sex, when I was too blissed out to think. "I don't even know who that woman was. She was reckless, and she must have been stuck in some post-orgasmic haze when she said it."

He squeezes my hip. "Well, then, how about I remind you and we bring Reckless out to play again?"

"That girl *doesn't* exist. She was a product of too much giddy girl talk and alcohol." I peel his hand off my body, and as I climb out of bed, more chimes ring out. "I have to go. I have work to do, and someone needs something." *Someone needs something? I am really losing it.*

"That woman is very real, Pepper. You can't hide that kind of passion forever." He follows me out of the bedroom, and his arm circles me from behind. He spins me around, and our naked bodies collide, our eyes locking. "That someone who needs something is *you*, and what you need is to relax and be pampered." He kisses my lips, and Lord help me, I want so much more. "Worshipped." He kisses my jaw, holding me tighter, and I feel him getting hard. "Fucked so thoroughly, you can't think of anything else."

I know just how well he can fulfill those promises. That knowledge coalesces with the feel of his stiff cock, the seductive look in his eyes, and the heat of his hands on my back, and I nearly combust at the thought of it. "As incredible as that sounds, I can't." I sound as regretful as my body feels, but my brain knows better. I push from his arms, making a beeline for the door. "I have to go. This was fun, but it never happened."

"Yes, it did," he says, following me.

I turn on him. "Clearly it did. But nobody can know. I'm not a buckle bunny."

"I'll alert the cowboys. You do realize I play for the Giants, right?"

Of course you do with that giant python between your legs. "I don't care who you play for!" I snap. "You know what I mean. I don't want to be a notch on your belt. I'm a scientist. My name needs to be taken seriously, which won't happen if it gets slung through a public rumor mill with some kind of sex scandal."

He laughs. "Sex scandal?"

"I saw what happened to Sable, and I'm too busy to deal with that kind of chaos." I pick up my clothes as I speak. "And if you talk to Dash, you walked me to my room last night, and that was it. Nothing happened, and you haven't seen me since. I don't need my sisters making a big joke out of this. I'll never live it down." I reach for the door but feel guilty about being so dismissive. I turn to face him and huff out, "Thank you for a lovely time. I hope you enjoy the rest of your vacation. But really, this never happened."

"I've got memories, Pepper. Phenomenal memories that are etched into my mind. You can't take those from me."

"Then I'll develop something to erase them. I'm a scientist. I can do that." It's a ridiculous statement, but I'm not exactly thinking rationally with his nine-inch pleasure wand staring at me. "Until then, you keep those memories stowed away under lock and key."

"Yes, ma'am."

I reach for the door again.

"Pep?"

I look over my shoulder at him, standing there all hard bodied and beautiful. The bastard.

"If you go out in the hall like that, you'll give lots of other guests memories, too."

I look down and realize I'm still buck naked. "Damn it."

I drop my things and quickly get dressed. Then I steal one last look at him, because I know he's the most beautiful man I'll ever see naked.

"I had a lovely time, too," he says, handing me my blazer and jacket. "Feel free to brag about it."

I narrow my eyes. "This *never* happened." I tug open the door and stalk out, trying to ignore the niggle of longing in my chest.

Clay

Enjoy the rest of my vacation indeed, sexy girl.

If Pepper thinks I'm going to forget last night, she's sorely mistaken. I give her time to get to her room, and then I text her.

Me: *Hey, Reckless. My sheets smell like you. Want to make yours smell like me?*

Pepper: *You've reached a nonworking number.*

Me: *I'm officially in lust with your mouth.*

Pepper: *Don't think about my mouth.*

There's no way she's not craving me the same way I'm dying for more of her. Last night was too good, too fun, too *different.* But she obviously needs to feel in control this morning, so I let her off easy.

Me: *I miss you too.*

As I get ready for the day, I can't stop thinking about how incredible last night was and how adorably flustered Pepper was this morning. I got a peek behind her demure veil at a seriously sensual, fun woman, and I have a feeling that was a glimpse of the real Pepper Montgomery. I want to explore that side of her and see what else she's hiding from the world.

I grab my bomber jacket and head down to the café to meet Dash and the others for breakfast.

I walk into the café feeling on top of the world and scan the room for Pepper. I spot Dash and Amber at a table with Trace and Brindle and see Morgyn and Graham heading in that direction from the buffet. A pang of disappointment hits when I realize Pepper isn't here. Then I remember we didn't go to sleep until almost three this morning. She was so worn out, she fell asleep in my arms, mumbling about our deal not including sex. I stand a little prouder with the memory, feeling like a fucking king, and head over to the table.

"Oh good, you're here," Brindle says. "Was Pepper with you this morning? She's not answering any of our texts."

The caveman in me wants to beat my chest and announce my conquest, but I'm not a complete asshole, and the truth is, I don't see Pepper as a conquest. I've wanted her for a long damn time. She's screwed with my head in more ways than one, and after witnessing the way her siblings talk candidly about their sexual escapades and learning that Pepper keeps hers close to her chest, I want to protect her from their banter.

"No, she wasn't," I say as Graham and Morgyn take their seats.

"Brindle said you left the club together last night," Amber says.

Amber and Dash were on the dance floor when we said our goodbyes. "We did. She'd had a few drinks, so I walked her to her room to make sure she got there okay. She's probably sleeping in."

"Pepper doesn't sleep in," Morgyn says. "But she could be working and ignoring her messages."

I hike a thumb over my shoulder. "Why don't I go check on her? What's her room number again?"

"She's in 307, and—" Brindle waves toward the café entrance. "Never mind. There she is. She's with Axsel."

I turn around as Axsel heads for the buffet and take in Pepper and her stunning smile before she notices me. Her hair falls in gentle waves over the shoulders of her forest-green turtleneck sweater. Her curve-hugging skinny jeans are tucked into fashionable flat-bottomed boots. I can't help wondering if she's wearing silk panties again.

Our eyes connect, and her cheeks instantly pink up, her smile faltering. She might as well be wearing a billboard announcing our night together. Didn't she know I was invited to hang out with her family today?

"Hey, Pep. What were *you* up to this morning?" Brindle asks coyly.

Pepper points at me. "Whatever he said isn't true." She puts her coat on the back of a chair.

Brindle eyes the two of us. "Does that mean he *didn't* leave you at your door last night?"

Everyone looks at Pepper. "*Oh.* Yes. He did. I just thought...You know how he's always making jokes and how guys make stuff up."

Fuck. She's making it worse. "Damn, Pep, that stings. I'd never lie about you." I can't stop the grin tugging at my lips.

"That is, unless you ask me to."

She scowls. "I need coffee."

"It's at the buffet," Morgyn says helpfully.

"I'll go with you." I fall into step beside Pepper. "You look beautiful this morning."

"What are you doing with my family?" she whispers harshly.

"It's nice to see you, too," I say as we reach the buffet.

She deadpans as Axsel steps up beside us holding a plate piled high with food.

"Man, we just got here. How'd you piss her off already?" Axsel asks.

"Don't let that scowl fool you. She loves me." I grab two plates and hand one to Pepper.

Pepper rolls her eyes and turns her attention to the buffet.

"Good luck with that," Axsel says, and heads back to the table.

I follow Pepper along the buffet, leaning closer as she puts strawberries on her plate. "That's a good start, but be sure to get some cheese and a pastry. You'll need your energy for later." I toss in a wink for good measure.

She doesn't look amused. "I asked you a question."

"Always so focused on answers." I put a pastry on my plate. "This is why we should have stayed in bed this morning. We could've sidetracked that brilliant brain of yours with more pleasure."

She sighs exasperatedly, but her lips twitch into an *almost* smile as we move along the buffet, filling up our plates. When we get to the coffee station, I wait as she orders a French vanilla latte.

"We could go back to my room now," I suggest. "And take the edge off before we spend the day with your family."

That brings her serious eyes to mine. "You're spending the day with us?"

"Yeah. Isn't it great? I'm looking forward to getting to know you better." I whisper, "It'll give me a chance to prove to you that I'm more than just an orgasm donor."

Her eyes widen, and her lips press firmly together, those pretty hazel eyes moving nervously around us.

"Don't worry, Reckless. Your secret is safe with me." I grab black coffee and head back to the table.

A little while later, with food in her belly and caffeine in her system, Pepper seems a little more at ease. I listen as her sisters ask her about last night and the unanswered texts they sent this morning. Pepper claims to have turned off her phone and gone to bed early. She says she forgot to turn it on until she was on her way to meet them for breakfast. I wonder if her sisters can hear the slightly higher pitch in her voice with the lie, like I can.

"Hey, Clay. It sucks about the playoffs," Trace says, draping an arm across the back of Brindle's chair. "That last sack looked rough."

"Made even worse because it was that douchebag Gorecky," Dash says. "That guy has had it out for Clay for years."

"I should've seen it coming." *Fucking Gorecky.* He used to play for the Giants, and he's been after my ass ever since I caught him cheating on his wife and gave him hell for it.

"You played a great game, and there's always next year," Trace says.

"They can't expect you to be Mr. Perfect all the time," Axsel says.

I grit my teeth. "Sure they can." *And they do. Just like everyone else.*

Axsel rakes a hand through his hair. "If football ever falls through, you can always do more underwear ads."

"Right." As arrogant as I am, those fucking ads have become the bane of my existence. They get more attention than my humanitarian work, and that bugs the shit out of me.

"Speaking of ads," Dash says. "I hear Hawk is doing your Under Armour photo shoot."

Dash's brother Hawk is a highly-sought-after photographer. "Is he? I didn't know that. The shoot's not for a couple of weeks yet, but I look forward to seeing him."

"This is your contract year, isn't it?" Trace says. "Are you negotiating an extension?"

"Yeah." My muscles tense up. That's the last thing I want to think about.

"Aren't you getting a little long in the tooth for football, cuz?" Graham asks. "You're what? Thirty-four?"

"Thirty-five," I grit out.

"That's right. You've got a few years on me," Graham teases. "Decades of pushing your body to the limits and taking hits makes you what? Sixty in non-footballer years?"

The guys laugh.

A master at deflection, I turn up my arrogance. "My body is like fine whiskey. It just gets better with age."

"No doubt," Trace says.

"How's your shoulder holding up?" Dash asks.

Like shit. My fucking shoulder has been giving me trouble all season, and for the last few months, the muscle tension has been leading to migraines, but I'm not about to share that. I meet Dash's inquisitive gaze. "It's fine."

"No more headaches?" Dash asks.

I shrug. "Nothing I can't handle."

"That injury's been haunting you for a while now," Graham

says. "When are you going to retire and settle down with a nice woman? Go after a cushy announcer job and live the good life?" He drapes his arm around Morgyn, who snuggles into his side, kisses him, then goes back to chatting with the girls.

Despite the fact that lately my career has brought more stress than pleasure and the issues I'm having with my shoulder, I can't bring myself to consider retiring. I can't fathom going out on a loss. The guys are looking at me expectantly, waiting for me to respond. I try to bury my thoughts, but it's not easy. I glance at Pepper. My beautiful distraction. She's the only thing that has ever rivaled football for my attention. "The good life, huh?"

"Yeah. Take a play out of Flynn's playbook," Graham says. "I was floored when I heard he got engaged. I never thought I'd see the day when *he'd* settle down."

Flynn is a survivalist and documentarian who won national attention for being the youngest person to win *Wilderness Warrior*, a *Survivor*-style show. He hated the attention that earned and went off the grid for many years. Eventually he found his way back to society and became the program director for *Discovery Hour*, where he met his now-fiancée, reporter Sutton Steele. The funny thing is, before they got together, he tried to get her fired.

"None of us did." I take a drink. "Sutton's great, and she's perfect for Flynn, but that's not my kind of playbook."

"You're missing out," Trace says. "There's nothing better than coming home to your best friend and knowing she'll be in your bed every night."

Pepper glances over, like she's interested in hearing what else I have to say on the matter, but I'm not about to announce how enticing the thought of *her* in my bed every night is.

"We've got a big day planned. Is everyone about ready to go?" Amber asks. "Any questions about the itinerary?"

I nudge Dash. "Itinerary?"

"I emailed you a copy," Dash says.

"And you think I looked at it?"

Dash shakes his head. "I should've emailed it to Doogie."

"Always a good idea." Douglas Warsaw aka Doogie is my assistant. He keeps me organized, but he's currently enjoying a lavish honeymoon in the Maldives, which I gifted him and his new bride. I turn my attention to Pepper and brush my leg against hers, drawing her beautiful eyes to mine. "Want to be my bus buddy?"

She laughs softly. "We're walking."

"Even better. I can't wait to see what kind of fun awaits us."

Chapter Seven

Clay

The air is brisk, the sidewalks and streets are busy, and the sky is clear as we make our way to the first stop on our itinerary, Shakespeare and Company. Amber and Dash are leading the pack, and Amber is giving us a history lesson on the historic bookstore. "The original Shakespeare and Company bookstore was founded in 1919 by Sylvia Beach as a gathering place for expat writers like Joyce, Hemingway, and Stein, and for famed French writers, too. The shop we're going to see was founded in 1951 by George Whitman, and the original name was Le Mistral…"

Axsel is texting, and tossing out comments as if he's listening. Brindle and Morgyn are holding hands with their husbands, talking quietly among themselves, and Pepper and I are bringing up the rear.

We're in a city full of old-world charm, with intricate architecture and an aura all its own. I should be listening to every word Amber says, getting lost in the history and the beauty of our surroundings, but it can't even begin to hold my attention the way Pepper does. She looks beautiful in her navy peacoat, her cheeks pink from the chilly air, her eyes a little guarded. I know she's unsure whether she can trust my word to keep our secret, but I'm working on that.

"You can hold my hand if you want," I offer, and she gives me a pointed look. "Friends hold hands. It doesn't have to mean anything."

She looks amused. "No, thank you."

"Have it your way. It's just that your sisters seem happier when they're holding their husbands' hands, and I didn't want you to feel left out."

"That's awfully chivalrous of you."

"If you change your mind, just let me know. Have you been to Paris before?"

"No. This is my first time."

"What do you think of it so far?"

Her gaze sweeps over the cobblestone street and surrounding buildings as we walk down the sidewalk. "The architecture is pretty, and I like the cobblestone streets, but walking on them in heels would be nearly impossible. To be honest, I don't get why everyone thinks it's so romantic."

"What makes a place romantic isn't what it looks like. It has to do with who you're with and how you feel when you're with them."

"Well, yeah. Feeling romantic *is* a chemical reaction to pleasurable experiences based on a reward system."

"By that definition, last night was romantic."

"I can't comment on things that didn't happen," she says teasingly. "But being turned on is different from feeling romantic. There are overlaps, of course, but desire is driven by hormones, and attraction is created by dopamine, norepinephrine, and serotonin. Oxytocin and vasopressin mediate the reaction and the attachment."

I chuckle and shake my head. She's so fucking adorable.

"Sorry," she says softly. "Sometimes I forget a simple answer is enough."

"Don't apologize. I think it's sexy as hell that you know all that."

She rolls her eyes. "Do *you* think Paris is romantic?"

"I think the whole world can be romantic. To me, romance is catching the scent of your lover's perfume and thinking of all the things you want to do for them, with them, and *to* them. It's holding hands as you walk down the street without needing to talk because just being together is enough. It's learning the little things about someone you care for and then making the effort to do them and having such a good time together, you want the moments to last forever."

Her brow furrows, and she looks at me like I've confused her.

"What?"

"I didn't take you as a romantic guy."

"I told you there was more to me than just an orgasm donor."

She gives me an imploring look and glances at the others.

"Don't worry, Reckless," I say quietly. "They're all feeling too romantic with each other to listen to us. Except Axsel, but he's sidetracked with his phone. I'll try to be more careful with what I say."

"No, you won't," she says with a smile.

"Yeah, you're probably right." I can feel her tension easing as we follow the others around a corner.

"Have you been to Paris before?"

"Once, with my family when I was a kid, but we didn't spend much time in the city."

"No?" she asks with surprise. "What did you do here?"

"We mostly explored the Paris Region forests."

"Really? That's *different*. I didn't even know there were forests here. I don't think I've ever heard of anyone coming here to see forests."

"I'm not surprised. My upbringing wasn't typical by any stretch of the imagination."

"What do you mean?"

"My parents are wildlife biologists, and my mother is also a wildlife photographer. Our home base is in Ridgeport, Mass, but most of my childhood was spent traveling overseas with my family. We lived in remote villages for months at a time, in homes and tents and huts, exploring rainforests and jungles and learning about other cultures."

"Wow. That must have been an amazing experience," she says as we arrive at the bookstore, and the others start taking pictures of it.

"For some of us it was." I motion to the bookstore. "Do you want to snap a shot?"

She shakes her head. "This is for Amber. She's wanted to see this bookstore forever, and thanks to Dash, her dreams are coming true. But I don't need pictures of a building that'll just sit on my phone."

"Dash is the king of romance. Well, I'd like to get a picture." I pull out my phone, and before she can complain, I drape an arm around her shoulder and take a selfie of us.

"*Clay*," she chides.

"Don't worry, I'm not posting it anywhere." I text the picture to her and pocket my phone.

Her phone chimes, and as she checks the text, a smile crawls across her face. "What's this for?"

"So you don't forget me. Come on." I take her hand and follow the others inside.

Pepper doesn't pull away, and I don't let go as we explore the ancient bookstore, with its meandering rooms and narrow passageways. The worn floors and massive floor-to-ceiling wooden shelves bending under the weight of the books give the literary haven character. Stacks of books litter corners and tables, and greenery winds around structural posts elevated by small concrete blocks. There are plants in odd places, epigrams painted on stairs and above doorways, and the rooms seem to be never-ending.

We head upstairs, checking out reading nooks and a maze of rooms. "What do you think, Pep?" I ask as we walk through one room to another.

"It smells like old books," she whispers.

"Is that what that smell is? I thought it was dust bunnies. I keep expecting an old man with round spectacles to shuffle by talking to himself."

She laughs softly and whispers conspiratorially, "I can see him wearing suspenders and an old white dress shirt stained yellow with age."

"I think we passed him three rooms ago," I joke.

"I bet a guy like that lives here. This would be a great place to play hide-and-seek."

"We could get lost for days in here," I say as we meander into another room, the two of us whispering like kids. "I bet you had great hiding spots when you were little."

"They were only great because they were obvious and no-body looked there."

I picture her as a little girl, calculating her chances of getting caught in different places based on some mathematical equation. "Makes sense. What was your favorite one?"

"I'm not telling you all my secrets." She peruses a bookshelf.

"Ah, playing it mysterious, are you? I'll figure it out. It's got to be outside, because there were too many kids in your family to hide inside."

"You've got that right."

"Give me a minute. I'll get it." I think about her parents' property, which I've seen a few times while visiting Dash and Amber. They have a gorgeous Victorian with a wide front porch and a large yard, a barn for their horses, and another building for her mother's service-dog training business. There's a gazebo, where I can imagine her spending hours reading, but that would be too obvious. There are mature trees and a few manicured gardens. "Is it near a garden?"

"You're getting warmer."

"Being near you gets me warmer." I brush my hand along her back and catch a flash of desire in her eyes. "What's your favorite flower?"

"Roses, why?"

"Just curious." I mentally scroll through the gardens in her parents' yard, but I can't recall any with roses, which is probably why she gave up the answer. Then it hits me. The most obvious place. "I've got it. By the big oak tree in your parents' backyard. The one with the prickly holly bushes around it."

Her eyes widen. "How could you possibly know that?"

"Easy. I can't imagine you crawling under your parents' porch, which would be the best hiding place, or hiding out in the woods, and the barn and garage are *too* obvious. But no kid wants to go near holly bushes."

"Impressive deductive skills. How about you? I bet you were a wild thing when you were young."

"You're not wrong. I hated to sit still then, and I still do. I was always running around, imagining myself out on a football field. I think I drove my older sister and brother crazy. Victory and Seth were always trying to rein me in, but my younger brother Flynn loved to explore. If I couldn't get anyone to play football with me, I'd take off in the fields or forests, knowing Flynn would come after me, and we'd run around for hours, using sticks as swords and finding cool places to hide."

"You said you lived in remote places. Was it dangerous?" she asks as we wander into a room filled with literary memorabilia.

"Sometimes, but our parents gave us strict rules about where we could go and what we could do. They kept a pretty tight rein, and while I was just wild, Flynn was wild and careful. He's a world-renowned survivalist and a producer now, but even as a kid he was into survival, and he has this amazing ability to hear and read things once and know them forever."

"Does he have a photographic memory?"

"No. He's just super smart. He used to drive us nuts spouting facts about animals and plants, but I have no doubt that he did his part in keeping me safe. I was an impulsive kid, and I liked to push limits. My parents would tell me not to go into a pond, and the minute they turned their backs, I'd be in the water and come out covered with leeches."

"Ew." She wrinkles her nose adorably. "Sounds like you were rebellious."

"I was bored. I wanted to be playing football."

"Even as a little boy?"

"For as long as I can remember. The first time I saw a football game, I was five. We were eating lunch at an airport waiting for our flight, and I saw a game on TV. I was mesmerized, and according to my parents, I wouldn't shut up about it. My dad wasn't a sports guy, but when he realized my interest wasn't waning, he learned all the rules and positions and taught me everything he could."

"Wow. He sounds amazing."

"My old man? Yeah, my parents are super supportive of all of us. They definitely fed my love of football. When we were little, it didn't matter where we were living. If there were enough people to put together a game of football, I'd rally them. Kids, parents, even grandparents if that's what it took, and I'd teach them all to play. It didn't matter that half the time we didn't speak the same language, or that we were in some remote village in New Guinea or Indonesia or South America. I'd find a way to teach them the game." A rush of adrenaline hits with the good memories. "*Man*, I haven't thought about that in years." I haven't felt that type of passion for the game in so long, I wonder where it went. I tuck that question away to pick apart another time.

"You sound like you enjoyed it."

"I did. I loved teaching everyone to play and finding ways to communicate well enough that they all had fun. There's something about bringing a team together that has always fired me up."

"So you were a bored wild banshee?"

"Pretty much." My smile fades as more memories creep in. "But that wild streak got tempered when my youngest brother, Noah, followed me into the woods without me knowing. I was probably nine or ten, and he was only four or five. It took us a while to find him because he'd learned how to hide from playing with us. Not to brag, but we were pretty fucking great at it."

"You, brag?" she says sarcastically, grinning.

"He learned too well. I don't think I've ever been so scared.

That day changed me. I went from being a carefree kid to watching out for others before myself."

Pepper's expression turns thoughtful. "Hurting someone you love, or putting them in danger, can definitely change a person."

"You say that like you have experience with it."

She doesn't look away, but her voice softens. "I did something when I was younger and one of my sisters took the blame for it. It had a big impact on both of us." As if she realized she was exposing her underbelly, she waves a hand dismissively, quickly adding, "But that was a long time ago."

I want to know more about what happened, but she's looking around the room, avoiding my gaze, and I can tell she doesn't want to talk about it, so I reassure her instead. "Having each other's backs is what siblings do. I can't tell you how many times we covered for each other."

"Yeah, I know," she says too cheerily.

I let it go and motion to the literary memorabilia decorating the walls to try to lighten the mood. "What do you think of all this?"

She gazes up at it. "It's interesting, and I can see how it would be intriguing to Amber, since she owns a bookstore, and she's into all things literary. But famous writers aren't really my thing."

"Mine either. But I'm glad I have this time with you."

Her expression turns a little bashful, and it's an incredibly sexy look on her.

"You can admit you're having fun, you know."

"I'm not having a *bad* time," she says sassily.

"Damn, Pep. You sure know how to make a guy feel good."

"I think I proved that last night," she whispers, and then she giggles and covers her mouth, like she can't believe she said it, and it's the cutest thing I've ever seen.

A quick look around tells me we're alone, and I can't resist getting her a little worked up. "Ah, the sensual vixen I had the pleasure of devouring last night comes out to play." I lace our fingers together.

"*Clay*," she warns, her gaze flicking between the two entryways.

"There's nobody around, and I'm just holding a friend's hand." I tuck her hair behind her ear, speaking low. "Tell me, Pep. Do you want to kiss me as badly as I want to kiss you right now?"

Her lips part, lust simmering in her eyes, but she doesn't respond.

"You don't have to say it," I whisper, closing the small gap between us. "I can feel how much you want me." I slide my hand beneath her hair to the nape of her neck, bringing our lips closer together. "Tell me I'm wrong, and I'll back off."

She breathes harder, her eyes imploring me with as much desire as restraint. Her breasts brush against me with each breath. Her fingers curl tightly around mine, and she whispers, "Are you crazy? We can't kiss here. It's too open. Someone will see us."

I want to push her limits and drag her into one of the dark alcoves we've passed to show her just how much we *can* do here, but there's something about Pepper that makes me greedier than I've ever been. Wanting me isn't enough. I want to be the guy she can't stop thinking about. The guy she can't keep her hands off.

I want her to *want* to be reckless with me.

There's only one way to achieve that, so I take what feels

like the biggest risk of my life and crush my lips to hers in the kiss we both want. The kiss I've been dying for since I woke up with her in my bed. She stiffens, but her resistance is no match for the lust pounding between us, and she melts against me, her hands moving beneath my jacket to my chest, her fingers curling into my shirt as she goes up on her toes, eagerly returning my efforts. The feel of her surrendering to our passion makes me want to take it further. But that won't get me what I want. I want her to realize she *wants*, too.

Fighting that urge with everything I have, I pull back, leaving her hazy eyed and breathless. "Looks like you were wrong, sweetheart. We *can* kiss here."

Pepper

My heart thunders as Clay steps away, like he didn't just shatter my ability to think and leave me desperate for more. The man doesn't just kiss. He *consumes*, like kissing is his superpower.

I don't know how my rubbery legs make it through the rest of the bookstore, but somehow they do. Eventually we make it downstairs and out the front door. When the winter air hits my cheeks, my brain finally starts firing again. My body, however, is still reeling from that toe-curling kiss.

"Amber, where to next?" Clay asks, as casual as can be, as if he kisses like that every day.

For all I know, he does. *Shut up.* Why am I sticking up for him?

"The Notre-Dame Cathedral," Amber says excitedly as she

takes Dash's hand. "Let's go."

Clay falls into step beside me, and we follow the others down the sidewalk. "How're you doing, Reckless?"

"You're the reckless one," I whisper. "If my sisters find out we hooked up last night and I have to deal with their crap, you're going to pay for it."

"Careful tossing out promises like that. I might be into you punishing me."

I shake my head, smiling. *Smiling!* I should scowl, but *this* is what he does to me. The man renders me stupid, and I don't hate it.

"There's that gorgeous smile that keeps me up at night."

I'm sure my smile is the last thing keeping him up at night, but that's not something anyone has ever said to me before, and it's nice to hear it.

My family's voices mingle with the sounds of traffic as we make our way to a bridge over the Seine. I try to focus on the views of the city, the cobblestone streets, and the river, but I can't concentrate on anything other than Clay's proximity. When we start across the bridge, everyone else stops to take pictures. Clay touches my lower back, leaning close, like it's become a habit. His lips graze my ear, sending shivers of heat down my neck as he whispers, "How about here?"

"Here what?"

"This looks like a good place to kiss." He flashes those dimples.

I laugh. "Would you stop?"

"Why would I stop when it makes you smile? I've already told you how much I like that gorgeous smile."

I'm starting to like the things he says and does way too much. He doesn't leave my side as we go from one famous landmark to the next, exploring Notre-Dame Cathedral with its intricately carved gargoyles and Chimeras, and twin bell towers, and then Sainte-Chapelle royal chapel, where we admire the magnificent scenes depicted in the stained glass.

"The glasswork is incredible," I say as we walk around the chapel.

"Not nearly as incredible as my view," Clay says.

I glance over and find him looking at me with an intensity that makes my heart flutter.

He keeps me in that heightened state of anticipation and arousal as we explore the rest of the chapel and head to the next landmark. Amber tells us about each place we visit, but I've barely heard a word. I'm too sidetracked by Clay's furtive touches and whispered flirtations.

"The architecture here is out of this world," Trace says.

Everyone chimes in with their thoughts, but our late night is catching up to me, and my words are swallowed by a yawn.

"Does architecture bore you?" Clay asks.

"No. I'm just a little tired. *Someone* kept me up late last night."

He grins. "You're welcome."

As cheesy as he is, he has kept me smiling, blushing, and laughing at his silly jokes all afternoon. A little while later, we're heading to yet another site, when Clay says, "I'm going to hit the men's room in that café we just passed."

"Do you want us to wait?"

"No. I'll catch up." He jogs back to the café.

We stop at a corner, waiting to cross, and Axsel sidles up to me. "Did you scare Clay off already?"

"*No.* He went to use the bathroom."

"He's a nice guy."

Axsel is trying too hard to be casual. "And...?"

"Nothing," he says as we cross the street. "I just think you two look good together. He seems into you."

"There's no one else here for him to flirt with." I try to ignore the bad taste that leaves in my mouth.

Clay joins us a couple of minutes later and hands me a warm to-go cup.

"What's this?"

"A latte. We can't have you falling asleep on the tour."

My heart doesn't just flutter. It swells. "Thank you."

He nods like it was no big deal.

"Handsome and thoughtful," Axsel says. "No wonder they call you Mr. Perfect."

Clay's jaw tightens.

"Hey, Ax, come here," Dash calls out, and Axsel goes to him, leaving us alone at the back of the group.

I take a sip of the latte. "*Mm.* How did you know I like French vanilla?"

"I was with you at breakfast, remember?"

I didn't realize he'd paid attention to such a small detail. I'm starting to think there's more to this guy than the rumors let on.

His phone chimes with a text. As he pulls it from his pocket, it chimes again.

"Someone's popular," I tease as he thumbs out a text.

"It's my buddies. A group text about the game." The muscles in his jaw bunch as he pockets his phone.

"I'm sorry you lost the playoff."

"Thanks." The tension lingers in his jaw. "I hate that I blew it."

"I don't know much about football, but I'm sure it wasn't just you who blew it."

"I blew it when it counted, and that's what matters. I hate letting my team down."

"I wouldn't be too hard on yourself. Everyone must have a bad game now and then. Besides, you've won Super Bowls before. That's more than some quarterbacks can say."

"Yeah, but you don't win a Super Bowl and then sit back on your laurels and take it easy. You do better, work harder, so you can win another one for the team. Teammates come and go, and some of them haven't ever made it to the Super Bowl. They worked their asses off to get to the playoffs, and they were counting on me. And it's not just a loss for our team. It's a hit for our sponsors and a huge disappointment for our fans, who have cheered us on all season. It's..." His jaw clenches. "Never mind. I'm sure it seems silly to you. A bunch of grown men tossing a ball around."

He's been so casual, his passion takes me by surprise, and I realize it shouldn't. He's talking about his career, and clearly there's a lot more to his thoughts on the game than just winning. "No, I get it. I don't watch football, and I admit that I didn't understand all the hype before, but when you put it the way you just did, I get it."

"You do?"

"*Mm-hm.* It's like if I'm working on a contract and another scientist's research isn't up to par. The whole project can fail, making years of hard work all for naught."

"Yes, exactly. Can you recover from that without blaming that person?"

"Of course. We're a team, too, and it's not always the scientist's fault. Depending on the project, there are a multitude of factors that affect our research. All we can do is look at the data and try to figure out where we went wrong and what needs to change. It must be similar for you. Doesn't everything impact the game? Weather? Strengths and weaknesses of your teammates and opponents on any given day? Frame of mind? There are so many variables. You can't always be at your best. It's physically impossible."

"There's no room for less than perfect during a game."

The others start *ooh*ing and *ahh*ing, drawing our attention to the Panthéon as it comes into view. Its majestic dome and Corinthian columns dominate the streets of the Latin Quarter. But that magnificent sight holds my attention for only a few moments before my thoughts return to the man before me. *Mr. Perfect.* The man who I now realize is as dedicated to his career as I am to mine and also carries the weight of his team, his sponsors, and thousands of fans on his shoulders. I don't have fans, but I endure other pressures, like supporting my team financially and professionally and the scrutiny of the scientific and medical communities. It's a lot, and it can weigh you down.

"That sounds like an incredible amount of pressure."

"Nah," he says with a grin. "It's no more pressure than anyone else's career. That's enough work talk. Let's go see what kind of trouble we can get into."

This man is walking trouble where I'm concerned. He's already got me wanting to know more about him. What does he really think about that pressure? How does he handle it? How often does he get to see his family? Are they still close?

As we explore the Panthéon, he whispers things like, "*How about here?*" and "*I can't stop thinking about getting my hands on you,*" at the most inopportune times, knowing exactly how revved up he's getting me. He steals kisses behind pillars, and when no one is looking as we walk around, and I'm like a giddy teen, chasing that high. By the time we leave, I'm a heart-pounding bundle of desire, anxiously awaiting our next stolen kiss.

I don't know which is worse, that Clay has me acting like someone I don't recognize again or that I like it. But I know one thing for sure. If I'm not careful, Brindle will sniff out last night like a hound dog on a trail.

Chapter Eight

Clay

We stop at a quaint café for a late lunch, and Pepper moves swiftly to the other side of the table, planting herself between Morgyn and Axsel. *You can run, my secret vixen, but you can't hide.* I sit directly across from her, and while everyone talks at once about the places we've been and the places we have yet to see, I take out my phone and thumb out a text.

Me: *I miss you.*

Pepper pulls her phone from her back pocket and glances at the screen. Her hazel eyes flick briefly to mine, and then she lowers her phone to her lap, responding to the text.

Pepper: *I'm right across the table from you!*

Me: *You're too far away.*

I stretch my leg beneath the table, brushing my foot along her calf. I'm rewarded with a sexy blush as she thumbs out another text.

Pepper: *Stop it. Someone's going to notice.*

Me: *Does that mean this isn't a good time to lean across the table and kiss you?*

She presses her lips together, giving me that pointed look again, but betraying that disapproving facade is desire shimmering in her eyes.

Me: *I can't wait to get my mouth on you again.*

Her cheeks flame.

Me: *Rendezvous at the bathrooms?*

As she reads the text, that shimmer turns to flames.

Me: *Come on, baby. Be reckless with me.*

She bites her lower lip as she reads the text, and I know she's considering it.

Me: *Come on, Reckless, you know you want to.*

"Pepper, are you working again?" Morgyn asks, trying to glance at Pepper's phone.

Pepper startles and turns her phone over. "Yes. Sorry." She shoves her phone into her back pocket, shooting me a narrow-eyed glare.

"Pepper," Brindle chides like *she's* the responsible one.

"Look how tense you are from work texts," Morgyn says.

"Luckily Pepper has a friend who's good with his hands," I say with a smirk. "I'd be happy to work out that tension for you."

"Now we're talking. A little"—Brindle waggles her brows—"goes a long way in loosening me up."

Pepper glowers at me. "Thanks for *that*."

I hold my hands up in surrender. "Don't look at me. I was talking about giving you a neck rub or a back massage."

"A back massage is how we got Emma Lou," Trace says, referencing their adorable toddler and sparking jokes from the others.

Pepper spends the rest of lunch doing whatever she can to avoid looking at me. Every time I touch her leg with my foot, she tries to stop herself from smiling. Little does she realize, knowing she likes it makes me do it more.

We continue sightseeing after lunch. I'm having a good time

chatting with Pepper and her family, and I'm discreet with my flirting. I don't want Pepper to have to endure teasing from her siblings, but *man*, I'm ready to get her alone.

"There's a gift shop!" Morgyn points to one of the shops.

I hold the door for everyone, but Axsel doesn't follow them in. "You coming, Ax?"

"Nah. I'm going to hang out here."

"Everything okay?"

"Yeah. I've just had my fill of touristy stuff."

I let the door close and head over to him. "You want company?"

"Sure." He eyes me with a serious expression, which is rare for him. "You and Pepper really hit it off, huh?"

"Your sister's a trip when she's not running away from me."

"She's good at keeping to herself, but from what I hear, she books it out of town every time you're around. I've never seen her do that before."

Interesting. "Damn, I was hoping it was just a coincidence. I guess you don't believe her *work emergency* excuses?"

"If I believed it of anyone, it would be her, but they're a little too coincidental the way all her 'work emergencies' coincide with your visits. Then again, what do I know? It's nice to see her loosening up this weekend. But you should probably get in there before the girls pry the truth about last night out of her."

I try to play it off like I have no idea what he's talking about. "Last night?"

"Dude, don't even try," he says with a smile. "The girls might have bought that bullshit this morning, but I saw the way you two were looking at each other at the buffet."

I glance through the shop window and see the girls huddled

around Pepper. *Shit.* "You want to read me the riot act or something before I go in there? Tell me not to hurt her? Because I can tell you that I don't intend to."

"That's not my business or my style, and I don't worry about Pepper. She's not just the smartest of all of us. In a lot of ways, she's also the strongest."

I'm getting that sense, although I also think she might be the most sensitive, even though she hides it well. "Yeah? How so?"

"She's not known for making mistakes with her personal life. Whatever's going on with you two is happening because she wants it to."

I have no doubt about that. She is definitely not a pushover. "Thanks, man."

When I head inside, the girls scatter away from Pepper like pretty little roaches. The guys are checking something out on the other side of the shop. I debate heading over to them now that Pepper's not under scrutiny, but I take a moment to admire her as she looks through a display of scarves. I can feel restraint billowing off her like she's struggling not to look my way. The same way the other girls are trying too hard to appear as though they weren't just interrogating her.

"Look how cute this sweater is," Brindle says animatedly, holding up a child's sweater. "I think I'll get it for Emma Lou."

"She'll look adorable in that," Morgyn says.

"Emma Lou looks adorable in everything," Amber says.

Pepper holds up a colorful scarf. "Do you guys like this? It's silk. I think Mom would like it."

"Where is she going to wear silk?" Brindle asks. "I wouldn't waste your money, but you should get one for yourself."

Pepper sets the scarf down, and her shoulders droop in

disappointment.

Fuck the girls' scrutiny. I am not going to let them steal her smile.

"Pep, you should get one of these magnets with the Eiffel Tower on it since you didn't go up in it with us," Amber says. "A reminder for the next time you come here."

"I don't need a frivolous magnet to remember that," Pepper says flatly.

"I can't believe the top floor was closed," Brindle says.

"I told you before we came that they close it every January for maintenance," Amber says.

I walk up behind Pepper as her sisters lament the closing of the top floor of the Eiffel Tower, and my chest brushes her back. She inhales sharply, her fingers stilling on the scarf she'd held up. "Are you afraid of heights, Reckless?"

"No." I hear the smile in her voice. "I was on a work call. Eavesdrop much?"

"I didn't want to miss out on the juicy gossip about your hot new hookup."

Her fingers curl around the silk scarf.

"I must've missed the good stuff." I lower my voice to a whisper. "Did you tell them you had the best sex of your life last night?"

"*No*, I did *not*," she whispers.

"We can show them. How about it, beautiful? One scorching kiss, right here."

"Don't you dare."

The lust in her voice tells me how much she wants it. I let that desire simmer and trail my fingers over hers on the silk scarf. "I think your mother would love this scarf."

"No, they're right," she says, sounding deflated. "She has no place to wear it."

"Gifts aren't about that. I think she'd like knowing you saw that scarf and thought of her." I pick up a gorgeous emerald-green and gold scarf and brush it over her hand. "How about this one for you? It'll bring out your eyes."

She is quiet for a beat. "I don't have anywhere to wear silk either."

"My little fibber. I've seen your sexy silk panties," I rasp in her ear, and she shudders against me. I skim my hand up her hip on the side her sisters can't see. "I think the scarf would look nice wrapped around your wrists."

She turns, her wide eyes gazing up at me with the enticing mix of lust and restraint that has been warring in them all day. "I...*um*..."

"Like that idea?" I offer.

"I'm going to look over there" tumbles from her lips fast and breathy, and she scurries away.

I fight the urge to follow her.

I carry our purchases from that shop and others, and we spend the afternoon taking in more sights. I talk sports and joke with her brother and brothers-in-law, and she and the girls take pictures, chatting about who knows what. I love the way Pepper handles them, joining in with their jokes and rolling her eyes when they get silly. But when she looks at me, her smile heats up the brisk winter air.

As the hours pass, she and I dance around the sparks threatening to ignite between us. She does her best to give our mounting desires a wide berth, as if she can escape them, but our every interaction reels her back in. Hell, my every taunt, touch, and tease, meant to fray *her* restraint, eat away at mine, and I'm powerless to stop.

By the time we reach the last landmark on Amber's itinerary, the Musée de Cluny, a museum of medieval art housed in a palatial Gothic-style hotel, I want Pepper so badly, I can practically taste her. We're taking a guided tour with a large group of people. As usual, Pepper and I hover near the back of the group. As we move from room to room, pretending to listen to the history of sculptures, tapestries, paintings, and other artifacts, Pepper and I whisper among ourselves.

"We could make good use of the baths," I say as the guide talks about the second-century Roman baths and the frigidarium we'll be visiting during the tour. "I'll wash your back, you wash mine."

She laughs softly.

"We could make our own history. Give you something to brag about when you pick up the shot glass the next time you play Never Have I Ever."

"That would be a *no*," she says as we follow the group into another stone room with several massive archways leading to dimly lit corridors.

The group stops to admire ivory carvings, and as the guide gives a history lesson, I whisper, "That sly grin tells me you're thinking of all the places we could sneak into."

"Do you ever behave?" she asks with a playful smile I want to see more of.

"Yes, *often*. But apparently it's impossible when I'm with you."

She gives me a *yeah, right* look.

I scoff. "You know you're taunting me with that high-necked sweater."

"How is this sweater taunting you?" she whispers with amusement. "It covers everything."

"Exactly. You know how much I like your neck."

"Why do you think I had to wear it? You gave me a hickey last night," she whispers harshly.

Some kind of primal satisfaction takes hold, and I want to howl at the moon.

"Get that look off your face," she says as we move around the periphery of the group. "You left your mark on my thighs, my breast, *and* my neck. It's ridiculous."

"If my memory serves me correctly, I marked your ass cheek, too."

Her eyes widen.

"Don't pretend you didn't like it."

She clamps her mouth shut but thinks better of it and leans into me, whispering, "I told you you're a bad influence."

"Do you want me to stop?"

"I didn't say *that*," she says quickly, and we both laugh.

We meander around the room exchanging heated glances. There's so much want in her eyes, when the tour guide starts leading the group out of the room, I slip my finger through one of Pepper's belt loops, keeping her from following them, and rasp in her ear, "I want to kiss you so badly right now."

"Not here." Gone is the adamancy she started the day with, replaced with a breathy, needy plea for me to find someplace safe from the eyes of others.

My reckless girl is back.

I take her hand, and we rush like horny college kids through one of the archways, into a dark corridor, and I pull her behind some sort of large storage cabinet. I drop our gift bags and haul her against me. As her arms dart around my neck, our mouths crash together in a feast of desires. There's no melting, no slowing down. She's grinding against my cock, and I'm pushing my hands under her sweater, groping and teasing her magnificent breasts. She arches into my hands, moaning hungrily. I'll probably go straight to hell for this, but I push my fingers into the waist of her jeans. She draws back, breathing hard, her eyes searching mine.

"Tell me to stop, or give me that mouth."

She pulls my mouth back to hers. *So fucking hot.* I tug open her jeans and push my hand into her panties. She inhales sharply as my fingers dip into her slick heat. I groan into our kiss, pumping my fingers, using my thumb on her most sensitive nerves as we eat at each other's mouths. She palms me through my jeans, and I grit out, "*Fuck*," working her faster. She strokes me through the denim, driving me out of my mind. "Keep doing that, and I'll fuck you right here."

Her eyes gleam with lust, but she releases my cock and pulls my mouth back to hers, riding my fingers. I fist my other hand in her hair, holding her mouth tight against mine, fucking it with my tongue as I stroke the spot that takes her up onto her toes. "I can't wait to get my mouth on you again," I grit out, and crush my lips to hers. It doesn't take long before she's spiraling out of control, moans sailing from her lungs into mine as her climax ravages her. The feel of her pussy clamping around my fingers makes my cock weep.

When she finally goes soft against me, she buries her face in my shirt, and I imagine sweet Pepper wondering how she could have let Reckless take over. I keep my fingers buried deep and lift her chin with my other hand, so she can see the man who made her feel so good.

Gazing into her blissed-out eyes, I tell her what she needs to hear. "No one will know."

I kiss her slowly, sweetly, and reassuringly and vow in that moment that I will do everything within my power to keep my word. Just as the thought hits, a voice comes from the room we just vacated.

"Where could they have gone?" Brindle asks.

Pepper's eyes fly open, and she jerks back, but I keep her close as I pull my hand out of her jeans and quickly button them. She watches me suck my fingers clean, her eyes flaming anew, despite the worry in them.

"Maybe Clay walked her to the bathroom," Morgyn says.

Pepper squeezes her eyes shut, and I embrace her, putting one hand on the back of her head, wishing I could take her embarrassment away, and at the same time, finding it incredibly appealing.

"I'm sure they'll catch up," Brindle says. "As long as they're together, we know she's okay."

Her sisters' voices fade as they walk away, and Pepper lets out a relieved breath. Her heart hammers against mine. I lean back to see her face, and when our eyes connect, we both laugh.

"What is it about you that makes me lose my good sense?" she asks, smoothing her hair.

"I think you mean *thank you*."

She swats me and steps out of our hideaway, but I pull her back in for one more kiss.

Chapter Nine

Clay

The brisk afternoon fades into a chilly evening. We're back at the hotel, taking a brief respite to shower and change before heading to dinner. My shoulder's been tight, so I do the physical therapy I've been doing all year. It doesn't help much, so I pop a couple of ibuprofen and jump in the shower.

My phone chimes twice while I'm getting dressed. I hope it's not my agent. Tiffany is excellent at her job, but right now I'm finding that annoying as fuck. She's hounding me to negotiate the offer to extend my contract, and that's not a decision I can handle making right now. I glance at my phone on the counter, prepared to ignore the text if it's from her, and breathe a sigh of relief at the group texts rolling in from my siblings. After nearly losing Flynn to a tragic accident last year, I never miss a chance to connect with them.

Victory: *Noah said you're in Paris. Are you behaving?*

Noah: *It's Clay, of course he's not.*

A devil emoji pops up from Noah.

Me: *Noah you're a worse gossip than TMZ.*

Me: *Vic in my world misbehaving is behaving.*

I send a devil emoji.

My siblings know I'm no longer the player some people

believe I am, but each of us has a role to uphold in our sibling circle, and this is mine.

Seth: *Clay how are you holding up after the loss?*

Me: *Can't fix what happened so I'm not stressing about it.*

It's a lie, but as president of BRI Enterprises, a major retail conglomerate, and co-owner of several upscale restaurants, my self-made billionaire brother has his hands full managing his empire. He doesn't need to worry about my career.

Flynn: *Did Pepper pull another disappearing act when you showed up?*

Noah: *I still think you should've brought me as your wingman.*

Flynn: *Clay doesn't need a wingman.*

Me: *Damn right, I don't.*

Me: *As for Pepper…*

I send the picture I took of us in front of the bookstore, and their responses are immediate.

Seth: *About time she realized how awesome you are.*

Victory: *You two are cute together!*

Noah: *Damn bro she's gorgeous.*

Flynn: *I'm happy for you dude.*

Noah: *Can I sell this? I've got my eye on a new boat.*

Noah doesn't need to sell a damn thing. Like most of us, he's got plenty of money. Even so, I feel compelled to squash that thought.

Me: *Only if you want me to end you.*

Noah: *Oops! Too late. Already sent it to Page Six.*

I mumble "Bastard" as I thumb out a response.

Me: *I'm not kidding. I don't want to screw this up.*

Victory: *Aw, our little boy's growing up.*

Seth: *Are you going steady?*

Noah: *Did you carve CB + PM on a tree?*

Flynn: *Did you give her your letterman jacket?*

"No, but I gave her a bunch of hickies." I laugh at how annoyed she was when she spilled those beans.

I send a laughing emoji.

Me: *We're not a couple but she's finally giving me the time of day.*

Victory: *If you want to keep her around, show her who you really are.*

Her statement gives me pause. I wonder who Victory thinks I am. I've been who the world wants me to be for so long, *I don't even know who I really am anymore.*

Noah: *I'm sure he already has.*

Noah sends another devil emoji.

Victory sends an eye roll emoji.

Victory: *I'm serious. You're a great guy, Clay. Show her the real you.*

Flynn: *I can vouch for the importance of that.*

Seth: *How to Win a Wife 101. Be yourself.*

What is it with everyone pushing marriage these days?

Me: *I'm not trying to win a wife. I've got to go. We're all meeting for dinner.*

Victory: *Have fun! Love you!*

I'm pocketing my phone when another text rolls in.

It's from Seth, and not on the group thread.

Seth: *You've been trying to get Pepper's attention for a long time. My guess is that means she's more than just a hookup.*

Seth: *I'm not saying marriage, but I vote for being yourself and giving Mr. Perfect a rest while you're with her.*

Victory is the oldest sibling, and she exudes all the hallmarks of a responsible firstborn, but Seth has always acted like he is the oldest. He's been doling out sage advice and watching out for all of us for as long as I can remember. Since I have a tendency to be hyperfocused on goals, Seth's ability to slow down and see the bigger picture has always served me well, even if I thought it made him boring when we were kids.

But tonight I'm not in the mood to be schooled, and I definitely don't want to think about me versus Mr. Fucking Perfect.

Me: *I have no idea what you're talking about. I've got to run. We'll catch up when I get back.*

I pocket my phone and put on my shoes. I don't know exactly what this is between me and Pepper, and I don't know where it will lead. But I know this. I'm in Paris for three more days, and when Dash invited me to join them, he said they were staying for ten days. That means Pepper is here for the rest of the week, and I don't want to spend our time together hiding our connection from her family.

Now I just have to convince her of the same.

Unfortunately, while I'm hoping to talk with Pepper about not hiding our attraction, it appears she has other ideas. She's wearing a killer black dress with a silver design running through it, which I hoped she chose for my benefit. But she's been acting distant during dinner, barely making eye contact with me, and my attempts at humor are met with a soft smile that feels almost apologetic.

I don't get it. I thought we connected and had gotten past this game of cat and mouse.

On the walk back to the hotel after dinner, I try to get a minute alone with her, but she stays close to her sisters, in constant conversation with them.

"I'm excited to go to London tomorrow," Amber says as we walk into the hotel. "Don't forget you guys, we're leaving at seven thirty sharp tomorrow morning."

"You're going to London?" I ask Dash.

"Yeah," Dash says. "It was on the itinerary I sent you. You know, the one you didn't look at."

Shit.

"I can't wait to go to Barcelona," Morgyn exclaims.

"We're going to have the greatest time, Sunshine," Graham says.

I sidle up to Pepper as the others chat about their next destination and decide to play it cool. "So, where are we singles heading tomorrow?"

"I'm heading back to Charlottesville." That apologetic softness shows in her eyes again.

Everything seems to move in slow motion as I process that new information, and disappointment sinks in.

"This is Pepper's first vacation since graduate school," Brindle says. "And she isn't even staying for a full week. You should give her crap about that. We even told her we'd go to Greece just for her, because it's the one place she *really* wants to go."

"Brindle, *enough*," Pepper says softly.

"Clay, are you sticking around?" Dash asks.

"Only for a few more days," I say absently, unable to take my eyes off Pepper, who seems unable to take her eyes off me, too.

"Do you want to hit London with us?" Dash asks.

"Or you can come to Barcelona with us," Graham suggests.

"No, thanks. I think I'll stick around here."

Pepper tears her gaze away from me and waves her hand

nervously. "I guess this is goodbye. I'm going up to my room to pack. I have an early flight tomorrow. I love you guys."

"We're heading up, too," Amber says.

Pepper hugs everyone, and the others promise to send her pictures from the rest of their trip. She stands awkwardly in front of me, fidgeting with her hands. My chest constricts at the idea of this being it for us. I don't know why it's hitting me so hard, and I hate that she looks so uncomfortable after all we've done. I want to pull her aside and talk about it, but that's not an option without causing her trouble, so I open my arms and say, "Get in here, bus buddy."

The others laugh, and she gifts me a genuine smile and steps into my embrace. Hell if it doesn't feel like she belongs there. There are so many things I want to say, but I have to keep it light with the others listening. "Thanks for hanging out with me."

"It was fun," she says too animatedly, and starts to pull away.

I tighten my hold just long enough to whisper, "You can run, but you can't hide, Reckless."

Chapter Ten

Pepper

I toss my suitcase on the bed, catching a glimpse of myself in the mirror. The low-cut, easy-access wrap dress I'd hoped would drive Clay mad clings to my body, my favorite black lace thong and matching bra going to waste beneath it. My heart hasn't stopped racing, or aching, since we met for dinner, which is when it hit me that my time with Clay was over, and it wouldn't be fair to pretend otherwise. That ache shows in my eyes. They look so dull, I have to turn away.

I hated saying goodbye to him, and I hated doing it in front of everyone else, which shouldn't matter, since I wouldn't have told him that his kisses were the best I'd ever had anyway or that I can't stop thinking about last night or how much fun it was to spend time with him. I force myself to begin the arduous task of packing, tugging open the dresser drawer, absently unfolding and refolding my clothes, telling myself it's just as well. It's not like he's my forever person. This was just a fling.

My stomach knots up. It didn't feel like a fling.

I squeeze my eyes shut against the pain and tilt my face up to the ceiling, groaning. *Why is this so hard?* Why can't I be like Sable used to be? Able to walk away without looking back. Why did she get all the fling-resilient genes? I imagine my twin in our mother's womb, gathering and hoarding those genes, thinking she's protecting me from heartache.

Ugh. Now I'm just being ridiculous.

I sink down to the edge of the bed, clutching the shirt I wore last night and press it to my nose, soaking in the faint scent of cedarwood and the unique smell of Clay. I don't know how his scent could have seeped into my clothing, but I'm glad it did. I smell it again, and then I force myself to put the shirt in the suitcase and go back to folding my clothes. But his face is all I see. His playful smile, the dimples that make my insides go hot. *Tell me to stop, or give me that mouth.* A shudder of heat follows his voice in my head.

I may not know anything about flings, but I know my battery-operated boyfriend will never satisfy me again.

What am I doing?

I am not someone who pines for a man. I'm a scientist. I deal with facts, not chemically induced lust or runaway hormones. I need to think rationally. Tomorrow I'll go back to my real life, and Clay will probably find some other woman to hang out with here in Paris. A stab of jealousy hits me, but I refuse to give in to it. I tell myself there's nothing wrong with him being with someone else. That's what people do after having flings. They tuck away the memories of their fun times and carry on.

I can do that. I can do anything.

I mentally bundle up those happy, sexy memories and stomp them with my pointy heels, but they keep popping back up like freaking jack-in-the-boxes.

"I'm *so* not built for flings."

I grab my belted sweater and concentrate on folding it, startling when a knock sounds at my door. Sure it's my sisters, I set the belt on top of my sweater in the suitcase and take a deep breath, trying to compose myself. I don't need them asking me why I look frustrated. It was bad enough when we were in the gift shop and they tried to get me to confess that I was into Clay. I played it cool and said what I have every other time they've said things to me about him. *He's obviously handsome, and he's a nice guy, but I don't go out with athletes.* Thinking about it now, I get the same burn in my chest as I did when I said it to them. Kind of like when I make a statement about a scientific fact that I've heard a time or two and then second-guess myself on the accuracy of it.

Trying to ignore that discomfort, I make my way to the door and peer out the peephole.

It's *Clay.* My heart beats even faster as I take in his tight jaw and serious expression. I don't blame him for being irritated with me. He looks so handsome in that slate-gray dress shirt, I could barely look at him during dinner for fear of not being able to take my eyes off him. I wasn't exactly gracious tonight, and he's been nothing but good to me.

Good isn't the right word.

He's been exciting and thoughtful and fun. He made me feel beautiful, wanted, sexy, and *alive.* He made me feel more than anyone ever has. The truth is, he's been pretty damn perfect.

That's when it hits me.

Of course he's been perfect. There's a reason they call him Mr. Perfect, and he has enough experience to have mastered the game of flings. I need to keep that in mind and not let my naive heart take over. I open the door and immediately regret not giving myself time to let that resolve sink in and take hold. Without the buffer of the door between us, that magnetic pull is in full force. I don't like feeling out of control, but at the same time, with Clay I want to chase that high.

"Hey, Reckless. How's the packing going?"

The nickname that at first had conjured troubling memories from when I was younger no longer does. I've become as fond of it as I have of him. He makes it sound special and exciting, but his gaze is still serious, which is a little unnerving. "Okay."

"I got you a few things today." He hands me a gift bag.

"You didn't have to do that." I look in the bag and see two slim boxes, one with a pink ribbon, one with a red ribbon, and the Eiffel Tower magnet Amber said I should get. "You got me a magnet?"

"Everyone needs a frivolous magnet on their fridge to remember their trips."

He doesn't miss a thing. I can practically hear my resolve chipping away.

"The box with the pink ribbon is for your mom."

"You got my mom a gift?" *Oh, my heart.*

"No," he says warmly. "I got you the scarf you picked out for her so you could give it to her. I think it'll mean a lot to her coming from you."

Chip, chip, chip.

"That was really thoughtful. Thank you. I've actually been regretting that I didn't buy it for her." I take the box with the red ribbon out of the bag and open it. My pulse quickens. It's the green and gold scarf he suggested for me in the gift shop. *I think it would look nice wrapped around your wrists.* I lift my gaze to his, and holy mother of hotness, even with that tight jaw, he possesses a wickedness that takes my breath away.

"It'll bring out your eyes." He cocks a brow, his lips curving up. "Are you going to invite me in?"

"Yes. *Sorry*. We should talk." I step back, trying to get my brain to work so we can clear the air. "My room isn't as nice as your suite."

He steps in front of me, his gaze softening just a tad. "It's nicer than mine, because you're in it."

He leans in, and I close my eyes as his warm lips touch my cheek and his words touch my heart. Closing the door, I follow him in and put the gift bag on the dresser.

His gaze sweeps over the suitcase. "If I hadn't asked about tomorrow, were you going to leave without telling me?"

"No. I just..." I try to think of something to say other than the embarrassing truth, but I don't want to lie to him. "I've never done this before. I don't know how to navigate a fling. I thought that's what people did. They have fun, then move on."

He rubs the back of his neck, giving me a look somewhere between amusement and disappointment. "I gotta say, that makes me feel a little cheap. You were just using me for a few orgasms and going to take off like it meant nothing?"

"I wasn't *using* you. I mean, no more than you were using me, but—"

"Ouch." He puts a hand over his heart, feigning pain. "I might be strong, but I'm still human. My ego can be bruised."

I try to give him a stoic look, but he's so damn endearing, with those sexy dimples and a playful glint in his eyes, I can't maintain it, and I laugh. "You're a fool. What am I supposed to do with you?"

"I can think of a few things." He strides toward me like a panther stalking prey, and my pulse quickens with every powerful step. "That is, unless you didn't want one more night to kiss me?" His breath warms my lips, sending heat prickling down my limbs. His hands slide over my hips, resting hot and heavy on my ass as he draws me to him. "Another night to explore each other's bodies?"

Forget talking. I want *exactly* what he's offering. One more night, for closure. "I never said I didn't want that."

"My bruised ego needs to hear you say you want me."

He brushes his scruff along my cheek, and I feel him getting hard. Lust coils tight and hot in my core as I wind my arms around him. "Your *ego* feels solid to me."

He smiles against my lips. "Maybe I'm a greedy bastard with you and want to hear that you want me as much as I want you."

"Maybe?" I taunt, emboldened by his desire.

"You know damn well how greedy I am for you." His gruffness sends a shudder of desire through me. His hand slides along my stomach as he moves behind me, leaving me facing the mirror. Our eyes lock in our reflection. "Tell me you wore this sexy dress just for me." His hard heat presses against my ass as his hands move up my stomach. "That you *want* me to touch you."

Anticipation stacks up inside me. "You know I want you to touch me," I pant out.

He holds my gaze in the mirror, wickedness gleaming in his eyes. "Watch me touch you."

The demand is low and gruff. I've never watched myself with a man. It feels dark and dirty, heightening the thrill as he palms my breasts, teasing my nipples through the thin dress, sending bolts of lightning between my legs. I feel myself go damp, and he must see it on my face, because he rubs his cock against my ass, whispering, "You like this, Reckless. You like being naughty with me."

There's no holding back the "*Yes*" that rushes lustfully from my lips.

PLAYING MR. PERFECT

"I should've known one night with you would never be enough for either of us." He grazes his teeth along the curve of my neck and shoulder, and I gasp with the shock of pleasure it brings. "And this sexy dress?" He lowers his hands to the knot at my hip.

"I wore it just for you."

He's untying the knot before I even finish the sentence, and my dress falls open. He slips it off my shoulders, and it glides to the floor, leaving me in nothing but my matching thong and bra and heels. He swiftly removes my bra, and his gaze moves lazily, lustfully down the length of me in the mirror, lingering on the bite mark he left on my breast, making my nipples throb with need. Those all-seeing eyes move lower, hovering at the mark on my inner thigh. The raw satisfaction on his face makes me breathe harder. He steps back, admiring my backside, and makes an appreciative sound as he caresses my ass.

"Look at you, wearing my marks everywhere." His breath is hot and tantalizing against my neck. "It should be illegal to be this sexy."

I can do little more than watch him in the mirror as he undresses. He fists his cock, his eyes on me as he strokes it. I bite my lower lip, itching to touch and be touched, but he steps behind me and gathers my hair over my shoulders. "Where is it, Reckless? Where's my mark on your neck?"

I touch the tender spot I've covered with makeup near the back of my neck.

He drags his tongue over it, then wipes off the makeup with his hand, bringing the evidence of our passion into view, and flashes a wolfish grin. He licks that tender spot as light as a feather, sending shivers of heat rippling through me. I lean my head to the other side, giving him better access. His eyes never leave mine in our reflection as he lightly licks and sucks my neck, groping one breast, teasing me through my thong with his other hand. A needy sound escapes me, and I don't even try to stop it. I want him to hear what he does to me.

"You're so wet for me, your thong is drenched." He seals his teeth over my neck, sucking hard as he continues teasing me through the damp material and squeezes my nipple. A mix of pleasure and pain whips through me, and I cry out, grabbing his wrists. But I don't stop him. It feels too good. He eases the suction on my neck.

"*Again*," I beg.

He does as I ask, and my hips shoot forward, thrills whipping through me anew. He continues his masterful assault until my entire body is quivering like a bundle of live wires. I'm lost in his ministrations, panting, clinging to his wrists in an effort to remain upright. Then he's pushing his fingers beneath the thong, my legs are giving out, and I'm swamped with pleasure so vast and all-consuming, my eyes slam shut, and a stream of indiscernible sounds sails from my lungs. He doesn't relent, sending a surge of pleasure crashing over me. I cry out and ride that high to the very end.

"Eyes open, sweetheart."

My eyes flutter open as I float down from the peak, and our gazes lock in the mirror.

"When you go home and you're fixing your hair or putting on makeup, I want you to remember *this*. I want you to see my face, feel my hands on you, remember how it felt when I made those marks on your body and the pleasure only I can bring you."

His words burrow into me, bringing a whole new type of thrill, because I am memorizing every one of them. I want to remember all of this, but I can't let him know that. "You really are greedy."

His eyes narrow. "I never was before. Not like this."

Those words burn into me as he turns me gently in his arms and takes me in a sensual, mind-numbing kiss that leaves me moaning for more. His eyes darken. "Those sexy sounds make me crazy." He bites my lower lip, and I gasp at the sting of pleasure racing through me. "*Fuck.* I'm going to hear those noises in my sleep." Just as the idea of him thinking of me when we're apart starts to take hold, his tongue glides along my lower lip. "This gorgeous mouth will be what I see every time I fist my cock."

The breath rushes from my lungs.

He sinks lower, dragging my thong down to my thighs, and gazes up at me. "Look at this pretty pussy, begging to be eaten." He licks my sex, and my knees buckle, a moan pushing from my lungs. He grabs my thighs and presses a kiss to my clit, drawing another needy sound from deep inside me. But he doesn't continue. The master of anticipation drags my thong down to my ankles and helps me step out of it. Then he presses another kiss to the apex of my sex, causing more scintillating sensations, and rises to his full height. Those blue eyes bore into mine. "Are you in a *giving* mood, sweetheart? I'd love to see you on your knees with those sexy lips wrapped around my cock."

The way he asks and the depth of emotion staring back at me feel strangely intimate, making me eager to please, bringing that boldness that only exists with him. "With an invitation like that, how can I resist?" I step out of my heels, wanting to make him feel as good as he makes me feel, so he really *will* think of me after I'm gone. I kiss his chest and tease his nipple with my tongue.

"Christ, that feels good," he grits out.

I take his thick length in my hand, stroking him as I graze my teeth over his nipple. He hisses, and I sink my teeth into it. He grabs my hair and yanks my head back, his volcanic eyes blazing into mine.

"Sorry," I say lamely. "Too hard?"

"No. So fucking good. Careful, Reckless, or you'll make it hard for me to hold back."

"I don't want you to hold back." The words come unbidden, but they're true. It makes no sense, but I trust him more than I've ever trusted any man in an intimate situation. I know I'll never have another fling, or another night with Clay, so I give myself permission to go a little wild and give up control.

His brows slant. "What about that threat you gave me last night?"

"I know you won't hurt me." I kiss my way down his chest and abs, loving the feel of his muscles flexing beneath my touch and the appreciative sounds he makes as I sink to my knees. He gathers my hair in his hand, his eyes trained on me as I guide his heavy cock into my mouth, humming around it. He curses, and I work him with tight strokes, taking him deep, his hungry gaze and salacious sounds spurring me on. I grab his hips, pulling them forward, giving him a green light. He pumps his hips, quickening his efforts as I suck more rigorously.

"Touch yourself while I fuck your mouth."

I do it without hesitation, and the thrill of it takes over. I moan around his cock, and he tightens his fist in my hair. "So good, Reckless...*Fuck*...Look at your sweet pussy glistening for me." I work him faster, his words taking me closer to the edge. "That's it, baby," he grits out, thrusting faster, deeper. "Your mouth is fucking heaven." I cling to his leg with one hand, using my other on myself, letting him take full control as he fucks my mouth. An orgasm builds inside me, taunting me, just out of reach. My muscles flex, my core tightens, and I work myself faster, matching his thrusts. "Fuck, Pepper. *Fuck.*" I moan louder, digging my fingernails into the back of his leg, willing myself to come with him. Just as my orgasm careens into me, he roars out my name, his release spurting hot and salty down my throat, and we ride out our mutual pleasure.

When he withdraws from my mouth, I'm shaking, quivering with aftershocks. He caresses my jaw and lifts me to my feet on my rubbery legs. His strong arms circle me, his eyes gleaming with emotions I don't trust my lust-addled brain to decipher, and he kisses me tenderly.

"I didn't hurt you, did I?"

I can do little more than shake my head.

"Thank God." The relief in his voice wraps around me like another embrace as he lowers his lips to mine in a slow, titillatingly sensual kiss. Without a word, he moves my suitcase to the floor and guides me onto the bed. I watch him stride naked over to the gift bag and withdraw the green and gold scarf. My pulse spikes as he makes his way back to me and drags the cool silk along my body. "Do you trust me enough to play, Reckless?"

"*Yes,*" I manage, as nervous as I am aroused.

"Wrists or blindfold, baby?"

I worry my lower lip, trying to decide, and finally confess, "I've never done either. But I want to. Can we try both?"

"You, at my complete and utter mercy? Now, that's a fantasy come true."

His devilish grin has me squeezing my thighs together to quell the ache it causes. Those eagle eyes sweep over the room, and he picks up my sweater belt, stretching it between his hands. "Nice and long. Perfect." He snags his wallet and puts it on the nightstand.

My heart races as I move to the edge of the bed, offering him my wrists. He carefully binds them near one end of the belt, leaving a long tail. When he finishes, he puts a finger under my chin, lifting my eyes to his. "Are you sure you want to do this?"

"Yes." I'm so turned on, there's no way I'm backing out.

"You can tell me to stop anytime, and I will."

I nod, swallowing hard, glad he's thinking of me and not just of what he wants to do to me.

He picks up the silk scarf. "Out go the lights, sweetheart."

He wraps the scarf over my eyes and ties it on the side of my head. The world goes dark. Anxiety prickles my chest and white-hot anticipation flares in my core. I'm sure he can hear my thundering heart.

"Still with me, sweetheart?"

"Uh-huh."

"I'm going to lay you down and put your hands above your head so I can tie them to the iron slats on the headboard."

"*Oh*....um...okay." Holy cow. I don't know how I feel about this. "I didn't know you were going to do that."

"We don't have to. There's no pressure to do anything."

I debate not doing it, and it only takes a second for me to know without a doubt I'll regret it if I don't. "*No.* I want to do it. I'm ready to go dark and dirty."

"Damn, Reckless," he says with a laugh. "I sure like you."

He helps me down to the mattress and guides my wrists above my head. As he secures the belt to the headboard, I feel more vulnerable than I ever have, but I know I'm safe with him.

The mattress shifts with his weight, and my other senses magnify. I feel the heat of his stare, taste his arousal more acutely than I did when he came in my mouth. The air vibrates with anticipation, the scents of sex and lust hovering around us.

"I feel you staring at me." I sound husky and shaky.

"Not staring. *Admiring*. You can't imagine how stunning you are." His hand trails down my breastbone and between my breasts. "Look at these gorgeous tits." His fingers glide lightly over one breast, circling my nipple, and all of my focus goes to that tantalizing touch. Goose bumps chase up my body, and my nipples harden to painful points. The mattress shifts again, and his tongue traces the same path. Pleasure courses through me, and I grit my teeth as his hand moves to my other breast, circling that nipple as his tongue circles the other. My insides go tight, every iota of my being rushing toward his touch. I arch up, wanting his whole mouth on me, but he draws back. The breath rushes from my lungs with his retreat. "*Clay*—"

"I want you needy." The mattress shifts, and his breath comes down over my nipple, hovering like a blowtorch. His fingers circle my other nipple, and the competing sensations have me writhing, bowing off the mattress again, but his mouth retreats. He continues taunting me, taking me right up to the edge and then pulling back, until I'm standing on a razor's edge, on the verge of shattering. His fingers trail down my body to my inner thigh, moving along it as light as a feather. His fingertips graze my sex, and I gasp, my hips rising.

"*Yes. Please.*"

"Soon," he promises.

His tongue circles my nipple again, his fingertips teasing between my legs, but no matter how I wiggle or move, he doesn't enter me, doesn't touch me where I need it most. Heat simmers in my core, my inner muscles swelling until I'm dizzy with desire, begging, rocking my hips, trying to *take* more. He refuses me, and it turns me on more than I could ever imagine. I don't know how long he continues the exquisite torture, but by the time he finally lowers his mouth over my breast and his fingers enter me, I'm a moaning, pleading mess of arousal. When his thumb hits my clit, I *detonate*. A hailstorm of sensations rains down on me, and I cry out so loud, I'm sure everyone on our floor hears it. Clay stays with me through every pulse and whimper.

The mattress shifts, and he spreads my legs. Embarrassment suddenly tries to break in, but it's no match for the onslaught of thrilling anticipation.

"Look at you, so fucking perfect." His rough hands skate up my thighs, spreading me wider, and then he's feasting on me, catapulting me into ecstasy again. He's rough and somehow also sensual, keeping me at the peak. I can't see, can't hear past the thrum of desire consuming me and the blood rushing through my ears. But I can *feel* every prickle and burn of the most excruciating pleasure I've ever experienced, and I revel in it, crying out, begging him not to stop, and he doesn't, until I sink boneless into the mattress.

As I come back down to earth, he says, "Time to play, beautiful."

There's more?

I'm not sure I'll survive it, but he turns me over, running his hands down my back and caressing my ass. I have a fleeting worry about what he's going to do to me, but his touch is electrifying. I feel him straddling my hips, his body heat radiating through my back as his chest grazes my skin. The length of his cock rests against the crack of my ass, and his warm breath coasts over my neck as he kisses me there. "I could do whatever I want to you right now, and you'd let me, wouldn't you, Reckless?"

I'm so lost in him, I hear *yes* in my head, but I don't dare say it.

"Don't worry. I only want to make you feel good." He moves down my body in an arousing dance of kisses, bites, and caresses, murmuring against my skin, *"So soft...so beautiful...so trusting..."* He moves off my hips, down the bed, his hands squeezing and caressing, and presses his warm lips to my ass cheeks. He drags his fingers between my legs, teasing me. "Has anyone ever touched you here?" He slides his fingers between those cheeks, teasing that private spot.

"No." I'm shocked to realize I want him to.

"Such a gorgeous ass." He continues teasing me there, sending new sensations scattering through me like white-hot ants. I moan and rock, and he spreads my cheeks, using his hands and mouth everywhere, driving me out of my mind. I rise up on my elbows and knees, needing more. "That's it, baby. Give me that ass." His finger breaches the tight rim of muscles slowly, and I lose my breath.

"I need *you*," I beg.

"You're not needy enough yet." He pumps his finger, going deeper with every push, and uses his other hand on my clit. I rock against his fingers. "That's it. Chase your pleasure," he says gruffly, and sinks his teeth into my cheek, hurling me into a kaleidoscope of pleasure. He stays with me, licking and teasing, his fingers working me through the very last aftershock.

My head falls between my shoulders, and he lowers me to the mattress, turning me over.

"You're fucking amazing," he rasps, kissing my lips, jaw,

and shoulder as he unties my tether and unbinds my wrists. I reach for the scarf covering my eyes, but he grabs my hand, stopping me. "Leave it on for one minute. It'll make everything more intense for you." He kisses me deeply and passionately, and then the mattress dips, and I hear the tear of a condom wrapper.

He moves over me, and I feel the broad head of his cock against my entrance. He laces his fingers with mine, pressing them into the mattress on either side of my head, and nudges my legs open wider with his knees. His head dips beside mine, and I hear him breathing. I revel in the erotic, sensual sound, in the heat of him hovering over me, his thighs pressing down on mine, and the erratic thundering of our hearts as his hips press forward slowly. I welcome the delicious intrusion. He was right. I'm intensely aware of his thickness stretching me, the heat our bodies create, the way Clay holds his breath as he takes me deeper, and how our hearts calm as we come together fully. When he finally exhales, I hear his smile in it, and he whispers, "Breathe, baby."

I hadn't realized I was holding my breath, too, and it rushes from my lungs.

He removes the scarf from my eyes, and it takes me a minute to adjust to the light. When I do, I feel myself getting as lost in him and the emotions staring back at me as I am in the sensations engulfing me. I pull his mouth to mine, not wanting to overthink any of it or think at all. He's right there with me, thrusting and gyrating, stroking that magical spot inside me. We're fueled by passion so bright and hot, it coils around us like molten metal. His kisses are merciless, his thrusts just as ruthless. "Need to see you," he rasps, and rolls us over without breaking our connection.

He clutches my hips, helping me ride him. His eyes bore into me with the hunger of a ravenous lion. He feels so big from this angle, so thick and incredible, prickling heat sparks in my limbs, gathering speed and pressure, invading my core like a stampede of wild animals. He thrusts harder, and I know he's close, too. "*Fuck*," he grits out. "You're so tight. So fucking beautiful." He reaches up, tugging my mouth to his.

My hair tumbles forward, curtaining us in darkness. He grabs my ass with both hands, driving up from beneath me. Pleasure scorches through me, and I tear my mouth away, crying out as he gives in to his own powerful release. We rock and thrust, our noises echoing off the walls. The pleasure comes in waves, and we ride them out until we have nothing left to give. I lean over him, trying to catch my breath, our bodies spasming with aftershocks.

As the last shudders ripple through us, he cradles me in his arms, rolling us onto our sides and raining kisses over my lips and cheek. I snuggle into him, unable to tell where my body ends and his begins. He holds me tight until our breathing calms. Only then does he whisper, "I'll be right back, beautiful." He kisses me again before climbing off the bed.

I can't stop smiling as I watch him walk into the bathroom, all lean muscles and the sexiest butt I've ever seen. When he closes the door, I throw my arm over my eyes, feeling so *alive*, so invigorated, I'm sure I'm going to burst. It's like someone new has come to life inside me. Someone fun and sexy, who isn't afraid to let go. I never knew I could feel so uninhibited. That I could trust anyone with my body the way I trust him.

I squeeze my eyes closed, pressing my arm tighter over them in an effort to suppress it, but it bursts out in a flurry of kicks and a ridiculously giddy sound.

"Can I take that as a five-star review?"

My eyes fly open, and I clamp my mouth shut, but he dives onto the bed, pinning me beneath him, making us both crack up. My cheeks are hurting from smiling so hard. "Can we pretend you didn't see that?"

"Not a chance, Reckless."

I bite my lip.

"Do you call that a happy dance? Because it looked like pure and total elation to me."

"Shut up." I bury my face in his neck.

He lifts up just enough that I can't hide my face and grins down at me. "Stay with me."

"We're in *my* room, remember?"

"No. I mean stay with me in Paris. I'm here for three more days. *Stay.* Your family will be gone, and it'll be just us."

My heart seems to have turned giddy, too, because it screams *yes!* But my head speaks louder. "I have to get back to work. I'm starting a new project at the end of the week, and we have a kickoff meeting on Wednesday."

"Then give me *one* more day. One day of just us."

I consider the project preparations I have planned for the beginning of the week. I've already done most of my own, but I wanted to look over my team's preparations to make sure they're ready to go, too.

"Don't overthink it, Pep. I know you haven't taken a real vacation in years, and you own the company. Isn't flexibility one of the perks? Surely you can spare an extra day. Just call your assistant and tell them to cover for you."

"I don't have an assistant. We lost our front-desk person two weeks ago. Even if I want to stay, I can't just change an international flight at the last minute."

"Leave it to me. I'll make the arrangements."

"It's not that easy."

"It is for me. Come on, beautiful. Be reckless with me. We'll have a great time. When else will you be in Paris with a handsome quarterback who thinks you're the coolest woman he's ever hung out with? *Wait.* You're not into athletes. When else will you be in Paris with a regular guy who adores you?"

I laugh, my head spinning with the things he said. *Cool? Beautiful? Adores me?*

"What do you say? I guarantee you'll have an unforgettable time."

"You're serious," I say incredulously. "What if you can't get me a flight?"

"My cousin owns a private jet. If his pilot is busy, I'll hire another one. I'll buy a fucking plane if I have to. I won't let you down. I know how important your work is."

Excitement bubbles up inside me. "You really want me to stay that badly?"

"*Yes.* More than anything. I like being with you."

"You like sex," I tease.

"*True,* but that's not why I want you to stay. I've been into you since we first met, and this time together has been incredible. I'm not ready for it to end, and I don't think you are, either."

"I'm not, but this is *crazy.* It's like something out of a movie. I want to do it, but can you promise me I'll be home in time to prepare for my meeting?"

"I'll do you one better. Don't move." He presses his lips to mine, then gets up and grabs his phone from the pocket of his jeans.

He paces as he makes a call, unfazed by his own nakedness,

while I'm mesmerized by it, by *him*. He stops at the foot of the bed, his eyes dancing with delight. I gather the sheet around me and sit up, anticipation building with every passing second.

"Treat?" He pauses, listening. "It wasn't my best moment, but I'm good. Thanks for asking. How are you and Max and the kids?" He's quiet. He smiles, laughs. "That's great. I can't wait to see everyone again. Listen, I'm in Paris with a very special lady, and I need to secure a flight to Charlottesville, Virginia, for her early Tuesday morning. Any chance I can hire your pilot?" He rubs the crook of his neck and shoulder as he listens. "Great. Okay. I'll text you her information. Thanks, man. This means a lot to me." He listens again. "Really? I didn't know Noah was there. Give him a hard time for me, and please give my love to your family and Uncle Hal. Thanks, Treat. Have a good night." He ends the call and sets his phone on the nightstand. "Looks like you're all mine until Tuesday morning. We've got the plane."

"*Seriously?* That was a real call? You booked a private plane that easily?" *Holy cow. Am I really doing this?*

He puts one knee on the bed. "I did, and you can't back out now."

"I've never done *anything* like this before."

"Aren't we lucky? It's a night full of firsts." He waggles his brows.

My cheeks heat. "I need to message my team. I can't believe I'm staying in Paris. I can't believe I'm staying in Paris with an athlete, of all people." *An athlete who just had his face and hands all up in my naughty business.*

"I'm just a regular guy, remember?"

"Right. Regular guys don't hire private planes. I don't even know who *I* am anymore."

"It's a good thing I do." He kisses me and takes me down to the mattress beneath him. "Pepper Montgomery, meet Reckless, my sexy European fling."

Chapter Eleven

Clay

"Those were the best crepes I've ever had," Pepper says as we walk out of the quaint café after breakfast Monday morning. "How did you find that place?" The blond streaks in her hair appear even lighter against her navy peacoat as she puts on the scarf I gave her.

A taunting reminder of our incredible night together.

"A gentleman never reveals his sources."

I feel like I'm on a first date and want to impress her. That's a new feeling for me, and it poses a challenge. Other than on the football field, I haven't tried to impress anyone in so long, I'm not sure I remember how. Especially when I know she doesn't give a damn that I'm one of the best quarterbacks in the NFL or that I've got more money than I could ever spend. But I know how big a decision it was for her to take off work, and I'm determined to give her the best day of her life. I made good use of my time this morning, doing research and making calls while she dealt with emails, and I've got a few more things besides the five-star café planned for us that I think she'll enjoy.

"Okay, Mr. Mysterious." She looks up and down the busy sidewalk. "Which way should we go?"

I nod to our right, and as we head in that direction, my

phone chimes with a text. I pull it out and open the text from my grandfather. It's a picture of a gorgeous sunrise, with the message *Can't get that on a football field.*

"Someone just made you happy," Pepper says with a curious lilt in her voice.

"It's from my grandfather." I show her the picture.

"That's beautiful. Almost as pretty as ours was."

"Almost." After we made love in the wee hours of the morning, I convinced her to watch the sunrise with me on the balcony. I don't know where the urge came from, but it was the most spectacular sunrise I'd ever seen.

"Where is he?"

"In Alaska on an archaeological expedition. He discovered an impression of dinosaur skin and several fossilized footprints last year. The expedition is ongoing."

"I think I heard something about that on the news."

"I'm sure you did. He's a renowned archaeologist and paleontologist, and he's made some big discoveries over the years. He's supposed to be retired, but he's always planning his next adventure. It drives my grandmother crazy."

"He sounds fun, unless she doesn't like it."

"She adores him. Back in the day, she was his assistant. That's how they got together. Anyway, that picture I just showed you? That's kind of our thing. He's been sending me pictures of sunrises forever. He likes to remind me there's a big beautiful world out there beyond football, with hopes that one day I'll slow down enough to enjoy it."

"You should send him a picture of the sunset from the Eiffel Tower and the one you took of the sunrise this morning to show him that you're not missing out."

"I sent him the sunset picture," I say as we cross a street.

"And I sent him a picture of you sleeping and said you were more beautiful than any sunrise."

"*Clay.* Tell me you did *not* send him that."

I laugh. "I didn't, but it would've been funny."

She swats my arm. "I still can't believe I stayed."

That's about the fifth time she's said it this morning. I can't believe she stayed, either, but I'm damn happy she did. Even after our intimate night, I wasn't sure what this morning would hold. But I got to wake up with this incredible woman in my arms, and I get to spend an entire day with her. I can't remember the last time I was this excited to spend time with a woman. *Wait.* Yes, I can. It was yesterday.

"In your defense, I am hard to resist," I tease.

She gives me a coy glance. "You *do* make it impossible to say no."

"You say that like it's a bad thing."

"It's not bad, but it's definitely a thing. You're persistent and very convincing. I feel like a rebel around you."

I laugh and reach for her hand as we stroll down the busy sidewalk, but she moves it out of reach. As cute and amusing as that was yesterday, it kind of sucks now.

"Pepper, it's just us, remember? Your family left. There's no one to hide from." She sent her siblings a text early this morning saying she was off to the airport, and we waited until they left the hotel to move her things into my suite.

"Sorry." She slips her hand into mine. "I told you I don't have experience with flings. I don't know the rules."

I haven't held anyone's hand in so long, I'm struck by how good it feels to hold hers and how perfectly our hands fit together. *Just like our bodies.* Jesus, she's really messing with my head. I never think about that stuff, and with her, I can't stop.

"I don't think this is a typical fling, so how about we make our own rules?"

"You must do this a lot to have a comparison. Which begs the question, if I'm your European fling, do you have flings by country, state, or…?"

"Don't do that." I squeeze her hand.

"What? It's a fair question."

"It is," I admit. "But don't put me in a box like that." I stop walking to explain. "I played around a lot and earned that reputation when I was in my early twenties, but I'm thirty-five, Pepper. Give me some credit. I'm not a sex-crazed kid without a conscience. A lot of those rumors are based on fiction, not facts, stemming from someone seeing me out to dinner with a woman, or talking to someone at an event. Neither of which means I slept with them. I'm not saying it never happens, but it's not as often as you think. Those *encounters* have been few and far between for a long time. I spend a hell of a lot more time with my buddies and my family than I do with random women."

She studies me in silence.

"It's true, Pepper."

"I believe you. I was just thinking that it must be difficult to overcome a reputation like that."

Relieved, I say, "I don't really care about it most of the time. But I do where you're concerned. So if you have any other questions about my past, let's get them out of the way now."

"I am curious about whether you've had any long-term relationships."

We start walking again. "I've had a couple that lasted for more than a few dates, but nothing I'd call long-term. The game has always come first, and that doesn't fare well with women who want my attention."

"I can understand that," she says as we cross a street. "It would be hard to compete with your love of the game."

"I guess I always figured with the right woman, there would be no competition. How about you? I know you don't do flings, but when was your last long-term relationship?"

"Oh, *gosh*. Forever ago."

"Why?"

She shrugs. "I'm busy, and relationships take time and attention."

"Does that mean you don't date often?"

"Not very. I'm sure you can tell by now that I'm not exactly the kind of person who goes out looking for guys."

"Sure, but what about dating apps?"

"My sisters made me try them, but I didn't like it. There's a lot of pressure that goes along with those apps. They're very looks oriented. I know I'll never be the prettiest girl in a room, but I might be the smartest, and you can't tell that from a dating app."

I stop walking and draw her into my arms. "That's the second time you've said something about not being beautiful, so I'm making our first fling rule. No negative self-talk."

"It's not negative self-talk. I just accept the truth. I grew up with gorgeous sisters, remember?"

"That's *your* truth, Reckless, not mine, and I can assure you, it's not a million other guys' truths, either. Guys have been checking you out everywhere we've gone. But that's beside the point. Negative self-talk affects everything you do. Imagine if every time you worked on a project, you told yourself you wouldn't do a great job before you even started."

Her expression turns serious. "I'd never do that."

"Exactly. So don't plant those seeds in your brilliant brain about your looks. When you walk into a room, you're all I see. You have been since the first time I set my eyes on you."

She studies me again, which she seems to do a lot, and I imagine her picking apart the things I say, dissecting their honesty.

I lift our joined hands and kiss the backs of hers as we stop at a busy corner, waiting to cross. "Think about how I see you every time you look in the mirror, and hopefully one day you'll see what I see."

Her cheeks pink up, and she steps closer, her voice hushed. "The image of us last night might render me unable to think at all when I look in the mirror."

We both laugh, and I steal a kiss before we cross the street.

"Where are we going?" she asks.

I'm not about to tell her everything I have planned, but I can give her a taste. "I thought we'd start with some window-shopping on Champs-Élysées, and then I figured you'd get a kick out of seeing the largest science museum in Paris."

She holds my hand a little tighter. "That's really sweet, but would it be okay if we didn't go to the museum?"

"Sure." So much for my plan to impress her. "Did you have someplace else in mind?"

"No, but I saw a ton of museums the last few days with my family, and I'm kind of museumed out. Unless you really want to go?"

"No. I was only going so you could see it."

"I appreciate the thought you put into it, but I've got one day of playing hooky with you, and I'd like to do things I wouldn't normally do. Like *not* follow a plan."

That's it, baby. Break out of your shell with me. "I like this rebellious streak."

"You should. You caused it."

"I take great pride in that. What are you up for? Walking around and figuring out where to go along the way?"

"That sounds fun."

"Want to really get risky and ask other people where we should go?"

Her eyes light up. "Yes! And we have to go wherever they say. No googling, either. We have to ask for directions, and let every place be a surprise."

"I love it. I'm in."

She beams at me. "But wait. There is *one* place I want to go."

"Today's your day, Reckless. I'll go anywhere you want."

"Last night at dinner, Brindle was bummed that she didn't get to see a show at a place called Crazy Horse. Maybe we can get tickets and go."

I have something special planned for later that I don't want to give up, but I'll find a way to work it in. "Crazy Horse, huh? What is that, a Western show or something?"

"I don't know, but that's the fun of it. *Plus*, my sisters always have great stories to tell about their adventures, and I *never* have adventures," she says mischievously. "It would give me a feather in my cap."

I wonder if that means she's not going to keep today a secret from them, but I don't ask, because I don't want anything to change the direction we're heading in. "You want to stick it to your sisters, don't you? You want to one-up them."

"I don't know if I'll ever tell them, but I love knowing I could." She wrinkles her nose adorably. "Is that bad?"

I can't help hoping one day she will. "No, I love it. I bet the concierge at the hotel can get us tickets." I pull out my phone and call the hotel.

After securing tickets for a champagne dinner and show at the Crazy Horse, we spend the morning meandering the cobblestone streets of Paris hand in hand. We ask random strangers where to go and take their word as gold as we head out on each adventure. We take pictures of the places we're sent as we explore interesting shops and check out cool galleries, showing each other things we like and things we don't. We gorge ourselves on the sweetest chocolates I've ever eaten, and Pepper likes them so much, I buy extras for her to nibble on throughout the day. We people watch and make up stories about them, and we laugh more than I have in a long time. I have never done anything like this, and I can't remember ever having so much fun.

As we leave a gallery, I pull Pepper into a kiss. Her cheeks and nose are cool, but her lips are warm. "Are you cold? Do you want to take a break?"

She shakes her head, her eyes glittering with excitement. "Who should we ask next?" She looks around and tugs me toward an older couple watching us from an outdoor table at a café. "Excuse me, do you speak English?"

"Yes, we do," the portly man says with a French accent.

"We're here for only one day," Pepper says excitedly. "And we're looking for suggestions of places to go and things to see other than museums."

The couple exchanges a look, and the gray-haired woman says, "A happy couple like you must see the Wall of Love."

Pepper's brows knit, as if a lightbulb in her head went off and she is wrestling with *fling* versus *couple*. I don't want her to overthink it, so I drape my arm over her shoulder and say,

"Hear that, honey? I guess we're going to see the Wall of Love."

"It's in the Jehan Rictus Square in Montmartre," the man says helpfully. "You can catch the métro."

We take the train, which smells like old sneakers, and we act like silly kids, joking about the smell and trying to guess what the Wall of Love is. "A mural of an orgy, of course," I say, making her laugh.

"Only if it was designed by a man. I think it's a graffiti wall, like the one at the Stardust Café in Oak Falls."

"I don't remember seeing any graffiti in town."

"It's inside the café. We call it the Let It Out wall. It's covered with decades of proclamations of love, or more likely, lust."

"And what did *you* write on that wall?"

She arches a brow. "Nothing I'm going to tell you."

"You giving me sass, Reckless?" I put my hand on her thigh and squeeze. "I'm not above coercing it out of you." I lower my lips to hers, taking her in a long, slow kiss that leaves us both breathing so hard, we go back for more.

When we get off the train, there's a massive number of steps to climb. Pepper huffs out a breath. "We should've taken the elevator."

"You don't get much exercise, do you?"

"I got plenty of exercise last night."

I laugh and hug her against my side. "Come on, Montgomery. Show me what you've got. I'll race you, and I'll even give you a head start. *Go.*" I smack her ass.

She squeals and bolts up the steps, her arms pumping.

She's so cute, I can barely stand it. I catch up to her in seconds. "Gotta go faster than that to beat me." I wrap my arm around her waist, lifting her off her feet, and race up the rest of the steps with her tucked against my side like a football. When we reach the top, we're both cracking up.

"I can't believe you did that!" she pants out between laughs. "Don't your thighs burn?"

No, but my shoulder aches like a bitch. "No, but I'd like to make your thighs burn."

She blushes a red streak, and I tug her into another kiss, which I can't seem to stop doing. Nor do I want to. Seeing her unguarded and carefree like this is as spectacular as watching a touchdown play out on the field. I keep my arm around her, wanting to be closer as we head into the garden, which is surrounded by tall buildings and iron fencing. The plants aren't green or flowering since it's January, but it's easy to imagine them with colorful blooms and lush greenery. There are several couples taking pictures in front of the Wall of Love, which is not a mural of an orgy after all or a graffiti wall. It's a massive, dark-tiled wall with elegant white calligraphy all over it in different languages, and several oddly shaped red areas. "What do you think, Reckless?"

"I think it's beautiful. There's a plaque." She points to it. "Let's read about it."

I snag her hand, pulling her back to me. "Isn't that like googling?"

She winces, and I press my lips to hers.

"I like when you try to break the rules." I can't resist stealing another kiss before turning to two middle-aged women, a blonde and a brunette, holding hands. "Excuse me. Do you speak English?"

"Yes, we do," the blonde answers with a British accent.

"What's the deal with this wall?" I ask. "Is there a meaning behind it?"

"Yes, a very important one," the blonde says. "It was designed by two artists, and it says 'I love you' in more than two hundred languages, symbolizing love in all its forms."

"See how the words cross over the lines between the tiles?" her partner asks. "Walls usually divide people. This is a reminder that love can overcome boundaries and connect all of us." She goes on to tell us more about the artists and the eight-year journey of collecting the *I love you*s in different languages. "The red marks represent a shattered heart, showing how the human race can be torn apart by a lack of love. If you pieced them all together, they'd form a complete heart."

"Wow. That's powerful," Pepper says, gazing at the wall like she can feel the messages behind it.

I pull her closer and kiss the top of her head, wondering if she's thinking about a past love. That's a surprising and uncomfortable thought, but now I want to know if she is.

"Would you like a picture in front of it?" the brunette asks.

"Yes, please." I hand them my phone.

When we stand in front of the wall, Pepper gazes up at me, and I feel something powerful, too. But it has nothing to do with the wall. Pressing my lips to hers feels as natural as breathing.

"Now, there's a great picture," the brunette says, reminding me we have an audience.

When she hands me back my phone, I thank her and offer, "Would you like me to take a picture for you?"

After I take their picture, we chat with them for a bit and ask them where we should go next.

"Have you been to Place du Tertre?" the blonde asks.

"No," we answer.

She tells us it's a square that was once a gathering place for famous artists like Renoir, van Gogh, and Dalí and is now used by amateur artists. "Ask one of the artists to sketch a picture of the two of you together. It's a wonderful experience. We still have ours from fifteen years ago."

"We'll do that," I promise. "Thank you."

On the walk to the square, I'm still thinking about the way Pepper looked at the wall. "Hey, Reckless, have you ever been in love?"

"No. I had a major crush on Ravi when we went out, and I might have thought it was love at the time. But we were just kids, so…" She shrugs.

"You mean the lucky bastard who got to pop your cherry?" As the words leave my lips, I bite back a sting of jealousy.

She looks amused. "I never said that."

"You didn't have to."

She rolls her eyes. "What about you? Have you ever been in love?"

"Yes."

"Really?" She looks up at me with disbelief. "What happened?"

"Nothing. I fell in love at five years old, and I'm still in love with the same game." *The business of it has gotten old, and it's taking a toll on my body, but my love for the game is still there.*

She squeezes my hand. "You're such a brat. I'm being serious. Have you ever fallen for a woman?"

"I have been in lust, but never in love." I pull her closer, trying to ignore the unfamiliar tug in my chest. "I guess those chemicals you mentioned haven't mediated that particular reaction yet."

We find a vintage photo booth on our way to the square, and I drag her into it, pulling her onto my lap. She smiles properly for the camera, and right before it takes a picture, I tickle her ribs, catching her mid-laugh, with her head back and her mouth wide open. I kiss her as the camera flashes again, and it catches us in various stages of silly faces and hilarity.

We walk away arm in arm, each with a strip of four black-and-white pictures, laughing at ourselves. It only takes a few minutes to reach the square, which is bustling like a street fair with artists and people and shops along the periphery. We visit all the artists, watching them paint or sketch, taking pictures of everything and of the two of us. We sit at a table outside a café sharing a croissant and having a glass of wine, people watching. My shoulder burns, and a dull ache radiates up my neck. I try to rub it out, praying it doesn't lead to a headache today of all days.

"Are you okay?" Pepper asks.

I lower my hand. "Yeah, fine."

"Did you hurt your shoulder when you carried me up the stairs?"

I scoff. "*No*. I could carry you for days."

"Are you sure? Yesterday at lunch, I heard the guys say you had a shoulder injury."

"It's nothing. They were just talking shit. I'm fine, really." I look out at the square and try to distract her. "This place is pretty incredible, isn't it?"

"I haven't seen anywhere like it since I got to Paris. I love the energy here. It's like a hidden village all its own." Her eyes shimmer in the sunlight, more beautiful than ever. "It's kind of magical."

I feel something magical, too, but I'm pretty sure hanging out anywhere with Pepper would feel that way.

"I can't believe I just said that." She laughs softly. "I don't use words like *magical*."

"Magic looks good on you, Reckless."

She gives me the sweetest smile, reeling me in for another kiss. I throw away our trash and reach for her hand. "Let's go, beautiful. Time to get our picture drawn."

There are lines for most of the artists, but we find an older gentleman who's sketching caricatures, and we don't have to wait for too long before sitting for our sketch. The artist speaks in broken English, telling us the history of the square, and we learn there's a ten-year waiting list to secure a spot there.

When he's done with the sketch, we rave about it and thank him for doing such a good job. We walk away, trying not to laugh. It's not just a sketch. It's a mix of shapes and angles and long flowing hair over bare shoulders. We've got sharp noses, large, lustful eyes, and plump lips.

"Is it just me, or did he make me look like Michael Jackson?"

"He *did*." Pepper laughs. "I've got to give him credit. You're the hottest MJ I've ever seen, but why did he draw us naked?"

"To go with those blowjob lips he gave you, of course."

We both crack up.

"I wish my lips were as full as he drew them."

"Your lips are perfect."

"I'm glad you like them."

"I don't just like them. I'm obsessed with them." I brush my lips over hers. "I think I might be a little obsessed with you, too, Reckless." I punctuate my point with another kiss, and before either of us can overthink it, I say, "Onward!"

On our way out of the square, we stop a tall, chicly dressed woman and explain that we're here for the day, and ask her where we should go next.

Her gaze moves assessingly over Pepper. "This lovely woman should be dressed in Dior. You must take her to Avenue Montaigne and buy her something beautiful." She gives me the same scrutinizing once-over and says, "You have handsome bone structure. It must be Armani for you."

"You have good taste," I say. "Thank you. Have a nice afternoon."

As she walks away, Pepper laughs. *"Dior?"*

"That's right, Reckless. Time to get a taxi." I take her hand and head for the street, excited to treat her like a princess and watch her squirm, and bloom, right before my eyes. Like she did in the bedroom.

"We are *not* spending that type of money."

"You're right. We aren't. *I* am."

"Clay." She gives me a stern look.

"You made the rules, and we're not breaking them. Besides, we need clothes for tonight."

Chapter Twelve

Pepper

The hours pass in a whirlwind. I can't remember the last time I had so much fun. I'm treated like a queen at Dior, and though I fight Clay every step of the way, I finally settle on a black cocktail dress with heels to match, both of which are shamefully expensive. I apologize for initiating the must-do game a dozen times, but he just smiles and kisses me, bringing wild flutters to my chest and stomach, like he's been doing all day. He arranges for my outfit to be sent to the hotel, and we hit Armani next, where Clay seems more than comfortable. I've never met anyone like him. He's a chameleon, acting like a carefree kid one minute and looking like a bigger heartthrob than James Bond in an Armani suit the next. He makes arrangements for his purchases to be sent to the hotel, too.

It's after two o'clock when we finish, and we realize we haven't eaten lunch. Clay asks the salesman for our next destination, and we head to Hôtel Plaza Athénée, an iconic luxury hotel and restaurant, where we enjoy an elegant champagne lunch.

"What do you think, Reckless? Are you glad you stayed, or are you worried about work?"

It's so easy being with him when we're not hiding from my

family, I realize I haven't thought about work once since we left the hotel. Well, it's been easy *other than* when he was making me spend his money. That wasn't easy for me. Although being treated like a queen was almost as fun as being with Clay. He makes me feel special every second we're together. He's so different from the man I thought he was.

That hefty realization momentarily steals my voice. But he's looking at me expectantly, and I want him to know the truth, so I find my voice. "I'm really glad I stayed."

He covers my hand with his, giving it a squeeze. "Good. I don't want to make you think about work, but I do want to know more about you and how you got into research and development. Have you always loved science?"

"Yes. I've always been a curious person, and science answers a lot of questions. When I was a kid, my parents would buy me science kits, and I'd spend hours working with them. My dad made the hayloft in our barn into a lab for me when I was in sixth grade. I had to swear never to use fire or flammable chemicals without him, but I was too smart to do that anyway."

"I'd expect nothing less. Your parents seem very support-ive."

"They always have been, for all of us. My dad was an engi-neering professor before he retired, and he used to come up with things for us to build together."

"I can see your dad doing that. What kind of things did you build?"

"All sorts of things. We made robots and boats and gadgets we could use around the house."

"Like what?"

"This won't seem like a big deal now, because technology is so easy to come by, but we built a detection system that turned the light on when I came into my bedroom, and a plant watering system, which worked, but it was too cumbersome to leave in place."

"That's amazing. Dash told me that when you were in graduate school, you developed the seizure-alert necklace Amber wears and that it's now sold all over the world. That's impressive. Is that how you got into making medical devices?"

"Sort of. I wanted to make a difference in people's lives, and R and D allows me to do that. I guess it was a natural fit. Probably like football is for you. What did you study in college?"

"Biology and physical education. I figured if professional football fell through, I'd become a biology teacher and coach high school football."

"*Biology*, really?"

"Why do you sound so surprised. You *did* think I was a dumb jock, didn't you?"

"*No.* You're obviously smart. It's just that a biology degree takes a lot of hard work and dedication, and the athletes I knew in college didn't care about anything but football and skating through their classes with a passing grade."

"That would've been a waste of time and energy. I like structure, and I have always enjoyed school. That's one of the reasons I fought to stop traveling when we were young. That and football, of course."

"I didn't realize you fought for that."

"I had to. I was going stir-crazy. I've always been competitive, and while my parents supported my love of football, signing me up for teams when and where they could and bringing in coaches from time to time, I wanted to excel at it. I also wanted to have clear academic expectations and goals so I could excel at that, too. We were homeschooled a lot, and I wanted the competition of kids other than my brothers and sister. It turned out I loved science, too. Why do you think I found your explanation of chemical reactions sexy?"

"I thought you were just flirting with me."

"I was." He picks up his glass and takes a drink. "But now you know it goes deeper."

"I have a feeling a lot of things about you go deeper than I thought. Are you a sapiosexual?"

He shakes his head. "No. I don't think intelligence is the most important quality in a partner, but it's damn sexy with you."

"It's pretty sexy with you, too." Our gazes hold for a long moment, and then I remember we were in the middle of a conversation and try to get back to it. "How old were you when your family stopped traveling?"

"We moved back to Ridgeport when I was twelve, but we still traveled during school breaks."

"How did your siblings feel about it? Did they resent you for asking your parents to stop traveling?"

"No. Victory and Seth wanted to go to a normal high school, so we were a united front. Flynn hated giving up travel, and Noah was too young to really know what he wanted. But we were brought up a little differently in other ways, too, and I think that kept Flynn from being too angry at us."

"What do you mean?"

"My parents had family money, but we never knew it until we were adults. We lived meagerly, fitting all of our belongings into a few small bags, and we were raised with family and giving back to others at the heart of everything. So when one of us got something that was important to them, the rest of us were genuinely happy for them, even if it meant we didn't get anything. We knew we'd get our turn. Of course, we had our moments when we'd lose our shit, but in general, we were happy for each other. Flynn knew football was my life and that Vic needed consistent friends and Seth needed bigger opportunities. He didn't resent us, but my parents made sure he got what he needed, too."

"How?"

"Flynn has always been tight with our grandfather. They're like two peas in a pod, and when Flynn was a teenager, he got to go on expeditions with our grandparents."

"That's incredible. Your parents sound like really special people. Your grandparents, too."

"They are. I'm lucky. But you're lucky, too. I've met your parents. They seem like they'd go to the ends of the earth for you and your brother and sisters."

"Yeah. They would. Was it hard to get good grades and keep up with football in college?"

"Yes, *very*. But as my grandfather always says, nothing easy is worth a damn." He pops the rest of his croissant into his mouth. "Did one of those athletes you mentioned have anything to do with why you don't date jocks?"

I fidget with my napkin. "Maybe."

"What happened?"

"I was naive. A star football player acted like he was into me, and I was stupid enough to believe him, when all he really wanted was for me to basically do his homework so he'd pass his classes and not lose his scholarship."

Clay's eyes narrow. "He used you."

"Mm-hm." *Why does that still sting?* "Before we went out, I wasn't someone people noticed, and I liked that. I had a small group of friends, and I was happy. But suddenly people knew who I was, and when finals were over and he dumped me, I became a laughingstock. I didn't even have the courage to give him hell for it. The worst part was that everyone in his friend group knew he was using me, and I was too naive to suspect it."

"That's not on you. That's on *him*," he says vehemently. "No wonder you don't trust jocks. How big of a star was he? Did he go on to play pro ball?"

The answer is yes, but I don't want to get into that, so I shrug, fidgeting with my napkin.

The muscles in Clay's jaw bunch. "Give me his name."

"*No*," I say with a laugh, surprised by his adamancy.

"Come on, Reckless. Who was it?"

"It was a decade ago. It doesn't matter."

He levels me with a serious stare. "It matters to *me*."

Heck if that doesn't make me feel good all over, but still. I don't want to cause trouble. "We were kids. It's water under the bridge. Can we please let it go and move on? I don't want to think about those awkward college years."

He's quiet for a beat, his jaw working overtime. He takes a drink, averting his eyes for a moment. When he meets my gaze, some of that tension is gone. "I bet you were adorable in college. I would've been into you."

I laugh. "You wouldn't have given me the time of day. Besides, you were out of college by the time I started. I'm only thirty."

"Are you calling me old?" he teases.

"No. I'm just stating a fact about our ages." I eat my last bite of quiche, which is heavenly.

He sits back, his expression turning serious again. "I'm sorry that asshole hurt you. I know a lot of athletes, and some are real pricks, but there are a lot of good guys in the league."

I think he's right about our fling being different than others', because according to Sable, flings are usually a onetime thing with no emotions involved. I'm feeling all sorts of emotions toward Clay. "If the guys you're talking about are anything like you and Dash, I'm inclined to believe you."

"Good. Speaking of Dash, he told me you started your own company last year. What was that like, going out on your own?"

"It was scary, giving up the security of a steady paycheck and a marketing team that worked on securing contracts. There were people I could go to with questions and issues, and I didn't have to deal with the business side of things, which takes up a lot of my time. Honestly, I was really close to not going out on my own."

"I can see how that would be intimidating. It sounds like it would be the equivalent of being the quarterback and managing the entire team at the same time."

"My company is much smaller than a football team. I only have a few employees."

"What pushed you over the edge to do it?"

"My dad said something that made me realize I couldn't *not* give it a shot, and I'm glad I didn't chicken out."

"What did he say?"

"Nothing groundbreaking. He told me to imagine myself twenty years from now still working for someone else and asked how I'd feel about it. When I looked at it that way, it made me take stock of what was really important to me. I've helped develop some amazing medical devices, and I'm proud of them and thankful for those opportunities, but I'm not looking to change the world. My heart lies in changing *lives*. Helping people with disabilities who are having trouble in their daily lives because they can't find relief through what's currently available to them. I couldn't make the decision to work on those types of projects while working for someone else. That's when I realized, if I didn't take the chance, I'd definitely look back at my career and wish I had."

"Your dad had a great point, and you and I have more in common than you think. I can't change people's lives the way you do, but I support several charities, and one cause that's close to my heart is my foundation, Fast Friendships, which helps improve the lives of people with intellectual and developmental disabilities."

"*Your* foundation?" I guess I should have taken a deeper dive when I googled him.

"Yeah. My high school coach's son, Ronnie, is intellectually disabled. He used to hang out with all the players, and seeing how he was treated by some people when we went places is what gave me the idea. I set up the foundation right after I started playing pro ball and pulled together a great team to run it. I made it our mission to help spread awareness to stop the social stigmas associated with people with IDD. We offer programs to help with employment and mentorship and have support groups for their families."

"That's amazing. I had no idea you were involved with that. Social stigmas are hard to overcome. Especially for kids. I saw it with Amber when she was first diagnosed with epilepsy. People are scared of what they don't understand. You're doing a good thing."

"Like I said, there's more to me than just an orgasm donor. But we're not here to talk about me. I just wanted you to know that we do have that in common."

We seem to have a lot more in common than I first anticipated.

"Now that you're in the thick of running your business, how do you like being your own boss?"

Switching gears, I sit back and sigh. "It's a double-edged sword. It's exciting and scary, knowing my staff relies on me for a paycheck, and like I said, keeping up with the business side eats up a lot of my time, which takes away from my research. But I love being able to go after contracts for devices I want to make, even though it's harder to secure funding for them."

"What makes it harder?"

I sip my champagne. "There's more of a demand for products that help a larger number of people, like the wireless heart-failure monitor and the pocket ultrasound that I helped develop, which is why the bigger companies go after them."

Clay smiles and shakes his head. "That beautiful brain of yours blows me away. I'm out there tossing a ball around and fans are screaming my name, and you're developing life-saving technologies but the general public has no idea who's behind them. That's not right."

"It wasn't just me. It was a whole team of people, and we weren't the first to develop either of those technologies. But ours are the most widely used on the market today."

"That's incredible. I assume you've been successful securing funding for the projects you want to work on through your own business, or you wouldn't have a company."

"So far," I say proudly.

"I'd love to hear about your work."

"I don't want to bore you."

"Pepper, I wouldn't ask if I thought it would bore me."

Wow. I like that. "Okay. We're working on two contracts that are funded by venture capitalists. A Smart Glove to help people with neurological conditions regain hand function and a wearable assistive device for people who are sight impaired, so they don't have to use a cane. And we've got a contract with NIH to develop a vagus nerve stimulator for seizure prevention in people with drug-resistant epilepsy."

"Those sound incredible. Is that the type of epilepsy Amber has?"

"No. Her seizures are controlled with medication, but seeing how epilepsy has affected her over the years makes me want to help others who aren't so lucky."

He asks a dozen more questions. His genuine interest and his knowledge of how bodies work spur me on to talk in more detail about my current projects, which leads to a conversation about my failures and my successes, and some of the projects I hope to work on in the future. It's so refreshing to talk to a man who's not only interested but understands the science behind what I do. Most of the guys I've gone out with ask generic questions about my work, and I can see their interest waning within the first three minutes of answering. Clay and I talk for nearly an hour, and when we leave, I feel closer to him than I have to anyone in a long time. Even my own family doesn't show as much interest in my work as Clay.

We take our waiter's suggestion and go for a walk along the Seine. It's breezy by the water, and when Clay pulls me close, I snuggle into his side. His scent mixes with the scent of the river, and I realize that when we were near the river with my family, I didn't even notice it had a scent.

I've never been one to dream about frivolous things. I haven't longed for romance or been starry-eyed over the idea of a white wedding or a picket fence. But in this moment, with this unexpectedly interesting and surprisingly thoughtful man, I think I know why I haven't dreamed of those things.

I never knew what romance felt like until *now*.

Everything about today, from laughing on the train and kissing in the cobblestone streets, to letting strangers control where we go and what we do and sharing a meal and good conversation, has been romantic. It's as if I'm seeing everything through new eyes. The buildings I'd previously thought were pretty and interesting have taken on a magical quality, like castles in fairy tales. The gentle flow of the river feels relaxing and beautiful, bringing more warm, fuzzy emotions. My rational brain wants to pick all of that apart, but I don't allow myself to analyze it.

I want to revel in the specialness and intimacy of it. I want to be free from overthinking just for today.

Fear tries to bully its way in against my efforts to abandon rational thinking, but my trust in Clay feels like a buffer protecting me. From *what*, I have no idea, but once again, I shut down the urge to overthink it, allowing myself to revel in *all* these remarkable, inexplicable feelings.

Unfortunately, my brain doesn't turn off that easily, and in the far recesses of my mind, I hear a whisper about this being fleeting, not real, *a fling*. I know that's all it can ever be. We live in different worlds, and they're very far apart in every way that counts. But for the first time in my adult life, something feels too good to ruin it with reality, and I cling to it with everything I have.

We walk in comfortable silence, serenaded by the gentle flow of the river and the sounds of life taking place around us. Clay holds me a little tighter each time people walk past, and I like that, too. Fling or not, it's a luxurious feeling to be this content, to feel this safe and special.

When he kisses my temple and lets go of me to pull out his phone, I long to be closer. He thumbs out a text, and as he pockets his phone, he says, "Time for our next stop, sweetheart."

Sweetheart feels different now, too. Bigger, more intimate. "Who should we ask where to go?" I look at the people around us.

"I already asked a guy."

"When? We haven't stopped to talk to anyone."

His dimples come out to play. "You didn't see me talking to a great-looking dude with excellent bone structure?"

God, he makes my cheeks hurt. "Does he happen to go by the name Mr. Perfect?"

"Not if he can help it. Come on, Reckless. Your surprise awaits."

My heart skips. "Surprise?"

His grin knocks my socks off as he takes my hand, pulling me along as he rushes toward the steps that lead to the road, and I get caught up in the whirlwind that is Clay Braden. We go from the river to a carousel. *A carousel!* Although it's not quite sunset, the carousel lights twinkle against the dusky sky. In the distance, the Eiffel Tower stands like a romantic sentinel watching over us. Now I wish I *did* climb the tower with my family, if for no other reason than to have known what the view of all the places Clay and I have visited today look like from above.

"I haven't been on a carousel since I was a little girl," I say as we choose our horses.

Clay helps me onto a horse. "I don't think I've ever been on one."

"Ever? I thought carousels were like a rite of passage."

He shakes his head. "I didn't have a conventional childhood, remember?"

When he told me about his childhood, I was so focused on the things he was sharing with me, I didn't think about the things he'd missed out on. "I'm glad I get to share this first with you."

"Me too." He climbs onto a horse and reaches across the space between us. "Give me that hand, Reckless."

It's ridiculous the way my heart flutters as I take his hand. The carousel starts, and I grab the pole with my other hand as my horse moves up and down.

"Look over here, beautiful."

I look over and he snaps a picture. *"Hey."* I'm sure he caught me with a goofy grin.

"I want to remember that smile in your eyes, and before you say I'm being cheesy, you should know I don't care if I am, because it's true."

He holds up his phone to take more pictures, and I make silly faces, feeling like a teenager with a crush. When we get off the carousel, he pulls me into a kiss. Then he's rushing us off again, leading me toward the Eiffel Tower.

"Are we climbing the tower?" I ask.

"Yes. You didn't get to do it yesterday, and you can't leave without getting the best view of the city."

Thrills sweep through me as we make our way there. "We need tickets."

"Already taken care of."

"We can't go to the top."

"I know the rules." When we get to the tower, he leads me around the line of people waiting for their turn and heads for a dark-haired man wearing a black coat.

"Mr. Blanchet?" Clay asks.

The man nods, a cordial smile gracing his angular face. "Mr. Braden." He shakes Clay's hand and turns that friendly smile on me. "Ms. Montgomery."

Thoroughly confused, I say, "Hello," and look questioningly at Clay.

"Right this way," Mr. Blanchet says. "We need to do a security check before we can go up in the tower."

Clay puts a hand on my back as we follow him, and I whisper, "What's going on?"

"We're following Mr. Blanchet."

"I know *that*."

He just flashes those dimples and keeps on walking.

After going through a brief security check, we're taken into an elevator by ourselves. I've never been afraid of heights, but my heart is already racing with anticipation, and watching the world get smaller as we ascend in the belly of the iron tower brings a hint of anxiety.

Clay's arm circles me from behind, pulling me against his chest. "You okay, Reckless?"

Better now. "Yeah."

We step out of the elevator on the second floor, and there are a lot of other people milling about. Mr. Blanchet tells us to take our time.

"Why did we ride up alone?" I ask Clay as we make our way to a railing.

"Because I didn't want to share you with anyone."

He kisses me like he didn't just say the most romantic thing I've ever heard. As we make our way around the perimeter, taking in the magnificent views of the city, he keeps me close, the way he has been doing all day. We both take pictures as I point out the Louvre, Montmartre, Notre-Dame, and more. "Look at the river," I say. "It looks like a ribbon running through the city." I snap a picture of it and glance at Clay, catching him taking pictures of me. "You're missing the view."

"I'm not missing a thing. I've got the best seat in the house."

I shake my head, but the more he says things like that, the more I believe he really feels that way. As we circle the tower, the sun is hovering just above the horizon, like a mother watching over her children as evening sets in.

"Time to go, sweetheart." Clay takes my hand again.

"But the sun is about to set. Do you think Mr. Blanchet would mind if we stay to watch it?"

"No, but I will." He leads me to a different elevator, where Mr. Blanchet is waiting for us.

"Why?" I ask as the elevator doors close.

"Because you deserve the best view of the sunset," Clay says, and the elevator starts going *up*.

My pulse skyrockets. "I thought the top floor was closed?"

"It is. But I promised you an unforgettable time, and I am a man of my word."

The magic of the evening must be getting to me, because I full-on *swoon*. My heart feels too big for my chest, my body tingles with happiness, and I feel a little dizzy.

I hold on to Clay as we step out of the elevator and are met with a cold wind. He tucks me beneath his arm and kisses my temple, keeping me close as we choose the spot with the best view to watch the sunset. As the sun makes its gentle farewell, painting the sky with gorgeous streaks of pinks, oranges, and purples, the lights of the city bloom to life in twinkles and bursts of gold and white, until they're all we see.

I'm so overwhelmed by the magnificence before us, "*Clay*" comes out just above a whisper. "This is extraordinary."

"It sure is," he says huskily, those piercing blue eyes locked on me.

I want to memorize the rush of emotions swirling inside me, but it feels a little too dangerous, because our time together, our fling, will soon be over. I try to shut down that rational part of my brain again, but without the light of day, with Clay looking at me like he truly believes *I'm* extraordinary, I'm stuck in some middle ground between caution and the wind.

But then he lowers his lips to mine, holding me possessively, and kisses me so thoroughly, every ounce of me aches to be closer to him, and my caution flits away in the wind.

Chapter Thirteen

Pepper

I take back everything I said about Paris not being romantic.

I feel like I'm living in a fairy tale. Not only did Clay literally lose his breath at the sight of me in my new Dior cocktail dress, but he also hired a driver to take us to the Crazy Horse in a vintage Bentley. I was floating on cloud nine in the back of the ritzy car with this beautiful man who has been making my heart sing all day. Imagine my surprise when we pulled up to the venue and saw bright red, illuminated *lips*. It turns out we're *not* seeing a Western show, but a cabaret featuring female nude dancers, and Clay knew exactly what the Crazy Horse was the entire day.

Needless to say, he got a kick out of seeing my shock.

It's a good thing we had dinner before the show. It gave me time for the idea of watching a nude show to settle in. Although I was too nervous to eat much of the lavish meal, I did indulge in champagne to help calm my nerves. Our time together truly is an experience of firsts. I've never pictured myself watching nude dancers, but here I sit under dizzying lights, utterly mesmerized by the tantalizing cabaret of perfectly sculpted, long-legged women perched on sky-high heels, wearing nothing but red lipstick and a few straps of strategically placed leather, which covers absolutely nothing. The stunning dancers look identical, save for their vibrantly colored wigs.

"This is incredible," I whisper to Clay, surprised by how much I'm enjoying the show.

"Yeah," he says, a little clipped.

I glance over and see him rubbing his neck. I noticed him doing that during dinner, too. When I asked if he was okay, he said rubbing his neck is just a habit. But now his curt tone has me wondering if it's more than that.

"Hey," I whisper, bringing his eyes to mine. They're a little stormy, and that worries me, too. "Are you sure you're okay?"

"*Yes.* Just watching the show." He flashes a wolfish grin and squeezes my hand. "I hope you're taking notes, because I want a private show with the prettiest woman in here later." As I try to work out whether he means me or one of the dancers, he says, "Stop overthinking. I'm talking about you."

I swear he can read my mind.

We watch a number of performances with short magic shows in between each set while the dancers change from one alluring costume to another. Their current costumes consist of leather straps crisscrossing over their shoulders and ribs, leaving the rest of their bodies exposed. Thigh-high fishnets and mid-calf high-heeled boots finish off the scant outfits.

After an hour and a half of watching back-arching, body-baring, provocative dancing, I'm embarrassed by how turned on I am. Applause rings out at the end of the show, and as the lights come on, I notice Clay rubbing his temple, but his eyes brighten as he takes my hand and we follow the crowd out of the building.

When we're safely in the Bentley, he says, "What did you think?"

His voice is tight, but I don't ask if he's okay. It's obvious that he doesn't want to talk about whatever is bothering him. "I thought it was fantastic. Those women were gorgeous, and so fit. They must practice all the time. Did you like it?"

"Yeah. It was good." His brows are knitted, but he gives me a half smile and pulls me into a kiss. He threads his fingers into my hair, which I love, and in between kisses, he brushes his lips along my cheek, whispering, "I'm so glad you stayed."

When we get up to his suite, I reach for the light switch, but he intercepts my hand, pulling me into his arms. "No lights."

The discomfort in his voice is too harsh to ignore, and when I take a good look at his eyes, they're shadowed with pain. "Clay, what's going on?"

His hands slip down to my ass. "We're about to have an unforgettable night."

Knowing he's pushing through whatever is causing him pain for *me* kills me. "The night has already been unforgettable. The whole day has been better than anything I could have dreamed of, but *you're* obviously not okay, and that worries me. If you don't want to tell me what's wrong, that's your prerogative, but if you're trying to brave whatever this is for me, you don't need to."

"I'm *fine*," he insists.

I can see he's not even close to fine, and that's when a harsh and unwanted realization hits me. "If you're trying to act fine just to keep your man card in place, you don't have to worry. I'm not going to tell anyone you couldn't perform." It hurts to say it, but my rational brain refuses to ignore the truth anymore. This *is* a fling, and I need to keep that in mind.

He rubs the back of his neck, wincing as he grits out, "Is that what you think?"

"I don't know what to think. I trusted you with *all* of myself, and I can see you're hurting, but apparently you don't trust me enough to be honest about it."

"It's not that I don't trust you." He pauses, the muscles in his jaw bunching. "It took me a long time to get you to give me the time of day. I just don't want to let you down."

"Let me *down*?" I laugh incredulously. "How can you say that after the wonderful day we've had?"

"I don't want you to go home unsatisfied and regret staying."

"How can I possibly be unsatisfied when—" Understanding hits me like a brick. "You mean *sexually*?" Ohmygod. What is wrong with men? "I've had more sex with you than I have had in the past year, and better sex than I've had in my entire life. I'm more than satisfied. But even if I weren't, your well-being should come before my sexual satisfaction." I soften my tone. "Please tell me what's going on with you. I refuse to ignore it."

"It's just a migraine. I get them sometimes from my shoulder injury. I'll take some Tylenol, and I'll be good to go in no time."

He heads into the bedroom, leaving me to stare after him in disbelief. *Good to go in no time?* Most migraines are not that friendly, and I have a feeling his has been building all day.

I grab a bottle of water from the mini fridge and find him in the bathroom, lights off. He's leaning on the sink with one hand, rubbing his temple with the other. He straightens the second he notices me, grabs a bottle of Tylenol from his toiletries bag, and shakes a couple of pills into his hand.

"I brought you water." I hand him the bottle.

"Thanks." He takes the medicine. "I'll be good to go soon."

"Clay, you're not on the field. Your fans aren't watching."

He manages to cock a brow. "Too bad. I was hoping you'd become a fan today."

"I am, of *you*, but you don't have to impress me with your virility. The lights at the show must have wreaked havoc with your head."

"It was fine."

"Why are you so stubborn? We've established that you're not fine, and I'm just pointing out a fact. I wish you'd told me that you weren't feeling well. We could've left early, or skipped it altogether."

"I'd never disappoint you like that. It's really not a big deal. I'll be fine." He slides an arm around me.

I'm touched by his efforts, but now that I'm looking for it, the tension in his face and body is inescapable. All I want is to take that pain away, and the way he's acting makes me wonder if anyone has ever cut him a break and let him bring less than his A game. The thought of that makes my heart hurt.

"Let's make a deal." I put my hands on his chest and slide them up to his shoulders, rubbing gently. "You forget about having sex tonight and lie down, and I'll take care of you."

His brows knit. "That's a sucky deal for you."

"It's a better deal than you know. It's hands-on research. I've been working on a new pressure point device to alleviate migraines."

"No, you haven't."

"Yes, I have, and if you lie down, I'll tell you about it."

He gathers me in his arms, speaking low, the way people with migraines do when the pain becomes overwhelming. "Sex is *not* off the table, but I'm not about to turn down your hands on me." He presses his lips to mine and gives my ass a squeeze. "How about we get this dress off."

I move his hands from my butt to my waist. "Getting your blood pressure up isn't going to help your migraine."

"Touching you will help."

"Clay…"

Several negotiations later, I convince him to lie down. I wash off my makeup, brush my teeth, and change into my silk sleeping pants and matching cami. He's lying on the bed in his black boxer briefs when I come out of the bathroom carrying a bottle of lotion. His arm is draped over his eyes, the blanket and flat sheet bunched up at the foot of the bed. He has definitely awakened something carnal in me, because as I drink in his broad, muscular body, and the bulge between his thick thighs, a sexual hunger takes hold.

He's lying so still, I'm pretty sure he's fallen asleep, so I crawl carefully onto the bed, trying not to wake him.

He reaches for me, his eyelids heavy, his lips curving up despite the pain written all over his face. "Aren't you a sexy sight for sore eyes?"

The strain in his voice underscores that pain, and the hunger I felt morphs into a bone-deep desire to ease his discomfort. I've never been a caretaker like Amber and Grace, who always seem to know exactly how to help people feel better. But it feels natural, as if I have always been one, as I run my fingers through his hair and say, "Thank you. How about you tell me where you hurt?"

He gives a half-hearted eyebrow waggle, his hand resting on my hip.

"I doubt *that* hurts. Come on. Let me help you." I trail my fingers over his shoulder. "I know your neck and shoulders hurt, but tell me about the migraine. Is the pain in one area, like your temples? One side? Or…?"

"I don't know. It hurts everywhere."

My heart squeezes. "Okay. There are several pressure points that might help, but why don't I try to ease some of the tension in your shoulders and neck first? Can you turn over?"

"Are you sure you don't mind doing this?" he asks as he turns over, and I can see that even that motion is hurting him.

"It is a chore to touch you," I tease, moving closer, tucking my legs beneath me. "But I guess I can deal with it." I pour lotion into my hand, warming it between them, and begin massaging his shoulders. His muscles are so tight, I wonder how much of his pain is caused by the insurmountable pressure he's under with his career. "Wow, you're all knotted up."

"I've got a beautiful woman touching me and telling me not to touch her. Of course I am."

I don't want him to continue trying to keep up the charade, so I don't respond, and apply pressure, kneading the knots with my thumbs. He winces. "Sorry. Are you always this tense?"

"Not when I'm buried deep inside you."

"Nice try." I apply more pressure, kneading and massaging, working my way across his shoulders and up the back of his neck.

"That feels incredible." He's quiet for a minute. "You can straddle my hips if it'll help with leverage."

"That'll make your back muscles tense up, and I'm pretty sure it might make other things take notice, too."

"Trust me, sweetheart, the second your hands touched me, my entire body went on red alert."

I smile and deepen the massage.

"*God*, Pep," he says gratefully. "I think I like your hands as much as I like your mouth."

I laugh softly and continue massaging his shoulders. "How

did you hurt your shoulder?"

"It wasn't any one thing. Years of overuse, and enough direct blows to make it worse."

"When did your headaches start?"

"A few months ago."

"Have you gone through PT and tried migraine meds?"

"I've done it all. It's fine, really. Don't worry about me. This is just a minor setback."

I apply pressure to a knot and hold it. He sucks in air between clenched teeth.

"That doesn't sound fine to me," I say gently.

"I don't usually have anyone pushing on me like that."

"Sorry. Applying pressure limits the blood flow. When it's released, more blood flows in, which should help the muscle relax."

"I hear ya, Dr. Pepper. That's cute. *Dr. Pepper.*"

I've been called that so many times, I thought it had lost its cuteness. But coming from him, I kind of like it. "You need to stop talking and relax, or your headache won't go away."

He's quiet as I work out the knots in his shoulders, neck, and back. I take my time, touching him lovingly. I get the sense that's what he needs, and it's definitely how I want to touch him. When he's breathing easier and is visibly more relaxed, I ask him to turn over and begin working my way through the pressure points. Starting with the simplest, I apply pressure to his hand between the base of his thumb and index finger.

"That pinches."

"I know. *Sorry.* This one doesn't always help, but I thought it might be worth a try." I don't want to make him uncomfortable, so I skip some of the others and move to sit against the headboard. "Come lie on your back with your head between my legs."

"It usually works better if I'm on my stomach, but I'm game." He moves into position, gazing up at me. "Hey there, beautiful. Want to come here often?"

Yes plays out in my head. "What I want, is for you to close your eyes and relax."

"Should we get the scarf and use it as a blindfold?"

"I might be tempted to use it as a gag if you don't stop flirting and let me help your headache. Now close your eyes." When he does, I use my thumbs to gently massage his face. Starting at the bridge of his nose, I press gently, easing them down the sides and across his cheeks.

"That feels nice."

"Shh." I work my way over his entire face, relieving the tightness in his jaw and mouth, giving extra attention to where the bridge of his nose meets his brow bones, around his temples, and along his forehead.

"You're really good at this. It's helping."

"I'm glad," I say softly. "But you should try not to talk."

"I will if you tell me about the migraine device you're working on."

"It's just something I've been fiddling with during my off hours. It's a device that alleviates muscle tension while stimulating the nerves that cause migraines. There are devices that stimulate the nerves separately, but I'm looking at enhancing them and possibly combining two of them for people who react well to the individual stimulation."

"That sounds complicated."

I finish massaging his face and begin massaging his scalp. "Like your grandfather says, nothing easy is worth a damn."

"Why are you doing it after hours?"

"Because I have to work on the projects that are funded, and this isn't one of them."

"Are you going to develop it eventually?"

"That's the dream."

"Why not the reality?"

"Because it takes money and time I don't have, and getting funding is hard. I'm glad you're interested in my work, but *please* stop talking."

"I'm okay. You took the edge off. Thank you." He starts to sit up.

I stop him with a hand on his chest. "I'm not done. Can you scoot down a little?" When he does, I massage the base of his skull.

He winces. "That hurts. Like my skull is bruised."

"That's because you carry a lot of tension there. I'm going to try a pressure point release. It may hurt a little at first." I place my index and middle fingers on the pressure points at the base of his skull and hold them there. "Relax your head and neck. Just let your head fall back."

He groans as his head falls back, and my fingers press against the pressure points.

"I know it's uncomfortable, but the pain you feel is the release."

"How do you know how to do this?"

"I studied reflexology. You're a difficult patient. Please stop talking and relax." I release the pressure and run my fingers lightly over his forehead.

"That feels really good," he says just above a whisper.

"*Shh.*" I do the pressure point release two more times, and he exhales with so much relief, I can feel it. When he opens his eyes, he looks half-drunk, and I know he's on the mend. I gently massage his head and shoulders again. "I want you to close your eyes and just breathe. Let any remaining tension bleed out."

I expect him to fight me on it, but to my surprise, he says, "Can I put my head on your lap?"

"Of course."

He repositions himself, moving out from between my legs, and rests his head on my lap. He pushes one arm around my back and drapes the other over my hip, holding me like he doesn't want me to get away. "That's better," he murmurs.

It is better.

"See? It's okay to be not so perfect," I say softly, and run my fingers through his hair. He makes a humming sound of appreciation. I love the friendship we've developed and the incredible sex we have, but I also really like this togetherness, and taking care of him. I realize I've never seen him simply relax. He's always *on*, upbeat, making sure I'm okay and happy. I think about the latte he got me when we were with my family yesterday. He noticed my yawn, for Pete's sake. Even the two mornings we woke up together, he was energetic from the moment he opened his eyes. I wonder if he knows it's okay to just *be* sometimes.

His hold on me eases, and his head becomes heavier in my lap.

He's fallen asleep, and I love that, too. I continue stroking his hair, listening to the peaceful cadence of his breathing, and I'm overcome with a sense of contentment I can't ever remember feeling. It makes me want more.

But this isn't real life. This is a fling.

A dull ache forms in my chest. As exciting as it is being with him, the person I am when we're together isn't *me*. I'm not someone who shirks her responsibilities and blows off work on a whim for a whirlwind day in Paris. This is some altered version of me that reacts solely to Clay's energy, his touch, his voice, the things he says.

The thought of our time together ending brings a wave of longing, and I have to force myself not to give in to it. I know better. I turn my thoughts inward, searching for the *real* me.

I know she's there. She's always at the ready.

But this time she's been pushed back to the shadows. I try to will this altered version of myself to retreat. It's not easy, but eventually she takes a step back, leaving sorrow in her wake. It takes a few minutes for the real me to find her way forward and settle in. When she does, I do what I need to in order to keep her there.

I pick up my phone and scroll through work emails, but there's no fire in my belly to handle them like there usually is. I open a report from Min and try to concentrate, but after reading the same paragraph three times and comprehending none of it, I know the effort is futile.

In a few hours I'll have nothing but time for work.

It's just one night.

I realize I'm still running my fingers through Clay's hair and set down my phone. I gaze down at his handsome face, so unguarded and serene. I wonder if that's how I looked falling asleep in his arms the last two nights. The first morning we woke up together feels like it was a month ago. I wish I hadn't run from him.

Too many emotions stack up inside me, and I toy with the idea of staying for another day. I can see us lazily welcoming the morning, exploring more of the city, or spending the day in bed, pleasuring each other. Just as I feel myself smiling, my hand stills in Clay's hair.

Have I lost my mind? I shouldn't even have taken today off work.

That's how dangerous Clay is for me. All it took was thinking about spending more time with him and I'm pondering shirking more of my responsibilities.

I take my hand out of his hair, but the need to touch him is too strong to deny. I put my hand on his back, feeling the sure and steady beat of his heart, and close my eyes, reveling in it as I accept the hard truth.

This wonderful man is far more dangerous than I thought. Not just to my heart, but also to the business I've worked so hard to build. Too hard to jeopardize it.

Chapter Fourteen

Clay

I wake to a dark room, with my head still in Pepper's lap, and remain still, waiting for the pounding in my head to start. When it doesn't, I'm more than relieved. I turn my attention to the incredible woman in my arms, feeling bad for the way our night ended. I'm also immensely grateful for her thoughtfulness. Nobody has ever taken care of me the way she did.

She stirs, moonlight illuminating her beautiful face as her eyes flutter open.

"Hey, sweetheart," I whisper, and slide her down to the mattress beside me, catching a glimpse of the clock on the nightstand. *3:45.* "I'm glad you're still here."

"Where would I go?" she asks sleepily, and touches my cheek. "How's your head?"

"Better, thanks to you. I'm sorry about last night."

"Don't be. You can't help it if you have a migraine."

"No, but I can make it up to you now." I lower my lips to hers, kissing her tenderly.

"Yes, please," she whispers.

Her arms circle me as our mouths come together in a slow, sensual kiss. I savor the taste of her, memorizing the feel of her soft curves against me, knowing this is our last morning together. The longer we kiss, the fiercer our passion becomes, and soon we're desperately groping, grasping, *clawing* at each other. Her needy moans spur me on to earn more of them.

"I can never get enough of you," I grit out as I strip off her top. I tease her breast as I push her pajama pants down, and she wiggles out of them.

She tugs at my boxer briefs. *"Off."*

I strip them off, need coursing through my veins, and I snag a condom from my wallet, quickly rolling it on. Our eyes lock as I come down over her. She grabs my forearms, her hazel eyes drilling into mine with so much emotion, it's inescapable. Without sneaking around, without alcohol messing with my senses, this feels intensely intimate, amplifying every scintillating sensation as I thrust slowly, taking her inch by inch. I watch her, wanting to see her passion brewing as our bodies become one. Her lips part, her fingers tightening around my forearms and her eyes widening as I bury myself to the hilt. I'm swamped with that feeling of completeness again, and the wonder in her eyes tells me she feels it, too.

"Clay" falls desperately from her lips at the same time a rough growl escapes mine.

I stroke into her again, loving the hunger in her eyes. The rampant beat of our hearts roars between us like a ravenous beast. Her fingernails cut into my flesh with every thrust of my hips. The pleasure is so intense, so excruciatingly perfect, it consumes me, shattering my restraint. I take her in a brutal kiss, pounding into her. She's right there with me, rocking her hips, moaning as we feed our carnal desires.

"Come for me." My demand is harsh and unrelenting, and the staggering pleasure in her eyes has me clutching her ass so hard, I'm sure I'll leave marks. I'll probably go straight to hell for thinking it, but I fucking love marking her, and as my name tears from her lungs and her pussy clamps around my cock, I know she loves it, too. I crush my mouth to hers as her climax ravages her, feeling every pulse and gasp.

She shivers and shakes as she comes down from the peak, and I take her right back up. I want to stay buried inside her forever, but she feels too fucking good. I wrap her long legs around my waist, angling my hips, driving deeper into her, gritting my teeth against the climax that's barreling toward me.

"*There. Ohgo—*"

Her words are lost to a cry of pleasure that sends the world spinning on its axis, carrying us both into oblivion. We pump and grind, clinging together, draining each other of everything we have, until we're too spent to move.

I bury my face in her neck, breathing her in. I've never felt so in sync with someone in and out of the bedroom, and somehow I know this unstoppable connection is only the beginning.

"Jesus, Reckless. You fucking destroy me."

She hums a sweet, satisfied sound.

I roll off her, gathering her against me. Her eyes are at half-mast, her sweet, sated smile tugging at something deep inside me. "Still with me, baby?"

"*Mm-hm.*" She nestles into the crook of my neck.

I kiss her forehead. "I'm really glad we had this time together."

"Me too," she says softly.

I run my fingers through the ends of her hair, wishing she wasn't leaving in just a few hours. "I know you'll be busy when you get back home, but I'd like to keep seeing you."

She's quiet for a long moment before resting her head on

my arm and pressing her hand to my cheek. "I don't think that's a good idea."

"*Yeah, right.* Because the sex is too good?"

She rolls her lower lip between her teeth, the apology rising in her eyes, gutting me.

"You're *serious?*"

Her brow furrows, and she nods.

"I don't understand. I thought we had a great time together."

"We did. You're an amazing guy, and this has been a once-in-a-lifetime adventure, but everything I said in the beginning still holds true. My life is in Charlottesville doing research and working in my lab, and yours is…I don't even know where. Playing football, traveling, and being famous." Her eyes are sad, her voice strained. "I *really* like you. It's scary how much I like you. But we would never work long term. I'm so busy, I have to be at work every day, and we don't even live in the same city. I'm not this carefree person. I was being honest when I said I don't know who I am when I'm with you. I just think it would be better if we part with all our wonderful memories intact instead of ruining them by trying to make it work and ending up unhappy and resenting each other."

I'm rendered momentarily speechless.

"I'm sorry," she says pleadingly.

There's a crushing pain in my chest, but I suck it up, because I can see and hear how hard this decision was for her and I'm not about to make her feel worse. "Don't be. It's fine. I get it."

"You're not mad?" she asks tentatively.

"How could I be mad? I feel lucky to have had this time with you. Besides, 'we'll always have Paris.'"

Her smile doesn't reach her eyes. "Yes, we will."

"The sun will be up soon. Think you can give me one last sunrise?"

"I'd like that."

"Be right back, beautiful." I kiss her cheek and climb out of bed, heading into the bathroom, trying to wrap my mind around what just happened.

Chapter Fifteen

Pepper

The office phone rings as I click *print* on an article I want to bring home to read tonight.

"I'm taking off," Chris Wharton says as he appears in my office doorway. His curly brown hair is as messy as ever, his beard is unkempt, and his clothes are wrinkled, but his disheveled appearance is a small price to pay for his top-tier scientific brilliance.

The phone rings again. "One sec." I hold up my finger as I answer it. "SynTech."

"I have to run. I'll email you the data from the simulation," Chris says in a rushed voice as the guy on the other end of the phone says, "Is this...*Wait*...what company did you say this is?"

I give Chris a thumbs-up, and as he leaves, I say, "SynTech Research and Development," into the phone.

"I'm sorry. I must have the wrong number," the man says, and the line goes dead.

I hang up, and as I reach for the documents on the printer behind my desk, the phone rings again. I turn to grab it and knock a stack of papers onto the floor. I take a deep breath and put the phone to my ear. "SynTech."

There's grumbling on the other end of the line. "It's me again," the man says. "Sorry. I'm trying to reach Westerly

Appliance Repair."

"Their number is one digit off from ours. I believe you dialed a three instead of a five." It happens just often enough to be annoying.

"Sorry. It won't happen again."

Not by you, maybe. "No worries. Have a good night." I hang up the phone and pull up the email I've set up to receive résumés from the employment site where I listed the receptionist position. I'm pleased to see three responses and quickly peruse them. My hopes deflate. The first is overqualified and asking for twice the going rate. The second has no experience, and the cover letter from the third applicant is too poorly written to even consider.

I delete them all.

"*Open a business,* they said. *It'll be great,* they said."

If I have to answer one more call...

As if the gods are testing me, my cell phone chimes with a text. I swear, if it's one of my sisters again, I'm going to throw my phone into a sewer. They've been bugging me about Clay ever since they got back from overseas, asking if I've heard from him despite the fact that I have repeatedly told them we only hung out because *they* were all paired off. I don't know if they can tell I'm lying, but thank God they haven't found out that I stayed an extra night with him in Paris. I'd never hear the end of that.

I snag my phone from my desk, and my heart skips and aches at once at the sight of Clay's name in the text bubble. The same way it has the last several times he texted. It's been a week since I saw him, and one day since his last text. But he's always on my mind. Not only does our time together play on repeat in my head like my favorite freaking movie, but Clay has been sending me gifts. Two days after I got home, I received a package of chocolates from the shop in Paris where we gorged ourselves with a note that read SO YOU DON'T FORGET HOW SWEET IT WAS. Two days later I received his football jersey with a note that read I THOUGHT YOU'D WANT TO WEAR IT TO BED, SINCE I'M SURE YOU'RE DREAMING ABOUT ME.

He's not even in the same state, and I feel his presence like he's right here with me *all* the time. And *yes*, I wear his stupid jersey to bed every night, and damn it, it's his voice I hear lulling me to sleep and his face visiting me in my dreams. I'm pretty sure I'm on the fast track to losing my mind.

I take a deep breath, mentally preparing myself for the onslaught of emotions to come, and read his text.

Clay: *I can feel you missing me.*

I don't want to like his sense of humor, but I can't help it. I smile as I thumb out my response.

Me: *I'm sorry, who is this?*

Clay: *The guy who can't stop thinking about you.*

Tingles chase up my chest.

Me: *Ben or Jerry?*

A picture of us kissing in front of the Wall of Love pops up. My insides melt, and the dull ache of missing him claws its way up to the surface. It's torture, but I know how this will end. He has time off now, but then he'll be traveling again with his team, and I'll never be the kind of woman who will leave my work behind and follow a guy across the country. Not even a guy as wonderful as Clay. And I know there would be pressure to do that, and it would tear us apart.

Me: *Sorry. Doesn't ring a bell.*

Another picture pops up. We're in front of a gallery. Clay's arm is hooked around my neck and he's kissing my cheek, his eyes smiling at the camera as he snapped the selfie. The ache of missing him turns into a painful throb. I love flirting with him, but it's not fair to either of us. My life is already overloaded. I could never fit a long-distance relationship into my schedule and make it work, and he deserves someone who can.

Me: *Ah yes. I remember you now. The distracting guy I met through my brother-in-law.*

A devil emoji pops up.

My pulse races, and I'm tempted to keep flirting, but I know this will lead to the same place his previous texts led. To him asking when he can see me again and me saying I'm too busy. I can't keep riding this emotional roller coaster of wanting what I know will just hurt me in the end. Steeling myself against the lump forming in my throat, I force myself to do what needs to be done, thumbing out, *I'm working like a madwoman and I have to run, but we'll always have Paris.* I read it again, and I know it's not strong enough to get my point across. I have to stick to my guns. I delete the message and start over, hating every word I type.

Me: *I'm really busy, and I know you probably are too. Neither of us needs to be distracted by something that won't end well, so we should probably stop texting. But we'll always have Paris.*

I add a heart emoji.

Trying to swallow past the lump that is now clogging my throat, I push to my feet and shove my phone into my bag, knocking it off the credenza in my rush to leave my office before he texts again.

Don't cry. Don't you dare cry.

My hands curl into fists. I'm not a crier. Until last week, I hadn't cried over a boy since that unfortunate circumstance with that jerky jock in college. But I shed more than a few tears when I was sitting in the lap of luxury on Clay's cousin's private plane on the way home from Paris, and I swore I wouldn't shed any more.

The sting of tears has me ducking into the bathroom.

I pace, reminding myself that I'm the one who ended it. Clay would be happy to continue our fling. Until he gets bored or it's football season again, which is another reason I need to protect my heart. I stop pacing and look in the mirror, struck for the umpteenth time since returning from Paris by the woman staring back at me. Something about me is different. It's like I left an invisible piece of myself behind, and it changed the way I see myself.

My sisters would have a field day with that.

There's no room in my life for these kinds of distractions. I have a business to run, and the bottom line is, I don't make good decisions when I'm with Clay. I don't regret staying in Paris with him. That was the happiest day of my life, but it wasn't the smartest decision. I was so jet-lagged when I got home last week, it took me three days to catch up, and I was less than my best at the kickoff meeting. I can't afford to not be on top of my game.

I draw my shoulders back, shoving all those feelings down deep for the hundredth time in the last week. It takes an enormous amount of effort to force my thoughts away from Clay and back to work.

Feeling a little more in control, I leave the bathroom in search of my staff, because if I return to my office, the precarious lid I put on those feelings might pop off.

I find Ravi shutting down a computer in the lab where we work on prototypes and simulations. Unlike Chris, Ravi has impeccable taste, and he's always well put together. Today he's wearing a fitted dress shirt and slacks that show off his lean runner's frame. With thick black hair, a peppering of manicured scruff, and coal-dark eyes, Ravi is strikingly handsome and a dead ringer for the actor Manish Dayal. But his good looks are background noise to me. When I look at him, I see the friend who has been there for me through the hardest and the best times in my life. The lanky teen who, like me, wanted to see what all the hype was about and treated sex like an experiment. I see my best friend and the perfect distraction from the fissure in my chest.

He looks up as I walk in, his pearly whites gleaming against his dark skin. "Hey, Pep. What's up?"

"I thought I'd come check on things. Did you reach Dr. Bowry?" Dr. Bowry is a neurologist consulting on one of our projects.

"Yes. We have a meeting scheduled with him Friday afternoon. I put it on the group calendar."

"Great. I'll be ready. Was Min able to help with the coding issue you were trying to work out?"

"Of course."

"Excellent. I'd like to see this week's progress report before—"

"Before we submit it. I *know*." He looks amused and slightly annoyed, which is par for the course when I ask to review data before it's given to our funding sources.

I look around the lab, filling with pride as my gaze skates over the worktables, computers, and neatly organized supply shelves.

"Nothing is out of place," Ravi says with exasperation as he steps beside me.

"I wasn't looking at that."

He arches a brow. "You've been extra neurotic since you got back from Paris."

"I have not. We just have a lot going on."

"We always have a lot going on. Maybe you should go see Clay for a little stress relief."

I roll my eyes, regretting divulging our fling to him, but Ravi was a big part of the reason I went on the trip in the first place. We had a lot going on at work, and I almost canceled my trip, but he refused to let me. "I never should have told you about that."

"You were dying to tell someone, and you knew your dirty little secret would be safe with me."

That is true. Ravi knows more of my secrets than Sable does. In fact, Sable doesn't know about what happened between me and Clay yet. She and I haven't spoken since we saw each other in Paris. Her tour was extended, and I'm trying desperately *not* to think about Clay. Hopefully she's doing better with the tour than I am with my efforts.

Ravi nudges me. "So? Any more gifts from your hot European fling?"

"No, but he's texted a few times," I say more casually than I feel.

"And?" he asks eagerly.

"I told him the same thing I told you. I don't have time for whatever it is he's looking for. Why are we talking about him anyway? We've got work to do."

"We've been here until after nine every night since the kick-off. My eyes feel like sandpaper. I'm heading out to grab some dinner. Come with me. Min and Chris already left, so there are no more whips to crack."

"Thanks, but I'm not hungry. I didn't eat lunch until after

three. I want to look for a few more employment sites where I can list the receptionist job, and I want to go over the data files Chris is working on, and a few other things."

"You can do all of that in the comfort of your own home after we eat dinner."

Yes, but I think about Clay even more when I'm home. At least in the office I've got visual cues applying silent pressure to focus on business. "It's easier here."

"Want me to stick around?"

"No. Go enjoy your night."

"All right, but for the record, I think you should give *fling boy* another go."

I cross my arms. "Why would you say that? You don't even know him."

"I don't need to." He cocks a grin. "Any guy who can get you to blow off work *and* rattle the unflappable Dr. Montgomery must have rocked your world."

"Did I *ask* for your advice?" I snap.

"That's the great thing about our friendship. You don't have to ask. But that testiness is a definite indicator that you could use a little more rattling."

"Out." I point to the door, trying to keep a straight face.

"I'm just saying—"

"Ten. *Nine.*" I stalk toward him like I did when we were kids and he would say things just to yank my chain.

He grabs his jacket from the chair and walks backward, laughing. "He really *did* rattle you."

"Eight." I speed up my steps. *"Seven."*

He stumbles into the hall, walking faster as I close in on him. "Can you just give me his number?"

"Why? Are you suddenly into hot guys?"

"*No.* I haven't seen you this worked up since we were kids. I want to thank him."

"I swear on all that is holy, Ravi Bhandara, I will give you the mother of all titty twisters if you say one more word about that man." Another childhood threat. My favorite, because he hates it.

"Okay, fine," he relents. "I'll get his number from Dash!" He turns and bolts down the hall, his laughter trailing behind him as he flees out the office door, setting off the chimes above.

"Fool." I laugh and head back to my office.

As I come around my desk, I nearly step on the contents of my bag strewn across the floor. The mess is far too similar to my chaotic thoughts lately. I kneel and start gathering my things. My gaze catches on the strip of pictures Clay and I took in the photo booth.

I pick it up, taking in the black-and-white images of us laughing, kissing, and making silly faces. I miss him so much, it hurts. I don't understand how it happened so fast. Tears spring to my eyes, and just like that, he's rattled my world again.

Chapter Sixteen

Clay

"You're avoiding me," Tiffany says when I answer my cell Wednesday evening.

I look out the window of the New York City cab, on my way to meet Seth, Victory, Flynn, and Sutton at one of Seth's restaurants for dinner and imagine my cutthroat agent pacing her office on four-inch heels, her blond hair flowing over her shoulders. "Hello to you, too, Tiff."

"Don't *Tiff* me. I've been texting you for days."

"Didn't Doogie text you back?"

"Don't pull that shit with me, Braden. You know damn well Doogie doesn't get back from the lavish honeymoon *you* sent him on until next Friday."

Shit. "Would you believe I've been so busy with sponsorships, I totally forgot?"

"*No.* I'd be more likely to believe that you've been shacking up with a hot young thing you hooked up with in Paris."

Don't I wish. But the only woman I'm interested in will once again barely give me the time of day.

"What's going on with you, Clay?" Tiffany asks. "You're usually one of my most reliable clients, and suddenly you're ghosting me."

It was easier to avoid her calls when I was distracted in Paris, but Tiffany has been my agent for years. She's one of the best in the business, and she deserves better from me. "I'm sorry for not returning your messages."

"We need to talk about your extension."

I rub the knot in the back of my neck. "I've had a lot on my mind the last few months. I'm not ready to sign on the dotted line."

"Finally, a little communication. Thank you. I know you've got a lot going on, with Staley chomping at your heels, your shoulder acting up, and the playoff loss. Let's set up a time to discuss it. That's what I'm here for."

"I'm not ready to do that yet. I need you to buy me more time." The cab pulls over in front of the restaurant. I swipe my credit card to pay for the fare and thank the driver as I climb out of the car.

"Clay—"

"Sorry, Tiff, but I've got to run. I just need a few more weeks to figure it out. I'll be in touch." I end the call feeling like a dick, but I push that discomfort down deep and put on a winning smile as I walk into the restaurant.

The young hostess's eyes light up like I'm her favorite candy. "It's nice to see you again, Clay."

"You as well, Gretchen." I scan the dining room, with its elegant candle-style chandeliers and two-story brick walls, and spot Seth and the others sitting at Seth's usual table in the back by the arched entryways to the bar.

"Melanie should be right back to take you to your table," Gretchen says. "She was just seating a group."

"That's okay. I can seat myself. Have a good night." As I make my way to the table, hushed voices ring out. *Is that Clay Braden?* and *Is that the quarterback for the Giants?*

I didn't miss this attention in Paris. I smile for the eager fans. I appreciate them, but while I used to get off on being recognized, the lack of privacy has worn thin.

Seth is the first to stand to greet me, sporting gray skinny slacks and one of his nerdy old-man sweaters—a thick olive green with lapels and a patterned orange-and-gray stripe across the lower chest and arms. Like me and our other brothers, Seth is over six feet tall and athletic. His hair is dark and wavy, like Victory's, but it always looks windblown, while Flynn and Noah have lighter hair, and mine is somewhere in between. Noah will be sorely missed tonight, but we're a long way from Colorado.

"Bonjour, little brother," Seth says, tugging me into an embrace. "Here's to another great season."

I scoff. "We had a shitty loss."

"It was a good loss, and we're all proud of you," he says.

"We sure are. Welcome back," Victory says as she hugs me. "Did you miss me?"

"Like a splinter. You look great." She and Sutton are fashionistas, and dressed to the nines. Like me, Flynn looks casual in a Henley and jeans. I eye Sutton, motioning to Flynn's collar-length hair. "Get this guy a haircut, will ya, Sut?" I push him out of the way and hug her.

"Never," Sutton says. "It's nice to see you again."

"You, too. You look as beautiful as always. Is my little brother treating you well?"

"Like a queen he wants to fire," she teases.

"That's one way to keep the spark alive, bro."

"Whatever it takes, right?" Flynn embraces me. "Good to see you."

As we settle in around the table, the waitress takes our drink orders. I wait for her to leave, then say, "Catch me up. What's going on with everyone?"

"Oh, no, you don't," Victory says. "We've been waiting for you to get here. We want the scoop on you and Pepper." She leans forward, folding her arms on the table and looking at me expectantly. "Spill that tea, baby brother."

They're all looking at me, eager for details, but I don't need them dissecting our relationship. And yeah, I know Pepper doesn't think we have one, but she's wrong. "We had a great time. She's an amazing person."

"She must be," Victory says. "That was a bold move you pulled, calling Treat to hire his pilot and use his private plane."

Seth's brows slant.

"Dude, that's *huge*," Flynn says.

"Take notes, Flynn," Sutton says. "My standards have just been raised."

Jesus Christ. I look at Victory. "How did you find out about that?"

"Noah told me."

"Fucking *Noah*." He called me last week and gave me shit about it. I'd forgotten he was at Treat's house for dinner the night I called about the plane. "I would've called Seth if he *had* a frigging plane." In addition to everything else my overachieving brother has done, Seth got his pilot's licenses a few years ago to fly helicopters and airplanes. He bought a helicopter a year later, but he has yet to choose a plane.

Seth flashes a shit-eating grin. "I'm narrowing it down."

"You've been narrowing it down for three years, you picky bastard." I shake my head.

"So? Give us the scoop. What's happening with you and Pepper?" Flynn asks.

"Nothing. She's back at work in Charlottesville, and I'm here taking care of my own shit." *Or rather, doing what I can to keep my mind off her and my own shit.*

"I half expected her to show up here with you tonight," Victory says.

I wish she were here, but I haven't even texted her today. I'm respecting her decision, but I miss the connection, and I'm hoping she'll miss it, too, and realize she made the wrong choice.

"I was hoping she would come," Sutton adds excitedly. "I'd love to see her again."

"You know Pepper?" I ask, remembering too late that Dash's younger sister Andi is Sutton's assistant at *Discovery Hour.*

"It's more like I know of her," Sutton says. "Amber and I lived in the same house in college, and I met Pepper a few times when she came to visit. From what I remember, she was beautiful, a little quiet, and super smart."

"She still is," I say, missing her even more.

"What's the deal with you two?" Seth asks. "Are you going to see her again?"

"I guess that depends who you ask," I say as the waitress brings our drinks. She goes over the dinner specials, and we take a moment to order.

When the waitress walks away, Victory says, "We're asking *you.*"

It takes me a second to remember Seth's question. "I'd like to continue seeing her, but she thinks our lives are too far apart, and she says she's too busy."

"*Ouch.* She turned down Mr. Perfect?" Flynn says. "That's got to sting."

"It wasn't my favorite moment," I grit out.

"Especially after you got her a private plane home from Paris," Victory says.

"Do you think it was just a fling for her?" Sutton asks.

"*No*," I say firmly. "It was more than that. I could feel it, and I know she felt it, too."

"That sucks," Seth says. "I'm sorry."

"Yeah." I take a drink. "I don't get it. We connected on every level. It's never been like that for me."

"Can I play devil's advocate for a minute?" Victory asks, but she doesn't wait for a response. "In all fairness, even if she felt a connection, I understand where she's coming from. It takes a lot of time and energy to run a business. I can't imagine trying to fit in a relationship and still run Blank Space. There are only so many hours in the day."

This coming from our sister who, when she was only twenty-six, fell in love with her boss, Harvey Bauer, who was sixteen years her senior, and would stop at nothing until they were together. They'd married a year later, and Harvey treated her like gold until the day we lost him to a heart attack. If anyone can understand what I'm feeling, it would be her.

"Vic, do you remember what it was like when you and Harvey got together?"

"Like it was yesterday," she says with a slightly sad smile.

"When you were trying to get his attention, we all tried to talk you out of it, but you were head over heels, bound and determined that he was the greatest love of your life. It turns out he was, and even though you were both workaholics, you made time for each other."

"Always," she says. "No matter what was going on at work, we left it behind and had dinner at our favorite restaurant every

Friday night like clockwork. Because when you care about someone, you find time for them. Gramps taught me that."

I happen to know she still has dinner there every week. "Exactly. I know Pepper is as into me as I am into her." *I feel it in my bones.* "So, yeah, I'm sure she's busy, but something isn't adding up. I think there's more to it."

"Do you think she has a boyfriend?" Flynn asks.

"No. She's not the type to cheat."

"Wait a second. Are you saying you think she's *the one?*" Victory asks.

Holy shit. Am I?

They're looking at me with bated breath.

"I don't know. I hadn't thought about it that way. All I know is, there's something real between us."

"I *love* this for you," Sutton exclaims. "You've been Mr. Cool since I met you, and suddenly you're hiring a private plane and pining after a woman. I am totally invested. Let's figure out how to get you your girl. I can talk to Andi, and she can talk to Amber."

Flynn laughs. "Clay's own personal cheerleader." He tugs Sutton into a kiss.

"Thanks, Sutton. I don't need a cheerleader," I say. "I just need to figure it out."

"Is there any chance Pepper is scared?" Seth asks.

"Of *what?* We had a great time."

"Maybe that's the wrong word," Seth says so fucking calmly, it's irritating. He's always been the king of calm. The voice of reason. "Could she be intimidated?"

"By *what?*"

"You," my siblings say in unison.

I look at them like they've lost their minds. "What the hell does that mean?"

Seth levels me with the big-brother stare he's used since we were kids. The one that says he has something important to say and I need to listen. "You have a tendency to barrel into situations and make things happen the way you want them to."

"Yeah, because I'm a strategic thinker on my feet. You know damn well I'd never put a woman in a situation she didn't want to be in. I'm not a prick."

"Of course I know that," Seth agrees. "I'm just saying that patience is not your virtue, and that can be intimidating."

I grind my teeth, knowing he's right.

"In Clay's defense, that comes with being a public figure." Victory turns her attention to me. "But it's still true. You walk into a room and people take notice, which in part is why you expect to snap your fingers and make things happen. But it's also who you are. When you set your sights on something, you get tunnel vision and make it happen. Remember how you used to put together football teams overseas?"

"He didn't even speak the language half the time," Seth adds.

I smile at the memory. "That wasn't easy."

"Nothing easy is worth a damn," we all say in unison, and then we laugh.

Flynn lifts his glass. "To Gramps and his words of wisdom." We all drink to the toast.

"What I'm trying to say," Victory explains as she sets down her glass, "is that laser focus can be intimidating to someone who needs time to ruminate."

"I'm sure Mom and Dad bringing in coaches for personal training added to that sense of privilege," Seth says evenly.

"They did shit like that for all of us," I remind him. "Or did you conveniently forget all that investing crap Dad set up for you when we were kids and living overseas? I'm not saying you're wrong, but we're successful *because* they supported us and taught us that where there's a will, there's a way."

"I agree with you," Seth says. "I'm just saying there are reasons beyond fame that make you, and the rest of us, who we are."

"No shit. How does that help me figure this out?"

"Can I say something?" Sutton asks carefully.

"Yeah," I say, thankful for the breather.

"I don't think any of you could achieve the levels of success you have if you weren't overly confident," Sutton says.

"Exactly my point." I take a drink.

"That said," she continues, "Victory is right. You're a charming, gregarious guy, Clay, and that in and of itself can be intimidating to someone who's not used to it. If Pepper was avoiding you before Paris, and then suddenly she was in your bed and being flown home on a private plane, that could make a woman's head spin. When Flynn and I first got together, I was like, *What the hell is happening here? Can I trust it? Do I want it?*"

"You wanted it," Flynn says confidently.

"Yes, I did, but it was confusing. You know that," Sutton says. "And if Pepper connected as deeply as Clay says, I agree with Vic. She probably needs to process it."

I grit my teeth, wishing that was the case. *She's not trying to process it. She's trying to end it.* I'm not about to admit that or let Pepper make that mistake. "Maybe all of you are right, but I didn't come here to analyze my personal life, so can we give it a rest?"

"We're on your side, Clay," Seth says.

"Always," Flynn says.

"I know. I appreciate that, but I'm still processing it, too, so let's turn the page. What did I miss during playoffs? Flynn, I heard they delayed the debut of *Heart Stories* by a week. Are you and Sutton excited to see it?" *Heart Stories* is a monthly series of special-assignment documentaries they're producing.

"*Yes*," they exclaim.

"It's too bad you guys can't make it to Mom and Dad's for the debut," Flynn says.

"Yeah, it sucks. Tiffany's got me doing a talk at a charity event that weekend, but I'm looking forward to seeing the show." Seth and I exchange knowing glances with my little white lie. Flynn and Sutton have no idea we're planning to surprise them at our parents' house.

"So am I," Victory says. "Seth and I are going to watch it together. We're both going to be in LA that week."

"I'm sorry I can't be there to watch it with you guys, but I'm excited to see it," Seth says.

"No worries. We know everyone is busy." Flynn takes Sutton's hand and says, "We're just hoping the viewers will like it."

"Well, *he* is," Suttons says. "I'm hoping they love it."

"Smartass." Flynn pulls her into another kiss.

Seeing them so happy makes me miss Pepper even more. "Of course they're going to love it. Just like they loved the rainforest episodes." Last year, Flynn and Sutton were tasked with surviving three days in the Amazon rainforest for *Discovery Hour*, which is where they first got together, and the viewers still haven't stopped raving about it.

"Fingers crossed," Sutton says.

"How about a wedding date? Have you picked one yet?" I ask.

"We just settled on one last night," Sutton says, exchanging a loving glance with Flynn. "We booked the last weekend in June at my family's winery on Silver Island."

"That's great. I'll get it on my calendar." I may not know what my future looks like with my team yet, but they don't need to worry about that.

"I already sent the info to Doogie," Flynn says.

"Thanks, man."

"Flynn, I'll book you and Sutton the honeymoon suite at the Silver House if you haven't done it yet," Seth offers.

"Thanks, man. But the Silvers are comping it for us as a wedding gift," Flynn says.

"That was nice of them. Then I'll get my buddy T to get the rest of us rooms," Seth offers.

"Seth, you do realize it's bizarre to call an assistant you've never met your *buddy*, right?" I ask.

His brow furrows in confusion. "Taylor is my buddy. He's worked for me for years, and he's always got my back."

"Yes, but you've never *met* him or even spoken to him on the phone," I reiterate.

Seth holds my gaze, unfazed, and takes a drink. As he sets the glass down, he says, "You want him to get you a room or not?"

"Of course. It'll save Doogie the hassle. I was just pointing out that it's a little weird."

Ignoring my comment, Seth looks across the table at Sutton and Flynn. "What time do we need to be there for the rehearsal dinner?"

"We haven't nailed that down yet," Flynn says.

"We're still trying to decide between having it at the Silver House or at Rock Bottom Bar and Grill," Sutton explains.

"Rock Bottom?" Seth eyes Victory with an amused expression. "Isn't that the place your boyfriend owns, Vic?"

Victory shoots him a warning glare.

"That's *right*," I exclaim, remembering the guy who had flirted with her relentlessly when we visited Flynn and Sutton on Silver Island last Christmas. "What was that guy's name?"

"Wells Silver," Seth says.

"That's it. He was definitely into you, Vic," I say.

"I have a feeling he'd be into *any* willing woman, and I am definitely *not* one of them." Victory takes a drink, eyeing us over her glass.

We'd all like to see her find love again, but that narrow-eyed stare has us falling silent as the waitress brings our meals. Flynn and Sutton share more of their wedding plans as we eat, and before we move on to other subjects, Victory raises her wineglass in a toast. "To Sutton and Flynn for grabbing that brass ring and enjoying every second of happiness while they can."

I hear the implication she's drilled into our heads—*Tomorrow is not guaranteed*—and I'm sure Seth and Flynn do as well, but my thoughts return to Pepper. I wonder if there *is* more to her decision than just our lives being too far apart or hers being too busy. Could Seth be right? Is she intimidated by me? Our connection *is* electric, and she was honest about not trusting athletes.

I think about our last night together. *Wrists or blindfold, baby?* Pepper's voice whispers through my head. *I've never done either. Can we try both?* The image of her blindfolded, her wrists bound, blooms to life.

You trust me, Reckless.

The question is, do you trust yourself?

Chapter Seventeen

Pepper

Focus, I tell myself for the millionth time Thursday afternoon and stare down at my notes.

Ravi and I have a conference call in twenty minutes with the executives of a major medical supply company to pitch the concept for our migraine device in hopes of securing funding. This meeting has to go well, and I'm definitely not at my best. I haven't been sleeping well. I can't stop thinking about Clay, wondering if I made the right decision. Every time I start reading my notes for the pitch, it brings back our last night in Paris, when he had a migraine. It still boggles my mind that he was going to play it off like he wasn't in horrible pain just so he didn't disappoint me.

I glance at my phone and tap the screen. It lights up, revealing a few unread messages from my family, but nothing from Clay. It's been two days since I've heard from him, and even though I'm the one who severed that connection, a pang of sadness moves through me. I keep telling myself the longing will pass. It has to. I can't function like this. I glance at my notes again, trying to concentrate, but it's Clay's smiling eyes I see, and in my warped brain, they intensify, the way they did over the weekend when he looked at me like I was all he saw. Nobody has ever looked at me the way he does.

Did. The way he did.

I blow out a breath, trying to clear my head. I must be really exhausted, because it's like his face is etched in my brain. *Coffee.* That's what I need. I push to my feet and head out of my office. The chime above the front door rings out, so I head for the lobby to see who it is.

A man wearing a black jacket is standing just inside the doors with his back to me. "Can I help you—"

He turns around, and my mouth goes dry. It's *Clay*, holding a bouquet of gorgeous red roses.

A slow grin that says *There you are* spreads across his handsome face. "Reckless."

My thoughts stumble at the mix of longing and relief in his voice.

He closes the distance between us. "These are for you." He hands me the vase of roses.

"Thank you." I sound as stunned and confused as I feel. He puts his hand on my hip, leaning in to press a kiss to my cheek. Cedarwood, vanilla, and the unique scent of *him* envelop me like a favorite blanket. "What are you doing here?"

"I missed you," he says like the answer is obvious. As if anyone who missed me would show up out of the blue at my work.

My heart hasn't taken notice of a man for years, and he makes it do somersaults every single time. "You came all the way from New York just to see me?"

"I live in Jersey, but yes. I also wanted to bring you this."

He hands me a framed picture I didn't realize he was holding, and my breath catches. It's the sketch of us from Paris. I've relived that day too many times to count, and I wondered what he'd done with the sketch. He's giving me that look again, like

I'm all he sees, making it hard to concentrate, but I manage, "You don't want it?"

"I'm hoping I'll still get to see it."

My thoughts are reeling, but the clock is ticking for my call with Ravi, and I can't make sense of anything. "I wish you'd texted. I'm about to get on an important call."

"Texting doesn't get me very far with you, but no worries. I know you're busy. Take your time. I can wait."

He shrugs off his jacket, and holy cow he's gorgeous in a fitted navy button-down and dark slacks as he lays his jacket over the arm of one of the lobby chairs and sits down. He crosses his ankle over his knee, as casual as can be, picks up a magazine, and starts leafing through it, while I try to remember how to breathe.

"Just about ready, Pep?"

I startle at Ravi's voice and spin around.

I must look as rattled as I feel, because Ravi comes to my side, his gaze moving curiously and protectively between me and Clay. "Everything okay?"

No. My worlds are colliding, and I think I might throw up. "Yes. *Fine.* This is Clay. He just showed up…out of nowhere."

Ravi looks relieved, and amused, which annoys the heck out of me.

Clay rises to his feet and offers his hand. "Clay Braden."

"I recognize you." Ravi shakes his hand. "I'm Ravi Bhandara, a big fan. Too bad about the playoffs, but you played a great game."

"Thanks, *Ravi.*" His gaze flicks to me briefly, then back to Ravi. "I appreciate that. Pepper has told me a lot about you."

"All good, I hope." He drapes an arm over my shoulder. "Pep and I go way back."

"So I've heard." Clay eyes Ravi's arm around me, his jaw tight. "She and I are more recently acquainted."

Why does this feel like he's trying to one-up Ravi? He's not jealous, is he? Why does that turn me on? My cheeks burn. *Ohmygod. What is happening right now? This cannot happen.* I duck out from under Ravi's arm. "Okay, well, Ravi and I have a conference call to make. Clay, do you want me to text you when I'm done working? It might be late."

"That's okay. As I said, I'll wait. Good luck on the call. It's nice to meet you, Ravi." Clay nods to him. Then he sits back down and picks up the magazine again.

"There's coffee in the break room, which is just down that hall." Ravi points in the direction of the break room.

I look imploringly at Ravi. *Don't say that. He'll never leave, and I'll have mush brain forever.*

"Thanks," Clay says.

"Are we good to go, Pep?" Ravi asks, snapping me from my stupor.

"Yes." I stalk toward my office, my mind reeling.

Ravi keeps pace with me, but he doesn't say a word until we're behind closed doors. "Whoa. That was hot."

"What are you talking about? This is a nightmare." I put the vase and the picture on the table in my office and wring my hands.

He laughs. "More like a fantasy. There were so many sparks flying between you two, I thought the lobby would go up in flames."

"This isn't funny. There are no sparks."

He scoffs.

"Okay, there *are* sparks. But he can't be here. Look at me." I hold out my trembling hands. "He makes me stupid."

"That's called turned on, babe."

"I am *not* turned on."

"Is that what you're telling yourself? Because the way you two were looking at each other tells me you must have been burning up the sheets in Paris."

I close my eyes, fisting my hands, and groan. When I open my eyes, Ravi looks even more amused. "I hate how well you know me. What am I going to do?"

"*Him*, I hope."

I narrow my eyes. "You're not helping."

"Pepper, what's the problem? Did something bad happen that you didn't tell me about? Because I'll go set him straight."

I take a deep breath, trying to pull myself together. "*No.* He's been nothing but wonderful to me. But I told you. He makes me forget my good sense."

"You could use a little more of that in your life."

"You don't get it. I don't even know who I am with him." I hand him the sketch. "Who is that? *Huh?* It's not me. It's some naked chick with sexy lips and dazzling eyes. Even the artist could see that I wasn't myself."

He studies the sketch, then sets it on the table and studies me. "Listen, you know I love you."

"What does that have to do with *him*?" I fume.

"Because you're not going to like what I have to say, and I'm going to say it anyway, so I want you to remember that you love me." He softens his tone. "As you've gone out with guys and brushed them off, I've supported you one hundred percent. I didn't think any of them were good enough for you. They didn't make the efforts you deserve, and you never seemed overly excited about any of them. I don't know Clay from Adam, but I do know this. You blew off work to be with him, and I say *blew off* lightly, because we both know you deserve a hell of a lot more time off than that one day. But you've been different since you got back from Paris. You've been distracted and edgy. I think he lit you up like a firecracker, and that scares the hell out of you because it reminds you of who you were *before.*"

I swallow hard. *Before the accident that changed everything or before the asshole in college, or both?*

"I recognize the girl in that sketch, and there's something really special about her. I'm glad you get the chance to experience her again. Even if she scares you."

I swallow hard, fighting tears. I have no idea if they're tears of anger, or for the girl I said goodbye to years ago, or sheer frustration, but I fight them with everything I have, trying to get my head to focus.

"Showing up here is an aggressive move by a guy who can have any woman he wants," Ravi says. "Which means he knows that *you* can have any man you want, and he's not taking any chances. I *like* that."

I hear what he's saying, but I'm too out of sorts to deal with any of it. "Then *you* go out with him." I huff out a breath and walk around my desk.

"Pepper—"

"Don't." I hold up my hand, silencing him. "We have a call to make, and my head is all over the place. Maybe we should reschedule."

"Are you fucking kidding me?"

"*No*," I snap.

"It took us six weeks to set up this call." As we've done dozens of times for each other, Ravi's demeanor morphs from best friend to determined business associate. His eyes go serious, his jaw tightens, and he places both hands on my desk, leaning across it, staring me down. "You are Dr. Pepper Montgomery, a leader in our field. You started this company with the goal of making medical devices you care about. Are you really going to let a little chemistry get in the way of doing that?"

"*No?*"

He scoffs with a smile and shakes his head. "Cut the shit and pull up your big-girl panties. It's showtime."

More than an hour later, we end the conference call, and Ravi and I sit back as the rejection sinks in. "Well, that sucks," I lament. "I thought I pulled myself together and gave a solid pitch. Did I say something questionable or sound like I wasn't confident in our abilities?"

"Of course not. They wouldn't have spent that much time with us if they weren't interested in what we were doing. The VP is just old school. You heard what he said. He's hesitant to give money to a company that hasn't been around very long."

"I'm glad I didn't screw it up, but that annoys the heck out of me. Our reputations should speak for themselves." As I say it, I look across the room at the roses and the sketch of me and Clay in Paris beside them, thinking about how badly I had misjudged him based solely on his reputation. "Actually, I take that back. Reputations can be manipulated. But ours isn't. Over time our products will speak for themselves, and they'll regret their decision."

"Exactly. We'll find the right investors." A corner of his mouth quirks up. "There are plenty of fish in the sea."

"You've got to kiss a lot of frogs."

We both laugh at the advice we've been given over the years at which we have privately rolled our eyes.

"Who do you think came up with those ridiculous sayings?" Ravi asks.

"A fisherman and a very smart woman." I push to my feet, and he follows. "We gave a great pitch."

"Yes, we did, despite Mr. Perfect making you remember you're a sexy babe with needs right before the call."

I narrow my eyes. "Have you been hit on the head recently? Because I don't recall you having a death wish."

He laughs.

I lower my voice, eyeing my closed office door. "It's six forty-five. Do you think he's still out there?"

"Do you want him to be?"

I look at the man who has been my best friend since we were kids, who has seen me at my best and my worst and knows all of my secrets, and I'm thankful I can share this one with him. "I think so," I whisper.

He whispers, "Why are we whispering?"

"Because I know it's not the smart thing to do, and I'm afraid if I say it too loud, I'll overthink it."

He hugs me against his side. "For a smart girl, you can be really dumb."

"That's not very nice."

"What can I say? Sometimes the truth hurts. Are you ready to do this?"

I'm not, but I nod, and my nerves flare as we head for the lobby. Laughter floats down the hall that leads to the lab. It's such a rare sound, Ravi and I stop walking and exchange confused glances. Clay's voice rises above the laughter.

My stomach knots up as we make a beeline for the lab. I don't talk about my personal life with Min or Chris, and I hope Clay hasn't said anything to them about us.

When we get to the lab, I stand by the entrance trying to get my bearings and listening for any hint of what's been said. Clay is sitting on the edge of a worktable talking with Chris and Min. I only have a side view of them, but I can tell that Chris and Min, a petite brunette with straight shoulder-length hair and glasses, have stars in their eyes.

"Let me ask you a serious question," Clay says. "How far and fast do I have to throw the ball for you to scientifically prove that I'm a superhero?"

Chris and Min laugh, and they all turn to look at us as we walk into the room.

"There they are," Clay says, pushing from the table to his feet.

"I see you met the rest of my team." I search their faces for clues of what's been revealed, but I can't read them.

"I was looking for the men's room and ran into Chris." He claps a hand on Chris's shoulder like they're old buddies, and Chris beams. "He was kind enough to show me where to go, and then we got to talking."

"You've been holding out on us, Pepper," Chris says, and I hold my breath. "You didn't tell us you knew one of the best quarterbacks in the NFL."

Relief washes over me.

"That's because she's got better things to talk about, like the important work you do here," Clay says, saving me. "How did your meeting go?"

"It wasn't a good match," I say, as upbeat as I can. "But we'll find the right funding source."

"Bummer," Chris says.

"I have no doubt you will." Clay motions around the lab. "I hear this is where the magic happens."

"More science than magic, but yes," I say, trying to sound casual.

"Don't let the boss fool you," Ravi says. "Plenty of magic happens here."

"Scientific magic," Min chimes in, perkier than usual.

"Are you guys done for the night? We were just talking about all of us grabbing dinner together," Clay says.

"Oh." There's no hiding the surprise in my voice. I don't know what I expected this evening, but it certainly didn't include everyone else.

"It's probably the only time in my life I'll get to have dinner with one of my sports heroes," Min says excitedly.

"You have sports heroes?" I didn't even know she liked sports.

"Doesn't everyone?" Min says, like I've asked a ridiculous question.

"Chris got her into football a few years ago. They watch all the games together. She knows all my stats," Clay says. "Pretty cool, huh?"

"Yeah." I didn't even know Chris and Min spent time together outside of work. Why does Clay know so much about them?

"When we watch his team, Min wears his jersey," Chris says.

What the...? Jealousy snaps my brain into gear. No wonder she's mooning over him. "Really? How fun."

"And to think you didn't know you had a Giants fan under your roof all this time," Clay says. "They said there's a good

Italian restaurant around the corner that we can walk to. What do you say? Can you two get away?" He looks at me *and* Ravi, clearly extending the invitation to both of us.

"We told him that you usually eat at your desk and rarely leave the office before eight," Min says to me.

"We don't have anything pressing tonight," Ravi announces, his dark eyes urging me to accept. "It'll be a nice break, and I'd like to get to know Clay."

"Sure," I say, uncomfortable with the idea. Before I sit around a table with everyone, I have to find out what Clay told them about us. "I just need to get my coat. Clay, why don't you come with me to my office so we can catch up, and we'll meet them in the lobby."

We head down the hall, and as soon as we're out of earshot of the others, I say, "Please tell me you didn't tell them about Paris."

"They know we were both in Paris, but give me a little credit. Did you really think I was going to tell them that I had you tied to my bed while I ravaged you?"

My entire body ignites, and I hurry into my office. Clay closes the door behind us, his expression serious as he turns to me and says, "You failed to mention that you and Ravi work together. Are you two still an item? Is that why you didn't want to see me?"

I can't hide my shock. "Do you really think I'd sleep with you if I were in a relationship with Ravi or anyone else?"

"I don't know what to think right now. Plenty of women conveniently forget that they're in relationships when they're around me."

My jaw drops. "You've slept with women who are cheating on their boyfriends or husbands?"

"Not intentionally, but *yes*. It happened a time or two when I was too young and too stupid to realize it. But I learned my lesson. I'm not proud of being a player or of being played. I don't condone that behavior. I respect relationships. My parents and grandparents have been married forever, and that's what I eventually want."

I appreciate his honesty. He could've lied about sleeping with women who were in relationships, but the rest of what he said gives me pause. "You *do?*"

He rakes a hand through his hair, averting his eyes, and makes an incredulous sound. "Yes, I do, and based on that look on your face, it shocks you as much as it shocks me. I didn't realize how much I wanted that until just now." He scrubs a hand down his face, and his gaze softens with a hint of confusion. "What are you doing to me, Reckless?"

My heart squeezes, but I remind myself to be smart. "I could ask the same of you, showing up here unannounced, bringing me flowers. They're gorgeous, by the way. Thank you."

"So are you." He closes the gap between us and slips his arm around my waist, gently pulling me against him, holding me loose enough that I can step away if I want to.

I don't.

"When I thought you and Ravi were a couple, I nearly lost my mind." His tone is gruff but somehow also tender. "I tried to glean what I could from Chris and Min about you two without being obvious, but learning how close you and Ravi are only made it worse."

"You were jealous?" I ask with disbelief.

"Yes. That's a new feeling for me, and I've got to say, I'm not a fan of fantasizing about doing physical harm to a guy I don't even know."

I laugh. "Sorry. I don't mean to laugh. You shouldn't wish Ravi harm. We haven't been together since high school, but he's my best friend. He always has my back, and I trust him explicitly."

He touches his forehead to mine. "Drive that stake a little deeper, why don't you?"

"What do you mean?"

He lifts his head, gazing deeply into my eyes. "I want to be the guy you trust."

My pulse quickens, and the honesty and longing in his voice make my insides go soft and warm. I don't know what this is, and I know making it work would be impossible, but I want *him*. I want all the joy and goodness of what we had, and I *don't* want to fight it anymore. My heart races as I put my arms around him. "You're the only man I've ever let tie me up. That should tell you something."

"That I'm the luckiest guy around?" He brushes his lips over mine, whispering, "I've missed you," and then he kisses me slowly and sweetly and not nearly long enough.

"I might have missed you a little, too."

He smiles. "One day I'm going to teach you that phrases like *kind of* and *might have* are jagged little buggers."

I laugh softly.

"We'd better get out there before they figure out we're more than just friends who hung out in Paris."

"Ravi knows about us."

His brow furrows. "You told him?"

"He knows all my…" I stop myself, realizing Ravi doesn't know all my secrets anymore. "He knows we got together, but I didn't share the dirty details. I'd like to keep my personal and professional life separate around Min and Chris. I don't want to muddy the waters."

"I expected as much, but just so you know, it's going to be hard for me to act like I don't want to kiss you after not seeing you for so long."

"In that case, here's one to hold you over." I lean in and kiss him, knowing it will be just as hard for me.

Chapter Eighteen

Pepper

I have walked to work nearly every day for years, but walking down the brick-paved sidewalks with Clay and my colleagues feels a little like I've been plunked down in an alternate universe. As shocked and happy as I am that Clay is here, Charlottesville is my safe space, and Ravi, Min, and Chris are my people. We may not socialize outside work much, but we work so many hours, I probably spend more time with them than most married couples spend together. We make a good team, and I don't want anything to upend that.

I'm anxious as we settle around the table, hoping dinner won't be awkward, but conversation comes easily, and I'm reminded of all the reasons I'm drawn to Clay. He's funny and interesting, and he makes everyone feel special. Those were some of the same reasons I shied away from him before Paris. Now that I know who he is, I see his efforts are genuine. I like that he's taking the time to get to know my friends as we eat, asking about their families and the work they're doing. But there's no missing the handful of people who are stealing glances at him, some of them whispering. I guess that's what happens when you're a professional quarterback in a college town where people live and breathe football. It makes me a little uncomfortable, and I do my best to ignore it. I can't imagine what it feels like for Clay, but to his credit, his attention never strays from our group.

Throughout dinner, his leg brushes mine, and he holds my hand under the table. I missed those simple touches, and they leave me wanting more.

After dinner, he picks up the tab, and I'm a bundle of live wires, anxious to be alone with him as we walk back to the office. The approving glances I catch from Ravi only make me more nervous. When we get to the parking lot, Ravi, Chris, and Min thank him again for dinner and say their goodbyes.

As they head for their cars, Clay turns to me. "We did good, Reckless. I don't think they suspect I'm your boy toy."

I laugh. I missed how easily he makes me smile and laugh, too.

"Seriously, they're great, and they obviously have nothing but respect for you. I hope you know I'd never do anything to jeopardize that."

"I appreciate that." As I say it, I realize there's something else I need to know. "Does Dash know you're here?"

"No. Why?"

"My sisters have been asking about us. I didn't tell them about Paris, and I just don't want to deal with their gossip or pressure. Would you mind not mentioning it to Dash until we know what this is?"

"I already know what this is, but sure." He nods toward the office. "Do you need to go back up to your office to finish up?"

I always have work to do, but he came all this way to see me, and I want to spend more time with him. I consider going up to get the roses but decide to leave them there so I can see them tomorrow. "No."

"Then I'll walk you to your car."

"It's not here. I don't like driving at night, so I usually walk to work."

"Really? What bothers you about driving at night?"

"Nothing in particular. I've never liked it, and I only live a few blocks away."

His brows knit. "What do you do when it snows?"

"I wear boots."

He laughs and looks around. "Is it safe to walk alone at night here?"

"I wouldn't do it if it weren't."

"Okay, Pep. What are we dealing with here? Does riding in other people's cars at night bother you?"

"Not at all."

"Well, then, Dr. Montgomery, may I drive you home?" He offers his arm.

"I'd like that very much, Mr. Braden." I take his arm, and he leads me toward a black Land Rover.

"This is a great location. I noticed your company name isn't on the directory, and you don't have a sign in your reception area. Did you just move in?"

You really do notice every little thing.

"No, we've been here for a while. I'll get a sign for the reception area eventually. I was sort of dropped and running when we moved in and just haven't gotten back to looking for one. As far as the directory goes, I got tired of hounding the property manager to get my company name on it. But it's not that big a deal. We don't get many visitors. Did you have trouble finding my suite?"

"Not really. I just went door to door asking if anyone knew where I could find the hot scientist I slept with in Paris."

I laugh and climb into his Land Rover. It's clean and luxurious, and it smells like leather and *Clay*. I give him directions, and a few minutes later we're parked in front of my cozy two-bedroom historic home.

He helps me out of the vehicle and puts a hand on my back as we head up to the front porch. "This is cute. I like the yellow."

"Thanks. I would've preferred more land, but housing is expensive here, and there's no place with land in walking distance to the office." The neighboring houses are not much more than a car width away, and my backyard is tiny. My nerves prickle as we ascend the porch steps, and I focus on unlocking the door instead of on how much I want to kiss him. "I'm lucky to have found this place. The alternative was a condo. They don't have many windows, and there's no yard. I would feel like I was living at work." I realize I'm rambling and make myself stop.

"Am I making you nervous?"

I put my keys in my bag and face him. "Is it that obvious?"

"Adorably so." He puts his arms around me and kisses my forehead. "I enjoyed getting to know your friends and spending time with you. Thanks for fitting me in."

"Thank *you* for driving all this way even though I told you I was too busy to see you, and for bringing me flowers and paying for everyone's dinner."

"I'd pay for dinner for everyone in this town if it meant I got to spend time with you." He kisses me softly. "I've missed your lips." His mouth finds mine again, lingering longer, kissing me deeper. He draws away slowly, whispering, "So sweet, Reckless," and kisses me more demandingly. *God*, I've missed kissing him. Desire builds hot and insistent inside me. I go up on my toes, taking more. He tightens his hold on me, making a greedy sound that steals my ability to think. I cling to him, feeling like a champagne bottle ready to pop, and grind against his erection. Without breaking our connection, I reach for the doorknob, ready to drag him inside, but he tears his mouth away.

A needy sound rushes from my lungs.

He smiles, his lips too far away as he says, "Good night, beautiful."

It takes me a second to realize he's descending the porch steps. "You're *leaving*?"

"Yeah." He hikes a thumb over his shoulder. "I'm going to stay at my place."

"You have a *place*?" I have definitely entered an alternate reality.

"You said we lived too far apart, so I'm staying nearby." His brows slant. "You didn't think I came here just to sleep with you, did you?"

"You don't *want* to sleep with me?" My words come out stilted and confused.

"Of course I do. But rule number one for getting a woman to fall for you is to always leave her wanting more. Sleep tight, sweetheart. I'll be in touch." He heads for his Land Rover.

Fall for you?

Dumbfounded, I watch him drive away, fully expecting him to turn around and tell me he's only kidding and rush back to me. I don't know how long I stand there waiting for the headlights to reappear, but it's long enough for the lust to clear from my head and embarrassment to settle in. I look at my neighbors' houses, hoping they didn't witness me practically climbing Clay like a tree.

After failing to distract myself with work, television, and ice cream, I'm lying in bed, wearing Clay's jersey, overthinking. I can't believe he's here in Charlottesville, much less that he just left me on the porch. Why would he leave if he's here just for the night? Even if he's here for the weekend, wouldn't he want this time together? In Paris he wanted *more* time with me, not less. I can't make sense of it. Is he waiting for me to ask him to come back?

Ohmygod. I'm such an idiot. Of course he is! He made a monumental effort. Now it's my turn.

I grab my phone and thumb out a text. *Do you want to come over?* That makes me sound desperate. I delete it and type, *What are you up to?* That sounds too buddyish. I start over. *Dinner was great. Are you hungry for dessert?*

Ugh. I delete the cheesy offer.

I officially suck at text flirting when not prompted by him.

I thumb out, *I had a great time tonight. Want to make it even better?* That sounds cheesy, too. I go through a half dozen more bad iterations and finally settle on something that feels less pushy.

Me: *Hi.*

Clay: *Hi beautiful. Thinking of me?*

Me: *Overthinking.*

Clay: *I'm a lot to think about.*

Me: *Yes you are.*

Me: *What are you doing?*

Clay: *Working off some pent-up energy.*

My thumbs hover over the keyboard, and I debate texting, *I can help you with that.*

A picture pops up of him wearing shorts and a T-shirt, taken in a mirror at a gym. He left me to go work out? That doesn't make me feel very good.

Me: *I didn't know gyms were open this late.*

Clay: *It's a home gym.*

Me: *You mean at the hotel?*

Clay: *No. I'm renting a house. It has a full gym.*

He rented a whole house for the weekend? I guess that's what you do when you're a big-time quarterback.

Me: *Are you really here just to see me?*

Clay: *Yes.*

Clay: *You said you were too busy for a long-distance relationship. Now we're in the same town.*

Clay: *You can get your work done and when you have downtime I'll be right around the corner.*

Shocked, I read his messages again. He did that for me. For *me.* After I tried to end things. *Twice.* That takes a minute to process, and happiness blooms inside me.

Me: *How long are you here?*

Clay: *However long it takes.*

My pulse quickens.

Me: *Takes for what?*

Clay: *For you to realize we're more than a weekend fling.*

Chapter Nineteen

Clay

 After a fitful night's sleep spent convincing myself not to drive back to Pepper's house, I'm up before the sun, getting my PT and workout done. I head out before the sun comes up for a run. The brisk air is exhilarating as I hit my stride. Few things center me like running does, and this morning I need centering. Leaving Pepper last night was not easy, but it was the right move. She needs to see that I'm into all of her, not just her body, and that I respect her career and her concerns.

The second I saw her in her office, I knew I made the right decision coming to see her. Not only had the chaos of the last week instantly fallen away, but I could *see* and *feel* how much she missed me, too. I don't know if she tried to end us because of her schedule and where we live, or because our chemistry scares her, or for some other reason altogether, but after last night, I know she couldn't fool herself into believing we were over any better than I could.

The house I rented isn't far from the University of Virginia, and the sun is just starting to rise when I reach the campus. My first thought is that I wish Pepper were here to watch the sunrise with me. I never gave much thought to my grandfather urging me to get out and enjoy all this world has to offer, but after spending time with Pepper, that's changed.

I take out my phone and snap a picture, texting it to him. No words necessary. I consider texting it to Pepper, too, but worry it'll get us both sidetracked, and I have a schedule to keep to this morning. I put my phone in my armband and head for the track. I figured I'd have it all to myself this early, but there's a young Black guy running. I hit the track, and not thirty seconds later he blows past me, saying, "*Morning.*"

The competitive bastard in me comes out, and I kick up my speed, waving as I sprint past him and call out, "*Mornin'.*"

I hear him laugh, and he blows past me again with a cocky grin.

Game on.

Adrenaline courses through my veins as we race around the track, flashing shit-eating grins with every pass. But he can't be more than eighteen or nineteen years old, and I run out of steam before he does. I slow down to catch my breath and wave him on, but he doubles back, a little starry-eyed, and I know he's recognized me.

"Hey! You're Clay Braden."

"That's right. And you are?" I offer my hand, and he shakes it eagerly. He's tall, lean, and fast, with a strong grip. In a few years this kid will burn up the field faster than lightning.

"Ben Clauson. Wide receiver."

"I recognize that name. You had a hell of a season."

"*Bro!*" He grabs his head with both hands and looks up at the sky, his short dreads poking out between his fingers as he practically shouts, "This is unreal. No fucking way you know my name."

I laugh, remembering the thrill of meeting NFL players for the first time.

"*Man*. I can't get over this!" Ben exclaims. "*Clay Braden*. What're you doing *here*?"

"I'm trying to keep my time here on the down-low." I have no idea what possesses me to admit the truth.

"Yeah. I swear it, man. I've got you."

"I'm here to see my girl."

"You're dating someone from my school?" His brow furrows. "Bro, how old are you?"

"Far too old for *that*." I laugh. "She lives in the area. Why are you running so early?"

"Between keeping my grades up and working full time to help my mom with the bills, I have to fit my workouts in when I can. I got a full ride, and I want to come back stronger next year. Can't slack. I'm the first one in my family to go to college, and I want to do my mom proud."

"That's the way to do it. What about your father? Isn't he in the picture?"

"Nah, but my mom and I are good."

That sucks. Or maybe it's better, if his dad is a deadbeat.

"I remember how hard it was keeping up with school and football." Beyond classes and football, my biggest worry was which party to attend. "I can't imagine working full time on top of that."

He shrugs. "We got through the season, and when I go pro, she'll never have to worry again."

"You're a good man, Ben."

We talk about the game, and he tells me about the areas in which he's trying to improve. He asks me a hundred questions about what it's like to play for the NFL. I like this kid. He's got his priorities straight, and he's hungry for the game.

"If you want to run some drills while I'm in town, I'd be

happy to help you out," I offer.

His eyes widen. "Are you *serious*? That would be amazing."

"Absolutely, but you've got to do me a favor."

"Anything. You name it."

Thinking about Pepper, I say, "Think you can keep this off social media?"

"You've got my word. You said you're keeping it on the down-low." He holds his hands up in surrender. "Message received, bro. You can count on me."

"I appreciate that. I don't know what my schedule will be like while I'm here, but if you give me your number, I'll text you and let you know when I've got some free time. If you're available and it works out, great. If not, no worries."

"That would be awesome. I work tomorrow from four till eleven, and Sunday morning. I've got classes from…"

He goes on about his school and work schedules, but I cut him off. "I'll never remember all that. Why don't we start with a phone number, and we'll figure out the rest later?"

After he gives me his number, I tell him I'll be in touch and head out, excited to see Pepper and looking forward to working out with Ben.

I run straight to Pepper's house. She lives on a quaint residential street, with mature trees and well-kept homes with wide front porches, like hers. I don't know what time she leaves for work, but my plan was to get there by seven thirty, and I climb her porch steps at seven twenty-five. I wipe the sweat from my brow and knock.

My fucking heart beats faster at the sound of her footsteps nearing the door. She peers out the sidelight, and *man*, her smile is prettier than the fucking sun. She opens the door, stunning and professional in a sleek camel-colored knit dress and knee-high boots, but it's the heat in her eyes as her gaze moves down my body that has my heart feeling like it's going to beat right out of my chest.

"Hi," she says with surprise.

"Good morning, neighbor. You look beautiful."

"Thanks. Did you *run* here?"

"Yes. I wanted to walk my girl to work."

Her eyes light up. "Really?"

"Really." I lean in and kiss her smiling lips. "That is, if you don't mind being seen with a sweaty guy."

"I like you sweaty." Her gaze roams down my chest again.

"Careful, Reckless." I slip my arm around her, drawing her against me. "Keep talking like that and I might just make you late for work."

"Don't tell me that when I've been thinking about you all night." Her words fall fast and flustered, and she steps out of my grip.

"Get over here, you adorable thing." I step inside, pulling her close again.

She groans. "*Why* do you have to feel so good?"

"I should ask the same of you." I lower my voice. "So you've been thinking about me, huh?"

"*Clay*," she warns, but it's breathy and half-hearted.

"What? I'm just thinking about you thinking about me and wondering if you were thinking about kissing me."

"I was definitely thinking about that." Her cheeks pink up, and she whispers, "Among *other* things."

Is my reckless girl coming out to play? "Were you remembering how good my hands felt on your body?" I slide my hands down her back, palming her ass, and press my hips forward.

"*Yes.*"

I brush my lips over hers, and she inhales a ragged breath. "Did you miss me touching you here?" I bring my hand to her breast, brushing my thumb over her nipple, and feel it pebble through her dress.

"*God, yes.*"

I kiss the corner of her mouth, loving the whimper it draws. "Were you thinking about how good my mouth felt between your legs?"

"*Yes. So good.*" She grabs my arms, holding tight. "Did you think about me?"

There's my reckless girl. "Every second we were apart." I kiss her neck, and she moans. "You're killing me, sweetheart."

"*Same,*" she whispers.

"Were you thinking about how much you enjoyed being tied to the bed, at my mercy?"

She makes another needy sound, her fingers pressing into my arms. I didn't plan on getting dirty with her this morning, but fuck. I'm as hard as stone, and the want in her eyes is inescapable. I drag my tongue along the shell of her ear, rasping gruffly, "Were you remembering the feel of my cock taking you inch by inch as our bodies came together?" Another whimper escapes her lips. "And how good it felt when I was buried deep inside you, your sweet pussy squeezing me as you came?"

"*Clay.*" The breathy plea is drenched in need.

"*Fuck,* baby. I'm trying to behave, but it's not possible with you. Are you wet for me, Reckless?"

"*Yes.*"

"Can you be ten minutes late for work?"

"*Yes.*"

I push the door shut and back her up against it, crushing my mouth to hers, unleashing the desire I've been trying desperately to ignore. I pull up her dress and push my hand into her silk panties, cursing as my fingers slide through her wetness. "So wet, my sexy girl." I reclaim her mouth, pushing my fingers inside her and using my thumb on her clit, stroking her to feverish heights. She's moaning, rocking against my hand, and it's not nearly enough. "I need my mouth on you."

I tug her panties down to her thighs, keeping them bound by the flimsy silk, and spread her thighs far enough to get my mouth between them. Then I give her what we both need. She gasps and moans as I lick and suck, using my teeth and tongue. Her greedy sounds rocket through me. "So fucking sweet," I grit out, aching to be inside her, and use my hands and mouth to send her soaring, her sinful sounds echoing around us.

As her body quivers through the last ripples of pleasure, I lick every last drop and press kisses to her inner thighs. When I kiss her swollen clit, she inhales sharply, and I can't help going back for seconds. "Ohgod, *Clay*—" She clings to my shoulders, and it doesn't take long before she cries out, "Yesyesyes—" I stay with her, fucking her with my fingers, licking and sucking, memorizing every wanton sound. When she finally comes down from the peak, she collapses over me, trying to catch her breath.

I drag her panties the rest of the way down and help her step out of them. I push to my feet with those sexy panties in hand. Her eyes flutter open, intoxicatingly sated and impossibly gorgeous. "Feel better, beautiful?"

"Uh-huh," she pants out.

"You can't wear these to work with come on them." I show her the panties and lick her essence from them. Her eyes widen. "My favorite flavor."

I put them in the pocket of my sweats and fix her dress, before taking that sweet, willing mouth in a ravenous kiss. She comes away hazy eyed. "Don't wear panties to work today, baby."

She blinks several times. "I can't do that. Min and I are working on a prototype, and I have software training on my new accounting system and a meeting with a neurologist who's consulting on our project."

"Are you worried they'll get you hot and bothered?"

"*No*, but I've never gone without underwear to work or anywhere else."

"Another first." A grin stretches across my face. "I'll be hard all day thinking about you bare and ready for me, squirming in your chair every time you think of me."

Her cheeks pink up, but the heat in her eyes tells me she likes that idea.

"It's okay if you don't want to do it, but you should know that it's also okay if you do." I cradle her face in my hands and brush my thumb over her lower lip. "What do you say, sweetheart? Want to be reckless with me? It'll be our dirty little secret. Nobody will know."

"You are *such* a bad influence."

"You can say no."

"I don't *want* to say no," she whispers harshly. "That's *why* you're a bad influence. I would never even think about doing something like this, and now I can't *stop* thinking about it."

I fucking love that. "If it'll help, then after my shower, I'll go commando, too. Just for you."

"Don't tell me *that*. I can't unhear it. Now I'll be thinking about *that* all day."

I laugh.

"Don't laugh," she says, but she's laughing, too.

"I'm sorry. You're just so cute, and I'm not gonna lie. I love the idea of you thinking about me all day."

"I bet you do. I have to get cleaned up." She kisses me. "You need to wash your face so people don't smell *me* all over you. Ohmygod. I cannot believe I just said that." She heads upstairs, shaking her head, mumbling, "This is *so* bad."

I laugh again and take a moment to check out her place. The foyer opens to a high-ceilinged, sunny and inviting living room with yellow walls and white trim. The floors are light hardwood, the sofa is coral with yellow and light gray throw pillows, and two comfortable-looking floral armchairs sit on either side of a fireplace with a marble surround. Behind one armchair are built-in bookshelves littered with books and knickknacks. Pictures of her family, the university, and her parents' Victorian home decorate the walls, in sharp contrast to the stark walls in her office.

I head down the hall and find a powder room just before the entrance to the kitchen. I wash my face with cold water, willing my cock to deflate. When I leave the bathroom, Pepper is coming down the stairs. Her hair is freshly brushed, and her cheeks immediately pink up. That's how I know she didn't chicken out and put on panties.

"Don't look at me like that," she says with a nervous laugh.

"Like you're the most beautiful woman I've ever seen?"

Her brows knit. "Like you know I don't have underwear on."

"Oh, sorry. I'll try not to." I put a hand on her back and kiss her, tasting mint toothpaste. "Your place is gorgeous."

"Thanks." She grabs her coat and bag from the foyer closet. "How did you know what time I leave for work?"

I take her coat from her and help her into it. "I didn't, but I hoped I'd get lucky."

"I think I'm the one who got lucky this morning," she says as we head outside.

On the porch, I draw her into my arms. "I think we're both lucky. I missed you last night, sweetheart."

"I might have missed you, too."

"*Might* have?" I kiss her again and take her hand as we head down the steps and onto the sidewalk.

"Can I ask you something?" she asks carefully.

"Of course."

"Did you really put your life on hold to come see me for some undetermined amount of time?"

A dog barks inside a home as we walk past, and I see its adorable scruffy face in the window. It dawns on me that I can't remember the last time I walked around a neighborhood. It's nice walking with her. "I think this is the first time in years I'm *not* putting my life on hold."

"What do you mean?"

"My world revolves around football. I'm either gearing up for the season, in season, catching up with family and friends, or taking care of sponsorships, charitable commitments, and fan events." We turn onto another residential street. "I've lived in that cycle for a long time, and it's been great. It's everything I always wanted. But what I didn't realize until you and I got together was that I hadn't been doing anything about living my life *outside* all of that."

"Why not?"

"Because before you, there wasn't anyone I wanted to see badly enough to make the effort."

"Really?"

"You ask that a lot. Hopefully at some point you'll realize that I don't say things I don't mean." I lift our joined hands and kiss the back of hers. "Being here with you"—*feels righter than being on the football field lately*—"is the only place I want to be. And to be honest, it doesn't feel like it was a choice. It feels like it's where I'm supposed to be. Like I not only wanted to be with you but needed to be with you. I've never felt this way before, and I couldn't let you throw us away."

Her expression warms. "In that case, I'll admit that I'm really glad you're here."

"The orgasm didn't pull that out of you, but my honesty did?"

"Shh." She looks around us as we turn onto the main drag, but she's smiling hard.

I pull her closer. "It's not like I'm announcing that you're not wearing panties."

She glowers at me, and I resist kissing her again.

"I am glad you're here, although we have to work on your verbal discretion." She smiles. "I'm sorry work is so busy. I wish I could take today off."

"I know how important your work is. That's why I'm here, making myself available when you have time."

"Don't let this go to your head or anything, but you're pretty great for showing up for me."

"I know," I tease, earning an eye roll.

As we make our way to her office, she says, "Would you mind if we stopped for a latte at the corner café? I usually get one before work."

"Sure, but I think I saw a coffee shop around the corner yesterday."

"You did, but I like the way they make lattes better at the café."

"Small-town hidden gems. I love it."

We head into the café and get in line. A portly redheaded waitress is rushing from one table to another, taking orders and clearing plates, while a slim brunette hurries between the register and helping customers sitting at the counter. An adorable little girl with curly brown pigtails sits at the counter on a stool to the left of the register, coloring and watching the woman behind the counter rush around.

"Smells good in here," I say. "It reminds me of the café where we had breakfast in Paris."

"That place was delicious."

My mind sneaks down memory lane, bringing naked images of Pepper.

"What's that grin for?" she asks.

I whisper in her ear, "I was remembering the hours before, when I had *you* for breakfast."

She squirms, looking imploringly at me. "Now is *not* a good time for me to think about that."

I chuckle. "Sorry."

"You are *not*."

I hug her and kiss her temple. "I wasn't trying to get you hot and bothered, but now that you are—"

She shoots me a death glare.

The line moves quickly, and when we reach the register, the woman behind it says, "I'll be right with you," and hurries to a pass-through to the kitchen to pick up an order.

As she delivers the plates to customers at the other end of the counter, the little girl looks up from her coloring book and says, "Hi."

"Hi," Pepper and I say in unison.

The little girl flashes a toothy grin. "There's no school to-day. The teachers have meetings."

"Aren't you lucky." I glance at the couple beside her, wondering if she's their daughter, but they don't seem to notice or care that she's talking with us.

"I was supposed to sleep at my friend's house last night and play with her today, but she got sick," the little girl says.

"I'm sorry to hear that," I say.

"My brother Sammy had a sleepover at *his* friend's house," she says as the woman behind the counter returns to the register. "I wanted to go with him, but Mommy wouldn't let me." She looks poutingly at the brunette waitress, whose name tag says CLARE.

As Clare smiles at the little girl, I notice she looks to be about my age. "Trina, we talked about this. Sammy needs time alone with his friends." She glances at us. "Sorry about that. My daughter has strong opinions."

"That's okay. I'd be upset if my sleepover plans got foiled, too." I glance at Pepper, who's looking at the little girl with a sweet expression. She's a natural with kids, or at least with her niece. I wonder if she wants to have a family of her own one day.

Clare smiles at Pepper and says, "The usual? A French vanilla latte?"

"Yes. Nobody makes them better," Pepper says.

"Thank you." Clare glances at me. "And what would you like?"

"Four blueberry muffins, please."

"Coming right up."

As Clare goes to fill our order, Pepper says, "Running must make you really hungry."

"The muffins aren't for me. They're for you to share with your team."

"You don't have to get them muffins. I'm sure they'll eat breakfast before coming to work."

"That's okay. It shows appreciation and keeps morale up. Little things can make a big difference. You do still like blueberry muffins, don't you?"

"Yes, but how did you know that?"

"We had breakfast at your parents' house one time when I was visiting Dash, and you grabbed a blueberry muffin before running back here for a work emergency."

"Okay, here you go." Clare puts the latte and the box with the muffins on the counter and rings us up.

"Thanks, Clare. Have a great day." I turn to Trina. "Be good for your mama. She's working hard."

"I will. Bye." Trina waves.

"What a cutie," I say as we head out.

"She is, and she's a good girl. I've seen her here a few times." We walk the half block to her office, and she tips her face up to the sun. "What a beautiful day."

"Sure is." I hand her the box of muffins. "Have a great day at work."

She tilts her head. "What are you doing today?"

"I've got a hundred things on my plate. But don't worry. I'll see you later."

"Okay. Thanks for walking me to work, and for the latte and muffins. I'm sure everyone will be happy to eat them."

"My pleasure. See you later, girl boss." I lean in and kiss her, and then I open the door for her, catching another sweet smile as she walks inside.

I jog back to the rental house. My phone rings as I'm walking down the long driveway. I pull it out and see Doogie's name on the screen. "Hey, man. How was your honeymoon? I didn't expect to hear from you so early."

"I've got a lot to catch up on and figured I'd get an early start. The trip was fantastic." He tells me about the resort and the things they did.

"Sounds like a great time. I'm glad you enjoyed it."

"Thanks again. I wanted to follow up on your last message. You said you were heading out of town, and you didn't know when you'd be back. What's the scoop? Where are you?"

"I'm in Charlottesville, Virginia, and I'm not sure how long I'll be here, but I've got my schedule. I won't miss anything important."

"Dude, please tell me you're not stalking Pepper."

I scoff. "Give me some credit."

"When it comes to her, I'm not sure I can. Did Paris go that well, or did you follow her home when she took off to get away from you?"

"Paris went very well. I'm here visiting with her."

"In that case, I'm happy for you. You've been pining for her for a long time."

"Don't be an ass."

"But it's so *fun*. I mean, come on. How often does Mr. Perfect have to work for a year to get a woman's attention? I think Pepper Montgomery has just made history."

I rake a hand through my hair. "I can fire you, you know."

"But you won't. Okay, back to business. I've got shit to do while you're busy romancing your woman. Tiffany's pretty upset with you. Do you want me to get a meeting on the books with her about your contract?"

"No. I told her I need a few weeks. I'll deal with it."

"You're seeing her Monday evening."

"For *what?*"

"She set up a dinner meeting with In the Zone Sportswear for a sponsorship deal after your Under Armour photo shoot, which is at eleven. Should I book you a flight for Sunday night?"

Damn it. "No." I don't want to miss any more time with Pepper than absolutely necessary. "Set it up for early Monday morning, and please get me a flight back that night."

"It'll have to be late. You're not having dinner until seven."

Fuck. "Then make the return flight early Tuesday morning."

"Consider it done. I haven't gotten it on the calendar yet, but Johnson & Johnson booked you to film a commercial the week before the Charity Bowl."

"Great." They're one of my largest sponsors.

We go through a few more scheduling items, and after we end the call, I text Pepper—*I can still taste you*—and head inside to shower, knowing she'll be squirming in her seat.

Chapter Twenty

Pepper

I'm putting the muffins in the break room when Ravi walks in. He eyes me curiously, making me even more aware of my missing underwear. I try to pretend my insides aren't twisting into knots over my dirty little secret and act normal. Although I don't even know what *that* normal is anymore.

"Hi, Ravi. Clay bought muffins for everyone." I open the box and show him.

"Now I like him even more." He plucks one from the box and takes a bite. "Dinner was fun last night. He seems like a really good guy."

Relief washes through me. If Ravi had any idea that I wasn't wearing underwear, he'd call me on it without hesitation. "He is. Do you think Chris and Min figured out that I'm seeing him?"

"Of course. You can't hide those sparks." He takes another bite of his muffin and leans his butt against the counter.

"I figured as much. I just don't want them to think differently of me."

"Because you have a personal life? Come on, Pep. You're smarter than that, and so are they. Since you and Clay were together this morning, can I assume last night was as good as

Paris?"

I grab two plates, handing him one and putting a muffin on the other for myself. "Last night was different, but not in a bad way."

His eyes narrow with confusion. "Care to elaborate?"

"He took me home and gave me one of the best kisses of my life. Then he said he's not here just for sex and told me he rented a house here for however long it takes for me to realize we're more than a fling. Then he left and showed up to walk me to work this morning." I'm not about to tell him the other thing we did this morning, or that he walked away with my underwear in his pocket.

His brow furrows. "He left after just a kiss?"

"*Yes.* I was shocked, too, but it's kind of nice, right?" Clay's voice whispers through my mind. *One day I'm going to teach you that phrases like* kind of *and* might have *are jagged little buggers.* "It *was* nice. He was making his point, and it was appreciated...after I drove myself crazy over it."

Ravi grins. "There's the overthinker I know and love. It sounds like he's serious about you."

"He says he is."

"Why do you sound skeptical?"

I sigh heavily. "I don't *know.* I love that he's making this huge effort, and I want to believe him, but this is his off season. Once he's playing again, it could be a whole different story."

"That's true, but I wouldn't be too quick to assume it." He sets the remainder of his muffin on the plate and crosses his arms, studying me. "What's that thing you always say about men and pennies?"

"That a man needs to treat a woman like a diamond before he's treated like he's worth a penny?"

"That's it. There are sparkles all around you, Pep. I know it's scary, because he is a jock, but Morgyn would say you manifested your perfect man, and he sure knows how to pick muffins."

"All of my sisters would have a field day with this, but you know I don't believe in manifestation."

"Maybe it's time you did." He pushes from the counter, heading for the door. "Don't forget, I'm out of the office from ten to one, and we meet with Dr. Bowry this afternoon."

"I know. I'll be ready."

I think about what he said as I finish my muffin. Clay pushes buttons I never knew I had, and he makes me sexually feral. I like who I am with him, even if I don't understand it. But I never would have manifested a man who did those things.

And I would have missed out on a really special man and the best sex of my life.

Why is this so confusing? I clean my plate and head back to my office.

I'm greeted with the sweet smell of my gorgeous roses and feel myself swooning all over again. As I gaze down at the sketch of us from Paris, my cell chimes with a text.

Clay: *I can still taste you.*

My body ignites, making me even more aware of my nakedness under my dress. I may not believe in manifestation, but I know I'll never be satisfied with anything less than the button-pushing bad influence that is Clay Braden.

The morning is busy, and I get the same flash of panic about my lack of underwear every time I see my staff and when I work with Min in the lab. But the thrill of knowing they have no clue about my naughty little secret brings a new level of excitement. I get an adrenaline rush with every interaction from the risk of being discovered. Getting away with it emboldens me, and the high of it makes me even more productive, which is a good thing, since I've got hours of accounting software training ahead of me.

At eleven forty-five, I head to the lobby to wait for the software trainer, Jeanette Woods. I answer a phone call and send it to Min's voicemail since she and Chris are running simulations in the lab. A sharply dressed, middle-aged brunette comes through the door as I place the receiver back in the cradle.

"Jeanette?" I walk around the reception desk to greet her.

"Yes."

"Hi. I'm Pepper." I shake her hand. "Thanks for making the time to come out."

"You're a busy woman. I'm glad you could fit me in." We've been trying to coordinate the training for several weeks.

"Sorry things have been a little hectic around here. But you've got my attention now."

The door opens behind her, and Clay walks in carrying a shopping bag, looking handsome as can be in a gray sweater, jeans, and the sexy bomber jacket he'd worn in Paris. He flashes those dimples, sending my stomach into somersaults. I fight the urge to drop my gaze to see if he went commando like he promised, and just the thought of it has my neediest parts clenching. *Nonono.* "I'm sorry, Jeanette, can you excuse me for just a minute?"

"Of course," she says, and steps to the side.

I go to Clay and lower my voice. "Hi. I wasn't expecting

you."

"I know. I thought I'd see if you were free for lunch."

A voice in my head says, *You should have texted*, but my heart silences it, because I'm really glad to see him. Even if I'm not able to join him for lunch, I like that he thought of me. "I'm sorry, but I'm not. I have a software training session, and we're working through lunch."

"It was worth a shot. I also brought a little something for your team." He holds up the shopping bag. "Is it okay if I give it to them?"

They were so happy about the muffins, I felt bad that I hadn't thought of bringing them myself. It really *is* the little things.

"Sure, but—" The phone rings. "Just a second."

I answer the phone, and as I send the call to Ravi's voicemail, Chris walks by and sees Clay. His face lights up. "Clay, good to see you again."

"You, too, Chris. I brought something for you."

"Excuse me, you guys. Chris, this is Jeanette Woods from the accounting software company. We're about to go into training. I'm waiting to hear from MedForce about the proposal we submitted last month, and Dr. Bowry is coming in this afternoon for a meeting with me and Ravi. Can you keep an ear open for the phones in case he's running late or needs to cancel?"

"Absolutely," Chris says.

I turn my attention to Clay. "Thank you for the offer for lunch. I'll text you after work."

"Sounds good," he says with a nod.

I turn back to Jeanette. "Sorry about that. Why don't we go back to my office and get started."

As we head down the hall, I hear Chris and Clay chatting up a storm and wish I could be chatting with Clay, too.

Jeanette is patient and methodical, which I appreciate. I take copious notes as we work through the program and somehow make it through a few hours without interruption.

When we finish, I walk her out to the lobby and nearly trip over my own feet at the sight of Clay signing for a UPS package. "Thank you again, Jeanette. I appreciate your help."

"My pleasure. Feel free to reach out if you have any trouble, or if you need me to come back to train other employees."

After Jeanette and the UPS man leave, I turn to Clay, keeping my voice low. "What is going on? Why are you accepting our packages?"

"After I gave Chris and Min their gifts, they were showing me some of your projects, and the phone was ringing, so I offered to help."

My eyes widen. "You've been answering the phones?"

"Yes, but don't worry, Chris showed me how to send calls to the right extensions."

Oh my gosh. This guy. "But you said you had a busy day. You shouldn't put off your plans to answer my phones."

"I'm not. Chris logged me on to the computer so I could watch the game footage from my coach."

"Game footage?"

"It's part of my training. The coaches analyze our games, and we watch them, listening to their comments. It helps us see our strengths and weaknesses. But you don't have time for this right now, babe. Dr. Bowry showed up early. He's in Ravi's office, and they're expecting you."

"He's *here*?"

"Yes. He's a nice guy, too. A big football fan. I think I won you some bonus points. Go do your thing. I've got this."

"*Clay*, you don't have to stay. We're going to be a while."

"I like helping my girl."

My girl makes my heart squeeze, and that alternate universe I fell into yesterday is sucking me in at breakneck speed.

He steps closer and slides a hand down my back to my bottom, whispering, "Do you need me to help you take the edge off before you go in there? Five minutes in your office, and you'll be much more relaxed."

My insides turn to liquid heat, and I squeeze my thighs together. "No. *No*, no. I'm going." His chuckles follow me down the hall.

Chapter Twenty-One

Pepper

It's after six when we walk Dr. Bowry out, and Clay is gone. I try not to let my disappointment show and focus on how well the meeting went. Dr. Bowry mentioned my company to MS Enterprises, a group of investors who fund healthcare, pharmaceutical, and medical research and development, and they're open to reviewing a proposal for funding.

"That couldn't have gone any better," I say to Ravi. "I want to get on that new proposal opportunity with MS Enterprises right away. I'll review the reports again tonight and go over the budgets and documentation one last time this weekend, so we can reach out early next week to schedule a meeting."

"Don't you want to spend time with Clay?"

"Of course I do, but this is an opportunity we can't afford to miss out on by coming in too late. I'll find a way to fit it in. I'm sure he has other things to do while he's here. He knows I have a business to run and employees who count on me not to drop the ball."

"We count on you, but not if it's at the expense of your happiness."

"You know me better than that. My happiness has never been dependent upon a man."

"Maybe not, but I don't think you've known happiness like you do when you're with him."

"What are you, a mind reader?"

"Do you think I didn't notice how disappointed you were that he wasn't here when we walked Dr. Bowry out? Disappointment wafted around you like dirt around Pigpen from Peanuts."

"Ew."

"Hey, you guys," Chris says as he and Min walk into the lobby with their coats on, ready to leave. "Check out what Clay gave us." They each hold up an autographed football.

"We're going to get display cases for them," Min says proudly.

"That's wild," Ravi says. "He got me a bobblehead to go with my collection."

"Are you BFFs now?" I joke. "How did he know about your collection?" Ravi's collection of bobbleheads consists of everything from Star Wars to sports figures.

"I mentioned it over dinner, remember?"

No, but I was a little sidetracked.

But Clay is never too sidetracked to pick up on the little things. I swear he blew into my life like he belongs here, and in two days he's made everyone happier. Is he really this thoughtful? Or is he just playing Mr. Perfect for his fans?

I look at Ravi checking out Min's autographed football. The three of them are all smiles. At that moment, I realized it doesn't matter if Clay is playing a role for fans or not. Either way, he was thoughtful enough to think of my friends, and that says a lot about him.

But I do have to nip him answering our phones in the bud. "While we're on the subject of Clay," I say, drawing their attention, "Chris, you can't let just anyone answer the phones."

"Clay's not exactly *just anyone*, and it's not like I put him up to it," Chris insists. "I tried to dissuade him, but he really wanted to help."

"I was there," Min says. "Clay was very persuasive."

I know just how persuasive he can be.

"I don't see what the big deal is," Ravi says. "It's no different from when Chris's sister was visiting and helped out. Besides, Dr. Bowry was thrilled to meet him. He talked about Clay for ten minutes when we got into my office."

"I would've run it by you," Chris says. "But I didn't think it was worth interrupting your training session."

"It's okay. Ravi's right. It's not so different from when your sister helped." *Except that Clay is famous and can buy a hundred companies like mine if he wants to, and I'm sleeping with him, and trying to figure out why he's doing so much for me.* "It just threw me off. Hopefully we'll find a receptionist soon."

"It threw me off, too," Chris says. "But then I realized he's a great guy. I had fun showing him around. He actually understood a lot of what we're doing."

"That's great. Thank you for showing him around."

"Are we cool?" Chris asks.

"Yeah. Go get your display cases." As Chris and Min walk out, I exhale a long breath. "I overreacted, didn't I?"

Ravi holds up his finger and thumb an inch apart and mouths, *A little.*

"Why would Clay want to answer our phones?"

"Why don't you ask him?" Ravi nods in the direction of the door.

Through the glass, I see Clay coming down the hall carrying two large bags. Our eyes connect, and that *there you are* smile appears. Suddenly the questions don't seem worth worrying about anymore. I open the door for him. "Hi. I thought you were gone."

"I knew you and Ravi might be burning the midnight oil, so I brought dinner for all of us."

My heart swells. If he is only playing a role, he could win an Academy Award.

"Thanks, Clay, but I just remembered that I have a basketball game tonight," Ravi says. "I'm going to grab my coat and take off."

"You don't play on Friday nights," I say.

"It's a pickup game."

"Wait. Take this for later." Clay hands him a to-go container.

"Thanks, man." Ravi takes it and tosses me an approving glance before heading down the hall.

"I guess it's just us, sweetheart. Where should I set this up?"

"Let's eat in my office."

We set up dinner on the table in my office with the roses in the center. "This chicken marsala smells delicious," I say as Clay pulls a bottle of Pinot Noir, a candle, and a lighter out of the bag. "Oh my. Aren't you fancy."

"Just because you're busy doesn't mean you don't deserve romance." He lights the candle, turns off the overhead lights, and takes my hand, drawing me into a kiss. "How is it possible that I missed you so much today?"

He reclaims my lips, kissing me deeper, more thoroughly, holding me tight against him. I don't know what it is about us that makes us go from zero to a hundred in ten seconds flat, but we do, moaning and devouring. When he draws back on a series of feathery kisses, I stifle a whimper.

"God, baby, I've got no control with you. We need to stop, or I'll be having you for dinner."

A giggle slips out as he pulls out my chair. "Are you trying to take over the king of romance title from Dash?" I ask as I sit down. "Because you're doing a pretty good job of it."

He sits beside me. "Pretty good is not nearly good enough for you. I need to up my game."

Doesn't he know he's already sweeping me off my feet? I struggle to stay grounded every time we're together. "You *are* competitive."

"Even more so when it comes to you." He pours the wine and hands me a glass. "Here's to having more than Paris."

So much for staying grounded. We toast and kiss. It's just a sweet touch of our lips, nothing more, and it's absolutely perfect.

"This is delicious," I say as we eat. "Thank you for thinking of me and of Ravi, and thanks for answering the phones and bringing everyone gifts."

"It wasn't a big deal."

"It's a very big deal. Why *did* you answer my phones?"

"Because I wanted to help. The real question is, why don't you use an automated system to direct your calls like most companies do?"

"I don't like them." I sip my wine. "I think it's important to have a personal touch. Especially for a young company. It's frustrating when you can't reach a person or at least be told how long you'll have to wait to get a callback. It's just taking a while to find the right person."

"Why is that?"

I spear a piece of chicken with my fork. "I don't know. My ad is very specific, but everyone who applies is either over- or underqualified."

"What are you looking for?"

"Someone smart, with experience in an environment similar to ours. Someone who's capable of doing more than phones, but happy to answer them along with their other duties. A team player who can...You know what? Let me just show you the ad." I pull out my phone and scroll to the ad on the employment site. "This is what we need."

As he reads it, his expression turns serious. "I think I know what the problem is."

"You do? What is it?"

"You need a master's degree just to decipher this ad. It's too technical. Try to see this from an applicant's standpoint." He reads the ad aloud. *"Seamless orchestration of front-office functionalities within a dynamic environment focused on innovative technological solutions and data-driven methodologies."*

"Okay, I guess that *is* a little technical," I admit.

He glances at the ad again. "You talk about industry-specific vernacular and project initiatives. Come on, Pep. Does anyone even use the word *vernacular?*"

"Obviously *I* do."

"It sounds like you don't want a receptionist. You want a scientist that'll answer your phone," he teases. "I'm going to do you a favor and rewrite this ad. We'll find you someone smart and qualified."

"You've done enough already." I take my phone from him. "Don't you have anything better to do than hang around my work?"

"Stop worrying about me, and tell me about the meeting with Doc Bowry. How'd it go?"

Persuasive indeed. "It went great. He recommended our

company to a group of investors. Which reminds me, I'm sorry, but I need to go over a few reports tonight, so I can work on proposals over the weekend for the migraine device and a hands-free alternative to a mouse that's controlled by head movements and facial gestures for people with physical disabilities."

"Don't apologize. I think it's great, and I think *you* are nothing short of amazing. Do you usually work weekends?"

I push my food around on my plate. "If I say yes, does that make me a loser?"

"No. It makes you dedicated to a very important job. I usually work weekends, too."

"That's right, Sunday football. But not during your off season." I take a bite.

"I still work out in the off season, and I've got other commitments, and some of them fall on weekends. I've got a charity football game in March on a weekend, and I hope you'll go to it with me."

That surprises me. He's thinking about us being together in March? "Where is the game?"

"In Vegas."

"As in Elvis impersonators, slot machines, loud bars, and flashy lights? That's not really my thing."

"No, it's not. But it might be Reckless's thing." He covers my hand with his. "Don't make your decision now. Let's wait until you realize you can't live without me."

I laugh, but I don't think he's kidding, and I kind of love that confidence aimed at us.

"So, tell me, Pep, what do you do when you're not working?" he asks. "Do you have hobbies?"

"Not really. I like to read, but it usually leads to me thinking up a new project and doing research. I do like to watch *Jeopardy!*"

"No way. Me too. I told you we had things in common." He takes a bite. "What else? You seem crafty."

"I'm technically crafty, but not artistically. Are *you* crafty?"

"I'm not bad. We grew up making presents for each other instead of buying them, and that took a fair amount of craftiness. Although, my siblings would say they got too many turkey drawings."

"Turkey drawings?" I take another bite.

"Yeah, you know the ones where you trace your hand and make the fingers into feathers. Every holiday, that's what they got."

"Your Christmas present to your siblings was a hand turkey?" I laugh.

"The hand turkey was my gift of choice for many years, but we don't celebrate Christmas. My parents adopted celebrations of family and friends instead of religious holidays because we lived among so many different cultures when we were growing up."

"I love that idea. It's like the Wall of Love. Holidays that are inclusive, without divisions or boundaries. I think I'd like your parents."

He cocks his head, his eyes narrowing. "Now you're just trying to get to my heart, aren't you?"

I have a feeling my cheeks are going to hurt a lot from this man making me smile. "You are crafty. You spin everything into what you want to hear."

"When your parents make elaborate treasure maps that you have to decipher with your brothers and sister in order to find your holiday gifts, you learn many different types of craftiness."

"Seriously? What a great way to teach your kids to work together. Did they really do that?"

He sips his wine. "They did, and they still do. I look forward to it every year."

"That's amazing, although I'm sure it takes a lot of work to coordinate all those maps."

"Play your cards right, and I'll let you go on the treasure hunt with me this year."

Is he for real? "How about we make it through a weekend before thinking about holiday plans?"

He leans in and kisses me. "We're going to make it through much more than this weekend." He sits back. "But I have to warn you, deciphering the maps is complicated, since my brothers and sister and I don't all live in the same place. And if one of us or my grandparents or parents are traveling, then that's usually where we're going to end up. So you'll have to clear your schedule ahead of time."

"I'll make note of that." I drink my wine.

"I'm serious. Last year we surprised Flynn on Silver Island where his fiancée, Sutton, is from. You'd love Silver Island." He tells me about the small towns there, and then he tells me about Flynn and Sutton and how they work together at *Discovery Hour*, producing documentaries.

"I guess boss-subordinate romance is a family trend. Do Flynn and Sutton still work together? I can't imagine working with a romantic partner."

"They still work together, and they make a great team. Their newest series is called *Heart Stories*, and it's launching in February. We're all going to surprise them at my parents' house."

"Your family sounds very connected. I love that. Are any of

your other siblings engaged?"

"No. Vic was married to a great guy, Harvey Bauer. He was her boss, and sixteen years older than her."

"Wow, that's a big age gap."

"It was. She fell hard and fast for Harvey and went after him relentlessly. It worked out well. They had a shared love for the business, and they were really happy. Unfortunately, we lost him several years ago to a heart attack."

"That's awful. Your poor sister." My heart hurts for her. "The grief must have been unimaginable for her."

"I think it still is. After he died, she took over Blank Space Entertainment and threw herself into work with that same relentless determination she'd had when she was trying to get his attention, and she's never slowed down."

"Burying yourself in work is an easy way to hide from what you're missing."

"Is that what you do?" He holds my gaze.

There's something about Clay that makes me want to tell him all my secrets. I take a drink, considering my response, and decide not to go that deep. "Don't we all?" I hope it sounds off the cuff and go for a quick change in subject. "It sounds like relentlessness runs in your family."

"You have no idea how right you are." Clay tells me about his other relentless siblings, Seth, a business mogul with a serious side who was named *Forbes*'s Most Eligible Bachelor twice, and Noah, a marine biologist with a love of all things female who runs an exploratory park for kids. "Needless to say, you're not going anywhere near Noah."

"So…Seth is fair game?" I tease.

He scowls and pokes my ribs, making me laugh.

"Don't worry. One relentless Braden in my life is more than

enough."

"Damn right." He kisses me. "How did we go from hobbies and holidays to you and my brothers?"

"I don't know. But I like hearing about your family."

"I'm glad. But before you try to get me to marry you, you should know that my family likes to make up stories around bonfires, and you'll be expected to take part in them. There's singing and playing music and lots of homegrown fun."

"I'll keep that in mind while I'm trying to rope you in," I joke. "I love bonfires. Do you play an instrument?"

"Not well. My dad taught us all to play the guitar, but Seth and Vic are the only ones who are any good at it. What about you?"

I shake my head. "I'm sure it would be worse than my singing. What other hobbies do you have?"

"I don't have many beyond seeing family and friends, running, and working out."

"Running and working out are for your job. They don't count. What else?"

"I tried fishing out at Flynn's place. He lives on a lake in Port Hudson, New York. But I don't have the patience for it. I love snowboarding and skiing, but I don't go often because I can't risk an injury. Have you ever been?"

"No. I'm not very sporty."

"You'd look hot in ski pants." He leans in and kisses me. "But you'd look hotter naked by a roaring fire with the snow falling outside."

"You definitely deserve that king of romance crown."

As we eat and finish off the wine, we talk about family, hobbies we don't have, and things we've done or would like to do. We kiss between conversations, laughing and teasing each other. Every kiss makes me want more, and every laugh draws me deeper into him.

"That settles it," he says as we clean up. "Tomorrow we're going to knock around town and see if we can figure out hobbies for both of us."

"Okay." I have no idea what he thinks we'll find, but we had so much fun in Paris, I know we'll have a good time.

"Come to think of it, there is one more thing I like to do," he says as we clean up. "I mean, besides *you*."

A thrill skates through me. "What's that?"

He puts the last of the trash in the bag and sets it aside. "I was never into video games until they made me a character in one. Every once in a while I'll play that to get out of my own head, but it's not a go-to hobby."

"It must be cool to see yourself in a video game."

"It's a little weird, but it is cool. I'll show you one day."

"I know *nothing* about football, and I've never even played a video game." I finish my wine and set down my glass, leaning my hip against the table.

"I'll teach you everything you need to know. It'll be fun."

"Okay, but don't blame me if I suck."

He wraps his arms around me. "I love the way you *suck*."

His dirty talk is a match to my torch. I go up on my toes as he lowers his lips to mine, and our tongues start a sensual dance. He pushes his hands into my hair, his tongue probing and delving, reminding me of what he did to me this morning, and I'm here for it, arching and grinding into him. He tastes like sweet wine and white-hot passion. He's rock hard, and I'm vibrating with desire, but he slows his efforts from intoxicating ravishment to sweet tenderness. Just as I catch up, he draws away, whispering, "*Damn*, sweetheart," and touches his forehead to mine. "You need to get that report done."

My stomach twists. I don't want to stop, but I know if I don't get my work done, I'll think about it all night, and that won't be fun for either of us. "I *do*, but I won't be long."

"It's okay. Take your time. That's why I'm here, so you can get your work done and fit us in where you can. Can I use the computer in the lobby? I'll get a jump on that ad, and we can hang out when you finish."

"Yes, but you don't have to rewrite the ad."

He cocks a brow, amused. "I do if you want to find a receptionist." He steps back, his gaze dragging slowly down my body, leaving a trail of blazing heat. When his eyes meet mine again, they're fiery blue. "I need to get out of here before I bend you over that desk." He gives me a quick kiss and heads out of my office.

I stand frozen in place, my body whirling like a hurricane. How does he get me revved up so fast? Never in my life have I *wanted* the way he makes me want. I know all about chemical reactions and hormones, but as I stand here on shaky legs, this feels too big to be just that. I take a deep breath and huff it out, forcing myself to get to work so I'm not here too late.

I sit down behind my desk and pull up the reports for the products we want to pitch. But I'm not just swamped with lust. I feel guilty about working when he came all this way to see me. He's being so supportive.

And those kisses…

I squeeze my thighs together to quell the ache he stirs.

I can't just push work aside because a guy makes me hot. I have responsibilities.

But Clay's not just some guy. He's everything I never knew I wanted.

And he'll still be here when I'm done working.

His deep voice whispers through my mind, *I need to get out of here before I bend you over that desk.*

And *now* I'm picturing him doing just that.

Clay

I pace the lobby, trying to get my cock to calm the fuck down. I'm not here for that.

Then maybe you shouldn't have her panties stashed at your place.

My dick jerks with the thought, and I grit my teeth, looking down at the offending bulge in my pants. *Get control of yourself. You're like a fucking teenage horndog.*

I close my eyes, thinking about my contract extension, my aching shoulder, and the other quarterback gunning for my job. That takes the edge off.

Relieved, I rake a hand through my hair and go to the computer, needing a distraction to keep my mind off my gorgeous pantyless girl down the hall. I pull up a Word document and realize I have no fucking experience writing employment ads.

Time to call in the big guns. I pull out my phone and call Seth. He answers on the second ring.

"Hi, Clay. What's up?"

My fucking cock. "I need some help writing an ad for a receptionist job."

"Why?"

"Because I'm helping Pepper find a receptionist."

Seth laughs. "You're with Pepper, and *this* is what you're doing on a Friday night? Bro, you have definitely lost your touch. Maybe you do need a wingman."

"Shut the fuck up and help me."

"I'm a little concerned," Seth says with amusement. "She's a smart woman. Why is she trusting this to you?"

"Because I offered. Are you going to help me or—" I swallow my words as Pepper slinks down the hall like a seductive cat on the prowl. Her hazel eyes are locked on me as she comes around the desk and spins the chair I'm sitting in so I'm facing her.

"Clay?" Seth says as she grabs the button on my jeans and yanks them open.

"Yeah. Never mind. I've got to go." I end the call, and she unzips my jeans as I put my phone on the desk. "Done working already?"

She shakes her head. "I'll catch up with work in the morning. I was too distracted by thoughts of you bending me over the desk." She says it so innocently, my cock jerks again. "Commando," she purrs. "I see you're a man of your word."

"Don't ever doubt it."

"Seems like you should be rewarded for your honesty." She sinks to her knees and licks her lips.

"Such a fucking temptress." I push my jeans down, and she fists my cock. Then she uses that sinful mouth on it, licking and sucking, stroking and taking me deep. "That's my girl," I grit out through clenched teeth as she works me tighter. "That's it. Suck harder." She does, and it tears a primal growl from someplace deep inside me. "So fucking good." Her eyes are locked on mine, brimming with pleasure. "Scoot back, baby. I need to fuck your mouth."

She gives me space to stand, and I rise to my feet, caressing her jaw. She rolls her lower lip between her teeth, looking innocent and sexy at once. "You're so damn beautiful, on your knees for me. Tell me if I go too hard."

"You won't." She guides my cock into her mouth.

I tangle my hands in her hair, thrusting into her hot, willing mouth again and again. She moves with me, her eyes locked on me like a fucking fantasy. I drive into her harder, faster, until I'm ready to blow. "Your mouth is too fucking perfect." I grab the base of my cock and pull out. "I want to make you come, and I want to finish inside you."

Her wicked smile has my dick aching as I lift her to her feet and crush my mouth to hers, kissing the ever-loving hell out of her. Then I spin her around. "Hands on the desk, baby." When she does what I say, I yank her dress up, baring her beautiful ass, and sink down, needing to taste her. I lick her pussy. "*Christ,* you're so fucking sweet."

She looks over her shoulder, her eyes blazing. "*Fuck me,*" she demands, breathless and needy.

Hearing those words from that sweet mouth nearly does me in. I grab a condom from my wallet and make quick work of sheathing my cock and aligning our bodies. Clutching her hips, I drive into her. "*Yes,*" she cries out, her pleasure-drenched voice sending me into a frenzy of desire. I pound into her, reaching around to work her clit, earning moans and pleas. "*Harder...Ohmygod...Faster...Yes—*" Her pussy grips my cock like a vise, and my name flies from her lips as she rides out her pleasure. Her moans rise around us, and I grit my teeth against the need to come, staying with her until she shudders around me.

"I need your mouth." I pull out and turn her around, taking

her in a ruthless kiss as I lift her onto the desk. I guide her legs around my waist and bury myself to the hilt in one hard thrust. I curse at the excruciating pleasure consuming me, and she cries out, "*Again!*"

My restraint snaps, and we fuck like we'll never get another chance. We're rough and animalistic. I reclaim her mouth in a merciless kiss as she shatters, her pussy pulsing around my cock, her hips bucking. I'm enraptured in her, lost in a hailstorm of sensations, but the greedy bastard in me needs to see her face. I grab her hair, tugging her mouth away from mine. Her eyes are wild, and as her body clamps around my cock, a sinful sound flies from her lungs, shooting through me like lightning, catapulting me into sheer, mind-blowing ecstasy.

We thrust and grind, clinging to each other, our bodies jerking with aftershocks, both of us breathing hard. When we finally still, I lift my face from the tangle of her hair. Our eyes connect with a thrum of heat, and I swear I feel something deep and moving weaving between us. But in the next breath, we're laughing, and she's burying her face in my shoulder. I'm falling so hard for this incredible woman, and I'm so caught up in us, *I love you* nearly tumbles out, but my gaze catches on the security camera near the door, and reality comes rushing in. "Reckless?"

"*Hm?*"

"Does your building have security cameras in here, or are they yours? Because I think we just made a sex tape."

She gasps and whips her head around, looking up at the camera. "Shit. It's *ours*, but Ravi has access to it."

"Hey, Ravi," I call out, waving to the camera.

"*Clay!*" She smacks my chest. "We have to delete it!"

"No way. I'm taking that footage home with me."

She laughs. "You are *not*."

"Hell yeah, I am. Bet I can sell it for a pretty penny." I absolutely love making her squirm. "Just one more place to your ever-growing Never Have I Ever list."

"Ohmygod. Who have I become?" She presses her face to my shoulder.

I give her hair a gentle tug, bringing those shimmering eyes to mine. "Who you were always meant to be. My sexy scientist."

Chapter Twenty-Two

Pepper

I wake up Saturday morning to my empty bed but not an empty house. The faint smell of coffee hangs in the air, and the clothes we'd left strewn around the room in our haste to get naked are draped over the chair by the window with the sketch of us from Paris. It feels like a dream, that Clay is here, shattering my comfort zones one at a time. I've never had a man spend the night at my house. I lie still, surrounded by his scent on my sheets and my body, expecting to feel strange or anxious about him being here, but I don't. I *like* seeing his clothes on my chair and knowing he's downstairs. That should bring anxiety, too, but it doesn't. It's *that* thought that rattles me.

I climb out of bed, put on the T-shirt he wore under his sweater yesterday, and head into the bathroom. I use the toilet, and as I brush my teeth, I see the evidence of our wild night in the red mark peeking out from beneath the collar of his shirt. I touch it absently, thinking about last night.

After much back-and-forth, Clay somehow convinced me to let him download the footage of our sexy office encounter—*We'll laugh about it when we're old and gray*—before deleting the original and the backup. He talks like we're a given and we have a future, and he makes it easy to get caught up in it with him. I know we have things to talk about and figure out, but I've never felt like this, and I'm not ready to rock the boat.

I put on my fuzzy slippers and head downstairs. There's Motown music coming from the kitchen. I peer around the corner and see Clay dancing in his black boxer briefs by the stove, singing along with "Ain't Too Proud to Beg" as he cracks eggs into a pan. Holy cow, the man can dance, but he sings as off-key as I do! He cracks another egg and spins around, catching me watching him.

He grins and belts out the lyrics, dancing over to me. He takes my hand and spins me around, making me laugh. "Sing with me, Reckless."

"Trust me, you don't want that. I'm worse than you are."

"Impossible." He sings louder, holding my hand and dancing around me. "Come on, baby. Let me hear you sing."

I shake my head.

When the song ends, he turns off the stove and draws me into his arms. "You look adorable in my shirt."

"You look adorable in my kitchen."

"I took a picture of the sunrise for you."

Sadness moves through me. "You should've woken me up to watch it with you."

"I kept you up late. You needed your sleep so that brilliant brain can function at work this morning."

I'm touched that he remembered.

His lips find mine as "My Girl" comes on. We dance and kiss and laugh, and he sings every word to me. I *feel* like his girl, and I *like* it. When "Last Night" by Morgan Wallen comes on, one of my favorite songs, I have to ask, "What are you listening to that has Motown and country?"

"One of my playlists. My parents love Motown. I grew up

watching them dance to it." He starts singing the country song, about me calling my mom and him calling my bluff and how he wouldn't trade my love for anything else. It's just a song, but I get swept up in it, and in him, like I do with everything else he does, and I start singing about how we're not over yet.

"That's my girl!" He *whoops* and spins me around, and my insecurities about my singing fall away. When the song changes, he tugs me against him and runs his finger along the collar of my shirt. "You're marked again."

"Mm-hmm. I have an overzealous…" I scramble for the right word. *"Friend."*

His brows slant. "Like hell you do. You have an overzealous boyfriend."

"Aren't you a little old for that word?" I tease.

"I'll give you *old.*" He slaps my butt, then kisses me. We fall into a sexy slow dance. "I don't care what you call me as long as you know you're mine and are off-limits to other guys."

"Then it goes both ways."

"That's cool. I'm not into guys."

I roll my eyes.

"You know I wouldn't have it any other way." He kisses me again, his hands slipping beneath the back of my shirt. A wolfish grin appears. "You're naked under here. Are you trying to make me crazy?"

I laugh as he backs me up against the counter. "That was my plan."

"You wicked thing." He brushes his scruff along my cheek. "I could get used to mornings like this."

So could I, but…

That nugget of truth bears a reminder for both of us. "Don't get too comfortable, Braden. You have time now, but things will change when it's football season again."

"Let's not worry about that. We'll figure things out as we go."

"I'm not great at not having a plan," I say honestly.

"As I recall, not only were you excellent at not having a plan in Paris, but it was your idea."

"Yes, but that was a one-day fling. This is…something else."

"Yes, we are." He kisses my neck, sending tingles down my chest. "Figuring it out as we go *is* a plan. This is new for both of us. There's no playbook, and I know it's not what you're used to, but neither was having sex in your lobby, and you enjoyed that."

Boy, did I ever.

"Don't stress, babe. Let's just enjoy each other and see where it takes us. Think you can do that?"

"I can try."

"Good girl." He kisses me, then turns back to the stove. "Hope you like scrambled eggs."

"I do. Do you want toast?"

"Sure. How long do you have to work this morning?"

I put the bread in the toaster. "Just a couple of hours."

"Perfect. Text me when you're done, and I'll meet you at your office. You can show me around town, and we can go in search of hobbies."

"Hobbies," I repeat, thinking about how much I learned about him yesterday.

"Yeah, you know. Those things we don't have. Maybe we'll find something we'll both enjoy."

"I like that idea. What are you going to do while I'm at work?"

"I met a kid who plays for UVA yesterday at the track. His

name is Ben. I told him I'd run some drills with him when I have time. I'll text him and see if he's still up for it."

"That's really nice of you."

"I love working with kids, and he was excited to meet me. I think it'll make his day." He draws me into his arms again. "Now, how about I make yours?"

"Yes, please," I whisper, and pull his mouth to mine.

He lifts me onto the counter, kissing me like he can't get enough, and I'm pretty sure I never will, because the way he kisses makes me desperate for more. He whips my shirt off, lowering his mouth to my breast, sending heat searing down my core. Grabbing his head, I arch into him. *"Clay."*

"I've got you, baby." He moves a hand between my legs and crushes his mouth to mine, fracturing my ability to think. Our kisses are hot and hungry as his fingers work their magic, taking me up, up, *up,* until my entire body tingles and burns, and all at once my orgasm crashes into me. I cry out, and he lowers his mouth between my legs, using his teeth, tongue, and fingers, driving me out of my mind. My vision blurs as waves of pleasure pummel me. I'm gasping and moaning, each wave more intense than the last.

The smell of burning eggs hits me. "Clay," I pant out, but he's relentless in his pursuit of my pleasure, feasting and teasing, sending me right up to the peak again. I cry out as smoke billows from the stove, but we don't stop. He intensifies his efforts, and I bury my hands in his hair, rocking against his mouth, unwilling to be deterred from enjoying everything he has to give.

Chapter Twenty-Three

Clay

Ben is waiting for me at the field when I arrive, and he looks as excited as he was yesterday. "Hey, Ben. How's it going?"

"How's it going? I'm standing here with *you*. How do you think it's going? I still can't believe you texted."

I set down the cones I bought at the sports store when I picked up the balls for Chris and Min. "I told you I would."

"Yeah, but with most people, that doesn't mean shit."

"I'm not most people. If I say I'll do something, then short of an act of God stopping me, it's going to happen. You look a little tired. Were you out late partying last night?"

"No. My mother had to work, and my little brother got sick. I stayed over so she could get some sleep after she got home."

"Your mom works nights?"

"Sometimes. She works at a club when they need her."

"Sounds like your family's lucky to have you around. Is your brother okay?"

"Yeah. He just had a bug and felt like he was going to puke every time he lay down."

I eye him more closely. "Are you feeling okay?"

"Yeah. I'm just a little tired. I'll be fine once I start running.

I always am."

He reminds me of myself at that age. "In that case, why don't we hit the track and warm up?"

"You're running with me?" he asks.

"I'll start out that way," I say as we head to the track. "But I'm sure I'll leave you in my dust."

He scoffs. "In your dreams."

Ben and I practice for nearly two hours, working on tracking the ball, speed, and running drills. As I blow the whistle for the last of the footwork drills, he sprints straight toward the first cone. He maneuvers around it, runs toward the second one, and cuts to the right beyond the third.

"That's it!" I call out as he circles back to the fourth cone.

He cuts right, stopping on a dime when he reaches the cone, then sprints at a ninety-degree angle, simulating a drag route, which is when a receiver runs a few yards downfield, then turns toward center field and runs parallel to the line of scrimmage. His direction changes can use a little work, but they're strong.

"Finish hard!" I holler as he sprints to the next cone, stops, and cuts around the last one, finishing the drill with a hard sprint. "Great job."

Ben slows to a walk, his hands on his hips as he catches his breath. "Thanks, man. I know I need to work on changing directions."

"They're a little rough, but they're good. We can do some jab steps and shuffle drills and some other things that'll help with that."

His eyes widen. "You'll run more drills with me?"

"If our schedules align. You still think I'm going to leave you hanging?"

"No, man, but...you're a pro, and I'm just—"

"I'm going to stop you right there. No negative self-talk. I put my pants on one leg at a time, just like you. Nobody starts out as a pro. It takes hard work and dedication, and you've got both. I had personal coaches to whip my ass into shape." The second the words leave my lips, I regret saying them. This kid doesn't need a reminder of how much I had or the things he doesn't. "I needed those coaches, because I didn't grow up playing on Pee Wee teams and working my way up. I grew up overseas, and struggled to find teams to join."

"I know. I read all about you and how you grew up living in huts and shit. That must've been wild."

"Yeah, it was, but it didn't make for an easy path to learn the sport. Listen, I've got to run in a minute. I know you're busy with classes and work, but do you have any free time during the day when you can squeeze in a workout? Or do you want to stick to early mornings?"

We go over our schedules and find a few times when we can get together to train during the day. I have just enough time to get back to my place to shower and plan out my day with Pepper before heading into town to meet her.

"Stop apologizing. I'm glad you had to work this morning," I say as Pepper and I leave her office, heading for the shops. After noticing a few too many glances at the restaurant the other night and in the sports store yesterday, I decided to try to blend in. I didn't shave the last two days, and I'm wearing a baseball cap and an old sweatshirt instead of my expensive coat. I don't want to draw any extra attention while we're out.

"You needed a break from me already?" Her brow furrows.

"How can you even ask that after the way I ravaged you and burned our breakfast?" I hug her against my side and kiss her temple. "Well, your breakfast. I was busy eating mine."

"*Clay,*" she says in that adorably innocent and exasperated way she has.

I chuckle. "I meant I was glad you had to work because I had a great time working out with Ben. I miss working with kids, and he's incredible. He's got a full ride at UVA, but he's still working to help his mom make ends meet, and he's driven to be the best. He's out there every day pushing himself to be better on the field. We're going to try to work out more this week."

"That's great. You sound excited."

"I am. I had forgotten how thrilling it was to be on that side of the game."

"That's great, but what do you mean by *that side?*"

"Before going pro. When the game is your shiny brass ring, and you live and breathe for it. Just being around his enthusiasm and determination is invigorating."

"Does that mean it's not that way for you anymore?"

We walk around the corner, and I see the gallery I wanted to take her into. "I still love the game, but it's complicated. When you go pro, things change. At some point it goes from being all about the game to being about the game and the business of it, with sponsorships and other obligations. But I'm sure that's probably true of every profession in its own way. Look at how much you do now that you own the company."

"Yeah. It's a lot."

"Well, if you can keep your hands off me long enough, we'll get your ad done tonight and hopefully find you a receptionist quickly."

"I'll try to behave," she teases.

"Please don't." I kiss her as we come to the art gallery. "This is our first stop." I open the door and follow her in.

"I thought we were trying to figure out hobbies."

"We are. I've got a whole day of ideas planned, but your office has no pictures on the walls. I thought we could look for some."

"You really do notice every little thing, don't you?"

"When it comes to you, I do." As we walk through the gallery, we point out pictures, but I can tell Pepper doesn't love any of them. "Why is your office naked, when your home is dressed up so pretty?"

"I don't know. I've looked for artwork, but nothing speaks to me. I mean, look at this painting." She motions to a landscape. "It's beautiful, but I don't feel a connection to it. I don't know where that place is. I didn't grow up there or have anything meaningful happen there or dream of going there. It's just a pretty picture."

Ah, she's granting me another peek behind her veil. "Most people buy art *because* it's pretty, but you want to feel it in your heart. Like you did with the Wall of Love. Why did you feel so connected to that wall?"

"I think because it stands for the one thing that's important to me."

"Love?"

"In a broad sense, yes. But more specifically, overcoming boundaries and loving people for *who* they are first and foremost."

I remember what she said about dating apps and realize this is the true peek behind her veil. I wonder if the pain she experienced in college did more than turn her against dating athletes, and had also shaped her thoughts about love. Or if her views are driven by what she saw Amber go through when she was growing up with epilepsy. I have a feeling those are just two pieces of a much more complicated picture.

"It would make the world a better place, that's for sure. What's special enough to you to be forever memorialized in a painting or picture?"

Her eyes brighten. "That's easy. My mom's smile every time I walk into her kitchen, because it always makes me happy, and my dad's hand, because holding it has always felt safe. The lake near my parents' house where my dad and I used to sail the boats we built and the lab my dad built me in the loft of the barn. I can still remember what it felt like to sneak out there when I needed an escape. And the Stardust Café, because of all the great memories I have there with friends and family. The creek where Sable and I used to go for walks because she'd play her guitar and tell me all her secrets, which were always way more exciting than mine. I felt really close to her there." She gazes at the painting like she's watching a scene unfold within it. "And the tree on the hill by the old church in town."

"Why that tree?"

"Because while my mom was shopping, my sisters and Axsel and I would run around there and play tag and other silly games." Her expression warms. "Around that old tree, it didn't matter if Gracie was too serious, or Sable or Brindle too brash. It was okay for Morgyn to be lost in a dream and Amber to be reading under the tree, being her careful self, and Axsel to be the little yappy boy he was."

"And you?"

Her gaze softens. "I just remember feeling like I did when

we were in Paris. Like I could just be me."

"You were pretty stressed around your sisters and Axsel when we were there. You were afraid they'd find out about us."

She lowers her gaze for a second, and as she meets mine, that slightly bashful smile appears. "I wasn't talking about when I was with them in Paris. I meant when it was just you and me."

Suddenly my chest feels too small for the emotions I'm keeping trapped there. "Aw, sweetheart." I draw her into my arms. "That's how I feel around you. Like I can just be myself, and not who everyone else needs me to be. I want you to feel that way all the time with me."

"I do, most of the time." She lowers her voice to a playful whisper. "But you keep bringing out someone in me I didn't know existed, and that takes some getting used to."

"My hidden temptress?" I hold her gaze. "I happen to be very fond of that side of you."

"Me too."

That feels like a victory. I kiss her and take her hand, heading for the exit. "Come on, Reckless. We need to hit the craft shop before we try out our first potential hobby."

"Why the craft shop?"

"To get a boatbuilding kit. It may not have been a hobby for you, but it'll be fun. We can build it together and float it on the lake tomorrow."

"We didn't build them from kits," she says as we hit the sidewalk. "We designed them and built them from scratch, using Styrofoam and other things we had lying around the house. The only things we bought were the motor and batteries, a battery pack with leads, and a few other supplies we didn't have lying around."

"Of course you did," I say with a laugh. "Well, there's nothing like designing on the fly. Let's go see what we can come up with."

Her face lights up. "How about we make it even more fun?"

"And build it naked?" I waggle my brows. "I don't think we'll get much building done, but I'm game."

She laughs. "I'm sure you are. Seeing as you're ridiculously competitive, I was thinking about making it a competition. We each build a boat and see whose works better."

"Seeing as *I'm* ridiculously competitive? You were valedictorian of your graduating class in high school and at UVA. You're every bit as competitive as I am. You just cloak it well with sweetness."

"Did you google me?" she asks with shock.

"I might've peeked at a thing or two when I was researching places to take you today. I think you might have an edge with this one, my R and D queen."

"Are you afraid of a little competition, Mr. Perfect?"

"Never." I haul her against me. "But call me that again, and I might just have to show you who's boss. And for that, you *will* be naked."

"I don't know if I should be scared or turned on."

"Given how you loved being at my mercy in Paris, I'd say turned on."

Heat flares in her eyes. "In that case, whatever you say, Mr. Perfect."

"*Reckless*," I grit out, and kiss her senseless.

Chapter Twenty-Four

Pepper

Clay wasn't kidding when he said he'd researched places to go today. Our first potential hobby is bowling, and it's bustling with children's birthday parties and rowdy kids running to and from the snack counter, giggling and shouting. I didn't even realize there was a bowling alley here.

We scarf down hot dogs and nachos, and as we put on bowling shoes, I'm still reeling from our trip to the craft store. We had a blast taking separate carts and gathering supplies, trying to keep our design ideas secret. But my competitive man didn't play fair. He cornered me in the packing material aisle, smelling good enough to eat, talking dirty, and kissing me until my knees weakened and my ability to think wavered. I was *this close* to divulging my plans for my boat, but I held firm and pried myself out of his arms.

Clay is lucky. All he has to do is pull down the shirt he has on under his hoodie to cover his erection, while I'm stuck walking around with damp panties.

Damn him.

I have to admit, I love his taunts and the way he appreciates my intelligence *and* brings out my inner sexual being. I didn't know that was possible. In my experience, if I was seen as a sexual being, my intelligence went unnoticed, and vice versa. I'm starting to realize I'd drawn a hard line between the two, but Clay makes me feel whole and appreciated on both levels. What's even more amazing is that he noticed my competitive nature, when I thought I'd hidden it so well. Nobody has ever taken note of it except Ravi, and he only sees it in regard to my work. My family thinks I did well in school because that's who I am.

The truth is so much more complicated.

Now that the competitive cat is out of the bag, there's no need to downplay it. I finish putting on my shoes and pop to my feet. "Prepare to lose, Braden."

"I thought you said you haven't bowled since you were a kid."

"I haven't, but I'm still going to beat you."

"We'll see about that." He pushes to his feet, looking even more rugged with his shaggy scruff and baseball cap. I've never been into scruffy guys, but I have a feeling Clay could grow a thick and wild beard and a beer belly and I'd still find him impossibly hot. His quick wit, thoughtfulness, and intelligence don't rely on his looks. Of course, his charming dimples and piercing blue eyes don't hurt.

He puts a hand on my back, drawing me from my thoughts as he leans in and says, "Keep looking at me like that, and these little kids are going to see things they shouldn't."

The innocent faces of the little girls playing in the next lane should be enough of a reason for me to give him grief for even saying something like that. But the truth is, I love the way he sees my hidden thoughts and the way he wants me even at inappropriate times. Not only do I refrain from giving him a hard time, but I also can't stop the grin from tugging at my lips.

Oh God. I'm turning into Brindle.

"What's that grin for, Reckless?" He smirks. "Thinking about all the fun things I could do to you?"

I school my expression. "You might want to get your mind out of the gutter so your balls don't end up there."

"It's nice to know you're thinking about my balls." He pats my butt. "You're up first."

He sits down and types our names into the machine that keeps score—Reckless and Winner.

I choose my ball, and it takes a minute for me to remember proper positioning.

"Come on, Pep. You've got this," Clay cheers.

I take a deep breath, tuning out the din of the other players, the crashing of pins, and the rumbling of balls. I set my eyes on the center of the lane as I swing my arms back, step forward, and release the ball. It rolls straight down the middle of the lane, knocking over nine pins. Clay cheers, and the little girls beside us clap. I smile at them as I turn around.

"Are you sure you haven't played since you were a kid?" Clay asks as I pick up another ball.

"*Yes.* I didn't get a strike, did I?" I say matter-of-factly.

He looks at me incredulously. "Did you play me, Pep? Were you in a league?"

"No. I didn't like going to parties, so I'd go bowling with Ravi and some of our friends from Science Club." As I line up for my next shot, I notice the little blond girl next to me is trying to mimic my stance. "Hey," I say gently, bringing her eyes to mine. "The ball will go in whatever direction your thumb is pointing when you let go, but don't tell him that." I motion with my head to Clay.

The little girl giggles. "I won't. Thank you."

"Good luck." I wait for her to take her turn.

She knocks down four pins.

"Good job! That was awesome," I exclaim.

She beams at me as the other girls and the woman who's with them cheer her on.

I get myself situated again and take my turn, knocking down the last pin. Clay and all the little girls cheer. Now I'm the one who's beaming as I come off the lane.

"That's my girl," Clay says as he rises to his feet. "It's a shame I'll have to beat you." He grabs a ball and lines up. He looks so serious as he releases the ball. It starts rolling straight but veers left just before reaching the pins, knocking down five of them.

"That was great," I cheer.

"I'm just getting warmed up." He rubs his hands together and grabs another ball.

"It's okay. I kind of like you not so perfect."

"Don't get your hopes up, Reckless."

A brown-haired girl with pigtails is getting ready to take her turn beside us, and the blond girl is whispering in her ear. The brown-haired girl looks at Clay and says, "I won't," to her friend. The three other little girls run to the blonde, begging to know the secret she shared.

Clay looks at me with a knowing smile and winks.

As we play, we have good turns and bad turns. We laugh with the girls, cheering on each other and them, and learn it's the blond girl's seventh birthday. After I win the game, receiving cheers from the girls and accolades from Clay, he buys them each an ice cream, and they all hug us goodbye.

"That was so much fun," I say as we drive out of the parking lot.

He reaches over and takes my hand. "I have a feeling anything we do together will be fun, my sporty girl."

"Bowling is hardly sporty."

"Don't fool yourself, Sporty Spice. It takes strength and skill." He kisses the back of my hand. "Are you ready for our next adventure?"

"I can't wait."

We work our way through Clay's list of potential hobbies. We try miniature golf and Frisbee. I royally suck at both, while he plays like a champ, but it was fun. While we're at the park, he points to birds flying overhead and suggests birdwatching. We share a good laugh. Neither of us can imagine staring at birds for hours at a time. We end up at Paint and Sip, where we sit across from each other drinking wine while attempting to paint a vase of colorful flowers.

"How's it coming? Are you the next van Gogh?" Clay asks as I put more paint on my brush.

"I'm not going to win any painting contests, and I'm having flashbacks to almost getting a B in art class, but I am having fun."

"You say B like it's a bad thing."

"It was for me. I needed an A." I start painting the last flower petals. "I begged my teacher to let me redo the project, and I worked my butt off until it was perfect."

"What was the project?"

"To create a three-dimensional image using words as art. We couldn't draw lines. Everything had to be created using only words. Everyone else made these beautiful pictures of their pets and barns and landscapes and all sorts of things. I kept trying to draw something pretty the way everyone else did, but my brain doesn't work with soft, flowing images. When I redid the project, I had the hardest time visualizing anything so I could draw it. Then my dad found me crying, and he told me a B was good enough, but I knew I wouldn't make valedictorian without an A."

"And you think I'm competitive?" He arches a brow. "So what did you do?"

"I listened to my father." I dab my paintbrush in paint to put the finishing touches on my painting. "He said not to worry about drawing something pretty and to draw whatever I wanted to, even if I didn't think anyone else would like it."

"Dad to the rescue. What did you draw?"

"The lab he made me in the loft. It made me happy, and I didn't have to compare a dog or landscape to anyone else's drawing, because nobody else drew my lab."

"How'd it come out?"

"It was pretty spectacular, if I do say so myself. I got an A, but more importantly, I learned a valuable lesson about not comparing myself to other people. That lab made *me* happy, and I'm sure that's why I was able to draw it so well using words. I went from dreading the drawing to creating tangles of wires from the word *wire* written over and over, and fitting all the letters of microscope into the drawing of one." I set down my paintbrush. "But *this* is not going to get me an A." I hold up my painting.

"What are you talking about? That's fantastic. I'm framing that sucker and putting it up on my wall."

"Yeah, right." I set it back down. "Let me see yours."

"Okay, but it's not nearly as good as yours."

He holds up his painting, and my jaw drops. He painted *me*, and it's really good. In it, I'm smiling, and it looks like my eyes are, too. My hair is tousled, and it cascades over my shoulders in several shades of golden brown that look just like my real hair, right down to my natural blond highlights.

"*Clay*, you're really talented, but you were supposed to paint the flowers."

"I painted what makes me happy."

I get all warm and squishy inside. "Where did you learn to paint like that?"

"My mom taught me. I think it was out of necessity."

"Why?"

"She said I used to wake Noah from his naps because I was too rambunctious, and she figured out early on that if I had a project that took a lot of focus, I'd stick with it until I nailed it."

"That's another thing we have in common."

"Sure is. When Noah went down for a nap, that became my painting time. She'd set up pictures of football fields, football games, the players, and I'd paint them."

"It's amazing that you can still do it so well."

"I never stopped. When I can't sleep, it's my fallback to get my brain to settle down."

"How come you didn't mention it as a hobby when I asked if you were crafty?"

He shrugs. "I don't consider it a hobby. It's more of a vice."

"That's one heck of a vice." I walk over to admire his painting. "Can I have that painting?"

"It'll cost you." He pulls me into a kiss. His phone chimes, and he pulls it out of his pocket, glancing at the screen. "It's Seth. I was on the phone with him asking for pointers for writing your ad when you came out to the lobby last night. I forgot to call him back."

"You called your brother for help with my ad?"

"Yes. I wanted to write the best ad I could, and he's an expert at hiring people."

My chest warms at that. "You did that for me? That's so sweet."

"I'd do anything for you." He reads the text, then turns the phone toward me.

I'm still hung up on what he said, but I force myself to focus and read his brother's text.

Seth: *Still need help with that ad, or did Pepper realize you can barely spell your own name?*

"What? Give me that." I take his phone and thumb out, *Hi Seth, this is Pepper. Not only is Clay smart, but look what he painted.* I take a picture of Clay's painting and send it with the message. Clay's phone chimes a minute later.

Seth: *How much did he pay you to say he's smart?*

Clay chuckles.

I think about how Sable would respond and quickly thumb out a response.

Me: *He doesn't pay me, but I'm sure he'll thank me later.*

I send a winking emoji, and my heart races as his response rolls in.

Seth: *You should ask for money. I'm sure it will last longer.*

I'm so far out of my league, my head is spinning. I shove the phone into Clay's hand. "You'd better take this. I was trying to be coy, but I'm not good at that. I haven't even met him yet. What's he going to think of me?"

"He's going to adore you as much as I do." Clay reads the texts and responds.

Clay: *Stop flirting with my girl.*

"I don't give a damn what he thinks. Seeing you stick up for me like that turns me on." He pulls me into a hard kiss.

"In that case, give me your phone. I have more to say."

"There's my naughty temptress."

As he lowers his lips to mine, I notice the person who works there watching us and say, "Behave. We have an audience."

He lets out a frustrated growl, and we quickly clean up and leave with our paintings in hand, kissing as we hurry out to the Rover. We put the paintings on the back seat, and Clay pins me against the side of the vehicle, taking me in a ravenous kiss that makes my every nerve ending flame. His hardness is deliciously tempting, and his scruff tickles my skin, making me crave it between my legs. I *almost* forget we're in the middle of a parking lot.

I'm stuck in a mental tug-of-war, wanting more and knowing I should step back to keep from becoming an even bigger spectacle. Before I can gather the strength to break the kiss, he does it for me, and our eyes lock. The desire and restraint warring in his nearly unravel me.

"I think we found a hobby we both enjoy," he says.

I laugh softly, clutching his sweatshirt, telling myself to let go. But the desire burning in his eyes has me throwing caution to the wind and leaning in for more.

"Not here, sweetheart," he grits out. "You have a reputation to uphold, and I'm not about to spoil it."

"Right. Of course," I stammer, grateful one of us is thinking straight.

We stop on the way home to buy a gaming system and pizza because Clay is dead set on teaching me to play the video game in which he is a character, and we are both hungry. We start a fire in the fireplace, put a blanket and pillows on the floor, and eat the pizza in front of the fire. Then he teaches me how to play the video game.

Or rather, he *tries* to teach me how to play.

We've been playing for half an hour and laughing our butts off, because I am every bit as bad as I told him I would be. There are a million things to remember, and it's too much to keep track of.

"Throw the ball," he says *ever so helpfully* as his player rushes my quarterback.

"I'm trying!" I feverishly push the buttons. "Stop running at my guy!"

"That's how you play the game."

His player sacks my quarterback, and I yell, *"Nooo!"* He cracks up, and I throw a pillow at him. "This is so hard."

"You're doing great."

I roll my eyes. "I am *not*."

"I'll tell you what. I'll throw in some incentives. We'll play touchdowns for clothing. Every time one of us gets a touchdown, the other one has to take something off."

"That's hardly fair. I've gotten one touchdown to your five."

"Okay. I'll make it easier." He stands up and whips off his sweatshirt and the T-shirt he has on beneath it.

"What are you doing?" My gaze skids down his chest to the hard planes of his abdomen as he unbuttons his jeans and pushes them down.

"Making it fair." He tugs off his jeans and socks and sits down in his boxer briefs.

"*How* is this fair? You know I can't think beyond you sitting there practically naked." I hook my finger in the neckline of my sweater, pulling it away from my skin.

"What's the matter, Pep? A little hot?"

"If I were sitting here in my underwear, you wouldn't be able to concentrate, either." After I say it, understanding hits me. "That's exactly what you want me to do, isn't it? Well, you're out of luck, buddy."

He laughs and holds his hands up in surrender. "I'm just trying to make it fair. Now you only have to get *one* touchdown to win the game."

I narrow my eyes. "You'd love that, wouldn't you?"

"Is that a trick question?" He flashes a wolfish grin but quickly wipes it away. "Get your head in the game, Montgomery. This is your chance to score."

I raise my brows.

"In the *game*. Geez, one-track mind much?"

"It's your fault. You turned me into some kind of sex maniac."

"Maybe it's the other way around," he says with a ridiculously serious expression.

"I don't think so." I try to concentrate as we start playing, and I'm determined to win because...*Clay naked?* Yes, please. My player chases his down the field.

"The truth is, I've never been unable to keep my hands *or* my mouth off a woman the way I can't with you."

So much for my concentration. My guy tackles his runner, and I cheer. "Yes!"

"You got me sidetracked thinking about touching you."

"Stop talking about it," I say as my player chases his down the field, but his guy cuts to the right, and I can't catch up as he sprints into the end zone.

"Yeah, baby!" Clay pumps his fist and looks smugly at me. "That'll be one article of clothing, please."

I take off my sweater and throw it at him, leaving me in my bra and leggings.

He catches my sweater. "I prefer your panties, but this is a start."

"Get your head in the game, Braden. I'm about to obliterate you."

"We'll see about that."

I hike the ball, and my quarterback throws it to a runner, who catches it. "Yes!" I make my runner sprint down the field, blowing past Clay's guys. "I'm doing it!" One of his players dives for my guy, and I dart around him. "Ha ha! No way, sucker!" My player runs around another of his, and Clay's guys chase mine down the field, right into the end zone. I jump to my feet, wiggling my hips and pumping my fists in a victory dance, cheering, "Yes! Touchdown! *I did it! I did it!*" I look over at Clay just as he drops his drawers.

"Looks like we're both gonna score." He tackles me to the pillows, both of us cracking up.

"You *let* me win!"

"I'm no fool." He kisses my smiling lips, and we both laugh.

I look up at the man who's changing my world faster than I can process, opening my eyes to a happier life. *And a big, new love* whispers through my mind. I trap my lower lip between my teeth, trying to keep that thought in.

"What?" he asks.

I gaze into his gorgeous blue eyes, and another truth comes out. "I've lived in Charlottesville for years and have never done any of the things we did today."

"See? You need me in your life."

I don't know about need, but I *want* him in it. Every time we're together, I feel closer to him than I did the time before. Heck, than the *hour* before. I feel stupid for running from him for so long, when we could have been together all that time. I want to tell him how I feel. The words are right there on the tip of my tongue, vying for release. I'm afraid to bare my heart like that. But I don't know how long he's staying, and I'm *more* afraid that he'll leave town without ever really knowing how I feel. I scramble for a middle ground, a comfort zone outside my own but close enough to race back if need be. One without *kind of* or *might*.

My heart races, and butterflies swarm in my belly as I reach up and touch his cheek, needing the surety of him, as I gather the courage to reveal my heart. He's gazing so deeply into my eyes, I'm pretty sure he can read my thoughts as I say, "I *really* like you."

His smile broadens. "I really like you, too, Reckless."

My hand slides around to his neck as he lowers his lips to mine, and I give myself over to the emotions winding around us like a bow, binding us together, as the rest of the world falls away.

Chapter Twenty-Five

Clay

A cool breeze sweeps up Observation Hill, where Pepper and I are cuddled beneath a blanket watching the sunrise over the campus. She shivers, and I hug her against my side, pulling the blanket further around her as gorgeous streaks of yellows, oranges, and pinks paint the sky.

"We need a picture for your grandpa."

I love that she thinks of him, and I take a picture of the sunrise, and one of us, which I'll send to him later.

Pepper rests her head on my shoulder. "Do you think watching sunrises counts as a hobby?"

"According to the great Bradshaw Braden, watching the sunrise is the most important part of the day, and it should be a *habit* for all beings great and small."

"I'm starting to think he's right. I can't believe I never took the time to watch a sunrise before you and I got together. It's a calming way to start the day."

"Other than when my grandfather used to pressure me to watch them with him, I've never been able to sit still long enough to enjoy them. But I can with you. I think you're my calming force."

"That's funny, because you get me out to do more than I've

done in years. I guess that's kind of a calming effect, too, since my brain is usually too busy to focus on anything but work, and with you it's all about pleasure and fun."

I kiss her temple. "Pleasuring you is fun for me."

She smiles, and I know she's thinking about our sexy night in front of the fire, too. We made love and slept there all night. My shoulder is paying the price for sleeping on the hard floor, but it was worth it. I'd sleep on nails if it means being with Pepper, but I hope I don't end up with a headache.

"There's a hill like this back home that overlooks the Jerichos' barn. Brindle and Morgyn loved sneaking out to watch the Jericho brothers hold midnight rodeos. They'd drag us all with them. Sable would try to keep them in line, which never worked, and Grace loved going when we were young, since she and Reed were secret lovers in high school, and he was always there. Amber went just for the sisterly camaraderie, and Axsel went anywhere there were hot guys."

I love how she knows her siblings so well. "What about you?"

"I only went when they forced me to. It wasn't my idea of fun. Not that there's anything wrong with it. But I learned early on that getting too caught up in boys led to trouble."

"That's true in many ways, but what kind of trouble did you get into?"

"None on those nights."

"But…?" When she doesn't respond, my mind starts making up shit. "Did you get in trouble with Ravi?"

"Not *with* him. I let Sable talk me into going to a party one night so she could see Tuck—"

"The guitarist from her band?"

"Yeah. They went out when they were young. She really

cared about him. It was when I was seeing Ravi. He was away with his family, and I was waiting to hear from him. I didn't want to go to the party. I hated parties as much as I hate driving at night, but Sable was desperate to see Tuck, so I went. It started to get late, and I didn't want to be there anymore. I begged Sable to leave or at least drive me home, but she wanted to stay with Tuck, and she told me to drive myself home. I was on my way when I got a text. I *knew* it was Ravi, and I was crazy about him. You know how when you're young, everything feels like it's life or death? That's how it felt when that text came through, but I couldn't reach my phone on the passenger's seat."

There's a sinking feeling in my gut. I tighten my grip on her shoulder.

"I only took my eyes off the road for a few seconds to reach for the phone, and when I looked up, a deer was *right there*, just standing in the road. I was going too fast to go around it." Her eyes dampen. "I don't remember the accident, and I have no idea how I got out of the car. It was wrapped around a tree, and there was blood everywhere. On the broken windshield and the hood, and all over me." Tears spill down her cheeks. "The next thing I know, I'm huddled in the grass by the dead deer, shaking and covered in blood, and Sable is sprinting down the road toward me, shrieking."

My chest constricts, and I wrap her in my arms. "It's okay, baby."

She shakes her head against my chest. "I'll never forget the *fear* in her screams." Her voice is ragged. "She's always been fearless. But that night—" A sob steals her voice.

"It was an accident, sweetheart." I pull her to me, and she buries her face in my neck. "It's okay. I've got you."

"It's *not* okay," she says angrily, and pushes out of my arms, swiping at tears. "I could've died, and my family never would have gotten through that."

"But you didn't, baby. All kids get into accidents. My mother always said, *It's not if your child will get into a car accident; it's when, because kids are kids. They're always distracted and thinking of a million things.*"

"But *I* wasn't usually like that. I was reckless, and that night broke us. It changed the course of *both* of our lives." Her eyes dampen anew. "I *lied* to Sable about the deer. I told her it came out of nowhere, and I didn't tell her about the text. She took the blame because she felt guilty about making me drive at night, and I *let* her do it. I didn't know it would change her."

"Of course you didn't," I say gently. "You were just a kid."

"But I never told her the truth until last year, when a friend told me about something similar she went through and how it affected her."

I frame her face with my hands and brush away her tears with the pads of my thumbs. "Kids lie to cover their asses all the time, and from what I know about Sable, she's very protective of you. I'm sure she forgives you."

"She *does*." Pepper sniffles, managing a small smile. "But she blamed herself for wanting to be with Tuck. She broke up with him that night and never let a man get close to her again. Until Kane, and he had to bully his way into her heart. I hate that I made her into that person and stole all those years from her." More tears slide down her cheeks.

"You didn't make her into anything, sweetheart." I wipe the fresh tears away. "She made a choice to protect you, and she became whoever she was supposed to be. Is this what you were referring to in Paris when you said hurting someone you love or putting them in danger can change a person?"

She takes a shaky breath, nodding. "I was never very adventurous, but I wasn't as careful or rigid as I am now, either."

"You're not rigid, baby. You're disciplined, and careful is good. I'm not negating that you might have changed, but you're such a special person, I don't want you to lose sight of that. I love who you are."

She swallows hard and takes a deep breath. "Thank you. But I *did* change. You know how everyone thinks I did great at school because I'm smart, and it's just who I am?"

"Yeah."

"Well, it's not just that. I was always a good student, but I blamed my recklessness on being too boy-crazed about Ravi. I broke up with him and threw myself into schoolwork to keep from thinking about him or any other boy. It wasn't because I was smart. It was because I was scared. When I let my guard down in college and got hurt, it renewed my determination to keep my walls up and focus on making something of myself so I wouldn't notice my lack of a personal life."

"And then I came into your life and blew all of that out of the water."

She smiles. "Pretty much."

"I'm sorry you went through that. It must have been hard keeping all those feelings in check for so long. I wish I could go back in time and be there for you and help you through it. I'm sorry I called you Reckless. I won't call you that anymore."

"It's okay," she says earnestly. "I like it when you call me that. You make me feel reckless, and that scared me when I left Paris because I've worked so hard not to be that way. But you also make me feel safe, which makes me want to be a little reckless with you. I *like* who I am with you."

"That's good, because I like who I am with you, too."

That earns another smile. "Being with you has made me realize that I've either been suppressing a lot of myself, or maybe I just never allowed myself to grow, and change, and explore, in the ways I am with you. I think you were right when you said I'm becoming who I was always meant to be, but that's because you make me feel safe enough to do it."

I hug her again, trying to wrap my head around the emotions stacking up inside me. "I adore everything about you, Pepper. From the way you fidget when you're nervous to the way you communicate cautiously until you truly trust completely, and then you share the most intimate pieces of yourself clearly and purposefully, as if everything is on the line. And it is, because it's your heart you're exposing. I'm glad you feel safe with me, baby, and I will do everything in my power to make sure you always do."

"Thank you," she whispers. Blinking away a few more tears, she wipes her eyes dry. "It's a little scary, opening up like this. I'm not a crier, and I'm sorry for that."

"Don't ever apologize for showing me how you really feel. I want to know the real you, good, bad, happy, or sad. What we have is powerful, baby, and it's moving fast. It scares me, too. I've never cared about anyone outside my family as much as I care about you. You're right up there with football."

"Given who you are, I'm going to take that as a compliment. But I've spilled my soul, and I feel a step behind. You're here in my world, and you know all about my life, but I don't know that much about yours. You've been here for days. When do you have to go back?"

"Are you trying to get rid of me, Montgomery?"

"No. I'm just curious."

285

"Your curiosity has good timing. I was going to mention that I fly out tomorrow morning for a photo shoot. I have dinner with my agent and a potential sponsor tomorrow night, but I'll be back early Tuesday."

"*Oh*, okay," she says with a hint of surprise. "How long can you stay when you come back?"

"However long we want. There's nothing in Jersey that can't wait, and I like it here. I've got great company, a full gym all to myself, and a kid to mentor, which I'm really enjoying. If you get sick of me, you can let me know."

"Oh good. Then I'm not stuck with you," she says teasingly, and snuggles in against my side. "I'm glad you're coming back. I just don't want to hold you up from doing whatever you need to. I don't even know when your season starts."

"We report back mid-April, and we play through January."

"It must be nice to have so much time off. This might seem like a silly question, but is there a lifespan for your position? Do guys still get tackled at forty-five? And for that matter, what comes next? How do you top being Mr. Perfect?"

Hearing her call me that makes my gut twist. "Please don't call me that."

"You don't like it?"

I shake my head. "*No*. I used to. I got off on the fame and notoriety. I worked my ass off for years to get there, and I lived for that limelight."

"I think most people would."

"I don't know about that. Flynn gained national attention for being the youngest person to win *Wilderness Warrior* when he was twenty-one, and he hated the limelight so much, he disappeared and went to live off the grid for several years. Back then, I was in the thick of it. On magazine covers, getting more attention than anyone could ever hope for, and I couldn't understand his distaste for it. But the last few years changed that. It's turned into a dog and pony show. I can't even go out to dinner without people staring at me."

"I've noticed that. You're good at ignoring them."

"That comes with loads of guilt. I'm *Mr. Perfect.* I'm expected to play flawlessly on the field and be this charming, amiable, approachable guy off the field. But I'm not that indestructible kid anymore. My body takes longer to heal, and my throwing isn't what it used to be. Nobody else has noticed, but I can feel the difference, and my patience for the bullshit of being Mr. Perfect twenty-four-seven has worn thin."

"That's understandable. What's going on with your throwing?"

"It's nothing."

"Don't play macho with me." She bumps her shoulder against mine.

"It's just harder to get a perfect throw. It used to be like something would click in my head and I'd know when to release the ball. My shoulder injury has messed that up, making it easy to miss the release point. *After* I let the ball go, I know immediately if I've missed it, even by a fraction."

"Are there exercises or something you can do for that?"

"Short of having a buzzer go off when I'm in the perfect position, no. But that's just part of the game taking its toll. That will work itself out, but I've been who everyone else expects me to be for so long, I'm not sure I know who I'd be without it."

"Does that mean this"—she motions between us, her beautiful eyes suddenly cautious—"is all part of an act?"

"*Hell no.* You're one of only a handful of people I don't have to be Mr. Perfect with. That's one of the things that drew me to you from the beginning. You couldn't care less about my notoriety."

"That's not true," she says adamantly. "I don't care if you're rich or famous, but I'm proud of you for going after your dreams and achieving a level of success that not many people can."

"Thanks, babe."

"I'm sorry it's become stressful for you, but I get that. I made my dreams come true, and I'm proud of that. But I also want to have a family one day, and I have no idea how I'll ever get to have one and spend time with my kids without losing everything I've worked for."

"Women work and have families all the time. I'm sure owning the business presents certain challenges, but where there's a will, there's a way."

"I keep telling myself that, and I know I have plenty of time to figure it out. But every time I see Emma Lou, that clock ticks louder. What about you?"

"Emma Lou could make anyone think about having a family. She's adorable."

"It doesn't hurt that she loves you. She's always running into your arms."

"I am irresistible to females of all ages," I tease.

She shakes her head.

"I think about having a family a lot, too. Some of my buddies have kids, and most of the families travel with us, but there's a fair share of bitching among the wives."

"I can't imagine how hard that would be with kids, but I can't even figure out how I'll ever have kids and keep my business afloat, so there's that."

"Like I said, where there's a will, there's a way."

She sighs. "It sounds like you and I are kind of in the same boat. Not with fame, but in the process of discovering who we are and what we want. It's a strange feeling, isn't it? To be this age and just learning about who we really are."

"It sure is. But I'm glad I get to figure it out with you."

She looks at me with the sweetest smile. "Me too."

I lean in to kiss her, then look out at the sun rising high in the sky. "The sunrise is almost as pretty as you," I say as I stretch my injured shoulder, moving it in a circular motion.

"Is your arm hurting from all the activities we did yesterday?"

"Nah. It's just tight from sleeping on the floor. I'm fine."

"I brought ibuprofen. I was worried you'd be sore today." She digs a bottle out of her bag and shakes a couple of pills into my hand.

How can something as small as two little pills make me fall even harder for her? "Thanks for thinking of me." I take the medicine with my hot chocolate.

"You inserted yourself into every aspect of my life, making it impossible *not* to think of you." A tease rises in her eyes. "Besides, we have a boatbuilding competition today, and I don't want you to have any excuses when you lose. In fact, I'm going to rub your shoulders and neck, and then you're going to lie here with the sun on your face while I rub your head and get those pressure points that helped the last time you had a migraine." She moves behind me. "Maybe we can nip it in the bud and you won't get a migraine."

"I have a feeling my shoulder is going to be hurting every day from now on."

She laughs softly and starts massaging my shoulders, working her magic in more ways than one.

Chapter Twenty-Six

Pepper

I'm on a dead run Monday morning, and everything seems to be going my way. Ravi and I hammer out most of the proposal we hope to pitch to MS Enterprises, and I schedule a meeting with their acquisitions team for next week, which gives me time to research their investment history. But first I dive into researching a new project.

I'm poring over drawings, working on designs midafternoon, when a text rolls in from Clay. Just seeing his name on my phone makes my pulse quicken. He only got a mild headache yesterday morning. We relaxed at home after watching the sunrise, and once his headache eased, we had a great time building our boats and racing them in the lake. The temperature dropped in the afternoon, but we didn't let it ruin our fun. My boat won the race, and I gloated, doing a happy dance that put my previous night's touchdown dance to shame.

Clay definitely brings out my inner child, and I don't hate it. We called Seth later in the afternoon. I was worried that our text exchange from Saturday might make things awkward between us, but Seth and I hit it off right away. He's a little serious, like me, but he's funny, too. He and Clay heckled each other throughout the conversation, which reminded me of my siblings. Seth was incredibly helpful, and the three of us came up with a killer ad for the receptionist position. I placed it this morning, and I'm excited to see how well it works.

I'm also excited to see Clay tomorrow. After spending the weekend together, I wasn't sure how much I'd miss him today. But that time together only made the ache of missing him stronger.

I open the text, and a picture pops up of Clay standing beneath harsh studio lights, wearing nothing but a wicked grin and skintight black Under Armour briefs. My stomach somersaults, but it's the memory of our passionate night, and his voice whispering through my mind—*I'm going to fuck you so thoroughly, you won't be able to think about me without getting wet*—that has me squeezing my thighs together. Once again, he's proven himself right.

Another picture pops up. A perfect shot of his ass taken over his shoulder in the mirror.

Me: *You're making it hard for me to concentrate.*

Clay: *You make me hard, so it's only fair.*

Another thrill darts through me.

Me: *You know what you do to me.*

A squirt emoji pops up.

Me: *Don't you have to go smile for the camera or something?*

Clay: *Just didn't want to slip your mind.*

Me: *Impossible.*

I add a heart emoji and go back to my drawings.

"Hey," Ravi says as he walks into my office. "I'm heading out to meet the guys. Are you okay? I haven't seen you all afternoon."

I look up from the drawings. "I'm great. Is it time to go already?"

"For normal people. I take it Clay isn't coming back?"

"He'll be back tomorrow. Can I get your opinion on this before you go?" I come around the desk and hand him the drawings.

"What is this? Some kind of sensory glove?"

"Yes. Keep this between us, please, but Clay mentioned his throwing has been off."

"From the shoulder injury?"

"How do you know about that?"

He looks amused by the question. "Because I follow the game. It's not like it's a secret. He had trouble with his shoulder all season, but there's never been any mention of his throwing being off."

"That's because it's not that bad yet, but he feels a difference. He said it's harder to get a perfect throw than it used to be and that before his injury something would click in his head and he'd know when to release the ball."

"Rote memory."

"Exactly, but the injury has messed that up for him."

"Makes sense. I'm sure he's moving differently to compensate for the pain."

"Exactly. He said he can tell when he lets go of the ball if he's missed it by a *fraction* and that short of having a buzzer go off when he's in the perfect position to release it, he's not sure how to fix it. So I had an idea. I spent all morning researching the muscles used when throwing, the isometric activations for stabilization, and what happens if certain muscles aren't strong enough. I know he's got the best sports doctors and therapists, but I think by tracking the movement of his muscles from his fingers all the way down his arm and over his back and chest muscles, I can get him the signal he needs. That's why the apparatus extends down the right side of his chest and shoulder."

"But every throw is different."

"Yes, but I'm not trying to define every throw, and this wouldn't be used during games. I'm only trying to help him figure out where that new release point is when he's practicing. I'm hoping if we can target it, he can create new rote memory based on his current injury."

"It's an interesting idea." Ravi's brows knit, and I can practically see the gears in his mind churning. "By tracking the sensors and working with him, you'll figure out exactly where and when he hits the sweet spot."

"Yes! And then we'll make a signal for it. A vibration or something. I haven't figured that out yet. I don't know what would be helpful without throwing him off. But we've already got knowledge of the technology with our Smart Glove project."

"You're not thinking of skimming off that contract, are you?"

"Don't be ridiculous. You know me better than that. I just meant that we have the underlying knowledge to create this. The data and analysis will be different, as will the physical apparatus, but it won't take much to have a prototype made. You know Kenji will cut me a deal." Kenji is one of our subcontractors for the Smart Glove project. We create the technology, and he manufactures the physical gloves. "He loves working with us, and he's fast. Once I have the specs and sensors figured out, it won't take him long to make the glove and chest piece."

"If he can fit it into his schedule."

"Yes, of course. I haven't mentioned this to Clay yet, but I'm going to tomorrow night. If he thinks it's a good idea, I don't think he'll have an issue helping me pay for it, and if need be, offering an incentive to Kenji."

Ravi studies the drawings again. "This could work."

Excitement bubbles up inside me. "I think so, too."

"Not quite so rattled by him anymore, are you?"

"Shut up. He's done nothing but help me. I'm excited to be able to do something for him."

"What if it fails?"

"Then we figure out why and fix it."

He grins. "Like a tick with a vein. Welcome back."

I roll my eyes as he hands me the drawings, and my phone chimes several times in quick succession.

"Either one of your sisters just found out she's pregnant, or Clay really misses you."

"It's not Clay. He has a big sponsorship dinner tonight."

"Then I'll leave you to the family drama. Don't stay too late."

"Just long enough to catch up on some of the work I put off today. Have fun with the guys."

As he heads out, I put the drawings on my desk, and my phone chimes again. Hoping my sisters aren't going to keep this up all night, I grab my phone from the credenza and open the group text thread from my family.

Brindle: *WTH Pepper? You're with Clay and the whole world finds out before us?*

"What?" My stomach knots up as I scroll through screen-shots she sent of celebrity news social media posts with headlines like *ALL YOU NEED TO KNOW ABOUT CLAY BRADEN'S HOT WINTER FLING* and *IS DR. PEPPER MR. PERFECT'S FLAVOR OF THE MONTH?* The word *fling* cuts like a knife. My hands shake as I swipe through pictures of me and Clay bowling and making out in the bowling alley parking lot. "Nononono. This can't be happening," I say pleadingly to my empty office, and I read the other messages.

Morgyn: *I knew the universe would come through for you!*

Amber: *Why are you and Clay keeping this a secret? Dash didn't know about you either.*

Mom: *Pepper, are you okay honey?*

Axsel: *She's fine, Mom. She's hooking up with the hottest bachelor on the planet.*

Dad: *Princess, I'm here if you want to talk.*

My chest constricts at the childhood nickname. I'll be the talk of Oak Falls, and my parents will have to deal with it. I hate the thought of embarrassing them like this.

Brindle: *Were you hooking up in Paris?*

Dad: *Brindle, I don't think we need to discuss those types of details in a group text.*

Grace: *Pepper, you look so happy. Are you?*

Sable: *Want me to hunt down the people who took the pictures and break their fingers?*

My hands shake as I frantically type a response.

Me: *Yes, we were together in Paris. I can't deal with this right now. Please stop texting about it and let me figure things out.*

A flood of texts rolls in with *I love you*s and *I'm here if you need me*s. I pace the office, feeling like I can't breathe. Why hasn't Clay said anything? As I navigate to our texts, my phone rings, and Sable's name flashes on the screen. Her tour ended over the weekend, and I know she got back to Oak Falls last night. If I don't answer, she'll show up here.

I reluctantly put the phone to my ear. "I can't talk right now."

"I know it seems like your world is collapsing around you, but trust me, it's *not*."

"Are you freaking kidding me, Sable? I went from being a well-respected scientist to a *flavor of the frigging month*."

"Who gives a fuck what those idiots think?"

"I do!" I snap, wearing a path in the carpet. "My clients are going to see this!"

"Your clients know you're a professional."

"They won't *now*!" My head is spinning.

"What does Clay say about it? He can make a statement to the media and shut it down."

"I haven't talked to him. He's in New York on business."

"He hasn't called you? What the fuck? You know he has a PR rep or an assistant keeping an eye on this shit."

Pain slices through me at her anger, because that's exactly what is going through my head. "I don't know what he has, but it's a good thing he hasn't called. I don't want to talk to anyone," I seethe. "This is all *my* fault. I saw people looking at him the first night he was here. I should've known better than to hang out with a celebrity."

"Or at least not suck face in the parking lot."

I groan. "I can't talk about this right now. I just...I can't."

"*Fine.* I can be there in an hour."

"*No.* Please just let me be." Tears sting my eyes, but she knows I process better alone. "*Please.*"

"Damn it, Pepper."

"Please, Sable."

"Fine. Crawl under your rock, but if I don't get a text with proof of life tomorrow morning, I'm going to be on your doorstep before eight a.m. Now tell me where Clay is staying so I can go kick his fucking ass."

"*Sable*, I can't do this with you right now. I've got to go." I end the call, struggling against tears.

"I guess we're official."

I spin around at Clay's voice, and my stomach roils. "How can we be official when I don't even know what we are?" Too upset to stand still, I pace again.

"Yes, you do," he says calmly. "If you didn't, you would never have allowed me to stay."

"*Fine!* I *do*, but I can't think straight right now! I worked my butt off to gain a place in my industry and get a little recognition in my field, and you come to town for *one* weekend, and suddenly the whole world knows me as your frigging *flavor of the month. This* is why we should have left whatever this is in Paris. But *no*. You had to come here and woo me."

"You like my wooing," he says calmly.

"*Clay!* Are you trying to piss me off?" I know I'm being irrational, but I can't stop. "Listen to me. I'm yelling! I don't yell! This is not me!"

"Yes, it is. You're a passionate woman."

I glower at him. "Now is *not* the time to flirt with me!"

"I'm not flirting. You're passionate about work, you're passionate about family, and you're passionate about us." He opens his arms. "Come here."

"I don't *want* to come there."

"Yes, you do. Come here." His arms remain open, and he beckons me with his fingers.

I shake my head, trying to gain control of my runaway emotions.

He stalks toward me, his arms open.

"*Clay,*" I warn, but he just wraps his arms around me. My arms hang like a petulant child, but I immediately feel safer.

"It's going to be okay," he promises, and kisses the top of my head.

The tears I've been holding back spring free. "Nothing is okay," I say softly. "Why are you even here? You're supposed to be at a business dinner."

"I got on a plane the minute I heard about the social media storm."

"You can't just shirk your responsibilities because of *me.*" I try to push out of his arms, but he tightens his hold on me.

"Nothing is more important than you. When we were in Paris, you were adamant about not becoming part of a scandal. I didn't think it would happen, and I didn't take it seriously. Especially once we were here. People seemed respectful of my privacy. But I should have known better. I'm sorry, Pepper. I never meant to hurt you."

I tip my face up. His eyes are brimming with concern, and that takes the starch out of me. "It's not your fault. I just worked so hard to be taken seriously, and now I'm embarrassed."

"Because you got caught kissing your boyfriend, or because of the nasty headlines?"

"The headlines mostly. But did you see the pictures? I'm practically climbing you in the parking lot."

He smiles, speaking gently. "I told you you're passionate."

"I don't need the *world* to see it." I touch my forehead to his chest. "I lose my head when I'm with you."

"That's a *good* thing, sweetheart." He slides a finger under my chin and tilts my face up, bringing my eyes to his again.

"I'm sorry this happened. I hate that you got hurt because of my reputation. If I could go back in time to change it, I would."

"I know you would," I admit.

"I'd never choose for us to be outed this way, but I'm glad people know about us now. We're in this together. I don't want to hide from your family or anyone else. I'm *proud* to be with you, and I thought you were proud to be with me. But I understand why you're upset, and I know this kind of public scrutiny isn't for everyone. If this changes things for you, I should probably tell Doogie to take down my social media post."

"What post?"

He pulls out his phone, scrolls to one of his social pages, and shows me the picture he took of us watching the sunrise yesterday morning. My head is resting on his shoulder, and his head is touching mine. The rising sun casts a romantic glow on our faces, and our smiles shimmer in our eyes. If happiness could be captured in one picture, it would be that one.

The caption simply reads, MINE 🖤.

Emotions clog my throat.

"As long as we're together, there will always be some form of public scrutiny," he says gently. "It'll follow me until I'm old and gray. Unfortunately, that's the nature of the beast. I can't stop people from posting about us, but I will *always* have your back."

He kisses my forehead, and my throat thickens even more, because I know he will. It doesn't make sense that the man who makes me feel reckless also makes me feel safe and whole, but he does.

"I talked to my PR rep, Nolan Kenard, about the best way to handle this for your business."

"You did?" *Oh, my heart.*

"Of course. You can talk to him if you'd like to discuss it with a professional. He thinks we should let it go and wait for it to blow over. But there are other options. I can make a statement and ask for privacy, or you can make a statement so your clients see it, or if you want us to make a joint statement to cover all our bases, then I'll arrange it. Just tell me what you need, Pep, and I'll make it happen, but please don't throw us away because some kid got excited and posted pictures of us, and they happened to go viral. That's just social media nonsense. It'll fade away, but my feelings for you are real, and they're only going to get stronger."

"Stop sucking me into your fairy tale," I plead half-heartedly. "That's how I got into this mess in the first place. I get lost in your charm and attention and forget I'm a realist."

"You're a realist who deserves a fairy tale, baby. I know it doesn't feel like it right now, but it's okay to be reckless with the guy you care about."

He kisses me sweetly. In the safety of his arms, with the real world locked outside my office walls, I breathe a little easier.

"I don't want to think about any of this," I say softly. "I just want to go home, have a glass of wine, and be with you."

"I have a better idea."

A little while later, we're lounging naked in a hot tub on the deck of the elaborate home Clay rented, sipping wine. It feels more like a private luxury retreat than a home, with spacious rooms, high ceilings, wide-planked hardwood floors, two stone fireplaces, a two-car garage, and four private acres of winding gardens and mature trees.

Steam rises from the water as I gaze out at the yard, which seems endless. "This was a great idea." I set my wineglass on the deck and snuggle against his side. "Why have you been staying at my place, when you have all *this* waiting for you?"

"Because you're there." He kisses my shoulder. "I would have brought you here the first night, but I got the feeling you needed the security of being on your own turf."

"You were right, but maybe we should test this place out for a few nights."

"Sounds good to me."

"I'm glad you're here with me, but are you going to lose that sponsorship opportunity because you missed the dinner?"

"I don't think so, but if I do, fuck it. I wasn't about to make you deal with this on your own. If they can't understand that, then I don't want to represent their brand anyway."

"I appreciate that, but I don't want you to miss out on important opportunities because of me."

"Don't worry about that. If I never got another sponsorship deal, I'd be just fine. But are you still worried about your clients?" he asks carefully.

"A little, but only because I feel like a teenager who got caught in the back seat of her parents' car."

That brings out his dimples. "Why do you feel like that?"

"I don't *know*," I say, turning to face him. "Maybe because it's so *not* me to kiss like that in public, or because that's how my whole family found out about us. Hearing my dad call me *princess* when he's seen headlines about me being your flavor of the month is a little embarrassing."

"I'll apologize to them."

"That's really nice of you to offer, but no. You don't have to do that. Something tells me I need to get used to that type of attention, because apparently it *is* who I am when I'm with you, and I need to accept that or drive myself crazy trying to hold back when we're together."

"Fuck holding back. How can anyone expect you to hold back when you're with *me*? I mean, come on. Look at me." He says it as arrogantly as he does teasingly.

I'm thankful for the levity and the kiss that follows.

"Seriously, babe. This *will* blow over."

"I know. The embarrassment is already starting to fade. But now you have to go home with me for the Valentine's Day Festival to prove I'm not your flavor of the month."

"Is that your way of asking me to be your Valentine? Because I'm used to a little more romance. Some chocolate-covered strawberries, maybe some flowers."

God, I love him.

"You should just be honored that I asked. I haven't had a Valentine since Ravi and I went out."

"Ah, competition."

"Hardly," I say with a laugh.

"We're going to have such a great time at that festival, when we go *next year*, you won't remember any Valentine who came before me." He leans and kisses me.

"I'm holding you to that." I take a sip of wine and put the glass back on the deck. "With all the craziness, I forgot to tell you that I think I came up with something that might help you with your throwing."

He arches a brow. "Great sex helps."

"*Noted*, but this might help even more. You know how you said you can feel when you release the ball and it's a little off?"

"Yeah."

"Well, I was thinking. Your injury has been going on for a while, and you're trying to throw the same way you did for years before the injury. Since the pain is ongoing, your body naturally adjusts to throw differently in order to avoid the pain. That's why you notice a difference. You might be able to adjust enough now to fool everyone else, but you aren't fooling yourself. That mental pressure makes it even harder to perform at the level you need to, right?"

"I guess. Yeah."

"I think the key is working with your injury instead of against it."

"I'm not sure what you mean."

"Every time you tweak your shoulder and feel pain, it affects the way you throw, and that affects your mental state, which *also* affects your ability to focus on throwing. If we can find a new release point, or get to the old one from a slightly different angle, as you said, even a fraction of a difference, it might take that pressure off, which could result in better releases, less stress, and the confidence and focus you need to succeed."

"That would be amazing, but how? Are you talking about *therapy?*"

"No, but with all the pressure you're under that could help, too. I did some research and worked on an idea for a sensory glove that could be the answer." I explain the design and how it would work. "The hope is that we can take the data and your feedback and figure out your new release point. Then we come up with a signal. You mentioned a buzzer, but that might be too much, so a vibration, or something that'll cue you to release at that point every time you throw. If it works, then it would just be a matter of practicing enough that you can hit it consistently without further injuring your shoulder."

His brow furrows. "You just came up with this out of the blue?"

"Not out of the blue. You said you were having trouble, and I thought it might help. I'm not even sure whether you'll need it to go farther down your arm than your wrist. It might just be a positional thing that doesn't require us to analyze your shoulder and arm positioning. I researched throwing, but that's the kind of decision I can't make without your input."

He studies me with an almost incredulous expression.

"If you aren't interested, or if you think it won't work, then I don't want to waste your time." He doesn't say anything for so long, I fear I've missed something and the idea is foolish. "Am I way off base?"

"*No.* You're brilliant. I'm just blown away that you'd take time away from your busy schedule to think about helping me and come up with something like that so fast."

"It's your career, and it's obviously causing you angst. Of course I'll help you. Does that mean you think it might work?"

"Not only do I think it might work." He moves in front of me, guiding my legs around his waist. "But you just did the impossible."

I put my arms around his neck. "I haven't done anything yet."

"Yes, you did. I didn't think it was possible for you to get any sexier." He brushes his lips over mine. "But I was wrong." He nips at my lower lip, sending shivers of heat down my core. "That incredible brain of yours just turned up the heat."

"Let me think of other smarty-pants things to say."

His lips come down over mine in a soul-searing kiss, and like every time we're together, greediness sparks hot and sharp inside me. I wrap my arms tighter around him, my legs squeezing his waist. He growls into our kisses, intensifying his efforts, and his cock presses against my entrance. Need swells inside me as our kisses turn urgent. Our hands roam as we kiss, bite, and suck our way into a frenzy. "*I need you*," I plead. He starts to release me, and I don't let him. I know he's thinking about protection. "I'm on birth control."

The sound he makes is something between a moan and a growl as he reclaims my mouth and I sink onto his cock. Pleasure shoots through me like bullets, making every nerve ending flare to life. We both tear our mouths away, a moan sailing from mine and a curse from his. But in the next breath, we're devouring each other again, thrusting and grinding with everything we have. I cling to his shoulder as he grabs my waist with both hands, his thick fingers pressing into my skin, and drives me harder and faster along his shaft.

"*Don't stop*," I beg, chasing the scintillating sensations spreading through me like wildfire as the cold air hits my chest and the warm water sloshes around my body.

"*Never*," he grits out. "I'll never fucking stop." He pounds into me harder, and my vision blurs. "You feel too good. So tight, so fucking *perfect*." The raw passion in his voice has me standing on the edge of a cliff. "Come on my cock, baby." His dirty demand shatters my control, and I cry out as my body spasms around him. He drives into me time and time again, keeping me at the peak. I'm lost in the feel of his thickness possessing me, his growls and curses heightening every sensation. Just when I start to descend from the clouds, he crushes his mouth to mine in a ruthless kiss. I return it just as brutally, craving more, wanting him to possess every inch of me. As if he's read my mind, his hand slides down my body, and he pushes a finger into my ass as he thrusts mercilessly into me, sending us both spiraling into oblivion.

We thrust and moan, giving and taking with reckless abandon. And then we cling to each other, breathing hard as the real world comes back into focus. His grip eases the slightest bit, and I tighten mine. "Can we just stay like this forever?"

"There's nothing I'd like more." He tightens his hold on me, and in that moment I know there's no amount of embarrassment that could keep me from the only man who makes me reckless, safe, and whole.

Chapter Twenty-Seven

Clay

"I set up the meeting with In the Zone for Tuesday. I've already sent details to Doogie, and you'd better not flake on me again," Tiffany says through Bluetooth as I drive toward town to meet Pepper so she can take measurements for the sensory glove.

I woke up with my girl in my arms, the sun shining, and it's been three days since news of my relationship with Pepper broke, and things are finally settling down. I'm not about to let Tiffany's irritation ruin my day.

"I'm sorry for canceling the last time, but I didn't *flake* on you. You know damn well how social media can ruin relationships. I finally have someone special in my life, and she's a professional, not someone who gets off on drama. I wasn't going to let those vultures ruin what we have." Thankfully, the picture and comment I posted rose above the noise, and the fucking flavor-of-the-week headlines were replaced with headlines like HAS MR. PERFECT MET HIS PERFECT MATCH? On top of that good news, now that the world knows I'm here, I've been working out with Ben and his friends, and we've accumulated a small group of spectators and fans who cheer us on. I'm excited to meet them later to run more drills.

"That's very chivalrous of you," Tiffany says, not unkindly.

"Did you know Pepper's twin is engaged to Dylan's cousin Kane?"

"Yeah. Small world."

"Listen, Clay, I'm glad you've found someone special, but does your new relationship have anything to do with you needing more time to negotiate your extension?"

"No." I grit my teeth and stop at a red light.

"Then let's talk about it. Time is running out, and this doesn't look good. They expected you to jump on it."

A call from Dash rings through, giving me an excuse to cut Tiffany short. "I'm sorry, Tiff, but I can't right now. I've got to run. I'll see you Tuesday." I switch over to Dash as the light turns green. "Hey, man. Sorry I didn't call you back the other night. I was doing damage control."

"I figured as much. Pepper's family was really worried about her."

"I know. I was worried about her, too. Still am." Pepper spoke to her family Tuesday morning and explained the situation. My family has reached out several times. They're glad I got my girl, but everyone, including my grandfather, worries about how this type of attention will affect Pepper.

"How are you doing with all of this? From what Amber says, it sounds like things between you and Pepper are getting serious."

"They are." I turn into the parking lot by Pepper's office. "You know how long I've been into her. When we got together in Paris and she agreed to stay an extra night with me, I felt like I'd won the lottery. Then she tried to end it when she left, and I nearly lost my mind. I finally understand how you fell so fast for Amber. I've never felt this way about anyone. That's why I'm here. I know how important her work is, and I want to be the guy she knows she can count on in good times and bad. I want to be the guy who makes her happy and makes her life easier. Then this shit hits the internet, and her life becomes a fucking spectacle."

"I get it. For what it's worth, she told her family she's not happy about the headlines, but she's happy with you."

I park and cut the engine. "I know she is, but you know how social pressures can become too much. Nolan is doing what he can to shut down any negative noise, and Kane's team is doing the same because of Sable being her twin. I'm just glad we're in Virginia. It's not like there are paparazzi hanging around."

"One of the benefits of being in a small town. Just so you know, I asked Shea to monitor it as well." Shea Steele is Dash's PR rep. "I don't want any of this negatively affecting Amber."

"I appreciate that, and I'm sorry about all of it. How'd you two skate under the radar when you got together?" I ask as I climb out of the vehicle.

"I was never a playboy like you. Your reputation sells." There's a reason Dash was never that guy. After his father abandoned their family, Dash became a father figure to his siblings and helped his mother in every way he could, much like Ben. In our buddy group, Dash was always the voice of reason, like Seth, but with a boisterous personality.

"If I could go back and warn my younger self…" I scoff. "Who am I kidding? Seth, my old man, *and* my grandfather warned me not to play the field the way I did. I was too arrogant to listen."

"I remember telling you that, too, but give yourself a break. Most guys who are thrown into fame go that route. You got it in check, and you haven't been that guy for a long time. This will pass. But you know what's *not* in the news?"

"What?"

"Anything about your extension. What's going on with that? I figured you'd have it sewn up by now."

"Not even close."

"What do you mean? Are you thinking about retiring?"

"Fuck no" comes out on instinct.

"Really?" He sounds a little surprised.

"Yes. *No.* I don't know what I'm thinking, man." I push a hand through my hair, gritting my teeth against the worries eating me up inside. Football is all I know, but the social shit and business end can be draining, my arm is turning to shit, and as fucked up and egotistical as it is, I want to go out a winner, not a fucking loser. And the worst part is that my decision will impact my team, my fans. *Pepper.* I know I can talk to Dash about this, but even the thought of trying to figure it out is overwhelming.

"Remember how scared I was when I first started thinking about retiring?" Dash reminds me. "Retiring was the toughest decision I ever made. I had no clue what I'd do after writing that book. But then Amber and I got together, and life figured itself out. I have zero regrets, and now Amber and I are hoping to start a family soon."

I'm surprised by the unexpected pang of envy I feel. Not necessarily about having a family, although I do want one eventually and I've been thinking a lot about that ticking clock Pepper mentioned, but I think it's more that Dash has his life figured out. He's made it to the end zone, and I'm stuck midfield. Like I got the snap, but I'm unsure whether to pass it or run it in myself.

"That's awesome, Dash. I'm happy for you and Amber.

You'll be amazing parents. Sorry, man, but I've got to run. I appreciate you checking in, and don't worry, Pepper is in good hands."

After we end the call, I head over to the café to get a latte for my girl.

The redheaded waitress is busy with a group of chatty older ladies sitting at a table, each with the same book in front of them, and Clare is serving a Black couple at the far end of the counter. There's a light-skinned young Black boy who looks to be around eight or nine sitting by the register making his way through a milkshake as he plays a handheld video game. I remember being a little kid and feeling like a big kid when I could sit away from my parents.

"Which football game is that?" I ask.

"*Wild Card*," he says without looking up, his brows pinched in concentration.

"Cool. Looks like you're good at it."

"Mm-hm. I play football."

"Really? What position?"

"Running back." His attention remains on the game. "My brother says I'm fast as lightning."

"I bet you are. Do you enjoy it?"

"Mm-hm. I'm gonna go pro when I grow up."

Clare heads my way, slowing in front of the boy. "Finish that up, Sammy. We're leaving soon."

I remember Trina mentioning her brother Sammy, and I realize he must be Clare's son.

"Mm-hm," Sammy says.

"Hello again." Clare flashes a sunny smile. "Flying solo today?"

Pepper and I had lunch here on Sunday. "I'm on my way to

see my girlfriend and thought I'd bring her a French vanilla latte and pick up a half dozen chocolate chip muffins for her officemates."

"That's sweet of you."

"Is this your son?"

"Sure is. Sammy woke up with an earache. I swear elementary schools are like petri dishes."

Thinking about when her daughter came to work with her, I ask, "No sitter?"

"Do you know what sitters charge these days? It was either a sitter or a doctor's bill. We're heading to the doctor as soon as my shift is covered."

"Your boss doesn't mind you bringing the kids to work?"

"He doesn't have a choice. He owns three businesses, and I *usually* work in the offices handling the administrative side of things like payroll, inventory, and everything else under the sun. But the man's a cheapskate, and there's a revolving door in this place. Which is why I'm working as a waitress, and he's got to take what he can get."

Her employer sounds like an ass. "How long have you worked for him?"

"Too long," Sammy drawls.

"You're not wrong, honey, but let's keep that to ourselves, ya hear?"

"*Yes*," he says reluctantly.

Her kind eyes find mine again. "I've worked for one of his businesses or another for seven years. Started as a waitress and went wherever he needed me."

"That's a long time. Why do you stay?"

"I can't afford not to."

"*Clare*," the cook calls out from the other side of the pass-through to the kitchen. "The delivery guy needs your signature."

"Can he wait a minute?" she asks with irritation.

"No, I cannot. I'm already late for my next stop," a man, who I assume is the delivery guy, says from behind the cook.

She turns back to me. "I'm sorry. Can you excuse me for just one minute?"

"Take your time. I'm not in a rush." I watch her go into the back and have a sharp conversation with the delivery guy and the cook as she signs whatever was so important.

She returns looking a little harried. "I'm sorry to keep you waiting. One latte and a half dozen muffins coming up."

As she goes to fill the order, I'm surprised to see Ben walk into the café. "Hey, man. I thought you had class this morning."

"I do, but my mom has to take my little brother to the doctor, so I'm covering for her. Don't worry. I talked to my professor. He's cool with it."

Sammy spins around at the sound of his brother's voice. "Ben!" He runs to Ben and throws his arms around his waist.

"Hey, buddy." Ben pats his back. "How's your ear?"

"Hurts like a *somebitch*."

Ben looks at him disapprovingly. "What did I tell you about that language, Sammy?"

Sammy hangs his head. "Not to use it."

"That's right, little man. And it's *son of a bitch*, not *somebitch*."

"Can I say that?" Sammy asks excitedly.

"*No*," Ben says sternly, and his little brother pouts. "Little man. Do you know who this guy is?" He motions to me, and Sammy shakes his head as their mother returns with my order.

"Hi, honey," she says.

"Mom, *this* is the guy I told you about last night. Clay Braden. The quarterback for the Giants."

Mom? Pieces of Ben's life are coming together like a puzzle in my head.

"You're a real live quarterback?" Sammy exclaims. "Can I have your autograph?"

"*Sammy,*" Clare chides.

"It's okay," I say. "I'd be happy to give him one."

"Yes!" Sammy does a fist pump and runs behind the counter. "I'll get paper!"

"All right, settle down," Clare says as Sammy darts through the kitchen doors. "That's awfully nice of you, Mr. Braden."

"Clay, please."

"Clay, then," she says sweetly. "Ben told me you've been practicing with him every day. Thank you for spending so much time with him."

"It's my pleasure. Ben's a good kid, and he's got real talent. He's sure to go far."

"Speaking of going, Mom," Ben says. "You better take off if you're going to make Sammy's appointment. I'll ring Clay up."

"Don't be silly, honey," she says. "This one's on the house."

"Thanks. I appreciate that."

Sammy runs out from the kitchen waving a piece of paper. "Wait! He's gonna give me an autograph!" He hands me the paper and pen. "Sammy is S-A-M-M-Y."

"Got it." I learned early on to use my fame to help kids stay in line, and I scrawl, *Sammy, study hard, be a good friend, and listen to your mother and your coaches. I look forward to seeing you play.* I sign my name and hand it to him.

Sammy beams as he reads it aloud, and Clare mouths,

Thank you.

As they head out, Ben says, "Thanks, man. You just made my little brother's lifetime."

"Happy to do it. Do you cover for your mom often?"

He lifts one shoulder. "Not really. Are you still cool with meeting me and the guys later?"

"Definitely. I look forward to it."

Pepper

"There's my girl," Clay says as he walks into my office carrying a box from the café and what I know is a latte.

My heart still trips up every time I see him, and this morning it's got an extra little something to trip over. "Hey, you." I come around my desk, brimming with happiness. I breathe him in as he kisses me. "I had a nice surprise about an hour ago, you sneaky thing."

"What kind of surprise?"

"I received a call notifying me that my company name has been added to the directory downstairs. How did you get that done so fast?"

His lips twitch like he's stifling a grin. "Who says I did anything?"

"The building manager."

"Damn. I was trying to keep that on the down-low."

"You're amazing. How did you do it?"

"Where there's a will..."

"*There's a way.* Yes, I know." I go up on my toes and kiss

315

him again. "Thank you. That was really sweet of you."

"I'm just making sure my girl gets the respect she deserves." He hands me the latte. "How's your day?"

"Better now." I peek into the box. "You don't have to bring goodies every time you come here."

"But I get to see that smile when I do."

"Let me clue you in on a little secret. My smile is not because of the treats."

"Mine is," Chris says as he walks by my office door.

"Hey, Chris," I call out.

He circles back in his wrinkled slacks and half-untucked dress shirt, flashing a warm smile. "What's up?"

"Would you mind taking these muffins to the kitchen?"

"Happy to, but I can't guarantee they'll all make it there." He takes the box from Clay. "Thanks for keeping us stocked up with the good stuff."

"My pleasure," Clay says.

Chris turns his attention to me. "I had an idea. Since Clay gets so much social media coverage, maybe he can talk up some of our work. That might help gain more funding."

It was a big relief not to have received any flak from our funding sources over those unflattering headlines. Although, I did have to resort to putting the phones on auto answer because of the media trying to reach me. As if I have something to say? *No, thank you.* The attention has also brought an even bigger influx of unqualified applicants for the receptionist position. But on the upside, Ravi, Chris, and Min rallied around me the morning after the news broke, and my family has checked on me a lot the last few days. When they realized I was past wanting to hide my head in a hole, they made light of the situation, which helped me move on from the sting of it. The new headlines are less obnoxious, pointing to a serious relationship, but they still make me a little nervous. If Clay and I don't work out, I worry I'll face more public humiliation. I said as much to Sable earlier, and she said not to let the public steal my happiness. One look at Clay solidifies how right she is.

"Chris, Clay is *not* our marketing rep."

"It's not a bad idea," Clay says as he shrugs off his coat and hangs it on my coatrack. "It could help with funding."

"No, no, *no*. I'm not going to turn you into a billboard for my company. Chris, we'll be in the lab." I take Clay by the arm and head out of my office.

"Why are you so against my help?"

"I'm not against your help. I'm against using you for my company's gain. I can just imagine the headlines. IS MR. PERFECT BEING PLAYED FOR HIS FAME? *No, thank you.*"

We head into the lab, and I set my coffee on the table where I laid out the measuring tools.

Clay takes my hand and pulls me into his arms. "I know you'd never play me for anything, but you're doing important work, and my face *does* sell. Maybe in this case headlines shouldn't matter."

"When it comes to my business, they do. I just think it's best to keep our relationship separate from my work. Now take your shirt off."

He grins wickedly. "Is this a personal visit, Dr. Montgomery? Because if you're asking me to take my clothes off *personally* and not in order to take measurements for research and development reasons, then I'm going to proceed a little differently."

My entire body goes into *heck yes* mode. My nipples pebble, my insides flame, and my mouth even waters at the thought of all the delicious things we could do.

"Cat got your tongue, sweetheart?" he says coyly.

"It's really unfair that all you have to do is imply something dirty and my brain turns to mush." That earns a bigger grin. I swat his chest. "Stop grinning."

"I can't help it if you're adorable."

"You make it impossible to be serious."

"Trust me, Reckless. I know you're serious about me."

I shake my head, but now I'm grinning like a fool. "Take your damn shirt off, Braden."

"That's it, baby, get sharp tongued with me," he says as he takes off his shirt.

He leisurely places it on the table, plants his hands on his hips, and draws his shoulders back, giving me a show and bringing with it flashes of our last few nights together. We've been staying at his place, and we not only christened the hot tub, but we got down and dirty in the kitchen, the living room, on the dining room table, and in the gym. Who knew a weight bench was so versatile? But it isn't just those things that have my heart thrumming. It's the small, unexpected things. The closeness of cuddling on the couch and watching a movie, the intimacy of waking up in the arms of the person who always makes me happy, and the comfort of holding hands as we walk down the street.

He grabs the button on his jeans, snapping me from my reverie.

"Don't even think about it," I warn.

"Always so controlling," he says in a low voice. "Just like in Paris when you tried to convince me our first night together didn't happen."

"Clay, if you don't stop it, I'll get one of the others to take your measurements."

"I'm just messing with you. I'll behave." He sits on the table.

I take a deep breath. "Thank you. Now, as soon as my heart stops racing, we can get started."

He laughs and tugs me between his legs. "You make it impossible not to fall for you."

My heart skips. "And you make it impossible for my heart to beat regularly."

"Well, then, Dr. Montgomery, you are utterly stunning when chemicals are mediating your attachments. The question is, are they mediating it to romantic or lustful feelings?"

"I plead the Fifth."

A while later, I'm almost done taking measurements of his hand and wrist, and ready to start on his chest. "I was thinking about skipping the shoulder and chest area, but I think we need it, at least to start. We'll put an inertial measurement unit on your wrist, to read the sensors on your fingers, and another one wherever it'll be the least intrusive, to read the sensors we place in the shoulder and chest area. Those measurements will be processed to give us a number of finger and arm positions, movements, and acceleration data, which will help map the results."

"I have no idea what you just said, but it sounded sexy as hell."

I wonder if he knows there's nothing sexier to me than the way he appreciates my mind. "Such a charmer. How was your morning?"

"Good. I had a great workout, and Tiffany called. She rescheduled the meeting for Tuesday to meet with that potential sponsor, which means another trip to the city."

"That's *great*. I'm glad you didn't lose the opportunity."

"They need me more than I need them." He smirks. "As you know, this face is a sought-after commodity."

"It's a good thing arrogance isn't hereditary, or your future children would be in trouble."

He swats my butt, and I laugh.

"Hey, you'll never guess who Ben's mother is."

"Who?"

"Clare, from the café."

"Really? That's wild. How do you know?"

"Ben walked in to cover her shift when I was there. He skipped class so she could take her other son to the doctor for an earache. She said she had to make a choice between paying a sitter and paying the medical bill."

"I can't imagine being in that situation. It's awful that Ben had to miss class to fill in for her. They've been understaffed for months."

"That employer should be ashamed of himself."

"Why doesn't she get another job?"

"She said she can't afford to. I didn't pry, but I really want to help them. I don't know what you're paying for your receptionist position, but I wonder if it's more than what she's currently earning. She said she usually works in the office handling bookkeeping and administrative duties."

"I'm offering a competitive salary, but if she does bookkeeping, I could pay more. That would save me from doing it, which would also give me more time for research."

"That's a good point."

"I wonder if she has health insurance through her company, because I offer that and retirement, too, which could also save her money."

"I don't know, but it sounds like it's worth a conversation."

"You're really something, Mr. Braden. I've probably seen Clare a hundred times over the past year, and I never slowed down enough to get to know her. Shame on *me*."

"Give yourself a break. You're a busy girl boss."

"That's no excuse. She makes my latte every day, and I appreciate it and go there because of it, but I don't see *her*. I see a woman who makes great lattes. That's not how I was raised, and it's not who I want to be. I'm going to make a concerted effort to change that."

"We're all guilty of it, babe."

"That doesn't make it right. I'll talk with her tomorrow morning, and if she's interested, we'll set something up." I guide his arm up above his head while I take more measurements. "You know what's sad?"

"That you made me keep my pants on?"

"*Yes*, you poor, sexually deprived man," I tease. "If you can get beyond that horrible deprival, think about how many other families are in the same position. Families who make ends meet the best they can, and then a kid gets a big break, and they have to continue to shoulder the burden of helping support their family. I bet there are a lot of families in that situation." I finish taking the measurements of his chest and move to his back.

"It's an eye-opener for sure. It makes me realize how privileged I was at that age. How privileged I still am. I'd like to give them money, but I did that when I first hit it big, and it was a huge mistake."

"Why? What happened?" I move his arm to another position. "Keep your arm still if you can."

"I got played by a young kid and his family. It cost me a lot of time and money, but I learned a hard lesson. Not all people are good or honest. That's why I set up the Playing it Forward Sports Scholarship. There are rules and criteria that have to be met in order to qualify, and it allows me to help young athletes without being taken for a ride."

"I didn't know you offered a scholarship. That's a great way to give back."

"I'm glad I can do it. I award a dozen scholarships a year, and I commit to doing it each of the four years they're in school if they maintain the academic and sports requirements."

"That's amazing. Couldn't you do the same type of thing through a foundation or something similar for low-income families like Ben's? You could set up criteria that have to be met just like you did with the scholarship program, only it would be for families of kids who receive sports scholarships, so the kids could focus on school and their sport."

His brow furrows. "You might be onto something. They could get a grant from the foundation equivalent to whatever that kid was contributing. Or more if it makes sense. I'll have to talk to my finance and legal guys to figure that out."

I finish the measurements and put down the instruments. "Do you really have enough money to do something like that?"

"More than enough, and after meeting Clare and Ben and her other kids, it really drives home just how much *extra* I have." He pulls me close again. "I love that brilliant mind of yours, Reckless."

The emotions I've been tamping down try to spring up and cling to the word *love*. He's looking at me the way he does so often. Like I'm the only thing he sees or wants, and I know it's true, because he tells me all the time. But that doesn't mean he's in love with me. He loves my brain the same way I love his body or his mouth. Not in the same way I'm falling for him—

deeper by the moment as his generous heart touches the part of me that has driven me into a lifetime of helping others.

Struggling not to reveal my hopeful heart, I say, "I'm glad, because it's the only one I have."

Chapter Twenty-Eight

Clay

Tuesday morning, I'm in Seth's Manhattan office talking with him and my father, who's joining us via video chat. I've just told them about Ben and his family and explained the concept for the foundation to help families of lower-income athletes who receive sports scholarships. "My legal and financial teams are ready to move forward, but before I proceed, I'd like to know what you think about the idea."

My father's brows pinch, his keen eyes serious behind his glasses. He's always been a strong influence in my life. He's patient, methodical, and supportive, and he thinks everything through before reacting, just like Seth. They are almost mirror images, except my father's thick, wavy hair was more salt than pepper, and he has better fashion sense than Seth. As proven by his blue button-down versus Seth's dark brown patterned sweater over a blue plaid shirt.

Seth sits forward, his elbows resting on the table, his fingers steepled. His gaze moves between me and my father, and he drums his fingertips. I know he's waiting for my father's response.

"I like the concept," my father finally says. "It's well thought out, and it can help a lot of families who aren't as fortunate as you boys were."

"That's the idea," I say.

Seth sits back, nodding. "I like it, too. You mentioned criteria. I assume the income of the kid and the adults will all be verified, but should there be parameters for the length of time they've been in that situation?"

"Yes. We don't want anyone gaming the system. I wanted your input on that. My attorney suggested three years of verified income for the adults and two years for the kids."

"I think that's reasonable for the burden of proof," Seth says.

"The kid would have worked through their junior and senior years of high school and kept up with their sports commitments?"

"That's right. Pepper and I were brainstorming all weekend about ways to help families without holding them back, and she posed an interesting idea about offering incentives so the adults have a chance to better themselves."

My father smiles. "I like the way she thinks. What kinds of incentives do you have in mind?"

"We thought about partnering with a career development company to offer job training, but that might be too limited and could be difficult to coordinate in certain areas. What do you think about offering to pay for classes for the adults and for childcare when it's related to those classes or other job training?"

"I think that sounds like something your mother would have come up with," my father says. "She always says if you're helping someone, you need to also give them tools to help themselves."

"I know. She and Pepper are very much alike in that way, always trying to help others."

"I think it's an excellent idea," Seth says. "Most of the people I know who have been in those types of situations have never been given a chance to get ahead."

"Will you rescind the grant if they surpass a certain income level?" my father asks.

I shake my head. "No. That feels wrong. Like we'd be penalizing them for doing well."

"Gramps would call you a bleeding heart," Seth says with a smile.

"Gramps calls everyone a bleeding heart."

"Yes, he does," my father says. "Then he'd pat you on the back and say he's proud of you while he doles out cash to the families who need it."

We share a laugh.

"We learned from the best," I say. "I was thinking that you guys might want to go in on this with me. Make the Fielding Futures Foundation a family endeavor. What do you think?"

"Get a load of this guy, Seth," my father says jovially. "He's banked multimillion-dollar contracts and he's *still* asking us for money."

"I guess he hasn't signed that extension yet," Seth adds.

"I don't *need* your money, and no, I haven't signed yet. I just thought it might be nice to do this together. Forget I asked. I'll see if Dash wants to go in on it with me."

"Like hell you will. You know I'm in, son, and I like the name you've come up with."

"Thanks. That was Pepper's idea."

"I'll message T and have him set up a meeting with my attorney," Seth says.

"While you're at it, ask Taylor to get you a woman, and maybe a little fashion sense," I joke.

"Ladies love my fashion sense," Seth says evenly. "Just because I don't flaunt my affairs doesn't mean I don't have them."

I scoff.

"A'right, boys, settle down." My father shakes his head with a laugh. "It's like you're teenagers all over again."

"Giving him a hard time adds a little joy to my day," I say.

"Speaking of joy," my father says, "it sounds like you've been doing more than just visiting your special lady in Charlottesville."

"Yeah, it's turning out that way. I'm really enjoying working with Ben and his friends. They're incredibly dedicated. It was pure coincidence that I met the rest of Ben's family, and it really drove home how good I've always had it. I wanted to help them, but I wasn't sure how I could. Pepper is the one who came up with the idea of a foundation. She planted the seed, and together we nurtured it until it grew into Fielding Futures."

My father arches a brow. "It sounds like you and Pepper are driven by the same things. It's nice to have that in common."

"It is. In fact, she's interviewing Ben's mom tomorrow for a job with her company."

"The receptionist job?" Seth asks.

"Yes, but Clare brings more experience to the table, which would be valuable for Pepper. She's thinking about redefining the position. Thanks for your help with the ad, by the way. She's interviewed three other candidates who came from it, and she has another interview today, but we're both hoping Clare will be the best applicant for the job."

"She must've been as touched by their situation as you were," Seth says.

"She was. She's made a career out of helping others, and she's helping me, too. In ways I didn't expect."

"How so?" my father asks.

I tell them about the migraine I had in Paris and how she'd helped me through it. "I had another one Saturday, and she took care of me. I'm not used to that, but she sat on the couch with my head in her lap for two hours reading over the pitch she's giving tomorrow to a group of investors, while I dozed off, trying to break the migraine cycle. She didn't mind that I was out of commission, and I've got to tell ya, she has a magic touch that makes everything feel better."

"Sounds like she cares about *you* and not just what you bring to the table," my father says.

Seth barks out a laugh. "She wouldn't give him the time of day because of his fame and reputation."

"I wondered why she kept taking off. That's a nice change," my father says.

"You can say that again. She's nothing like any other woman I've ever gone out with. She's sweet and funny, and so damn smart, I can barely keep up with her. I mentioned that my shoulder is giving me trouble when I throw, and now she's working on a prototype for a sensory glove to help with it."

Seth's brow slants. "Your shoulder is affecting your throwing?"

Fuck. I didn't mean to divulge that. "Just enough for me to notice. Nothing to be concerned about." I can feel him scrutinizing my reaction. "The point is, beyond my coaches, a few buddies, and family, nobody has ever given a damn about me and what I might be going through or wanted to be there for me in that way, to help me through the tough stuff. Pepper worries about me, my emotions, my physical state, my stress."

"You've never let anyone get close enough to see the real you before her," Seth points out.

"There's never been anyone who made me want to let my

guard down."

"She sounds like a remarkable woman all around," my father says. "I assume you're doing nice things for her, too? Adding value to her life, not just social media headlines?"

"Beyond sexual pleasure," Seth goads.

I smirk and give him a loaded answer. "I bring pleasure to her life in *and* out of the bedroom." He doesn't need to know that I also bring out her reckless side in *and* out of the bedroom, adding sexual pleasure to our lives and happiness to our hearts. I smile to myself thinking about the fun we had Sunday morning when I convinced her to go for a short run with me through the park, followed by a polar plunge in the lake. The run was more like a fast walk interspersed with jogging and stolen kisses, but I've never seen her smile as much as she did when she ran into my arms after the polar plunge, shivering and saying she wanted to do it again.

We also went to a pub with Ravi, Chris, and Min last night. We had a great time, and we're watching the Super Bowl with them this Sunday. I like this road of discovery we're on together, figuring out who we are as individuals and partners, and I look forward to a lot more of it.

"Your mother and I would love to meet her someday," my father says.

"You will."

"Any idea when?" my father asks.

"I'm all for meeting Pepper," Seth says, "but this guy needs to get those hearts out of his eyes and focus on that contract and the future of his career before the opportunity closes."

My fucking future.

I know I need to get my shit together and figure that out, but right now the only thing I'm certain of, is that I want Pepper in it.

Chapter Twenty-Nine

Pepper

 "I think we actually have a shot at this funding," Ravi says as we head for his car Wednesday afternoon after pitching our migraine device and the hands-free mouse alternative to MS Enterprises.

"I got that feeling, too. They also seemed interested in hearing about our other ideas."

He opens the passenger door for me and goes around to his side of the car. I pull out my phone as he settles behind the wheel.

"Sending Dr. Bowry a thank-you?"

"No, but I will. I'm texting Clay. He was so excited for us this morning. I want to let him know how it went."

"Look at you, excited about texting a man, and hardly working overtime anymore. I guess you're enjoying having him around after all."

I lower my phone to my lap and look at him. "What do you mean *after all*? You know I love being with him. You saw us at dinner the other night. There was no shortage of PDA." We met Ravi, Chris, and Min for pizza and wings at a pub Monday night. We played pool and darts, which I hadn't done since college, and we had a wonderful time. We're getting together with them Sunday to watch the Super Bowl, and I'm even excited about that.

"I also know you fought it tooth and nail for a long time, Little Miss If Anyone Asks, I Had a Work Emergency This Weekend."

"I didn't know who he was for all that time. I thought he was just a self-centered jock. Now I know he's someone who loves his family and cares deeply about other people, and he sees all of me, Ravi. Like you do."

"I assure you, Clay sees more of you than I have in a very long time." He flashes me a teasing grin. "I'm happy for you. It's good to see you smiling and not so stressed all the time. How long is he staying?"

"I have no idea, but I'll miss him when he leaves. I miss him when he's gone for a few hours. We have so much fun when we're together. Do you know what he got me to do the other morning after watching the sunrise?"

"Knowing you two, you had wild sex."

"Well, *yes*, but that was after he convinced me to go running with him. *Running*, Ravi. I don't *run*, and that wasn't the worst part. We did a polar plunge in the lake." I whisper, "*Naked!*"

He barks out a laugh. "Are you kidding? In the park?"

"Yes! Can you believe it? *Me*. Naked in the park! He makes me so reckless, and I don't even regret it."

He laughs. "I knew I liked him for you."

"It's *crazy*. Running? Skinny-dipping? I swear, when we're together, I don't recognize myself." I debate not saying more, but it comes out in a hushed voice. "But I kind of *do*, you know?"

"Of course you do. It's the old you. The one you tried to bury after the accident. I told you when you got back from Paris and I saw how you'd changed in a weekend, I knew he was someone who could make a difference in your life. Hell, who could breathe your love of life back into you. I'm so glad you didn't shut him out when he showed up at the office that first time."

"Me too. We're going to Oak Falls for the Valentine's Day Festival next weekend. I'm a little nervous about it."

"Why? Everyone knows about you and Clay, and he already knows your family."

"*That's* why. You know how my sisters are. Now that everyone knows, nothing is off-limits. Brindle is going to ask embarrassing questions, and Sable is going to be overprotective. I haven't been with a guy in front of my family since...*you*," I say with surprise.

"Well, don't expect them to like him as much as they like me. I mean, I'm *me*."

"You've been hanging around Clay too much," I tease. "I'm not worried about them *liking* him. They already like him. What if they go overboard and scare him off?"

He gives me a serious once-over. "I'll be there if you need backup, but you must really be falling for him to worry about that."

"*Shh*," I say softly. "We're not talking about that."

"Why not?"

"Because it's scary," I whisper.

"You survived being called his flavor of the week very publicly. Nothing is scarier than that."

That's what I tell myself, but when I think about not being with Clay, my chest hurts.

We make good time on the way back to Charlottesville, and when we get up to the office, there are two men on ladders hanging up a gorgeous black and gold SYNTECH sign on the wall behind the reception desk. "Excuse me."

The men look over their shoulders at me with questions in their eyes.

"Hi. Can you tell me who ordered that sign?"

The older of the two men says, "Um…Dr. Montgomery, I believe." He looks at the other man, who nods in confirmation and adds, "A guy named Chris signed off on it when we got here."

"Okay, thank you." As they go back to hanging the sign, I look at Ravi, and he's grinning like the cat who ate the canary. "Did you know about this?"

He stifles a grin.

"Oh my God. You *did*. This was Clay's doing, wasn't it?"

He shrugs, splaying his hands.

"*Ravi*," I say with amusement. "Now you're loyal to *him* before me?"

"When it comes to surprising you, I am."

I cross my arms, but I can't hide my smile. "I don't know if I like you two in cahoots behind my back."

"Yes, you do." He chuckles. "I'll be in my office. Let me know if you want me to meet with Clare or the other candidate after you're done interviewing them."

I thumb out a message to Clay as I head for my office.

Me: *I see the sign fairy has struck again.*

Clay: *I have no idea what you're talking about.*

Me: *Too bad. I had some sexy thank-yous in mind for him.*

Me: *I guess I'll have to give them to the guys who are putting up the sign for me instead.*

An angry emoji pops up.

Me: *Is that an admission?*

An angel emoji pops up, followed by a gift emoji and a red heart.

Me: *You are too much! I love the sign! It's beautiful. Thank you!* I add a smiling emoji surrounded by hearts.

Clay: *I'm glad you like it. Good luck with the interviews today.*

Me: *Thanks! Have fun with Ben and his friends. I'm going to stay late to catch up from this morning.*

Clay: *Sounds good. There are about a dozen guys meeting us at the field. Take your time and text when you're done. We'll celebrate your pitch.*

It makes him so happy working with those boys, I can only imagine how good a father he'll be one day. I sit down behind my desk and dive into my work, counting down the minutes until I'll see him again.

After a not-so-great interview with an applicant from the ad who asked if she would have opportunities to meet "Mr. Perfect," Clare shows up ten minutes early for our interview. Dressed in gray slacks, a cream sweater, and heels, she looks professional *and* nervous.

"Hi, Clare. It's nice to see you."

"It's nice to see you, too. It's always a little strange seeing customers outside the café. I feel like I should have brought you a latte."

"There's no need for that." I smile. "Let's go to my office and chat."

In my office, I hang up her coat, and in an effort to make her more comfortable, we sit at the table instead of across from each other at my desk.

"I brought you a résumé." She opens her purse and pulls out an envelope, which she hands to me. "I haven't applied for a job in a long time. I hope that looks okay."

"This is perfect." I scan the details of her work history. "You have a lot of office experience. Can you tell me about it?"

"Sure. I started working for Mr. Park, the owner of the café, as a waitress seven years ago. He also owns a convenience store and a night club, and he has an office in each establishment. From the beginning, when he needed help with any of the business offices, I would fill in answering phones and handling general office duties. His wife handled the bookkeeping, payroll, and inventory, but she trained me to do them a few months before she left him. That was three years ago."

"Sounds like it was a sticky situation."

"That's putting it mildly. Their divorce was messy, and that's when things started going downhill. Mr. Park has never been very organized. He had four people running the offices, and now he only has me and one other person. Unfortunately, he doesn't pay enough to keep waitstaff at the café, either, which is why I'm there a lot, as you know."

"Almost daily, if I'm not mistaken."

"Yes, but some of that is for extra hours. I also work in the evenings in the offices sometimes to catch up." She tells me about the software she uses, the hours she works, and how much she enjoys the work she does, both in the café and in the offices.

And then she tells me how much she earns, which isn't much above minimum wage. "I get tips, too, at the café, but they're never much."

I'm in awe of her resilience and her loyalty. "That's a lot to handle while raising your family."

"It is, but I'd do anything for my kids."

"From what I know, it sounds like at least Ben would do anything for you, too."

Her expression warms. "Benny is an amazing person. I hate needing to rely on him to help make ends meet, but we haven't had much of a choice. I had big plans when I was young. I wanted to become a nurse, but then I got pregnant with Ben and followed his father here. I had Ben when I was eighteen. His father left town with another girl six months later. In many ways, Ben and I grew up together. We had a lot of tough years, but we made it, and then I met Sammy and Trina's dad and thought things were going to get easier. But after Sammy was born, their father started drinking and never stopped. I had to ask him to leave."

"I'm sorry. Does he still see the kids?"

"No. Things got ugly before he left. I have no idea where he is, and I don't want to know. But the kids and I got through it, and we're stronger because of it."

"That says a lot about you. You seem very resilient."

"I had to be. Thank goodness for Ben. He loves the little ones so much, and he's always there to help with them. When he was sixteen, he started working to help with the bills. I didn't ask him to. He just did it, and thank goodness he did. With kids, there's always something that costs more than you anticipate. Do you have children?"

"No, but I come from a big family. I know how expensive

kids can be."

"It's the unexpected things that take a toll, some that are optional, like my boys loving football. Let me tell you, that is *not* a cheap sport, even when they're little. I know those expenses must seem frivolous, but I'm determined to make sure their lives are the best they can be."

"I don't think supporting your child's love of anything is frivolous, and it's paying off, at least for Ben."

"Yes, it is, and he deserves it. He is the first person in our family to go to college, and I am so very proud of him." That pride radiates in her brown eyes. "Then there are the expenses that aren't optional, like a medical diagnosis that sucks the wind right out of you."

"Are you referring to yourself? Are you ill?" *How much pressure can one woman take?*

"I wish it were me. Trina had a seizure in the bath a few months ago. I've never been so scared in my life. That's when we found out she has epilepsy."

"I'm so sorry. My younger sister Amber has epilepsy. She was eight when she was diagnosed, and it was scary for all of us. How are Trina and your other kids handling it?"

"Trina had a hard time accepting it. No child wants to be different than their friends. But she's a strong little girl, and she's doing okay now. Her brothers worry about her, of course, but we try really hard not to treat her differently."

"My parents taught us to do the same. It wasn't easy, though. We all wanted to protect Amber, but I'm sure it was even more difficult for our parents."

"Difficult doesn't even begin to describe it. I want to wrap Trina up in Bubble Wrap and carry her around with me." Clare smiles. "But my daughter would never put up with that. You saw her attitude over missing her brother's sleepover."

"She seems like a pistol. Are they able to control her seizures with medicine?"

"We thought they were, but she's had two seizures while she's been on it, and they're making adjustments."

"That's not uncommon. They're called breakthrough seizures."

"Yes, that's what they called them. We're hoping that's all it is. The doctor said there is a type of epilepsy that's drug resistant, which scares me even more. Life is hard enough. I don't want my baby to have to deal with that."

"Hopefully the medication will work. Do you know what we do here?"

"A little bit. I read that you do research and development for medical devices."

"That's exactly what we do, and one of our current projects is a device to help people with drug-resistant epilepsy. It'll take time before it's ready for trials and to be put on the market, but there are other options if it comes to that. I'm sure her doctor will go over them with you."

"Yes, he mentioned that. But...if this isn't fate, I don't know what is."

Before Clay and I came together, I might have rolled my eyes at that comment, but so much has changed over the past month, I'm starting to believe in fate. "It sure seems that way, doesn't it?"

She presses her hand to her chest and takes a shaky breath. "I'm sorry. I was so nervous about coming here, and I just realized I've rambled on about my family's problems. I'm sure that makes me the last person you want to hire, but please know that I have accepted that I have terrible taste in men, and I will *not* be going there again."

"You are not the last person I'd want to hire, and don't be too hard on yourself. We've all made mistakes and chosen the wrong partners."

"It seems like you have a great guy."

"Clay is wonderful," I say honestly. "But I had to kiss my fair share of frogs, too."

"Well, I'm *done* kissing frogs." She emphasizes her proclamation with a swipe of her hand. "I am happily single, and I have more than enough on my plate to keep me busy and happy."

I thought I did, too. "I understand where you're coming from, but you never know when someone remarkable will walk through your door. Like you walked through mine." The smile that earns warms my heart. "What are you looking for in a job? What's important to you?"

"Stability and working with honest people who appreciate the work I do. It would be nice to use my brain and maybe learn a little something along the way. I don't mind some overtime, but I'd really like to be home with my kids at night and earn enough money so Ben can focus on his life and not ours. I know that's asking a lot, but if you give me a chance, I promise I will be a dedicated, hard worker. I'm a good problem solver, too, and if I can help it, I'll never leave you hanging."

"With all you've been keeping up with, I have no doubt you'd be a dedicated employee. Let me tell you about the job, and then we can see if you're still interested." I explain what we're looking for, and we talk about the areas in which she could take on more responsibility as time goes on. Clare asks intelligent questions, and we get along well. I explain the benefits, and the salary, which far exceeds what she's currently earning. "Does that sound like something you would be interested in?"

"Absolutely. It sounds like a dream job. I love the office work I do for Mr. Park, and I'm good at it. I'm very detail oriented, and I never let anything fall through the cracks. You can call the references I have listed on my résumé. Melanie Park is his ex-wife. I spoke to her and to the others on the list. They're the other employees who left the company, and they said they'd be happy to talk with you."

"That's wonderful. I will call them. Do you have time to meet the rest of the staff?"

"Yes, I'd like that."

Clay

The sun is going down as Ben and his friends get into position for another play. These guys work together like a well-oiled machine. They're hungry for training and hungrier for success. I've been pushing each of them over the last week, and I love their energy and enthusiasm.

Kent, the UVA quarterback, catches the snap, and the small crowd cheers from the sidelines as Ben bolts down the field with two defenders on his heels.

"That's it, Jeremiah! Stay on him!" I holler as Kent throws the ball.

"Get it, Ben!" a group of girls yells from the sidelines.

Ben leaps into the air, reaching for the ball as Jeremiah jumps up in front of him. Ben catches it just above Jeremiah's fingertips, lands on his feet, and sprints toward the end zone with Jeremiah and Zack, another defender, on his heels. The people on the sidelines go wild, cheering and whistling.

"Get in there, Ben!" I shout, my heart racing.

Ben dives for the end zone, and Jeremiah and Zack dive for him. They go down in a tangle of limbs, and the crowd gasps. Jeremiah and Zack climb off Ben, and there's a beat of silence before Ben hollers, "It's in!" and jumps to his feet as his buddies shout, "Touchdown!"

"Yes!" I holler with the crowd as Ben and the guys throw their arms around each other.

The rest of their buddies run down the field cheering and shouting as Ben, Jeremiah, and Zack run toward them. They crash into each other, building each other up and cheering each other on. I laugh as they head my way, knowing just how invigorating that camaraderie is.

"Great play!" I holler.

"Woo-hoo! Good job!"

I turn as my girl's voice breaks through the noise and see Pepper, looking like a fucking wet dream wearing my jersey over a hoodie and jeans. She's with Clare, and they're each carrying several pizza boxes. Sammy and Trina are running toward us, hollering for Ben.

"Damn, check out the delivery chick," one of the guys says.

"You can have the pizza. I'll take her," Jeremiah says.

"Dude, you better not be talking about my mom," Ben snaps.

"No, man," Jeremiah says. "I want the hot chick in the jersey. She is *fine*."

I turn around. "Watch yourself, Jeremiah. That's my girl you're drooling over."

All the guys laugh.

"Sorry, man," Jeremiah says. "But *damn*. No wonder you're in Charlottesville."

I shake my head. "Go help the ladies, would ya?"

Trina throws her arms around Ben, and he lifts her up, swinging her above his head, earning giggles, while Sammy high-fives the guys as they head for Pepper and Clare, relieving them of the pizza boxes.

"Hey, guys," I say as they start walking away with food. "What do you say?"

A collective "Thank you" rings out.

"Try not to eat like animals," I say as they throw open the boxes and dive in. "Hi, Clare." I set my eyes on Pepper, wanting to haul her into my arms, but I hold back, so as not to embarrass her. "*Pepper*. What a nice surprise. I thought you were working late."

"I was, but I've learned that some things can wait, and others can't. Like celebrating the hiring of my amazing new assistant, Clare."

Clare is absolutely beaming.

"You got the job! Congratulations." I hug Clare and see Ben heading over.

"I can't thank you enough for connecting us," Clare says.

"I'm glad it worked out."

"Mom, you got the job?" Ben asks excitedly.

"Yes—" Clare barely gets the word out before Ben throws his arms around her and spins her around, shouting, "My mom got the job!"

Ben's friends converge on them, cheering.

I take Pepper's hand, pulling her off to the side and into my arms. "Look how happy they are. You have just changed their lives for the better."

"She's amazing, Clay, and I think she's a really good fit for our office. Did you know Trina has epilepsy?"

I glance at Trina, chatting animatedly with everyone, and my heart goes out to her. As I watch Ben's friends joking with her, something else occurs to me. Trina has a lot of people watching out for her. She has what I didn't know I was missing. Community. My teammates are my brotherhood, but in Jersey, I don't have community. I'm finding that here with Pepper, and I'm glad Ben and his family are part of it.

"I didn't know that. Is she okay?"

"Yeah. They're figuring things out. I texted Amber and introduced her to Clare, so she could ask her questions and get a sense of what it was like for Amber to grow up with epilepsy."

"That's great, sweetheart. I'm sure Clare appreciates it."

"She appreciates everything. She is ridiculously underpaid. I like knowing that soon she'll be earning what she's worth." Pepper gazes up at me, her eyes brimming with emotion. "But it's *you* who changed their lives. I meant what I said last week. I never would've thought to talk with her about the job if it weren't for you. You're teaching me to get my head out of the office and open my eyes to the people, and the beautiful world, around me."

"And I never would have met her or Ben if it weren't for you. We make a good team, Montgomery."

As I lower my lips to hers, cheers ring out, and Ben hollers, "Get it, Coach!"

"*Benjamin!*" Clare chides.

I gaze into Pepper's smiling eyes and cock a brow. "I guess we shouldn't give them an encore and show them just how crazy about you I am."

"Probably not, but I like hearing it." She kisses the center of my chest, and in a voice meant just for me, she says, "I'm kind of crazy about you, too."

"Kind of?" I crush her against me. "Guess I need to up my game."

Chapter Thirty

Pepper

I wake to the feel of Clay's warm lips moving down my neck. "Morning," I say sleepily.

"It's not morning yet." He nips at my lower lip, and I realize it's dark outside. "I just couldn't wait another second to taste you."

Thrills skitter through me like we didn't leave a movie early last night to ravenously devour each other. We barely made it into the house before tearing off each other's clothes and getting frisky with the silk scarf he bought me in Paris. It's hard to believe that was only a little more than a month ago. I swear time moves in a blur when we're together. We've done so much in the week and a half since I hired Clare, it feels much longer. Clay's working hard on moving forward with his foundation and practicing with Ben and the other guys, and I watched my first Super Bowl, beat Clay in his video game fair and square, and although I didn't get the funding for the migraine device, MS Enterprises is still considering funding the hands-free mouse alternative. Life is *good*, and while I know my work stands on its own, I also know the incredible man who is currently looking at me with emotion that feels a lot like love is the reason behind its wonderfulness.

"Then don't let me stop you," I say sassily. "Carry on."

He makes a gruff, appreciative sound and does just that. I revel in the feel of his hot hands caressing my breasts, his talented mouth nipping and kissing along the swell of them. He lowers his mouth over one nipple, rolling the other between his finger and thumb, and I bow off the mattress. *"Clay—"*

He smiles against my skin, then does it again, drawing a loud moan from my lungs. I push my hands into his hair as he drags his scruff along that sensitive skin, sending prickles of pleasure radiating outward from my chest, down my limbs to the tips of my fingers and toes. His hand skims my ribs as his mouth blazes a path south, obliterating my ability to think about anything other than the desire growing hotter with every touch of his lips.

He teases me, kissing my inner thighs and all around my sex until I'm drenched with desire, squirming and begging for more. When he finally lowers his mouth to where I need it most, the first slick of his tongue nearly sends me over the edge. But he's become a master at making me *want*, holding me at the verge of madness until my entire body pulses with need. He pushes my legs open wider, continuing the exquisite torture. I dig my heels into the mattress, my fingernails into his shoulders. "Clay, *please—*"

He takes my clit between his teeth and pushes his fingers inside me, masterfully finding that hidden spot that has my toes curling and my breath hitching. He does something incredible with his fingers, sending electricity arcing through me. My hips shoot off the mattress as pleasure explodes inside me like rapid-fire missiles. I cry out, and he pushes my hips down, devouring me as incoherent sounds fly from my lips. I'm pretty sure I'm speaking in tongues, but as I surrender to the pleasure bowling me over, I don't care.

As he does so often, he stays with me until I sink into the mattress, and then he kisses his way up my body. Every touch of his lips causes a sharp gasp of pleasure. "*Need you,*" I whimper, reaching for him as he aligns our bodies. His weight is deliciously familiar, and the feel of his hard length nestled against my center has me opening my legs wider. Those loving blue eyes reach deep into my soul, and *I love you* whispers through my mind. It doesn't shock me. I've felt it building for weeks, but that doesn't mean it doesn't scare me.

"My beautiful, brilliant girl," he whispers, his dimples coming out to play. "How did I get so lucky to have you in my life?"

"You charmed your way in and left me no choice."

"I'd do it all over again."

His mouth comes coaxingly down over mine and he thrusts, burying himself to the hilt. Pleasure consumes me, and "*Ohgod,*" comes out in one long breath, as he grits out, "*Jesus. How does it get better every time?*" He doesn't wait for a reply, reclaiming my mouth in a merciless kiss, which is a good thing, because I couldn't form a word if my life depended on it.

We thrust and grind, grasping and clawing, our moans and murmurs filling the air. He lifts my legs at the knees, driving into me deeper, rougher. "*Yes. Don't stop,*" I beg, and he makes a low, guttural noise as he pounds into me. I feel every blessed inch of him stroking that secret spot as our mouths reconnect in messy, urgent kisses. My body trembles with desire so hot it burns. I claw at his back, and he fists his hands in my hair, sending streaks of pain and pleasure whipping through me, unleashing a torrent of pure, explosive ecstasy. "*Clay—*"

He's right there with me, gritting out my name as our bodies shudder and pulse, binding us with something as true and vast as the dizzying world around us. And then I'm floating on a cloud of happiness, coming down from the high.

He kisses me tenderly and brushes his lips over mine. "Happy Valentine's Day, beautiful."

"*Mm.* To you, too."

"Are you still nervous about going home?" We're driving to Oak Falls after breakfast and meeting my family at the festival.

"I'm sure I will be later, but it's hard to be nervous about anything when I'm so blissed out."

He smiles, and we lie nose to nose, tangled together like mating snakes, whispering and kissing, his warm hand moving soothingly up and down my back. "If you're up to it, we can cuddle under blankets on a lounge chair on the deck and watch the sunrise."

We've been spending so many nights at his place, it's starting to feel as much like home as my house, which it shouldn't, since it's not even Clay's property. But it is for now. I've got clothes in the closet and in the drawers, and he even bought a latte machine. I like coming here after work, seeing his hoodies and shoes lying around and spending time in the hot tub and on the deck. He got me to work out with him a couple of times in the home gym, but we prefer horizontal workouts.

"I'd like that," I say. "But I need a minute to wash up."

"Let me brush my teeth, and then you can do your thing." He kisses me again, then heads into the bathroom.

I'm still lying in bed when he comes out. He pulls on boxer briefs and strides over to the bed, looking gorgeously lickable.

"What's that grin for, temptress?"

"I like looking at you."

"I like devouring you." He leans down to kiss me and then heads over to the dresser and puts on sweats and a hoodie. "Take your time. We've got about twenty minutes before the sun rises. I'll get the blankets and make you a latte. I'll meet you downstairs."

I lie sated and happy, thinking about how much has changed. It's been weeks since I felt the pressure to check email and catch up on work in my off hours. That's a little scary, but my work hasn't paid the price. If anything, I've been *more* productive lately. We finished the design for the sensory glove, and we pick it up this week from Kenji for a trial run. I had no idea that being happy could make me more focused in the time I have at work, clearing my plate to spend time with Clay in the evenings and weekends.

That man is good for me in more ways than I can count.

I get up and head into the bathroom. My heart skips at the sight of an envelope on the counter with my name scrawled across it in his blocky handwriting. I open it and withdraw a card with red hearts scattered around the message:

ROSES ARE RED

VIOLETS ARE BLUE

I HAVE A LIST

OF NAUGHTY THINGS

I WANT TO DO WITH YOU

I open the card, and there are several pictures of teddy bears in dirty positions. The male has hearts for eyes, and the female has long lashes and red lips. There's a picture with the female on all fours and the male taking her from behind, another of her riding him, and one of her on her knees in front of him. There's a picture of her lying on her back with his head between her legs and another of her hanging from a chandelier with him lying prone beneath her. Beneath the pictures Clay has written,

Happy Valentine's Day, Reckless. There's no one else I'd rather call mine than you. He drew a lopsided heart and signed his name.

I read it again, bubbling over with happiness, and look in the mirror. I'm *smiling* at nothing. I'm always smiling these days. Clay's voice whispers through my mind. *Nothing is as impressive as that unstoppable smile of yours.* I remember how much his words affected me in Paris, but that's nothing compared to how they affect me now. I study myself for a moment.

My hair is a tangled mess, and I look a little tired, but there's no mistaking the joy in my eyes staring back at me. I thought I looked different when I returned from Paris, like I'd left a piece of myself there. Now I see another change, and I know what was missing. Before going to Paris, I thought I was happy. But now I know I was happy *enough*—enough to survive and be content. I hadn't just left a piece of myself in Paris when I left Clay. In the short time we had together, I'd found true happiness, and I'd left that behind, too.

Now I look like myself again, only better. And that man downstairs is the reason.

I need to find a way to let him know.

After brushing my teeth and washing up, I pull on leggings, thick, fuzzy socks, and one of Clay's hoodies and head out of the bedroom. My pulse quickens at a trail of red rose petals leading down the stairs and into the living room. I lose my breath at dozens of bouquets of gorgeous red and pink roses on every surface, and there in the middle of the room, is Clay, with a coffee mug in one hand and a loving smile on his lips.

"*Clay…?*" I say breathily.

"Happy Valentine's Day, beautiful." He sets the mug on the coffee table and steps aside, motioning toward the couch he was standing in front of.

My gaze moves over several large photographs of my favorite things, with a big red bow on the corner of each elaborate frame. The frames could only have been decorated by Morgyn. I recognize her signature mix of colorful elements and repurposed metals, which are as eclectic as they are beautiful. Tears spring to my eyes, and I point at the picture of my mother standing in her kitchen, smiling warmly like she always does. "How did you...?" My voice cracks.

"I hired Hawk to take the pictures." He reaches for my hand, leading me over to them. "Your mom's smile, because it always makes you happy every time you walk into their kitchen and see it." He nods to the picture of my father standing by the barn, holding out his hand, as if offering it to me. "Your father's hand, because it makes you feel safe."

Tears spill down my cheeks as he motions to each picture, reciting what I told him about each one weeks ago.

"The lake near your parents' house where you and your dad used to sail the boats you built." The sun is glistening off the water, and on the side of the lake are the boats my father and I built together. "Your father saved all of your boats."

I laugh softly, more tears falling.

He motions to the picture of the lab in the barn. "I asked him why he kept the lab all these years, and he said, *So my princess can sneak out there anytime she wants to.*"

"I have a few times when life was overwhelming," I admit, wiping more tears.

He nods to the front of the Stardust Café, with its old-fashioned sign and big picture window. "Because you have so many great memories there." He points to the next picture, the sun setting over the creek. Sable's old guitar is leaning against the rocks we used to sit on. "The beautiful creek where you and Sable used to go for walks."

"And she'd play the guitar," I say as more tears spring free.

"And tell you all her secrets. You felt closest to her there." He motions to the next photograph. "And the tree by the old church in town, where you felt like you did when we were in Paris."

"Like I could just be me. In the moment," I say just above a whisper.

"That's right, baby." He guides me in front of the last two photographs, of the Eiffel Tower and the carousel we rode in Paris, both taken in the dusky morning light without any people around them. "I thought you might like them for your office even though they weren't on your list."

"I *do* want them there. I love them all." I turn to hug him, but he holds up his hand.

"We're not done yet." He goes behind the couch and picks up two more picture frames. "I thought you might like these for your house."

He turns them around, and my heart nearly stops. One is a picture of us at the top of the Eiffel Tower as the sun sets. His arm is around me, and we're gazing at each other. The adoration in our eyes is as palpable and real as the emotions clogging my throat. The second picture is of us holding hands on the carousel, both of us laughing.

My throat thickens anew. "Who took those?"

"I can't divulge my sources." He sets them in front of the couch.

"I can't believe you did all of this and remembered everything I said. Thank you." I throw my arms around him, holding tight.

"I'm glad you like them."

"I *love* them, and I love my card." *And I love you.*

He gazes into my eyes, and he looks so serious, it feels like he's going to say something important. But the seriousness fades, and his dimples appear. "I wish I could have taken the pictures myself." He kisses me softly. "Ready to watch the sunrise? I put the blankets outside."

"Yes. I have a gift for you, too, but I can't give it to you until we're in Oak Falls."

"That's intriguing." He hands me my latte, and as we head out to the deck, he says, "Christening your lab in the loft of the barn?"

I shake my head, laughing softly.

"Revisiting the site where you lost your virginity to obliterate those memories with better ones?"

God, he loves to make me laugh, and I love that about him. "You're impossible."

He wraps me in his arms and kisses me. "And you're my reckless girl, which means anything is possible."

Chapter Thirty-One

Pepper

 Oak Falls is home to horse farms, coffee shops, and quaint restaurants where customers are greeted like family and treated like treasured guests, whether or not they're from the area. That's one of the things I love most about my hometown. The people might be nosy and spread gossip faster than the wind, but as we drive through the town where I went from being a curious child to a careful teen, and finally to the woman I am today, a funny thing happens. I realize I didn't become the woman I am today in Oak Falls. I found her in Paris with Clay, and she took root with him in Charlottesville.

As we near the festival grounds, my nervousness about seeing my family in our newfound coupledom morphs into something else. I'm proud to be with a man who adores me for who I am, with all my meticulousness and overthinking. A man who has shown me that life is so much bigger than proving to the world I'm more than just a smart person or a scientist. A man who has helped me overcome my fears and insecurities. But that doesn't stop butterflies from swarming in my belly when we reach the crowded fairgrounds.

We're blessed with a sunny, almost-sixty-degree day, and it looks like the whole town came out to enjoy it. Hordes of people are milling about the lawn and moving in and out of white tents decorated in pinks and reds, selling arts and crafts, jewelry, clothing, and other wares. The scents of barbecue and popcorn carry in the breeze. Bells and chimes ring out in the distance from carnival games, and heart-shaped red balloons with #TEAMPLAY printed in white on one side and #LOVE printed on the other dance from ribbons tied to tents and tables.

As we make our way through the crowds, parents chase after sticky-faced children eating cotton candy and ice cream. Couples sit on blankets listening to Sable's band play on the stage. Surge came together for one last hometown event before Tuck and two other bandmates leave for LA. Couples hold hands and take pictures beneath a giant oak tree that has red streamers wrapped around its trunk, and dangling from the branches by red ribbons are large red hearts with SWEETHEART, LOVE, KISS ME, LOVE YOU, BE MINE, and other sentiments written across them in white.

I know my mother and Amber are running a booth for my mother's service-dog training business, and Morgyn has a booth for her eclectic and repurposed jewelry, clothing, and home goods. I scan the crowd looking for my other family members and notice people glancing our way, recognition lighting up their faces.

Clay lifts our joined hands and kisses the back of mine, giving me his full attention, as usual. "This reminds me of home. Ridgeport has festivals for every holiday."

"Charlottesville has quite a few, too, but I try to come home for them when I can."

"Do you ever miss living here?"

I wrinkle my nose.

He chuckles. "Not so much?"

"I miss my family, but a day or two every now and then is enough. I could never move back like Grace did. She was a playwright in New York City, and after she and Reed got a second chance at love, she moved back, he renovated the local theater, and now she does what she loves with the man she adores. But I need a bigger city, without the craziness of it being too big. Do you ever miss Ridgeport?"

"I've never thought about it. Like you, I miss my family, and there's that sense of comfort when I go home to see my parents. But I usually get edgy staying in one place too long."

"*Oh.* You've been in Charlottesville a while. Are you getting itchy to leave?"

"Not yet." He stops walking and pulls me into his arms with a playful twinkle in his eyes. "You getting sick of me, Reckless?"

"Not even close. You?"

"I never get sick of myself. I'm a fun guy."

I roll my eyes.

"I'm in no rush to be away from you, babe."

He kisses me, and as we start walking again, I see my father coming away from a funnel cake vendor with a plate full of the powdered-sugary treat. He spots us, and a smile stretches across his handsome face. He heads in our direction. My father is the most stable man I know, and that trait carries over to every aspect of his life, from the way he wears his fair hair short and side parted to his khakis and navy sweater.

"Hungry, Dad?" I ask.

"This is for your mother. You know how much she loves funnel cake." He draws me into a one-armed hug. "I missed you, princess."

"I missed you, too."

"It's nice to see you again, Mr. M." Clay extends his hand.

"You too, Clay." My father glances at his hand and shakes his head, drawing him into a one-armed embrace, too. "I think you've earned the right to call me Cade."

"A'right. Cade it is. This is quite a turnout."

"The sunshine brings everyone out. How was your drive?" my father asks.

"Not bad. We didn't hit much traffic," I say as a child runs by wearing a red sweatshirt with #TEAMPLAY on it. "What's team play?"

"Oh, that's just something the town's doing to encourage people to think like a team and support one another," my father says.

"That's nice," I say. "Where is everyone? Did Axsel make it home?"

"He didn't make it, but Grace and Reed and Brindle and Trace are around here somewhere. Morgyn and Graham, and Amber and your mother, are manning their booths, and Dash is running that football throwing game again this year, raising money for the youth football league. Everyone's looking forward to seeing you guys. Clay, now that you're dating my daughter, I look forward to getting to know you better."

"Maybe we can chat over a boatbuilding lesson sometime," Clay suggests. "I could use a few pointers. Pepper and I had a boatbuilding contest a few weekends ago. We took the boats out to a lake to race them, and she kicked my butt."

My father looks at me, surprise shimmering in his eyes. "You made time to build a boat and race it?"

"Yes." I glance at Clay. "This guy has me making time for a lot of things lately."

"I like the sound of that." My father eyes Clay. "You must

357

be pretty special. She only makes time for the people she cares about."

"Dad, I'm standing right here," I remind him.

"Don't worry," Clay says to my father. "I know how unbelievably lucky I am to have roped your daughter into spending time with me."

"Hey, Braden!"

We all look over toward the games to see who is calling Clay, and through the crowd, I see Dash waving him over. Clay lifts his chin in acknowledgment and holds up an index finger.

"It's okay. Go on over," I say. "I'll catch up with you in a few minutes."

"A'right." He kisses my cheek, and then he points at my father and says, "I'm serious about the boatbuilding lesson. I can't let her one-up me for too long. It'll go to her head."

My father laughs. "I guess she failed to mention that by the time she was a senior, her boats blew mine away."

"Well, *hell*. I guess I'm crazy about a woman who'll always beat me at something."

Clay winks at me, and then I watch him make his way across the lawn toward Dash.

"I like that smitten look in your eyes, princess."

I take a deep breath. "Is it that obvious?"

"Honey, I could feel the difference in you from ten feet away." He holds up the plate of funnel cake, and I take a piece. "It's been a few weeks since the news of you two came out. How have things been? Does he come see you often?"

Why is my heart racing? I break off another piece of funnel cake. "Actually, he's been in Charlottesville the whole time." I pop the sugary treat into my mouth.

His brows lift in surprise. "When Clay called to ask if we'd mind if Hawk came out to photograph us, we assumed things were going well, but we had no idea he was staying in town. How's that going? You usually like your space."

I like my space better when he's in it is on the tip of my tongue, but a voice of caution whispers to keep it there. "Can I ask you something?"

"Always, honey."

I nervously brush the powdered sugar from my fingers. "How did you know Mom was the one?"

"That's a big question. Has Aunt Roxie been sending you body lotion?"

My mother's sister, Roxie Dalton, lives in Upstate New York, and she's famous for making personal products with love potions in them. "No. I've always used them, but not because I believe they have secret powers."

"I wouldn't be so sure."

"Dad, this is hard enough to talk about. Can you just answer the question, please?" I eat another piece of funnel cake, trying to catch a glimpse of Clay, but there are too many people walking by to catch more than a flash of the back of his head as he talks with Dash.

"In a second. Why is it hard to talk about?"

"Because it's big and new and scary, and we're moving fast, which you *know* is not my norm."

"Yes, but love is supposed to be big, and for many of us, it has to be scary."

"*Why?* Why can't it just be easy and not make my heart race and my mind follow?"

"Because some of us are too busy to see what's right in front of our faces. If it wasn't scary and didn't feel bigger than anything else we've ever experienced, it wouldn't rattle us to our bones, forcing us to give it the attention it deserves."

Ravi's voice tramples through my mind. *Any guy who can get you to blow off work and rattle the unflappable Dr. Montgomery must have rocked your world.*

"This is a big change from the girl who spent so much time running from him," my father says, bringing me back to the moment.

"I didn't run from Clay."

He gives me a pointed look. "Are you saying I don't know my daughter? Because every time he showed up, it sure looked like you were skipping town faster than the Road Runner running from Wile E. Coyote."

I pop another piece of funnel cake into my mouth. "Okay, *fine*. Maybe he *did* rattle me."

"That's a good thing, honey, and maybe it's moving fast because that's what your heart wants."

I mull that over, nervously eating the funnel cake as we make our way toward Clay. When we break through the crowd, nearing Dash's booth, it's swamped with kids. I spot my mother, Grace, and Reed talking with Clay, who's holding Emma Lou. I'm pretty sure my ovaries are going to explode at the sight of my sweet little niece in his strong arms.

"That's quite a sight, huh?" my father says.

Realizing I stopped walking, I wince inwardly. "Yeah."

"He looks good with a baby in his arms."

"Yeah, he does." I look at my father, and it suddenly feels important that he hear the truth from me. "Dad, I like my space better with Clay in it."

He gives my hand a squeeze. "I know you do, princess. Otherwise he wouldn't be here. For what it's worth, we all really like him, too."

I nod, relieved that my family is supportive of us. "You never told me how you knew Mom was your one and only."

He glances at my mother with the same depth of love I've always seen in his eyes, and then he turns that loving gaze on me and says, "I liked my space better with her in it, too."

My throat thickens.

"Gwampa!" Emma Lou shouts, breaking the moment. She's beaming at us, with red hearts painted on her cheeks. "Auntie Peppa! Clay's he*ah*!" She wriggles from Clay's arms and runs to us, adorable in red-and-white striped leggings and a white sweater with a big red heart on the front.

I scoop her up and hug her. "Hi, sweets. Are you having a fun day?"

Nodding energetically, she pats my cheeks with both hands and presses her tiny lips to mine. "Love you!"

"I love you, too." I catch Clay watching us with a new expression I haven't seen before. It's warm and enticing in a different way than all the others, and I *like* it.

Emma Lou leans toward my father, her arms outstretched. "Gwampa!"

"Here, let me take that plate." Clay takes the empty plate from my father, and I hand Emma Lou to him.

"Pepper, honey. It's so good to see you." My mother looks pretty in a V-neck wine-colored sweater and jeans. She embraces me, and her brown hair tickles my cheeks, her familiar scent enveloping me.

"Sorry I ate your funnel cake."

She waves her hand dismissively. "There's plenty more where that came from. Clay was just telling us how you helped come up with the idea for his new foundation, and you hired someone new to work in your office, *and* you're close to getting funding for another project. Honey, it sounds like you're on *fire*."

"There's been a lot going on." I look curiously at Clay, surprised he'd say so much about me.

"I was just catching them up on how hard you've been working," Clay says.

"Bragging is more like it," Grace says teasingly, moving her thick brown hair over her shoulder before hugging me. "It's good to see you." She lowers her voice, whispering, "He adores you."

"I adore him, too," I whisper, and boy does it feel good not to hold it in. I step back, taking in her rosy cheeks and bright eyes. "You look beautiful, Grace. How are you feeling?"

"Amazing, and the doctor says everything looks good." She holds up crossed fingers.

"I'm so glad." I hug her again.

"But she's still going to take it easy," her strappingly handsome, renovations expert husband, Reed, says, and opens his arms. "Get in here, Pep."

I hug him. "Thank you for taking such good care of her."

Reed drapes an arm over Grace's shoulder. "Gracie's my world."

"These Montgomery girls have some kind of magic, don't they?" Clay takes my hand, pulling me to his side, and kisses my temple.

"You can say that again," Dash calls over from behind Clay.

"Ready for my help yet?" Clay asks.

"No, I'm good. We just needed you for that photo op," Dash says. "Hey, Pep. Want to take a shot?"

"I think I'll save myself the embarrassment and skip it. Thanks, Dash."

Clay arches a brow. "You don't even want to try, babe?"

"No, and there's a pack of kids heading his way." I nod to a group of teens hurrying toward Dash.

"Trust me, she's doing the right thing," Grace says.

"He knows I'm not great at sports," I say. "But I did kick his butt in bowling."

"You are an excellent bowler," my mother says. "Cade, remember when we signed Pepper and Sable up for soccer?"

I groan. "Do we really have to relive this?"

"Now we *definitely* do," Clay says.

"You two were adorable," my father says with Emma Lou in his arms. "When Pepper got the ball, Sable would tear down the field, knocking kids out of her way so her sister could make the goal."

"Now, *that's* loyalty," Clay says.

"Sable is loyal, but our sweet, smart Pepper would get all the way down the field and *stop*," my mother explains. "Then she'd stand there trying to figure out the best angle to kick the ball into the goal."

Clay hugs me against his side. "My girl just wanted to do it the best way possible."

"Yes, but then kids would try to steal the ball from me, and Sable would push them out of the way. She got kicked off the team because of me." I look up at Clay. "She was my own personal defender."

"She still is," Grace says. "Needless to say, unless it's bowling, Pepper's not great with anything that requires a ball."

The guys stifle laughs.

"What's this about my sister handling balls?" Sable asks as she struts over with Kane, causing more laughter. "Hey, sis, is Braden giving you a hard time about something? Because I'll set him straight."

"*No*, he's not."

Sable points at Clay. "You and I need to get better acquainted."

"Here we go." My father shakes his head.

"*Sable*," I warn.

"It's all good, babe," Clay says. "Sable, you and Kane should come visit us in Charlottesville. You can do a polar plunge with us."

The shocked look on my family's faces makes me laugh, and *come visit us* makes me swoon.

Sable scoffs. "Yeah, right. Pepper doesn't do polar plunges."

"I do now," I say, grinning as Sable's jaw drops. "Clay's opening my eyes to a lot of things I've never done before."

"I bet he is," she says with a smirk.

Hours pass with laughter, stolen kisses, and fun with friends and family. Clay and I play games, and when we run into Ravi and his family, they join us for lunch. We visit every available booth, and Clay buys his mother a necklace from Morgyn. He takes pictures with eager fans and signs autographs when asked, and I'm surprised to realize I no longer feel uncomfortable by that attention. It feels good to see him appreciated for his hard work.

By midafternoon, we're having so much fun and I'm on such a high, I don't want to wait another minute to give him his gift. "Are you ready for your Valentine's Day present?"

His gaze turns seductive. "I'm always ready, baby."

"It's not *that*. Come on." I take his hand, hurrying toward the exit.

"Where are we going?"

"You'll see!"

Soon we're running and laughing, sharing a kiss here and enduring a swat on my butt there, which makes me squeal and run faster. When we reach Main Street, I'm out of breath. We slow to a walk, taking in the banner hanging above the road announcing the festival and the big red bows tied around the old-fashioned streetlights. Shop windows are decorated with reds and pinks and boast signs that say OAK FALLS SUPPORTS #TEAMPLAY.

"Don't ever say you're not sporty." Clay hauls me into a kiss. "You can haul ass when you want to. Where to?"

Butterflies swarm in my belly again. I can't believe what I'm about to do, but I refuse to chicken out. I pull open the door to the Stardust Café and wave him in.

"Pepper Montgomery," Winona Hanson, an effervescent redhead, says from behind the counter, drawing the attention of a few customers sitting on red vinyl stools by the counter and a couple sitting in a booth. "I was wondering if I'd see you this weekend with your famous beau."

"Hi, Win." I wrap my arm around Clay's. "This is Clay Braden. Clay, this is Winona Hanson. She runs the café."

"It's a pleasure to meet you," Clay says. "I bet you're privy to all sorts of juicy gossip."

"They don't call it Gossip Central for nothin'." She grabs a plate from the counter and holds it up, offering us heart-shaped sugar cookies that have #TEAMPLAY written on them in red icing. "Cookie? They're on the house today."

"Thanks." Clay and I each take a cookie, and he says, "I love how the community is supporting teamwork."

Some guy at the end of the counter yells, "Go team play!"

"Oak Falls always pulls together," Winona says. "Do you want to take a seat, and I'll be right with you?"

"Thanks, but we're not here to eat," I say. "I just want to show Clay the Let It Out wall."

"It's quite a sight," she says. "Let me know if you need anything."

I take Clay's hand, and we head to the back of the café.

He eyes the graffiti wall. "Does this mean I get to see what you wrote on here?"

"Yup." We stand in front of the wall as he looks it over. "This café is legendary. Nearly every kid who ever lived in Oak Falls has worked here for some period of time, and anyone who's lived in the area has probably written on that wall."

"Did you work here?"

"Yes, for one summer. It was fun, but it was a lot of hard work keeping up with everything. Did you ever work as a waiter?"

"No, but I worked in a sports store one summer. The customers drove me nuts, but it was great for meeting girls. If you came into the store, I definitely would have asked you out."

"That would never have happened," I say lightly.

"What are you talking about? I would have asked you out."

"I have my doubts about that, but that's not what I meant. I meant I would never have gone into a sports store."

He cocks a grin. "You would've if you knew I worked there. You wouldn't've been able to resist me."

He tugs me into a kiss, and I can't help teasing him.

"I think I know why your shoulder hurts. It's from carrying around that big head of yours."

He laughs. "You like my big noggin. Now, stop distracting

me so I can figure out who was special enough to be on this wall with you." He moves along the wall as he reads the graffiti for a solid fifteen minutes before pointing to a heart with partially occluded names inside in the upper-left corner. "Is that your parents'?"

"You have eagle eyes."

"Not good enough, apparently. I don't see your name or your initials."

"Keep looking."

While he scours the wall, I worry with my hands, mustering my courage to push past my insecurities, past my need to stay behind the emotional walls that have protected me for so long. My heart races, and I feel like I might puke, but I want to give him this more than I've ever wanted anything. I grab a permanent marker, pull a chair over to the wall, and climb up on shaky legs.

"Careful." Clay hurries behind me, putting his hands on my legs to keep me from falling. "What are you doing?"

I can't answer. It takes all my focus to keep my hand steady enough to draw a big heart and write RECKLESS LOVES MR. NOT SO PERFECT inside it. I know he can't see it from where he's standing, and as he helps me down off the chair, I touch his cheek, keeping his attention on me. "The reason you can't find my name is that I've never written on the wall before."

"Not even about you and Ravi?"

I shake my head.

"Why not?"

"I don't know," I say honestly. "I never really knew why I didn't write on the wall like everyone else. I just never wanted to. But now I think maybe it's because my heart was waiting for you." That last part comes out shaky and quiet, sounding as nervous as I feel.

He holds my gaze for a long moment before stepping back and looking up at the wall. I can barely breathe as he stares at it, then turns slowly toward me, his eyes serious.

"You don't need to say it back" rushes from my lips. "I just wanted you to know before you go back to your real life, whenever that is."

"My *real* life?" he says low and a little gruffly.

"You know what I mean. When you're practicing or in season or whatever you call it."

His jaw ticks, and silence stretches between us. Just as my insecurities start to get the better of me, he steps closer and runs his fingers down my cheek. "Reckless," he says earnestly, his eyes searching mine as the warmest, most loving smile crawls across his face. "You *are* my real life. Don't you know I've been falling for you since day one?"

Relief swamps me, tears threatening. "You have?"

"How could I not? You know how much I love a challenge."

The tease in his voice is overshadowed by the emotions pulsing between us as he lowers his lips in a kiss so lovingly tender, it roots him deeper into my heart.

Chapter Thirty-Two

Pepper

After we leave the café, Clay says he wants to see the town through my eyes, which makes me love him even more. I love all the parts of us, but this part, where we can walk hand in hand and conversation comes easily, without awkward silences or the need for entertainment, is one of my favorites. Every now and again, I look at him, trying to figure out how we got here, or we look at each other with incredulous expressions, like we can't believe we've fallen for each other. We don't say a word. He just pulls me into a kiss, or we both laugh. I love that about us, too.

He lets my overthinking brain come out to play without picking it apart.

I take him to the site of my first kiss, and my competitive guy tries to kiss away those memories. When I show him the tree on the hill by the old church, he takes a picture of us there. I remember how stunned I was when he took that first picture of us in Paris in front of the bookstore. I never would have guessed we'd end up here, and now I can't imagine my life without him in it.

When we get back to the festival, Surge is onstage playing "Do I Make You Wanna?" Clay walks backward, pulling me toward the area in front of the stage where people are dancing, asking me if I want to do each of the things the song calls out. But he changes the lyrics—*Do you wanna stay up to watch the sunrise? Make love in the moonlight? Make out in the mornings?*—and a handful of other things that he definitely makes me want to do.

We weave through the crowd, and he twirls me into his arms. He sings off-key as we dance. When they start playing "Lose Control," Clay tugs me into his arms and says, "They're playing our song, Reckless."

His blue eyes hold me captive like they do so often. "You remembered?"

"Every second we've been together."

I bundle that up in a ribbon and tuck it away to moon over later. Our bodies move in perfect sync, and heat builds between us as swiftly as it always does. I try not to get lost in it, loving the way he makes me feel so much.

As if he's thinking the same thing, a wicked grin curves his lips. "Do you think everyone can tell I'm thinking about stripping off your jeans and dropping to my knees right now?"

My thoughts stumble, and I can tell by the gleam in his eyes that's exactly what he was trying to accomplish. "What if I say yes?"

"Then I'd say we should give them a show."

"You wouldn't dare."

He presses his cheek to mine and says, "No, but I'll make it up to you tonight."

Shivers of heat move down my spine. "Is that a promise?"

"You know it is."

The song comes to an end, and he keeps me close. I hold my breath waiting for his kiss, but as his mouth nears mine, he twirls me around. A laugh tumbles out, and he draws me into his arms again.

"*God*, baby. That smile gets me every time," he says roughly, and lowers his lips to mine, kissing me breathless.

As the band plays "My Person," we slow dance, and Clay sings every word to me, swapping some of them, like *mai tai* for *mojito*, and singing about how we never stay in bed to sip coffee, and how he likes it when I steal his hoodies. I join him, making up my own words. Singing about him making my heart race while we dance and how I want to stay in bed but not sip coffee, *wink, wink.* That earns a husky laugh.

"I'm crazy about you, Reckless."

My heart feels like it's trying to break through my chest to get to him. "I'm crazy about you, too."

He leans down to kiss me as the song comes to an end, but stops short again, his gaze catching over my shoulder, his brows slanting. "Um, Pep. You might want to see this."

I follow his gaze and realize we're the only ones standing in front of the stage, and everyone else is wearing a red sweatshirt with #TEAMPLAY across the chest.

Applause and cheers ring out, and the crowd starts chanting, "*Team Play. Team Play.*"

I look around expecting to see a Little League team or something and lower my voice. "Maybe we should move away from the stage." Trying to make sense of it, I look at Sable. She and her bandmates are pulling on red sweatshirts, too.

Sable steps up to the microphone, and the crowd quiets as she announces, "Ladies and gentlemen, I give you Team Play!"

The crowd goes wild again. Clay and I clap, looking around and walking backward to clear the way for the team.

"That's you, Pep!" Brindle shouts as she struts out of the crowd with Morgyn and Amber.

I freeze.

"You and Clay have your own hashtag!" Morgyn shoves sweatshirts into our hands. "Brindle thought it up!"

"Team *Play!*" Amber says. "*P* for Pepper and *lay* for Clay!"

The crowd bursts out in hysterics, and someone yells, "Mr. M can't unhear that!" causing more uproarious laughter.

Clay is laughing, pulling me against his side. "Our own hashtag, baby! I love it!"

"Ohmygod. *Brindle!*" My cheeks burn. "You got the whole town involved in this?"

"Don't look at me like that," Brindle demands, the din of the crowd quieting. "If it weren't for our matchmaking, you'd still be running away from Clay."

"What are you talking about? You didn't have anything to do with us getting together."

"Not alone, I didn't." Brindle turns to face the crowd and shouts, "Matchmakers unite!"

I watch in stunned silence as my parents, Grace, Dash, and Ravi step out of the crowd, and Sable comes off the stage, joining the gaggle of them.

"Wha…you *all…Grace? Ravi?*"

Ravi holds his palms up to the sky. "Someone had to make sure you didn't cop out of going to Paris because of work."

That's when I remember that Grace talked me into going to Paris in the first place when I was wavering.

"I'd say sorry," Grace says, "but I'm not."

"We had to do something to make sure you couldn't run from Clay anymore," Morgyn supplies.

"And Clay needed you," Amber adds. "He'd just lost the playoffs."

"We knew you were the only person who could have gotten

his mind off the game," Dash says.

"Thanks, you guys!" Clay says, and I glower at him. "*What? I got my girl. I'm happy.*"

"I'm happy, *too*," I insist. "But I can't believe there was so much scheming going on behind our backs. *Mom?* You and Dad were in on this?"

"Honey, it was so obvious that you were attracted to Clay, but you were standing in your own way," my mother says. "All we did was think up a few extra reasons for Dash to invite him to visit this past year."

"Dad!"

My father hikes a thumb at my mother and says, "It was her idea."

The crowd laughs.

"What are you upset about?" Sable steps forward. "You got the guy you've been drooling over. Shut up and kiss him already!"

The crowd cheers, and Clay draws me into his arms. "What do you say, Reckless? Should we show them how right they were?"

I know out of everything I have ever done, or will ever do, this moment will be the one Oak Falls residents remember me for. My rational brain says to be low key, but my loving heart says *eff that*. "Kiss me like you never want to stop, or don't kiss me at al—"

Whistles and cheers explode around us as my words are lost to his delicious lips. Clay crushes me to him, and I return his efforts with vengeance *and* possession, wanting everyone to know I'm his and he's mine. He intensifies his efforts, and I go up on my toes, his muscular arms holding me so tight, I can barely breathe. But I don't need to, because he does it for me.

His hand snakes into my hair, and my thoughts flit away, the din of the crowd turning to white noise, and I'm overcome with a sense of freedom I've never known before.

Our lips part on a series of feathery kisses, and as the cheers come back into focus, the rational woman in me can't believe I did that.

But Reckless is all smiles as my family converges on us in hugs and embarrassing comments that make me blush despite myself. I give my siblings a hard time but tell them I forgive them, and Dash says he's not sorry and that he and Amber knew we belonged together at their wedding.

When the chaos finally calms and the crowd begins to disperse, Sable and her band head for the stage, and my father makes his way over to me. "I'm sorry to trick you, princess."

"You're lucky I like him, or you'd be on my shit list." We both laugh. "I'm sorry about the PDA. I know it was a little over the top."

"Don't ever be sorry for showing the world your heart."

The sound of a helicopter drowns out the blood rushing through my ears, and Sable announces, "Team Play, your ride is here!"

I spin around toward the stage. "What?" I see Clay jogging over.

"Sorry, Cade, but we've got to go. Come on, Pep." He takes my hand, heading for the field where the helicopter is landing.

"Have fun," my father calls after us. "Dash and I will get your car home!"

My family and friends shout their goodbyes and wave.

"Where are we going? And why does everyone know about this but me?" I ask, hurrying to keep up with Clay. "Whose helicopter is that?"

"Seth's. He's flying it."

"Your brother is a *pilot?*"

"Overachievers run in our family. We're going to meet my family in Ridgeport."

I stop running, my heart thundering. "We're meeting your *family?* Why didn't you tell me? I'm a mess."

The wind from the helicopter blades blows my hair around my face. He puts his hands on my cheeks, setting his excited blue eyes on me, talking over the noise. "You're always beautiful. My family is going to be as crazy about you as I am, and our bag and coats are in the helicopter. It's really hard to get my family in one place, and tonight is the debut of Flynn and Sutton's *Heart Stories* documentaries. I want you with me when we surprise them. I'm sorry I didn't tell you about it. I just didn't want to freak you out."

"News alert! I *am* freaking out!" My head is spinning, but my heart is reeling. "I'm glad you want me there, but next time something big comes up, can you *please* give me notice?"

"Noted! Let's *go.*"

We head over to the helicopter, which is insanely loud. Clay helps me climb in and hands me headphones. We put them on, and as we settle into our seats and put on our seat belts, Seth turns to greet us. He's got thick dark hair, and he's wearing glasses and a freaking red #TEAMPLAY sweatshirt. "Welcome aboard Team Play," he says through the headset.

"You, too?" I exclaim, turning wide eyes to Clay.

"Don't look at me," Clay says.

Seth laughs. "Dash left no stone unturned. It's nice to meet you, Pepper. Let's see if we can make this bird sing."

I grab Clay's hand as the helicopter rises into the air. "Are you sure he knows how to fly this thing?"

"I sure hope so!" Seth says through the headset.

"Oh my gosh. You heard that? I didn't mean—"

Clay saves me with a hard press of his lips, and his brother's deep voice comes through the headphones. "If clothes start coming off, I'm hitting the eject button."

Chapter Thirty-Three

Clay

"Another flight without a crash," Seth jokes as we head off the tarmac toward the parking lot. "That makes two for two."

Pepper's eyes widen. "You've only flown that thing *twice?*" She looks at me, appalled, and too fucking pretty in her peacoat and the green and gold scarf I gave her.

"He's *kidding.*" I shift our bag to my other hand and put my arm around her. "I'd never put you in danger."

"That's a lie," Seth says. "You're about to feed her to a lion." He nods to Noah talking with our grandparents by a shiny black Navigator. Victory is pacing a few feet away, talking on her phone.

Noah looks over, flashing that boyish smile that melts women's hearts, *and* their panties. "There they are!" He swaggers toward us in jeans and a puffy black jacket, his eyes gleaming with their usual mischief. His sandy hair is short on the sides, longer on top, and as windswept as Seth's. "Clay, nice of you to bring me a gorgeous date."

Seth laughs. "Told you."

I shake my head, and my grandfather chuckles. Victory ends her call and struts purposefully over to join us, her dark hair spilling over the shoulders of her sleek brown coat.

"Hi," Pepper says. "You must be Noah."

"And you must be *mine for the night*," Noah says as he draws her into an embrace.

"Dude, have a little respect," I say.

"Did I just hear the pot calling the kettle black?" Victory asks.

"I think you did," Seth says.

I put a hand on Pepper's back. "Don't listen to them. They're just causing trouble."

"I have a feeling there's going to be a lot of that going around this weekend," my witty, plump grandmother says, her eyes full of love. "Pepper, honey, I'm Lara, Clay's grandmother, and this is my husband, Bradshaw." She touches my grandfather's arm. "It's such a pleasure to meet you."

She goes in for a hug, and Pepper smiles over her shoulder. "It's nice to meet you. I've heard a lot about all of you."

"Don't believe a word he says," Victory chimes in, before my grandfather can greet her. "I'm Victory, and I'm *so* happy you're here." She hugs Pepper. "I need someone to help balance the testosterone around here."

"All right, that's enough female bonding," my grandfather says. He hasn't changed much over the years. His voice is still as gritty as gravel and as warm as a summer's day. He's still thick chested, with collar-length hair that's more snow than sand and a trim beard. "You women are smarter than we are, which makes you dangerous when you team up. Pepper, after months of listening to this guy complain about how you wouldn't give him the time of day, I finally see why. You're twice as pretty as he is."

"That's saying a lot. Thank you," she says as he embraces her.

I hug my brother and grandparents and put our bag in the back of the Navigator. "Okay, guys. We need to make a plan before we get there. Huddle up." I hold my arms out and wait for them to come into the huddle. "We don't have many chances to surprise Flynn and Sutton, so let's do this right," I say in a hushed voice.

"We need to catch them off guard," Victory says.

"Why are you talking so quietly?" my grandfather asks.

"Why are we in a *huddle?*" Seth asks.

"I don't know, but I'm liking it." Noah's arm is around Pepper, and he flashes that damn smile at her again. "Stick with me, Pep. We'll do some surprising of our own."

"Like hell you will." I grab the back of Noah's coat and haul him away from her, making everyone laugh.

Victory sidles up to Pepper and says, "I'd say they're not usually like this, because Clay never brings women home to meet us, but they're like this all the time about everything. I wouldn't blame you if you want to get on a plane."

"We just came from an event where my big, mischievous family had everyone in the entire town from kids to grandparents wearing sweatshirts with the hashtag *teamplay* on them. *P* for Pepper and *lay* for Clay."

Seth opens his coat, showing them his sweatshirt, and everyone laughs.

"They had balloons and cookies, too," Pepper says. "It was wild."

"Sounds like you're used to this kind of thing," Victory says.

"Yes, but that's not why I'm staying." Pepper sets a loving gaze on me that gets me all twisted up inside and says, "If I go back alone, they'll have to change all those sweatshirts to say *team lay*, and that's not appropriate for kids."

Laughter rings out again.

"Guess she's stuck with you, Clay," my grandfather says. "How about we get this show on the road so we don't miss dinner?"

As the others climb into the vehicle, I draw Pepper into my arms and kiss her. "You're only staying because of the sweat-shirts, huh?"

"Well, that and your cute brothers," she teases, and slides into the vehicle beside Noah, who immediately puts his arm around her.

"You're killing me, Reckless."

I breathe in the salty sea air as we climb out of the vehicle and look up at my parents' sprawling two-story home overlooking the picturesque coastline. I'm met with warm memories of running around with friends, wrestling in the yard with my brothers, and telling stories around late-night bonfires with my family.

"This is gorgeous," Pepper says. "Is this where you lived when you stopped traveling?"

"Yeah."

She gazes thoughtfully up at the house. "It must be beautiful inside."

"It's all open. There are two staircases and a massive kitchen with an island that seats six and overlooks the great room, which spans the back of the house. You'll love it. There are huge picture windows looking out at the ocean, and there's a big deck out back with a fire pit."

"I might never leave. No wonder you rented such a fancy house."

"I thought you loved the rental."

"I do, but it's still fancy."

"This house looks fancy from the outside, but trust me, the furniture is comfortably worn and bears the proof of our rambunctious teen years."

"I like that they haven't replaced it."

"And I like you." I kiss her.

As we head up to the house, Noah says, "Let's see where they are so we can surprise them." He crouches beneath the front windows and waves for us to follow him.

As we make our way around to the side of the house, Victory says, "I feel like a burglar."

"Do you guys do this a lot?" Pepper asks.

"We're kids at heart," I say.

"*Shh!*" Noah puts a finger over his lips, standing beside the windows to the great room, and motions for us to get back.

We press our backs against the side of the house. My grandparents hold hands, watching us from a few feet away.

Noah points two fingers to his eyes and shifts them toward the window. He peeks into the great room, then quickly presses his back against the wall again, speaking quietly. "We've got two in the kitchen and two in the great room."

"And two going through the front door," my grandfather grumbles, and he and my grandmother head around front.

"Stop him!" Noah whisper-shouts, and we all hurry after them.

My grandfather is already plowing through the door, hollering, "Where are ya, boy?"

We barrel in after him, and there's a flurry of shock and

surprise followed by hugs and warm greetings as I introduce Pepper to my parents, Flynn, and Sutton. We all help set the table, and dinner is full of lively banter, interesting conversation, and lots of heckling. I love how my family embraces Pepper, asking her about her work and her family. She talks to Seth and Victory about the trials and tribulations of owning a business, and I'm thrilled when she tells them she never thought she'd have time for a relationship, but she's glad she made it, and her business hasn't suffered in the wake of not working weekends and evenings.

After we all clear the table and clean up, everyone takes their drinks into the great room. I slide my arm around Pepper's waist as we follow the others. "How are you holding up?"

"I'm fine. Your family is wonderful." She looks around the room.

Sutton and Victory are chatting with my grandmother by the couches, Flynn and Seth are heading over to my parents by the fireplace, and my grandfather and Noah are gazing out at the ocean, talking. Pepper's attention shifts back to my parents, lingering on my mother. My mother rarely wears makeup, and tonight she's makeup-free. She's tall and slim but not willowy. She's strong inside and out, with a mix of blond and gray hair she wears loose and untamed to the middle of her back. I've always found her naturally beautiful, and tonight she looks comfortable in jeans and a cream shirt with a forest-green cardigan, but I wonder what Pepper sees.

I hug Pepper against my side and kiss her cheek. "What are you thinking right now?"

"Just how much your family reminds me of mine. Your mom has such an easy smile, and she seems unflappable. I think moms of big families have to be that way, and your dad is a little serious like mine. Victory reminds me of Sable and Grace combined. She's so strong. Not just to have survived losing her husband but to run the business she does. Noah reminds me of Axsel and Brindle when she was single. Seth reminds me of Grace, serious but fun, and your grandparents remind me of what mine were like before they passed away."

"So no more freaking out?"

She shakes her head. "No. It feels good to be here."

"Good."

As I lean in to kiss her, Noah says, "Hey, Flynn. Have you broken the news to Seth and Clay about me being your best man yet?"

"He's your best man?" Seth asks with disbelief.

"Everyone knows he's choosing me," I say.

"Nope," Noah says. "Tell 'em, Flynn."

"Nice try, Noah," Flynn says. "I can't choose, so we're going to have a *Wilderness Warrior* type of competition. We're dropping you three off in some remote location, and whoever makes it back first can be the best man."

"I'm in," I exclaim.

"Dude, you're afraid to get your hands dirty," Noah says.

"That's Seth, not me."

Seth's brows lift. "Says the guy who won't go rock-climbing with me."

"That's because you take too long," I remind him. "I'm halfway up the cliff before you're even ready to start. And, Noah, you can't do shit on land. You're only good in the water."

"That's what she said," Flynn chimes in, and we all laugh.

"You all are nuts if you think he's not picking me. Right, boy?" my grandfather says.

"No way, old man," I chime in. "He wants to stand next to this face in his wedding pictures." I point to my face.

"*Clay*," Pepper chides.

"It's okay, Pepper," my grandfather says. "Let the boy dream."

As we jokingly argue about being Flynn's best man, my mother and Victory saunter over. "Honey," my mom says. "Can we borrow Pepper for a minute?"

Before I can respond, Victory says, "We're saving her from the nonsense. Come on, Pep." She drags Pepper away.

"Don't believe a word they tell you," I call after them.

Pepper glances over her shoulder and smiles.

I watch them sit on the sofa with Pepper in the middle. My grandmother and Sutton join them, sitting on the love seat. They talk animatedly, and Pepper laughs at something they say. I expected my family to love her as much as I do, but to actually see it unfolding before my eyes? That's pretty fucking incredible.

My father sidles up to me. "She's something special, son."

"Yeah. She is. I'm a lucky guy."

"How's that glove you mentioned working out? Is it helping?"

"We pick it up this week. I guess we'll see."

"And your shoulder? Think it'll hold up for another season or two?"

I scoff. "Of course. But I don't want to talk about football tonight."

He glances at Pepper with the others and says, "No, I don't suppose you do."

We watch as my mother touches Pepper's shoulder, her hand lingering there for a moment. Pepper's smiling, nodding.

She looks down at her lap in that slightly bashful way she has, and then Victory says something that makes them all burst out laughing. Pepper looks over, happiness radiating from her, and our eyes connect with the same zing of electricity that grows stronger every day. But it's the thrum of love beating a path between us that has me wanting to go over and take her in my arms.

"I haven't seen that look in your eyes since you were five years old, when you saw your first football game on television in the airport."

My father's words mirror what I've been feeling all along, drawing me from my thoughts. "You think?"

"There's no thinking necessary, son. Happy, mad, guarded, or elated, you've always been an open book. But you've been living life with blinders on, laser focused on football for so many years, I wondered if you'd ever give your heart a shot at anything else." He claps a hand on my shoulder the way he's done my whole life, only this time the way he's looking at me makes it feel different, *bigger*, like he's initiating me into some kind of exclusive club as he says, "Love looks good on you, son,"

I glance across the room at Pepper again, sitting with the people I love most, and my chest expands as understanding hits me. Being in love *is* different and bigger. Until you're knee-deep and willing to drown in it, you can't have any idea what it really is.

I meet my father's steady gaze. "It feels good, too, Dad."

"It's time for *Heart Stories*," Flynn exclaims.

"Everyone down to the media room," my father says, sparking a gust of activity and commotion as we all head for the stairs.

And I head for the only woman I want to write my heart story with.

Chapter Thirty-Four

Pepper

I wake before the sun, in the same favorite position in which I'd fallen asleep. Being spooned by Clay. His arm is heavy around me, his big hand palming my breast. His erection rests against my butt, and his thick thighs cradle the backs of mine. I lie still, reveling in the gentle puffs of his warm breath on my shoulder and neck, the way his chest and stomach press against me with every inhalation. I want to melt into him and stay in his arms forever. But time is moving quickly, and before long he'll be reporting to his team. I'm still trying to work out what that will mean for us. I've never considered myself needy, but I've gotten used to spending so much time with him, I hate the idea of us being apart. And his family? I'm falling just as hard for them as I have for Clay. They're warm, loving, and kind, and they value the things I treasure most. Family and helping others.

Last night when we headed downstairs to watch *Heart Stories*, a truly incredible documentary about our fragmented world, I expected to find a posh media room. Because who has a *media room* in their home? But it was just a big room with a projection TV and several worn leather love seats, with butt indentations from years of use, blankets draped over the backs, and throw pillows with kids' names scrawled in permanent marker on them. The walls were covered with dozens of photos of Clay and his family throughout the years, but none of them as adults. There were pictures of him as a little boy sitting high up in a tree he'd climbed and arm in arm with his siblings, all of them covered in mud. There were pictures of Clay huddled in the grass with dark-skinned kids, holding a football, and of his family around bonfires and dinner tables with dozens of people of varying nationalities. I realized there were no pictures anywhere in the house of Clay playing professional ball or of his siblings in their careers, and I asked his parents why. His mother said, *Because at home we're not a producer, a football champ, or a woman who runs an entertainment empire. We're a family, and we leave all the noise behind.*

Talk about a wall of love. This house is built from them.

Clay stirs behind me, hugging me tight. "Your heart is beating fast."

"You're naked against me. Of course it is."

He kisses my shoulder, sliding his hand down my belly and between my legs. I inhale shakily, his touch alighting flames within my core. "Are you sure my girl isn't overthinking?"

He knows me so well now. It's a blessing and a curse. But I don't want to get lost in logistics when we're having such a beautiful weekend. "Only about how much I want you inside me."

He presses a kiss to my neck. "Think you can be quiet?"

"I can try."

He nips at my shoulder, and I shift higher as he guides his cock to my entrance and thrusts into me. I moan. "Shh, baby." He thrusts again, sending sparks shooting through me, and I swallow a moan, my inner muscles clenching around his shaft. A husky growl rumbles from his lips. "So tight and greedy for me."

He moves his hand from between my legs, guiding my hand there. "Touch yourself while I fuck you." He knows his dirty demands get me even hotter, and pushes two fingers into my mouth. "Suck them like they're my cock." My entire body ignites, and I alternate between sucking and swirling my tongue along his fingers as he pumps them in and out of my mouth. His hips thrust harder and faster, and I work myself to the same pace. He seals his mouth over the crook of my neck, licking and kissing and sucking. Scintillating sensations come at me from everywhere, riddling me with desire. It pulses inside me, burning beneath my skin, until my body aches and throbs with the need to come. I whimper around his fingers. He reads me perfectly, thrusting faster as he sinks his teeth into my shoulder, sending me spiraling into ecstasy. With the next thrust, he follows me over, pumping and grinding, his muffled groans coalescing with my stifled cries.

After we float down from the high, he turns me in his arms and whispers, "*My love*," and then he kisses me, holding me like I'm too precious to ever let go.

A long while later, we clean up and dress in our #TEAMPLAY sweatshirts to watch the sunrise. I put on leggings and he puts on sweats.

"Are you sure this is okay?" I whisper as we gather blankets.

"Absolutely."

We sneak quietly downstairs and out the French doors in the great room to the deck. We're met with the cold breeze from the sea and the scent of a bonfire, and find his grandparents cuddled beneath blankets on the circular sofa surrounding the fire pit.

His grandmother lifts her head from his grandfather's shoulder and says, "We wondered if you lovebirds would get up this early."

"Mind if we join you?" Clay asks.

"Not at all," his grandfather says in that endearing sandpaper voice. "Get comfy and keep your sweet gal warm. We've got about half an hour before the sun graces us with her beauty."

We settle in on the couch, bundling up beneath the blankets, with the fire warming us. As Clay puts his arm around me, drawing me tight against his side, his parents come out the French doors. They're wearing thick sweaters over turtlenecks and jeans and carrying their own blankets. It makes me happy to have more time with them.

"Looks like we weren't the only ones with a good idea," his father says. "Morning, everyone."

We all greet him at once.

Clay's mother kisses the top of his head. "Morning, honey."

"Morning, Mom," Clay says.

She puts a hand on my shoulder, squeezing gently. "Good morning, sweetheart."

"Good morning," I say as they come around the couch.

They sit between his grandparents and us, and his father tucks a blanket around their backs and another over their laps. Then he puts his arm around Clay's mother, drawing her tight against him, and kisses her temple, just like Clay did with me. I catch a loving look between his grandparents. It's no wonder Clay is so affectionate.

"What a nice way to greet the day," his mother says.

"It's the best way." *Second only to making love with your son.*

"I've gotten more sunrise photos from Clay this past month than ever before," his grandfather says.

"It's not the sunrise that's so special, Gramps," Clay says. "It's who you watch them with."

My heart squeezes.

"That is very true," his grandmother says. "I'm glad you get to share it with Pepper. I never heard the story about how you two got together."

"You know I had to chase her for a year, Gram," Clay says. "She wasn't interested in me. Can you believe that?"

I roll my eyes. "That's not exactly true, and I never wanted you to chase me."

"She did," Clay says. "She just didn't know it."

"Okay, I admit it. You're not wrong."

His grandmother watches us fondly. "What kept you from going out with him?"

"I thought I knew who he was based on his reputation, and I didn't give him a fair shot. Then I got to know him in Paris, and I realized how wrong I was."

"She tried to break my heart when she left Paris, so I chased her to Virginia, and I refused to leave until she admitted we belonged together." Clay flashes a coy smile. "Right, Pep?"

"You were determined."

"It was the only way to break down your walls."

"Sounds like someone else I know," his grandfather says, eyeing his wife. "This one made me jump through hoops to get her to admit what I knew from the very first time I saw her."

"Oh, Bradshaw. You got your girl. Let it go." His grandmother reaches up and touches his cheek. "You know I love you."

"I know you put up with me." He kisses her, and we all chuckle.

"If I've learned one thing about the Braden clan, it's that they are fiercely loyal and relentlessly determined," his mother says.

"When a Braden finds their true love, they'll stop at nothing to make them theirs," his father adds. "Just look at Victory."

"I believe that," I say. "My sister Morgyn is married to Graham, and he's been all in from day one."

"Well, they're not *all* in from day one," his mother says. "Flynn was so thrown off by his feelings for Sutton, he tried to get her fired. Some Bradens need more time to process and understand their feelings than others."

"So do some Montgomerys," Clay says, and then he kisses me.

"Your father told me he's going in on your new foundation with you and Seth," his grandfather says. "I understand it was Pepper's idea."

"No, it wasn't," I say quickly. "We came up with it together."

"Guess you're both bleeding hearts," his grandfather teases.

"You say that like you're not one," his grandmother says.

His grandfather scoffs.

"I'm proud to be a bleeding heart," I say. "And I'm glad Clay helps others. That's one of the many reasons I'm with him."

"Better keep the other reasons to yourself, babe. It would be inappropriate to name them," Clay jokes.

The doors open again, and we all turn to see Sutton, wrapped in a blanket and wearing fuzzy slippers, and Flynn and Seth, both dressed in hoodies and sweats. "Hey, look who's here," his father cheers.

"You're having a party without us?" Seth jokes.

"They're probably talking about us," Flynn teases as they all squeeze onto the couch.

The French doors open and Noah comes out wearing shorts and a hoodie, his hair askew. "So we're really doing this? At the butt crack of dawn?"

"Nobody made you come downstairs," Sutton says.

Noah comes around the couch. "I heard you guys going down the hall and had FOMO." He squeezes in between me and his mother, flashes an endearing smile, and lifts the blanket from my lap, scooting closer to get under it.

"Dude, you better keep your hands to yourself," Clay warns.

"It's not his hands I'd be worried about," Seth says.

Noah smirks. Clay glowers, and his brothers crack up.

The door flies open again, and Victory runs out of the house bundled up in a blanket, wearing a hat and fuzzy socks. "I was worried I missed the sunrise." She stands behind me and shoves Noah's shoulder. "Move over."

"If you say so." Noah scoots even closer to me.

Victory smacks his shoulder. "*Other way*, mongrel." He curses under his breath and scoots away from me. Victory climbs over the back of the couch and wiggles between us. She points at Clay and says, "You owe me one."

Everyone laughs.

"It's good to have everyone home to celebrate Flynn and Sutton's big event," his father says.

"Here comes a dad speech," Seth jokes.

"It's a short one," his father promises. "Your mother and I are proud of all of you, and not just because you're more competitive than we could ever be and have risen to the tops of your fields."

Clay and his siblings exchange incredulous glances.

"Did our father just say he and Mom aren't competitive?" Clay asks.

"Yeah. What kind of BS is that, Dad?" Flynn asks.

"Who do you think we learned from?" Seth asks. "You dragged us all over creation in order to discover new species of animals and get award-winning photographs."

"That's a different type of competitive," he says. "We weren't out there publicly clawing our way to the top against the world's best athletes or billion-dollar entrepreneurs or putting out documentaries for the world to pick apart. You kids have the type of courage that blows us away on a daily basis. And you've all used your success to help others. That's what we're most proud of."

"You taught us that, too," Victory says. "When we were traveling, not a day went by when we weren't doing something for another family or for animals or for the community."

"That's true, honey," his mother says. "I think what your father is trying to say is that as parents, we can lead by example, but how kids turn out is kind of a crapshoot, and we got lucky. We're proud of how you all turned out."

Clay holds me a little tighter, and I can tell how much his father's praise means to him. As I look around the fire, I see how much it means to each of his siblings, too. Having that support, someone who's always in your corner, is everything. I know how that feels, because my father has been that person for me. But now it's Clay. The apple did not fall far from the tree.

After watching the sunrise, while Clay helps his family make breakfast, I go upstairs and shower. I dry my hair and dress in my favorite leggings and a comfy oversized cable-knit sweater Clay packed for me. I still can't get over how sneaky he was to have pulled this off, or how incredible this weekend has been. I have no idea how we're getting home.

I head downstairs wondering if we're in for another helicopter ride. I hear his family talking, and then I hear Clay and Seth in a heated conversation and stop before I reach the bottom step.

"What the hell have you been doing all this time?" Seth asks sternly. "Distracting yourself with her to avoid making a decision?"

My chest constricts. *What decision?*

"Let it go," Clay seethes. "It's none of your business."

"Clay," Seth pushes.

"Jesus Christ, Seth. Maybe I was using her as a distraction. Who fucking cares?"

Blood rushes to my ears, and I feel sick. I run upstairs on shaky legs. Tears blur my vision as flashbacks to my college heartbreak slam into me. I can't think, can't hear past my hammering heart. I have to get out of here. I order a ride to the airport. The car is seven minutes away. *Thank God.* I throw my things into our bag with trembling hands and hurry into the bathroom to get my toiletries, shoving them into the bag. I thought this was real. I trusted him. Clay's voice roars through my head. *Maybe I was using her as a distraction. Who fucking cares?* I zip the bag, feeling like I'm going to throw up.

I rush down the front staircase and reach for the front door. But I stop myself. I'm not doing this again. I'm not running and hiding. I never made that jerk pay for what he did to me in college. I'm not going to be that scared girl again.

I drop my bag, lift my chin, and with my heart in my throat, I march into the kitchen. Clay is pacing, and his family is sitting at the table chatting amiably. That cuts me to my core. They heard every word he said. It's college all over again.

"Excuse me." My voice comes out strangled.

Clay spins around, his face a mask of distress. "Reckless? What's wrong?"

He hurries over to me, but I hold up my hand, stopping him. I look at his family, and my heart breaks anew. "Thank you for a lovely time, but I have to go."

"Go? Go where?" Clay asks as his family gets up from the table, confusion riddling their faces.

"Oh, honey, we're sorry to see you go. Is everything okay?" his mother asks.

Nothing is okay! It takes all of my strength to hold myself together. "I have to go home. I called for a ride." I rush out of the kitchen, making a beeline for the front door.

"Pepper, *wait.*" Clay follows me out. "What's going on?"

I turn on him, my heart shredding in my chest as his family piles out the front door, just as the car I ordered pulls into the driveway. It's all too much. Tears break free, and the truth pours out, fast and cutting. "I *trusted* you. You *made* me believe this was real."

He steps closer, splaying his hands. "What are you talking about?"

"I don't know what decision you have to make, but I am *nobody's* distraction." I head for the car.

One of his brothers says, "Oh, shit."

"Pepper, *stop!*" Clay runs after me. "Guys, block the car!"

His brothers bolt past me, and Noah dives onto the hood.

The driver gets out of the car, shouting at him. Flynn and Seth run to Noah's defense, and their words turn to white noise.

"Don't do this to me, Clay," I warn. "All I ever asked for was honesty. I heard you tell Seth you used me as a distraction, and I *heard* you say *Who fucking cares?* That's not love. That's…" I turn away and cover my face as sobs steal my voice.

"You're right. I did say that." Clay steps in front of me and moves my hands away from my face, his eyes imploring me.

I grit my teeth to try to keep them from chattering.

"But you didn't hear the rest of what I said. I said *maybe* I was using you as a distraction in Paris, because at the beginning it was probably true. I'd just come off a shitty loss, and my contract is ending, and I have to decide whether I'm going to keep playing football. With my shoulder acting up and another guy gunning for my position, I couldn't think straight. I *needed* a distraction. When Dash suggested I meet him in Paris, I said *no.* Then he said you were coming." The muscles in his jaw bunch, his eyes serious. "The *only* thing that got my head out of that fucked-up place was the thought of seeing you. And the reason I said who fucking cares is because the distraction didn't last. It might have started out that way, but I fell head over cleats in love with you. I told you I've been falling for you since day one, and I meant it. We are *real,* baby. If I'm guilty of anything, it's not telling you about the contract extension, but I didn't lie. My love for you is as real as the ground we're standing on."

"It's *true,*" Seth shouts. "He told me he's madly in love with you."

"He did," his grandfather says. "The boy's a goner."

Swallowing against my thickening throat, I swipe at my tears, choking out, "I don't understand. Why didn't you just talk to me about it?"

"Because I'm terrified of making the wrong decision," he says vehemently. "The egotistical asshole in me wants to go out on top and play another season. I hope the glove you're making will work, but I'm scared of permanently injuring my shoulder, or playing shitty because of it and letting everyone down. But I'm also sick of all the public bullshit that goes along with playing, which doesn't just affect me. It affects you. And football has been my life for so long, I'm afraid of retiring and not knowing who I am without it. But most of all, I'm scared of losing you."

More tears fall at the gut-wrenching pain in his voice and the overwhelming love in his eyes. "That's a lot for anyone to try to figure out alone. Why do you think you would lose me?"

"Because you made it clear that you don't want a long-distance relationship, and if I decide to play, we practice in Jersey. I'll be gone more than half that time."

"Don't you know that's changed? You've chased me. I think I can do a little chasing. I *love* you, Clay. I love *us*, and the life we're building together. I respect your career, and more importantly, I want you to be happy. If that means playing for another year or *ten*, then I support that and I'll make time to be there on the weekends."

One of his brothers hisses, "*Yes!*" and "*Aww*s" ring out from Sutton and the other women.

"If I play, the schedule is grueling," he says.

"Where there's a will…"

He smiles, his brow furrowing. "I can't promise there won't be more annoying headlines. Especially if I fuck up on the field. They'll try to blame you and our relationship."

"I survived being your flavor of the month and being embarrassed by everyone I grew up with. I think I can handle just about anything at this point." I take a deep, shaky breath. "You and I have both been alone for a long time. I had no idea who I was outside of work. You showed me that it's okay to figure things out as we go. Football isn't who you are. It's what you do. *I* know who you are, and your family does, too. You're a loving, smart, generous, competitive man, and you're allowed to be unsure when you make a big change. Love is supposed to be scary, and football was your first and longest-lasting love. It's going to be scary no matter when you do it, but you won't be doing it alone. Whether you retire tomorrow, next year, or five years from now, I'll be here to help you take the next step."

"God, I love you." He draws me into his arms, and as his lips cover mine, cheers and whistles ring out around us.

"So much for my chance with Pepper," Noah jokes, and his family converges on us.

"I'm sorry for the outburst," I say as his mother embraces me.

"No need to apologize, honey," she says. "Real love takes hard work. You just stole another piece of our hearts."

We're passed from one warm embrace to another. When I finally land back in Clay's loving arms and those blue eyes find mine, the pieces of my fractured heart come back together, and I know that no matter what Clay decides, we're on the same team.

Chapter Thirty-Five

Pepper

The warm Vegas air crackles with intensity at the Charity Bowl. There are seventeen seconds left in the fourth quarter, and Clay's team is down by three points. I've been on the edge of my front-row bleacher seat the whole game. I want this win so badly for Clay. It's been three weeks since he laid himself bare on his family's front lawn. The sensory glove has helped him find a new release point, but his shoulder is still iffy. Even so, he decided to play for another season, because my competitive, loyal man doesn't want to let his fans, or himself, down. He's announcing it after the game this afternoon, and his fans are waiting with bated breath to see if their Mr. Perfect will sign or walk away. This was a torturous decision for Clay, and I couldn't be prouder of him for following his heart.

As Clay's team gets into position, the opposing team calls a time-out. I turn to Sable, Kane, and Seth, who came out to support Clay. "I never knew football could be so nerve-racking. I don't know how the players deal with this."

"I think they get used to it," Seth says.

"It should be illegal the way Gorecky keeps going after Clay," Sable says.

"He got a penalty for roughing the passer," Kane says.

"He gets one every game when he plays against Clay," Seth says. "Clay caught him cheating on his wife when he played for the Giants and gave him hell for it. Gorecky's been all over him ever since."

"I should've kicked Jason Gorecky's ass when I had the chance," Sable says.

Seth arches a brow. "Did you have a run-in with him?"

Sable looks at me, her jaw tight, giving me space to respond.

Clay and I had dinner with several of the players last night. That's when I found out Jason was playing in the Charity Bowl. I avoided him like the plague, and I'm glad I didn't reveal to Clay that it was Jason who hurt me in college. He's worried enough about his shoulder. He didn't need to worry about me being uncomfortable.

"I knew Jason in college," I say. "He was a jerk then, too."

"Guys like that never change," Seth says as the time-out ends.

The crowd cheers as the players get into position.

"Seventeen seconds on the clock, and they're on their own forty-two-yard line," Kane says. "Clay needs one hell of a Hail Mary."

Fans begin chanting, *"Let's go, Clay! Let's go, Clay!"* We all join in. I chant as loud as I can, my heart filling up at the love pouring out for him.

Clay gets the snap and scans the field for his target as the defensive line charges. I watch the clash of men with my heart in my throat as Clay evades a defender and the clock ticks down. *Thirteen seconds, twelve, eleven…*

Their star wide receiver cuts toward the center with two defenders on his heels. Clay fires the ball like a rocket. I hold my breath as it bullets through the air with pinpoint accuracy.

The receiver leaps across the end zone, his arms outstretched, and the ball lands in his hands as he crashes to the ground. The crowd erupts, and we jump up and down, hugging each other and cheering for Clay. Clay looks over at me, his arms shooting up in the air, and I yell, "Way to go, baby!" as players barrel into him.

"Way to go, brother!" Seth hollers.

Time moves in a heart-thundering blur as the extra point is lined up, and the kicker nails it. The crowd goes wild again and players spill out onto the field. I'm so happy, I've got tears in my eyes.

"Go get him, Pep!" Sable yells.

In the next breath, Seth and Kane are lifting me over the railing. I don't have time to think as Clay sprints toward me and throws his helmet to the ground. Then I'm in his arms, and we're kissing and laughing, and he's spinning me around. Cameras are pointed at us, and reporters are shouting for Clay's attention. Players are everywhere, the crowd is cheering, and Clay is looking at me like I'm all *he* sees, as he says, "That was for *you*, Reckless. Just for you!"

"And this is for you!" I crush my lips to his for all the world to see.

"I love you, baby!"

As he lowers me to my feet, I see Jason coming up behind him.

Clay

The blood drains from Pepper's face, and she stumbles backward. I reach for her just as Gorecky sidles up to me, and she steps farther away. One look at the humiliation and anger warring in her eyes and Gorecky's smarmy smirk is all it takes for understanding to slam into me. I grit my teeth, my hands curling into fists. Media cameras are all over the fucking place, reporters are shouting at me about my Hail Mary, but all I see is red.

Gorecky lifts his chin in Pepper's direction and says, "Looking *good*, Pepper."

"Don't you fucking look at her," I seethe.

He flashes an arrogant grin, turns his back to the cameras, and says, "Enjoying my sloppy seconds, Brad—"

A crack sounds as my fist connects with his jaw, and he reels back. Blinded by rage, I get another punch in before he comes at me, his face bloody. Our fists fly, but guys drag us away from each other.

"Watch your back, Braden!" Gorecky shouts. "I'm gonna fucking kill you this season."

Cameras are in my face and people are shouting at me. I tear my arms out of my teammates' grips, searching the crowd for Pepper. I scan the sidelines and see Seth and Kane standing in front of Pepper like bodyguards. Sable has her arm around her, and my girl, my *love*, has fear written all over her beautiful face.

"Clay!" a reporter shouts. "Why did you go after Gorecky?"

I look into the camera and grit out, "Because he's an asshole."

"Are you worried about his threat for next season?" the reporter asks.

"Not even a little. But he'll have to come find me, because I'm done. I'm retiring."

There's a flurry of shouts and gasps as I stride toward Pepper, who looks as shocked as everyone else.

The reporter keeps pace with me. "What's next for Mr. Perfect?" He shoves a microphone into my face.

"Hopefully marrying the love of my life."

Pepper's eyes widen, and her jaw drops as Seth and Kane step aside, and I step in front of her.

"Clay, what are you *doing*?" she asks with a nervous laugh. "Are you okay? Did he hit you in the head? I thought you were signing the extension."

"I'm following my heart. The only thing I want to sign is a marriage certificate making you my wife."

Her eyes tear up. *"What?"*

"Baby, when I threw that winning pass, all I wanted was to get to you. I'm done being Mr. Perfect and living my life for everyone else. I want to live it for *us*. I want to help make your dreams come true, because if you marry me, my dreams will be signed, sealed, and delivered. I want to bring you lunches and spend our lives finding new hobbies and taking polar plunges and dips in the hot tub. I want to make out in parking lots with the woman I love and not care who sees it. I want you to be reckless with me, and I'll be not so perfect with you. What do you say, baby? Want to tie the knot today in Vegas?"

She laughs, tears spilling from her eyes. "Do I even have a choice? I mean, look at those dimples." Laughter rises around us.

"Is that a *yes*?" I ask.

"*Yes*, I'll marry you, you crazy man!"

The stadium explodes into whoops and cheers, and I crush

my lips to hers. "I love you, baby," I say between kisses, and she says it, too, her salty tears slipping between our lips.

There's a frenzy of commotion as I give statements to the press, and my teammates and coaches congratulate us and give me shit for retiring. But I know I'm doing the right thing.

When we finally carve out some space from the mayhem, Sable says, "I guess we're heading to the Chapel of Love."

Kane eyes me. "How would you feel about making it a double wedding?"

"*What?*" Sable says. "We can't crash their wedding."

"Yes, you can!" Pepper exclaims. "We started our lives together. It's only right that we start our marriages together! Right, Clay? Would you mind?"

"Not at all, baby."

Pepper squeals and hugs Sable.

"Mom's going to kill us," Sable says.

"That's okay. Our mom is going to kill Clay, too," Seth says. "We'll send pictures."

I turn to the brother who has always had my back and clap a hand on his shoulder, "Spoken like a true best man. What do you say, bro?"

"You just want an accomplice," Seth jokes, and everyone laughs.

I draw Pepper into my arms. "Ready to go ring shopping, baby?"

Her smile lights up the whole damn afternoon. "I'm ready for anything with you."

"That's my girl," I say, and lower my lips to my love, my life, my future wife.

Chapter Thirty-Six

Clay

As the sun sets off the coast of Silver Island, I take a drink, listening to my brothers' banter on the patio of the Steele family winery, unable to take my eyes off my gorgeous wife in a floral mermaid dress that hugs her curves. I know she has no panties on under that dress. The little temptress tossed that golden nugget out as we were on our way to the ceremony. She's dancing with Victory and Sutton, who looks beautiful in her wedding gown, and a handful of other women. There wasn't a dry eye in the place as Flynn and Sutton exchanged vows. As perfect as their ceremony was and as elegant as this reception is, with twinkling lights and dozens of flowers, I wouldn't change a thing about ours.

My mind drifts back to that whirlwind day three and a half months ago.

We picked out a gorgeous three-carat engagement ring with a princess-cut center diamond, haloed and flanked by round diamonds, and a matching wedding band, bought a veil at the chapel, and were married by an Elvis impersonator. I'll never forget the love in Pepper's eyes when she said *I do*, or the completeness I felt as I vowed my love to her. Our parents were sad to miss the wedding, but we sent pictures, and I bought the house I'd rented in Charlottesville and surprised Pepper with it after we got back to Virginia. We moved in two months ago and threw a small ceremony in the backyard for our families and close friends to attend. We're enjoying filling the walls with pictures of family and all of our favorite places.

Tiffany was not thrilled with me for retiring, but she was happy for me personally, which I appreciated. She said she knew when I delayed signing the extension that my heart had found a new direction. It took some time to get used to not living on a practice schedule, and there were lots of loose ends to wrap up. But I don't have a single regret. I'm enjoying working out with Ben and his friends, and Fielding Futures is up and running and taking applications for the first grants, which are rolling out next month. Pepper couldn't be more pleased with how well Clare has fit into their office, and MS Enterprises came through with funding for her hands-free mouse alternative device. Although she didn't want to use my notoriety to promote her business, I surprised her by pulling a few strings with Johnson & Johnson and was able to get her a meeting with them. She pitched the migraine device, and they just signed off on a contract to fund the project.

Seth lifts his glass, drawing my attention as he says, "Here's to another Braden man off the market. Congratulations, Flynn. We're all happy for you."

"Less competition for us," Noah says as we tap glasses.

We all drink. One of the benefits of retirement is getting to spend more time with family. I'm looking forward to running the summer football camp at the Real DEAL for Noah next month and hanging out with him. Pepper is going to take a couple of days off and we're going to meet my relatives there, and in a few weeks we'll be in Oak Falls for their Summer

Festival. We're also looking forward to taking a honeymoon to Greece in August, when one of Pepper's contracts winds down.

"You guys don't know what you're missing out on. Marriage is the best. Right, Flynn?" I cock a grin. "*Oh, wait.* You *just* got married. You can't answer that yet."

"Jackass," Flynn teases. "You're so competitive, you had to be the first one to the altar."

"Clay was afraid Pepper would realize she was too good for him and run to me," Noah says.

"Stop thinking about my wife. You're too thickheaded for her," I say with a laugh.

"I'm thick, but not in the head." Noah smirks. "You guys can have that holy matrimony stuff, anyway. I like being the flavor of the month for various sexy ladies."

"Jesus, Noah." Seth shakes his head.

"Give me a break. Like you don't?" Noah scoffs.

Seth takes a drink without responding, but his grin answers for him.

"If it takes Seth three years to choose a plane, can you imagine him trying to choose a wife?" I laugh.

Ignoring my comment, Seth gazes out at the vineyard. "I like this island, Flynn. Maybe I'll give T a trip here as a bonus."

"I'm sure he'll appreciate the time off from dealing with your neediness." Flynn nods toward the dance floor. "Check this out." Wells Silver is trying to break in and dance with Victory, but all the girls shoo him away.

Sutton's grandmother, Lenore, walks into my line of sight and heads our way. "Are you boys having a good time?" She's stylish with a blond pixie cut, wearing a peach gown and a short fitted jacket.

"Yes," we all say at once.

"There are quite a few single ladies eyeing you two," she says to Noah and Seth. "I'd be happy to give you an introduction."

"I think that's a stellar idea." Noah takes her arm. "You coming, Seth?"

"Someone's got to babysit him," Seth says under his breath to me and Flynn. Then, louder, "Right behind you."

As he follows them, I clap Flynn on the back. "I'm happy for you, bro, but if I don't get my arms around my wife soon, I'm going to lose my mind."

"Guess the honeymoon isn't over."

"She's married to me. The honeymoon will *never* be over."

I head for my wife, and I swear she has Clay radar, because she turns and our eyes connect. Her lips curve up in a sweet smile, but the heat in her eyes tells me she's dying to be in my arms, too. She should, since I've been whispering to her all night about the dirty things I'd like to do to her.

"Excuse me, ladies, but I'd like to dance with my wife." Sutton's friends watch with rapt attention as I draw Pepper into my arms and we begin to dance. "How's my girl?"

"Better now."

"Have I told you how beautiful you look tonight?"

Her eyes shimmer in the moonlight. "Only a dozen times."

"That's not nearly enough." I kiss her softly as we slow dance. "Are you having fun?"

"Mm-hm. Everyone's really nice. I love getting to know Sutton's family and friends."

"Any regrets about not having a big wedding?"

"No way. Our wedding was perfect, like us."

"You're perfect, baby, but we both know I'm not so perfect."

She runs her fingers along the back of my neck. "Your not

so perfectness is *perfectly* perfect for me."

"God, I love you."

She meets me halfway in a sweet kiss, and we dance to another song. I see my grandparents and my parents step onto the dance floor. "Remember when I said I wanted what they have?"

"Yes, and you always get what you want."

"I got something so much better. I got you." I kiss her again, deeper, more sensually.

As our lips part, she whispers, "Take me for a walk."

"Is my temptress coming out to play?"

She steps out of my arms and takes my hand. "I guess you'll find out."

As we hurry off the patio, leaving the lights of the reception behind, I thank my lucky stars I can stop playing Mr. Perfect and enjoy a lifetime with the special woman who loves me for the not-so-perfect man I am.

Get ready to fall head over heels for Seth Braden

Come along for the fun, sexy ride as this business-savvy, pleasure-oriented billionaire gets the shock of his lifetime and finds out his ever-efficient virtual assistant is not the man he thinks he is but a beautiful businesswoman who knows many of his secrets and has some of her own in *Sincerely, Mr. Braden*.

Want to read Pepper's siblings' books?

Start with *Embracing Her Heart*, the first book in the Bradens & Montgomerys series, or buy the discounted bundle from Melissa's shop (shop.melissafoster.com) and binge the series. To read Flynn and Sutton's story, pick up *Enticing Her Love* (The Steeles at Silver Island).

Binge the series that started the Love in Bloom sensation

THE BRADENS AT WESTON

"Family knows no boundaries"

If you loved the Bradens at Ridgeport, you'll adore their fiercely loyal and wickedly naughty cousins, the Bradens at Weston, the family that kicked off the legendary Bradens. Start the series with *Lovers at Heart, Reimagined.*

Billionaire Treat Braden fell in love over one magnificent evening, but one mistake sent Max away. Now he's determined to win her heart forever, and she's forced to face her hurtful past head-on for the man she can't help but love. But can true love really conquer all?

SHOP.MELISSAFOSTER.COM

New to the Love in Bloom Big-Family Romance Collection?

If this is your first Love in Bloom book, there are many more love stories featuring loyal heroes and strong, sassy heroines waiting for you. The Bradens at Ridgeport is just one of the series in the Love in Bloom big-family romance collection. Each book is written to be enjoyed as a stand-alone novel or as part of the larger series, and characters from each series make appearances in future books, so you never miss an engagement, wedding, or birth. A complete list of series titles is included at the end of this book. Find one that looks fun and dive in, or download the reading order and start with the very first series in the entire Love in Bloom collection, the *Snow Sisters*.

Get Discounted Bundles (Ebook, Audio, Paperback)
shop.melissafoster.com

See the Entire Love in Bloom Collection
shop.melissafoster.com/pages/shop-all

Download Series Checklists, Family Trees, and Publication Schedules
www.MelissaFoster.com/rg

More Books By Melissa Foster

STANDALONE ROMANTIC COMEDY
Hot Mess Summer
Mr. Right Checklist

LOVE IN BLOOM BIG-FAMILY ROMANCE COLLECTION

SNOW SISTERS
Sisters in Love
Sisters in Bloom
Sisters in White

THE BRADENS (Weston)
Lovers at Heart, Reimagined
Destined for Love
Friendship on Fire
Sea of Love
Bursting with Love
Hearts at Play

THE BRADENS (Trusty)
Taken by Love
Fated for Love
Romancing My Love
Flirting with Love
Dreaming of Love
Crashing into Love

THE BRADENS (Peaceful Harbor)

Healed by Love
Surrender My Love
River of Love
Crushing on Love
Whisper of Love
Thrill of Love

THE BRADENS & MONTGOMERYS (Pleasant Hill – Oak Falls)

Embracing Her Heart
Anything for Love
Trails of Love
Wild Crazy Hearts
Making You Mine
Searching for Love
Hot for Love
Sweet Sexy Heart
Then Came Love
Rocked by Love
Falling For Mr. Bad

THE BRADENS (Ridegeport)

Playing Mr. Perfect
Sincerely, Mr. Braden

THE BRADEN NOVELLAS

Promise My Love
Our New Love
Daring Her Love
Story of Love
Love at Last
A Very Braden Christmas

THE REMINGTONS

Game of Love
Stroke of Love
Flames of Love

Slope of Love
Read, Write, Love
Touched by Love

SEASIDE SUMMERS

Seaside Dreams
Seaside Hearts
Seaside Sunsets
Seaside Secrets
Seaside Nights
Seaside Embrace
Seaside Lovers
Seaside Whispers
Seaside Serenade

BAYSIDE SUMMERS

Bayside Desires
Bayside Passions
Bayside Heat
Bayside Escape
Bayside Romance
Bayside Fantasies

THE STEELES AT SILVER ISLAND

Tempted by Love
My True Love
Caught by Love
Always Her Love
Wild Island Love
Enticing Her Love

THE SILVERS AT SILVER ISLAND

Flirting with Trouble

THE RYDERS

Seized by Love
Claimed by Love

Chased by Love
Rescued by Love
Swept Into Love

THE WHISKEYS: DARK KNIGHTS AT PEACEFUL HARBOR
Tru Blue
Truly, Madly, Whiskey
Driving Whiskey Wild
Wicked Whiskey Love
Mad About Moon
Taming My Whiskey
The Gritty Truth
In for a Penny
Running on Diesel

THE WHISKEYS: DARK KNIGHTS AT REDEMPTION RANCH
The Trouble with Whiskey
Freeing Sully: Prequel to For the Love of Whiskey
For the Love of Whiskey
A Taste of Whiskey
Love, Lies, and Whiskey

SUGAR LAKE
The Real Thing
Only for You
Love Like Ours
Finding My Girl

HARMONY POINTE
Call Her Mine
This is Love
She Loves Me

THE WICKEDS: DARK KNIGHTS AT BAYSIDE
A Little Bit Wicked
The Wicked Aftermath
Crazy, Wicked Love

The Wicked Truth
His Wicked Ways
Talk Wicked to Me
Irresistibly Wicked

SILVER HARBOR
Maybe We Will
Maybe We Should
Maybe We Won't

WILD BOYS AFTER DARK
Logan
Heath
Jackson
Cooper

BAD BOYS AFTER DARK
Mick
Dylan
Carson
Brett

HARBORSIDE NIGHTS SERIES
Includes characters from the Love in Bloom series
Catching Cassidy
Discovering Delilah
Tempting Tristan

More Books by Melissa
Chasing Amanda (mystery/suspense)
Come Back to Me (mystery/suspense)
Have No Shame (historical fiction/romance)
Love, Lies & Mystery (3-book bundle)
Megan's Way (literary fiction)
Traces of Kara (psychological thriller)
Where Petals Fall (suspense)

Acknowledgments

I hope you enjoyed spending time with the Bradens and Montgomerys as much as I enjoyed writing them. Writing a book is never an easy process. There are ups and downs and *aha* moments. I am grateful to my friends and family for their patience and support on the good days and the more difficult ones. I would like to thank author Elise Sax for her humor and a very special friend and incredible author, Melisse Shapiro, aka MJ Rose, for sharing her knowledge of Paris. Unfortunately, Melisse passed away unexpectedly. She will be remembered fondly for her bright light, creative mind, and kind, generous soul. If you haven't checked out Elise's or MJ's fictional worlds yet, I highly suggest doing so.

Many thanks to Becca Mysoor for helping me plot, and loads of appreciation go out to my daily sounding boards and shoulders to lean on, my sisters at heart, Sharon Martin, Lisa Filipe, Amy Manemann, Natasha Brown, and Sue Pettazzoni.

I am continually inspired by my fans, many of whom are in my fan club on Facebook. If you haven't yet joined my fan club, please do. We have a great time chatting about Love in Bloom characters and the stories I'm writing. You never know when you'll inspire a story or a character and end up in one of my books, as several fan club members have already discovered. www.Facebook.com/groups/MelissaFosterFans.

To stay abreast of what's going on in our fictional worlds,

new releases, and sales, follow me on social media and sign up for my newsletter. www.MelissaFoster.com/Newsletter.

As always, I owe heaps of gratitude to my incredible team of editors and proofreaders: Kristen Weber, Penina Lopez, Elaini Caruso, Juliette Hill, Lynn Mullan, and Justinn Harrison. Thank you for helping make my books shine. I truly appreciate each of you.

Meet Melissa

www.MelissaFoster.com

Melissa Foster is a *New York Times, Wall Street Journal,* and *USA Today* bestselling and award-winning author. Her books have been recommended by *USA Today*'s book blog, *Hagerstown* magazine, *The Patriot,* and several other print venues. Visit Melissa on her website or chat with her on social media. Melissa enjoys discussing her books with book clubs and reader groups and welcomes an invitation to your event. Melissa's books are available through most online retailers in paperback, digital, and audio formats.

Shop Melissa's store for exclusive discounts, bundles, and more. Shop.melissafoster.com

Printed in Great Britain
by Amazon

58101589R00249